WICKED LOVERS OF TIME

THE SINISTER SAGA OF BALTHAZAR AND ALINA

BLADE OF SHADOWS
BOOK 3.5

SARA SAMUELS

BLADE OF SHADOWS

BOOK 3.5

Wicked Lovers of Time

SARA SAMUELS

Wicked Lovers of Time

Book 3.5 in the Blade of Shadows series

Published by Sara Samuels

Denver, CO 80237

First Edition

Copyright © 2024 by Sara Samuels

All rights reserved.

Cover image copyright Krafigs Design

Editing by Rainy Kaye

Formatting Storytelling Press

"To the shades of darkness, where villains are born of wickedness or forged by circumstance. Come closer, dear reader, fear not, for within these pages, we unravel the tangled threads of their stories, finding echoes of pain, whispers of redemption, and the haunting truth that even the darkest hearts can yearn for salvation."

" To my past self, who dreamed boldly and fearlessly; to my future self, who continues to believe against all odds; and to you, dear reader, for accompanying me on this journey through the chronicles of time."

AUTHOR'S NOTE

Dear Reader,

Thank you for joining me on this thrilling adventure. You are about to delve into the villain's story of the series, a tale darker, spicier, and without a redemption arc. It's crucial that you have read the first three books before starting this one to fully grasp the unfolding mysteries and the journey of our characters. I've crafted this series with great care, aiming to take you on an unforgettable journey. Each book brings you closer to the ultimate reveal, and I hope you enjoy every moment.

With all my love,
   Sara

PROLOGUE

940 A.D.

The grim sky was swollen with boiling storm clouds as I rode my horse home, intoxicated by the thrill of victory. As one of the most feared Hersir warriors in the Viking army, I could easily lay waste to entire hordes with my blunt mace that crushed armor and my battle ax that cleaved through bone. Killing with such ferocity made me forget who I was—a creature spawned from the darkness. It gave focus to my treacherous existence.

My mind raced with adrenaline as I reflected on the defeated foes. They were a ruthless group known as the "Timehunters," their name evoking images of unstoppable predators. Led by the fearsome Chronosbane, they fought with unrelenting ferocity, determined to claim victory at any cost. But in the end, we emerged triumphant, our blades stained with their blood and our hearts still pounding from the intense battle.

As I urged my horse into a trot, a frigid shiver violently

jolted down my spine, sending goosebumps prickling over my skin despite the winter sun. A foreboding sense of impending doom loomed over me like a dark cloud ready to unleash its fury. My gut twisted with the certainty that life as I knew it was about to come crashing down, and I could do nothing to stop it.

I tried to push away the dark thoughts that threatened to consume me. I had been living a respectable and honorable life, but lately, the weight of my existence was taking its toll on me. There were so many things I didn't understand. Who was I? Did I have a purpose? Was I fooling myself into thinking I was happy? The inner turmoil was paralyzing.

The Havenshield Fjord glistened in the distance. Bordering the edge of the fjord sat my village's many dwellings and places of business. Havenshield was a bustling coastal village with fishing and trade from neighboring towns.

My journey had been long and demanding, but my heart swelled with happiness as I reached the hilltop, revealing my cherished abode cradled in the valley beneath. A sense of pride and affection surged as I gazed down at my longhouse sanctuary. I had created this haven for my family and myself. But that same shiver of doom ripped down my spine. Again, I cast it aside.

Guiding my horse down the slope, a heartwarming sight greeted me. My five cherished daughters rushed out of the dwelling, their faces radiant with delight. I nodded to our stable boy, Håkon, a ruddy-cheeked lad with golden curls framing his young face, who reached out to take the reins of my steed.

I dismounted and gathered the youngest, Freya, into my arms, showering her rosy cheeks with affectionate kisses.

WICKED LOVERS OF TIME

She giggled, wisps of her blond braids glinting in the sun like a halo.

The other four girls clamored around me and laughed, tugging at my woolen overcoat, loose-fitting trousers, and even my fingers, adorned with gold rings inscribed with runes and Viking knotwork for protection.

I smiled at my daughters, my heart swelling with love for them. I had been a warrior since I was twenty one and knew only battle and bloodshed. But in my daughters, I had found a new purpose. I threw myself into the role of a loving father and looked forward to sharing stories of raiding and adventure with them.

I crouched, setting down my toddler, and the children surrounded me, hugging, kissing, and peppering me with questions.

"Where have you been?"

"What did you see?"

"Did you bring us presents?"

I laughed and patted my leather pouch. "There might be some gifts for you."

A wisp of darkness flitted through my mind. Bloodshed. Crimson stains in the snow. I felt as if Odin, the god of war and death, whispered in my ear.

I shook my head and focused on my dear children.

"Show us, show us!" they crowed in unison.

"Not yet." I hugged them in turn.

I finally extricated myself from the children's embraces and made my way to the main hall of the longhouse, where my wife, Zara, awaited me. She had prepared a meal for me, and the children gathered around the table, eager to hear my stories. I set my satchel before the hearth beside where Håkon had placed my weapons. Then, I strode toward Zara and kissed her soundly, delighting in her lusty moan.

She pushed away from me, laughing. "I must tend to dinner, my love."

I waggled my eyebrows, plucking at her long tunic. "And I must tend to *you*! It's been too long."

She slapped my hands away, and her gaze slid toward the children. "After we put them to bed, Balthazar. Then, I shall serve your pleasures in bed."

I let out a growl and playfully bit her neck.

"Balthazar!" she squealed.

At the table, I recounted tales of fierce battles and epic feats of heroism. My children gasped and cheered, and their eyes sparkled with delight. I told of daring escapes and raids, brave warriors and cunning foes, and the children ate every word.

I spoke of my travels through distant lands, of the exotic cultures and customs I had encountered, and my children listened. As I spoke, I hoped each of the children felt a connection to me, as if they, too, had been there, sharing in the danger and the glory.

I concluded by telling of my final battle and how I had single-handedly slain the enemy's second-in-command. The children cheered and clapped, and Zara clasped my arm, beaming.

"Come now, my darlings. It's getting late," she said to the children.

"No," Freya protested. "More Papa stories! Presents from Papa, too!"

"In the morning, my sweets," I said, rising and hefting Freya and Tove.

Zara guided the other three before her, and we all made our way into the sleeping area of raised platforms covered with fur. The children climbed on their side-by-side platforms, snuggling together like puppies.

"Are you going away again?" Revna asked. "We always miss you when you're gone."

"I don't think so," I said, stroking her silken curls.

"Goodie!" Astrid exclaimed. "Papa's staying!"

"For a while," I said, pulling the fur under Astrid's chin.

After the children lay sleeping, Zara and I returned to the main hall, where we sat before the blazing fire on the fur rug.

"I'm glad your raid went well," she said, clasping my hand.

"It was a good fight. And what did you do while I was away?" I kissed the tips of her fingers.

She pushed my braids away from my face, then stroked my bearded jaw. "I missed you. What do you think I did?"

A touch of wistfulness filled her words.

"I missed you, too." I traced a heart on her pink cheek. "But I'm certain you did other things besides pine for me," I teased.

"Of course. I tended the sick, cared for the kids, the live-stock, the gardens... There's too much to do when you're gone." A frown creased her forehead.

I smoothed it with my thumb. "What troubles you, my love?"

She sighed. "Some of my patients didn't make it. I had to kill them and inhale their souls."

Zara, like me, was a darkness. Like me, she didn't under-stand why she had to kill to stay alive. She only knew that it filled her with joy to murder those who wouldn't survive their illness. She helped the others heal and sent them on their way.

"Don't beat yourself up. We do what we must. You kill those whose pain and misery have gone too far. You save them from needless suffering. I kill those whose lives aren't worth living," I said with a shrug. I crawled toward my satchel beside the hearth and retrieved the gift I'd brought her. When I returned, I held the leather-wrapped pouch in my cupped hands at her heart.

She opened the gift, her eyes sparkling with delight as she pulled out a shimmering ruby and moonstone necklace I'd traded for. "Oh! It's beautiful!"

"Allow me," I said, securing it with the gold clasp around her neck. A vision, dark and unbidden, tore through my mind. I could picture this necklace around another's neck—a woman far eviler than Helheim, the Land of the Dead. Where were these thoughts coming from? I shook them from my mind and focused on my dear Zara.

I kissed her neck as I removed the headscarf she'd tied around her honey-colored locks.

"Balthazar," she breathed as I unfastened the brooches holding the crisscrossed straps of her sleeveless apron dress.

I peeled away the garment, revealing her linen tunic. I let my fingertips push beneath her rounded neckline, tracing the lines of her collarbone and the hollow at the base of her neck. After months away, I craved Zara with a passionate yearning that normally would have me tearing her clothes from her body. But tonight, I wanted a slow exploration of her desires, passions, and intimate reactions. I urged the tunic over her head, revealing miles of golden skin. I caressed her belly and chest, feeling the heat of her body as it rose and fell.

Zara unfastened my belt buckle hesitantly before tugging off my tunic. She then moved to the fabric of my trousers, her hands slipping beneath the waistband to undo the drawstrings. I wriggled out of my pants, and she ran her hands over my legs.

I kissed Zara passionately, exploring the contours of her body with my hands. My touch was both tender and firm, arousing her with each caress. I ran my hands over her breasts and teased her nipples into hard points. She wrapped her hands around my neck, pulling me closer.

I kissed and licked my way down her stomach, exploring her curves and running my hands over her thighs. As my fingers moved toward her innermost secrets, she moaned, her body trembling beneath my touch. I teased her until she gasped before I finally entered her, thrusting my cock deep.

We moved together, exploring each other with a hunger and intensity that seemed to have no bounds. We clutched one another, our bodies melding together in perfect harmony. I moved inside her, pushing her to the heights of ecstasy as she clung to me and surrendered herself to my pleasurable assault.

More threads of darkness winnowed through my mind. Blood drops in the snow—the stench of burning flesh. I thrust myself into Zara with primal desperation, my body latching onto hers as if she were my last lifeline. Every movement was fueled by a desperate need to hold onto her, to keep her from slipping away from me. The intensity of our union was palpable. Each thrust brought me closer to the edge of oblivion.

I scolded myself for indulging in the negativity of my thoughts. They were like creeping shadows, trying to engulf me in their dark embrace. But I refused to succumb, knowing they were foolish and baseless notions.

As our lovemaking reached its climax, we both cried out. Afterward, we lay entwined together, savoring the intensity of our love and the warmth of the fire.

After a time, I murmured, "I need to restore my energy."

Zara smiled. "Mine, too. Where shall we hunt?"

I shrugged. "The nearby village. There are always hapless travelers lodging near the docks. The children will be safe enough with young Håkon watching the longhouse."

We proceeded to don our clothing.

"I wish I knew more of who and what we are," Zara said, smoothing her tunic over her curves. "We still don't know anything about who we are. All I know is we came into being and must kill to survive."

"And now we have to kill to protect our family," I said, yanking on my trousers. "Their necklaces are safe and secure, right?"

Zara nodded. "Safe around their necks, hidden from sight by their tunics."

I returned the nod. I never knew or understood why my children were born with these dagger necklaces on their necks. It was a mystery to Zara and me. "Let's go."

We headed outside into the starry night and rode my horse into the village. Not a single light shone in any of the houses. We sought out a few useless people, mostly vagabond travelers who were rumored to hurt their wives or beat their children, who drank too much, or were considered irredeemable. That same sense of invincibility thrummed through us as we inhaled the souls of the dead. But as my horse picked its way along the dirt road heading home, I turned to catch a glimpse of sorrow in Zara's expression.

"What is it, my love?"

"I wish we didn't have to kill," she said. "Lately, I feel like I have to kill all the time to sustain myself."

I had nothing to say that hadn't already been said. I knew my wife killed those with incurable infections or bones broken beyond repair. She killed those who were bleeding out, or their time on earth had come. Together, we murdered those considered depraved or beyond redemption. I was sorry she had regrets, but what could we do? If we didn't destroy lives and consume souls, we would die.

It was a harsh lesson learned when I first regained

consciousness as a young man, my naked body floating in the unforgiving ocean. My mind was blank, devoid of memory except for my name: Balthazar. Struggling to make sense of my existence, I dragged myself onto the shore, fueled by confusion, desperation, and insatiable hunger. It was then that I discovered my true nature—a predator driven by instinct to feed on the souls of the deceased. No amount of human or animal sustenance could satisfy me; only the inhalation of human souls could quell my endless craving.

If Zara and I died, there would be nobody to care for our children. My daughters meant the world to me, so I had to continue to kill to be in their lives.

Weeks passed before I was called to another raid. My earlier visions of darkness and doom had faded, leaving me to think they were all remnants of our last raid with the brutal men known as Timehunters.

"Please let me come with you," Zara pleaded, surprising me. She clung to my tunic in the front room as I sharpened my weapons before the fire.

I raised my eyebrows as I wrapped the handle of my battle ax with fresh leather, carefully avoiding the runes I'd branded in the wood for protection.

"Absolutely not." I hefted the ax up and down, testing the grip. It felt good in my hand—solid like I could slay the masses.

"Please, my love!" Her grip tightened around my arm. Tears welled up in her eyes. "We've become so close these past weeks. Please let me come. How could I bear the thought of losing such a strong bond?"

I looked deep into her eyes, pulled her hand away, and gently kissed her fingertips.

"Our connection is unbreakable," I whispered with conviction. "You'll never have to be afraid of losing me."

Zara continued to tremble. I brought my lips to hers and kissed her softly at first. She started to melt. I deepened the kiss, pouring all my love into her. She moaned and relaxed in my arms. I continued to kiss her until our energies were harmonious and connected. Only then did I ease away.

"Are you feeling better?" I asked.

"A little," she said, her cheeks flushed.

"Everything's going to be all right," I said.

She shook her head. "I can't keep living like this. You leave for weeks…months sometimes, and I'm alone. We must find out who we are and what our purpose is."

She fiercely gripped my tunic, her nails digging into the fabric. "We can't stay here and pretend everything is fine," she hissed. "Our children deserve to know the truth, and we need to find out who we really are before it's too late." Her eyes pleaded with me, desperate for me to understand. "I'll find someone to watch over them, to keep them safe while we uncover the secrets that have been hidden from us for so long. Please, Balthazar, trust me on this."

Her fingers dug into my chest.

"No," I said, removing her hands from my clothing. "It's not safe to leave. We should continue with our lives as we are."

"You're such a stubborn man! Every day, it gets harder. We kill to sustain ourselves. But our children don't have to kill. *We* do. I don't know why this is. I want answers, and you keep leaving us before we can get any insight!"

I picked up a sharpening stone and got to work on my blade in slow, rhythmical strokes. A chill ran down my spine, and goosebumps prickled on my arms. The visions were back. Something in the air felt different, like the calm before a storm. I glanced out the window. The trees swayed in an eerie rhythm as if foretelling the impending shift that was about to occur. My gut clenched with anticipation, bracing for what was to come. Everything was about to change, and there was no turning back.

Zara tugged her overwrap tightly around her slender frame. "I can't keep living this way. I can't go out and hunt on my own and leave the children," she said.

Where is this coming from? She's never reacted to my departure this strongly before when I've gone away.

"Surely you haven't forgotten about our stable boy, Håkon? He's a responsible lad." I resumed grinding the stone against the metal.

"What? No! Of course not!" Her gaze shifted away guiltily. "But Håkon is not a parent. He is a boy. He doesn't understand the disciplines of caring for a child."

I paused in my blade sharpening, the stone poised over the glistening metal. "But all you need him to do is watch over them when they sleep. Is that too much to ask?"

My words were met with an icy silence.

"Never mind." Zara threw up her hands and flounced from my side. "I have to get started with dinner."

Confused, I watched her depart. "Tonight, I'll be carousing with my comrades and will not require supper."

"There are others in this family who require sustenance." Her stern glare burned into me like acid as she trudged to the provisions cupboard.

The mood was celebratory as I sat at one of the tables in the wattle and daub-walled tavern. A blazing fire burned in the hearth, warding off the chill of the night. My fellow warriors and I were cups deep into our drinking, well beyond the point of good sense and reason.

"To victory!" I shouted, lifting my ale mug high.

"To kicking ass!" Ragnar bellowed.

The others roared their approval and hefted their tankards and horns as ale sloshed over the edges, splashing across the worn surface of the wooden table.

I drained my ale and slammed the empty tankard on the table.

"Ale-keeper!" I called out. "Refills all around."

Whoops and shouts accompanied my request as the barkeep nodded and rounded the crude wooden counter with a large jug. He poured the golden liquid into each mug and drinking horn as I traded insults and jabs with my men in good-hearted fun.

The massive door creaked open, its moaning hinges grating my ears like a thousand fingernails scraping across metal. I looked over, expecting to see Leif or maybe Bjorn. Instead, Zara sashayed through the doorway, her golden hair loose and flowing around her shoulders. Her tight-fitting long dress accentuated her curves, leaving little to the imagination. My men greeted her with lusty enthusiasm, their eyes lighting up like beasts in heat.

"Where are the other wives?" Ivar asked in his deep voice.

"Where are the *whores*?" Thorstein added with a snicker, and everyone laughed—everyone but me.

I bolted to my feet and rushed to my wife. "What's wrong? Are the children alright?"

She placed a palm on my cheek and smiled.

"Relax, love. I did as you suggested and appealed to Håkon." She leaned close and whispered, "I thought we could share one last kill before you depart."

My eyes flicked between Zara and my men, their faces rigid masks of alertness. What if they put two and two together when they discovered more killings in the village tomorrow? Then again, they would be dragging their asses on the heels of hangovers when we gathered in the morning at the Viking ship that sat waiting for us at the Havenshield fjord harbor.

I forced a smirk onto my lips as I coiled an arm around her shoulders. "Ale-keeper! Give us your strongest ale to celebrate this special moment!"

Everyone cheered.

When half the men had fallen into a drunken stupor with their heads on the table, I excused Zara and me. The few still upright looked at me with bleary, heavy-lidded eyes, lifted their hands, and bid farewell to us as I guided Zara out the door.

I forced an enthusiastic smile on my face as we scoured the village for people to kill. We took our sustenance from the many travelers who took shelter on the shores of Havenshield.

We consumed souls until sated. I helped Zara onto my horse to return home. She leaned against my back as the horse clomped through the night beneath a star-filled sky. A sense of contentment filled my heart. Despite my earlier resistance to her presence, I enjoyed connecting with this woman who'd captured my heart many years ago. We were bonded in this life and tonight's killing. Zara was everything to me: my soulmate, wife, and mother to my children. Some-times, we unleashed our darkness on each other and would have crazy, wild sex. But the question always remained: who are we, and why do we exist? We weren't humans—that I knew.

As our longhouse came into view, I was overcome with dread. Zara let out a scream—thick smoke billowed from the broken windows and charred wood. Flames licked the walls like a serpent's tongue, consuming every inch of our home. The smell of burning timber filled my nostrils as I spurred the horse forward, desperately racing toward the scene of destruction.

Zara and I flew from the horse's back as we reached the edge of our burning home. Håkon lay sprawled in the yard with an arrow through his chest. His sightless eyes stared at the Milky Way above. Several men, whom I recognized from a nearby enemy clan, raided the burning wreckage of our house, carrying handfuls of our supplies and food in their arms as they raced for their horses.

I seized my dagger from my waistband and charged. Before he could react, I plunged my blade into the chest of the nearest man. Zara gave a war cry and stabbed another man.

A chilling figure strode through my burning door— Chronosbane. How many others had he brought to exact his revenge? Grinning, he carried one of my children, now dead. He strode toward me and deposited Tove at my feet.

Horrified, I picked her up. My arms shook with rage as I clutched the lifeless body of my child to my chest. Hot tears rolled down my face, and anger coursed through my veins until the fire of wrath engulfed me in its inferno. My heart was hot with fury, searing my soul.

"My Tove," I whispered in her ear as I gently lay her behind me, away from the cruel gaze of the male before me. I closed her eyes with my thumbs so she could look within. "May Folkvangr welcome you into her arms."

I whirled to snarl at the self-proclaimed Timehunter. "I've heard the tales of your deeds, cruel and depraved beyond measure. You are monsters, possessed by some otherworldly force that commands you to wreak terror on the innocent. I have seen you slaughter innocent soldiers without mercy as if they were nothing more than a swarm of ants beneath your feet."

Chronosbane regarded me with a sneer. "I have watched you and your precious wife for quite some time. I have followed you. You both are incarnations of evil, monsters who feast on the blood of innocents to keep your depraved souls alive." He spat out the words with venom, his mouth contorted in hatred and revealing sharp, dagger-like teeth that glinted in the light. "We are your greatest enemy. We are Timehunters, and we kill your kind. We kill your children, who are Timebounds."

He raised his hand over his head, brandishing a gleaming blade.

I forced my dagger into his gut, slicing him apart. He fell, mouth agape, entrails spilling from his abdomen. As he collapsed to the ground, four of my daughters' necklaces tumbled from his grip.

"No!" I cried, scooping them up. I tore into the house, clutching the necklaces.

I stumbled over fallen timbers and the smoldering remnants of sleeping palettes. There, huddled in the corner, sat the charred remains of three of my other children.

"My babies!" I screamed and cursed the gods for taking them too soon. Crouching before the remains, I matched each necklace to its owner. "This one is Tove's. I'll rest it upon her when I am back by her side. This is Revna's. Astrid. Meya."

I laid Revna's, Astrid's, and Meya's necklaces on their burned chests and closed their eyelids, murmuring safe passage to Folkvangr. I lunged to my feet and began my search for my baby, Freya.

"Freya! Where are you? Papa's here to protect you. You can come out." Tears blinded me as I searched every corner of the room.

Freya was nowhere to be found.

By the mighty thunder of Thor's hammer, she is only three years old, so small and innocent. Where could she be?

Zara stumbled into the room with tears streaming down her face.

"Where is Freya?" I yelled, pointing an accusing finger toward Zara. "This is all your fault! You never listen to me! You should have stayed home!"

She trembled as she stood there, covering her mouth in a silent sob. Darkness filled her face as she lowered her hands.

"How can you say that, Balthazar? How can you blame me when I told you we must leave and find out who we are? But you and your stubborn mind wouldn't listen! And now you blame *me* that my children are dead." The words flew from her mouth like a torrent. "I love you so much! I only wanted to spend one last night with you and persuade you to stay behind for us. And for that, my children are dead, and you have the gall to stand there and blame *me*. It should be you to blame. They are dead. My babies are dead."

Tears streamed down her face, her sobs echoing off the night's stars. Through her cries, she managed to gasp, "We need to find Freya. She might still be alive!"

My face hardened as I looked her square in the eyes. "I will search for her. You lay the children to rest. Our children wouldn't be dead if you'd have stayed home!"

Tears cascaded down her cheeks as she screamed, "I left because I love you! I wanted to see you before you left. We don't know who we are!"

I roared, my voice shaking with fury. "We're monsters! We're pretending to be civil, to blend in. But at our cores, we're despicable creatures."

I relished Zara's anguished expression.

"We need to find Freya! She's all I have left!" I stormed past Zara, shoving her to the ground.

I trudged through the blinding snowstorm, calling out for Freya. My heart raced as I spotted a small pink shoe peeking out from under a mound of snow. My stomach twisted in fear as I saw a thin stream of blood trailing from the shoe. Panic set in as I dug through the snow, frantically searching for my baby girl. I followed the blood trail like an animal on the hunt, my face wet with tears. With dread clawing at my heart, I knew Freya must have fallen into the snow and been frozen there until death claimed her. But I refused to give up on my quest to find her.

Ahead, another Timehunter emerged from the blizzard. He lunged at me with feral eyes, his knife flashing in the pale light of winter's dawn. My dagger clashed against his, the metallic ringing filling the air. I dodged and parried each of his strikes, my muscles straining with adrenaline. Finally, with a swift thrust, I pierced his chest. His eyes widened in shock before he collapsed to the ground, lifeless. The smell of blood and sweat hung heavy in the air as I stood over my defeated opponent, victorious yet haunted by the violence of battle.

I executed each bloody Timehunter I found with precision and rage, then leaped onto my steed and flew like lightning into the village. My children had been brutally murdered. My heart raced as I frantically searched for the betrayer. Was it one of my men, envious of my power and willing to sell me out? Or perhaps one of their wives, bitter and resentful of our success? The villagers also came to mind—desperate and willing to do anything to survive. In a fit of blind rage, I let my emotions guide me as I vowed to make whoever betrayed me pay with their life.

Without mercy, I plunged into the homes of my people and slaughtered everyone. No one would escape. No one would be spared from my wrath. The raid tomorrow night would never come. All that remained in its stead was a blood-drenched, corpse-strewn massacre.

Spattered in blood, I rode home as dawn emerged, only to find Zara standing next to a man I'd never seen before. This man's presence radiated power and intensity that surged around him like a furious storm. He stood tall, towering over Zara, handsome and imperious.

I leaped from my horse and stalked toward him. I yanked him away from Zara. "Get the fuck away from my wife and get out of here right now!"

He stumbled but caught his balance.

"Balthazar, wait!" Zara screamed. "He's here to help!"

I whirled to face her, still enraged at what she'd done. My precious children were dead because of her.

"We do not require his help. It is far too late. My beloved daughters lie lifeless and still." Pain ripped through my heart like a jagged blade, spilling my soul's blood everywhere. "Why does he come here when the deed has been done, and they are dead? He should have come before."

Rage boiling in my veins, I squared up to the man again. "Or perhaps you sent these death-mongers here to brutally slaughter my children. What a stroke of luck that you appear from thin air and suddenly believe yourself capable of fixing this?"

"Balthazar, how can you accuse this blameless man of murdering our innocent babes when he came to help us?" Zara said.

I faced her, my eyes blazing. "You're correct, Zara. All of this is your fault. You are to blame. I loathe you, despise you, and am disgusted with you. I no longer want you in my life."

Zara gasped and stepped back, heartbreak filling her eyes.

"I don't *need* you, Zara. Freya, *my baby*, is dead too," I said. "And who is at fault? *You*! You had to come and say goodbye to me when you could have stayed home and protected them."

A silence, weighted and smothering, spread between us.

I took a few steps back, gasping for air as pain lanced my heart. My beard was damp and tangled from the exertion. Zara stood before me, her skin pale and illuminated by the moonlight, resembling the shimmering stars above us. She looked at me with a mixture of fear and agony.

The man cleared his throat. "My name is Mathias Alastair, and you both must come with me. I see the agony etched into your face and feel your misery even from here. You may wish to blame me for this tragedy, but I swear on my life that I had no part in the death of your children or the summoning of these Timehunters. I am here to help you, not harm you.

"But you must leave this place and come with me. It is not safe to remain. I know who you are, and I can help you. You can start over and have another family, and I will teach you how to understand your darkness and its purpose. But you *must* come with me. Fighting with each other will get you nowhere." He extended his arms to me. "Come with me and let me help you and Zara. You need my help more than ever."

"No! I don't trust you one bit! I refuse to go!" I yelled, my voice cracking like thunder.

Nearby lay Tove, Revna, Meya, and Astrid, all arranged with their heads touching, still and silent, never to laugh again. Pieces of wood had been piled on and around them.

Someone, presumably Zara, had prepared their funeral pyre, ready to cremate them and send their souls to the afterlife.

"There's nothing you can do to make me understand who I am," I said. "It's too late. My girls are gone. My precious, sweet babies are dead. What's the point of living when they are gone? I lived for them and only them."

The agony engulfed me, its flames scorching my innermost depths. A relentless fire ripped through veins and marrow, devouring my soul like a ravenous beast.

"They are gone. I no longer have a purpose but to get my ultimate vengeance on those fucking Timehunters. What good is knowing anything now? Now that my children are *dead*."

My children's laughter seemed to reverberate all around me in my grief before their faces became overshadowed by images of the Timehunters.

"I swear on my life that I will tear down the Timehunters with every ounce of strength I possess," I said as I clenched my fists, determination coursing through my veins. I strode toward their funeral pyre and fell to my hands and knees. I kissed my sweet Tove's forehead and brushed her hair with my hand. "Farewell, Tove. May Folkvangr welcome you into her arms."

I repeated the process with Revna, Meya, and Astrid, adding a silent prayer for Freya.

Tears blurred my vision as I reached for a smoking branch from the remnants of my former life. The heat seared through my skin, mirroring the burning pain in my heart. With shaking hands, I placed it against the dry kindling that surrounded my beloved children, taken from me in a cruel act of violence. As I watched the flames consume everything we had built together, a voice inside me screamed for revenge. But another part of me begged for forgiveness and questioned whether this was the right path. With one last shred of inner turmoil, I wrenched myself away from the inferno and plunged into the abyss ahead, torn between seeking retribution and finding solace. But the thirst for vengeance consumed me wholly, driving me forward with reckless abandon.

CHAPTER ONE
BALTHAZAR

"Come on, Balthazar," Zara pleaded, tugging at my arm. "We need to get out of here and start fresh."

All around us lay the shattered remains of my once-happy family. Blood drops spattered in the snow—the stench of burning flesh from the pyres. My house, built by my own hands, lay in ruins.

My mind raced with doubts and fears, but Zara was relentless. "Mathias can help us," she said, her voice urgent. "He knows things we don't."

"Yes, yes." Mathias said, with the backdrop of my children's burning bodies highlighting his dark hair. "I'm building a school for darknesses such as yourself. We can teach other darknesses to be at peace with themselves. Wouldn't you have loved to have a mentor when you came into existence?"

The memory of coming to consciousness in the surging sea, frightened and freezing, and knowing not where I'd come from, seized my mind. "Of course, I wish I'd had a mentor!" I shouted.

"Then, let me be that for you. It would be best if you came with me. Both of you." Mathias smiled broadly.

I hesitated, clinging to the fractured remnants of what I knew in Havenshield. But as Zara continued to beg and Mathias gave me promises, telling me he could help me understand myself, something inside me broke. I let them convince me to time travel to *1130 A.D.* London, leaving behind my old life without a second thought.

Part of me was grateful for the distraction from the over-whelming grief of losing my children, yet another part of me felt a deep sense of betrayal toward both Zara and Mathias. I couldn't shake off the feeling that Mathias was somehow responsible for my children's untimely demise, conveniently appearing on the eve of their brutal slaughter. If he had all the answers, why did he show up now? It seemed far too convenient.

It was a conflicting mix of emotions, but I had no choice. I needed answers, and Mathias claimed to have them.

Several years under Mathias' tutelage passed, each day feeling more monotonous than the last. I fought side-by-side with Zara, training the minds and bodies of Mathias' soldiers of darkness at his school. Yet, my heart was still shattered into a thousand jagged pieces. One part of me craved the familiarity and stability of my old life, while another burned with an unquenchable desire for revenge.

Rage consumed me as I pointed an accusing finger at Zara and Mathias, blaming them for every misfortune that had befallen me. But it was Mathias who ultimately betrayed me, his treacherous hands snuffing out the life of my beau-tiful Zara before my very eyes, for reasons I could not fathom. From that moment on, I burned with a seething hatred for him that could never be extinguished.

After Zara's death, my skin crawled every time I saw

Mathias, a feeling of unease and suspicion creeping up my spine. I couldn't escape the fact that I knew him from somewhere, but the memories were buried deep within me like shards of broken glass. He projected an idyllic life with his beautiful wife and new baby girl, but I could sense something sinister lurking beneath the surface. Why else would he have murdered my beloved? My gut churned with distrust and jealousy at his seemingly perfect existence—a life that used to belong to me before it was shattered into a million pieces. I couldn't shake the feeling that there was more to Mathias than met the eye, and it made me sick to my stomach.

We argued more and more as my dissatisfaction grew. It was always the same—I wanted to break free of his rules, and he wanted me to be bound and chained by them.

The argument between Mathias and I reached a boiling point one day as we stood outside in the shadows of the school. "Why must we wear this facade of goodness while secretly reveling in our darkness? It's like being a nursemaid to weak and ill prey," I spat out, my eyes blazing with rage. "I want to embrace my true nature and unleash my dark desires."

Mathias shook his head, his voice filled with determination. "We must correct our innate darkness. We may have been born this way, but it doesn't mean we have to live that way."

"It's like forcing a lion to eat vegetables! It goes against our very nature," I growled, clenching my fists.

But Mathias just patted me on the shoulder patronizingly. "These conflicting feelings are all part of the correction process. They will fade over time."

But I didn't want them to fade. I wanted to embrace my darkness and let it consume me completely, no longer confined by society's expectations or the false notion of control. Only then could I exact the revenge against the Time-hunters and Mathias that I so desperately craved.

Mathias excused himself, thinking I'd calm down. But I hurried to the training room, picked up a sword, and began to hack at a training dummy.

At the sound of footsteps, I lifted my gaze. I set the sword in a holder on the wall and made my way across the gleaming hardwood floor to peer through the doorway.

Mathias strode down the hallway toward the massive front door with his arm around his wife, Cora. Cora held their infant to her chest.

"When will you return?" Cora asked.

"As soon as my business is completed." Mathias flashed her a tender smile.

"You always say the same thing," Cora whined.

"And I always return, don't I?" He fished in his pocket and procured a gold coin. "Here," he said, thrusting it into Cora's hand. "Take this into town and buy something beautiful to wear."

Cora's hands clung to Mathias desperately, her lips hungrily seeking his in a desperate attempt to prolong their embrace. She gave him one last lingering kiss before reluctantly releasing him. He turned and left, leaving her alone in the immense, foreboding estate. She soon followed, closing the door with finality.

The deafening silence that followed echoed through the halls, a haunting reminder of my building anger.

My rage boiled over, and I let out a primal scream. The sickening sweetness of their loving exchanges was like salt in my wounds, especially since Mathias was the one who brutally murdered Zara. Every fiber of my being trembled with fury, and thoughts of revenge consumed my mind.

It was time to end things.

Enough was enough—I could no longer suppress the fire inside me that demanded justice against those who had wronged me. I refused to continue participating in Mathias' twisted school that trained soldiers of darkness only to eliminate those deemed evil. It was time for me to take matters into my own hands and exact my own brand of retribution.

I decided to start in his office. Since Mathias was gone again on one of his mysterious wanderings, what would it matter if I destroyed all his sacred books, hand-carved furniture, and handwritten notes? Having made that decision, my heart came alive for the first time in centuries.

The thunder of the war hammer hitting the wall echoed through the school, shaking the shelves from their foundations. The wooden panels groaned, splintered, and began to give way. Pieces of debris flew off the walls, some smashing against the windows in a cascade of glass shards.

I threw my head back and laughed maniacally as I watched the room crumble. Mathias' life work would soon be reduced to dust in my hands; his legacy was destroyed one piece at a time. My chest clenched with cold hatred as I remembered what he had done. The pain of losing my five beautiful daughters still weighed heavy on my heart. And Zara's brutal murder burned in my gut. For this, he would pay. Tears streamed down my cheeks as I surveyed the ruin around me, knowing that nothing would bring back the life I had lost because of him.

A hand rested on my shoulder. I turned to see my closest friend Amir standing there, his face grim yet filled with understanding. We had met when I came to London and quickly bonded over our respective darkness. I would never have survived these long, tortuous years had it not been for Amir. I frequently confided in him about my disgust over Mathias and this school, and he shared my sentiments.

I could have sworn a ghost of a smile crossed his lips.

"What are you doing?" he said.

"Remodeling. I hate this room." I gazed at the still-standing walls and gripped the war hammer with both hands. With Mathias gone and nowhere to be found, I'm taking over the school, destroying his office. I will teach these students to embrace their darkness, not resist it."

My eyes scanned the room, taking in the remaining cluttered shelves overflowing with books and the colorful paintings now strewn upon the floor. Each piece featured a different student, caught in vibrant moments of learning and discovery. They stood in various warrior poses, their expressions fierce.

When I took over and trained, my best students would be the darkest of the dark. No painter would dare capture their image.

"There will be time enough," Amir said, looking at me with a firm, steady gaze. "But, first, let's talk."

He led me down the stairs toward the formal sitting room where visiting dignitaries were served tea, libations, and other niceties. When I was the master of this school, we could serve flaming blood for all I cared.

Amir sauntered across the room and returned with a flagon of wine and two gold tumblers. We seated ourselves at an ornate table, the light of the full moon streaming through the stained-glass windows.

The table's oak surface, polished to a golden sheen, was adorned with designs and emblems of courage and strength. At its center was a giant kite shield delicately carved into the wood with a sword and shield motif, all representing the courage and skill of the generations of warriors who had previously called this school their home.

It was far too "good" for my liking.

The antique chair's arms were smooth, but the back was webbed with cracks and gaps between the aged planks. It smelled of old oak and leather and was dried and bleached to a pale shade of desert sand.

The chairs could stay. But the table, with its images of heroic deeds, would go.

Amir poured wine into each tumbler and handed one to me.

We each took a drink before continuing.

"I'm doing it," I said. "I'm taking over the school."

Amir looked at me sympathetically. "It is a bold plan, my friend. But how can I help?"

My expression hardened as I said, "You'll be my right-hand man. You will be the one to ensure that my students receive the best possible training. You will be their teacher, and it will be your responsibility to shape them into the perfect masters of darkness. Are you ready for this task?"

Amir's gaze appeared calculating. "While it would be an honor to serve at your side, I think your actions are reckless and foolhardy. Let's consider alternatives."

"Not a chance!" My anger was like a storm raging inside me, my words boiling with rage. "I'm going to take Mathias' school and make it mine. I will take Mathias' child and kill it. He will be left with nothing. Then he will know how I felt losing my precious daughters."

Amir's voice held a note of warning as he said, "You have been harping about how Mathias has killed your children and ruined your life. And now you're toiling away with a war hammer, trying to dismantle the school piece by piece. Perhaps you should do him the mercy of burning his precious school to the ground."

"I want this school for myself!" I said. "I will be the best!"

Amir took a couple of slow, deep breaths. "Think about it, friend. If we burned the school to the ground, all of Mathias' hard work would be in flames."

"No!" I said, baring my teeth. "That's too simple. I want to twist the students' minds and souls around my finger like a puppet master, molding them to serve the darkness. Let them become that evil Mathias seeks to end. This is far more important than what they are doing, trying to purify the world of wrongdoing. I will turn them into evil's very embodiment."

Amir shook his head. "You stubborn fool. I can see your mind is made up."

He took another long swallow of wine.

I did the same, conviction coursing through my veins. I drummed my fingers against the arm of the chair. "First things first. My plan begins with Cora's elimination."

"Mathias' wife?"

"Cora will try to thwart me. I must get rid of her."

"How are you planning to kill her?" Amir said, smirking. "And how may I be of assistance?"

I slashed my hand through the air, its wake causing a gust of wind to blow over us.

"Leave this to me! Focus on what you are meant to do," I said, my lips curled into a wicked smile.

A faint gasp, coming from just outside the room, followed by hurried footsteps, met my ears.

I sat up straight, wondering who had been listening to our conversation. "Is Cora here?" I asked. "I thought she was out doing errands."

"She arrived not long ago," Amir said, his dark eyes glinting. "You should take care of Cora and the child while you have the chance."

He drew an invisible line on the table with his finger, and a secretive smile lit his face.

Anger welled up inside me. *What is he planning?*

A piercing wail cut through my thoughts. All the fury seeped out of me, only to be replaced by urgency. Cora had indeed been listening to my plans. I flew upstairs to tend to the child and her mother.

Cora radiated innocence from her smooth, porcelain skin and wild, wavy hair. Her blue eyes were a vivid abyss that permeated into my soul. A relentless craving clawed at me, urging me to demolish the purity that seemed to ooze effortlessly from Cora's every pore. Her sweetness had a sharpness that cut through the air, creating a jarring effect, and I yearned to purge it from existence. My mind buzzed with an insatiable hunger to corrupt her innocence, to shatter the perfect facade she presented to the world. The urge pulsed through my veins like wildfire, consuming all reason and restraint as I plotted my next move.

At the top of the landing, I headed toward Cora and Mathias' sleeping room.

The infant was in Cora's hands, screaming as Cora raised the dagger born with the child, its hilt inscribed with ancient scripture.

I growled as Cora wrapped a ruby and moonstone necklace around her daughter's neck. That necklace had been a gift from *me* to *Zara*. As anger and regret coursed through me, I still couldn't deny how beautiful the baby looked in the exquisite necklace. But it was not meant to be hers. I unleashed a primal roar that surely shook Cora to her core, sending a wave of dark energy up her spine.

She gulped and looked up, wide-eyed with terror.

As quickly as lightning, Cora slashed the infant's tiny palms and chanted the forbidden verse.

"No!" I bellowed, but it was too late.

The baby had been transported to an alternate time and place far from reach, her cries fading into obscurity.

I growled under my breath and lunged for Cora. She beat at me, coughing and gasping, as I squeezed her neck.

"Now, you can't hurt my daughter. She is far away from you and your vicious ways. One day, Balthazar, someone will kill you," she wheezed through her sobs. "Light always vanquishes dark."

"That's where you're wrong," I snarled. "I shall rule the world with darkness."

I bore down on her slender neck, the bones fracturing beneath my grip.

After one last pleading look, Cora closed her eyes and accepted her fate.

Footsteps boomed like thunder toward me.

"Cora!" Mathias yelled, his voice echoing off the walls.

With a savage grin, I spun around to face him.

"What have you done?" Mathias said. "Where's my daughter?"

"Why don't you ask your wife?" My eyes locked on her still body. "Oh, looks like it might be too late for that."

Mathias slammed his fist into my jaw, sending me flying. He had already rushed to his dead wife's side when I landed.

"Oh, my Cora! My poor sweet Cora," he murmured as he kissed her face and hands. He turned back to me, rage etched into his features. "All these years under my tutelage, I knew you'd try to betray me. You're nothing but an egocentric son of a bitch. I swear to take revenge on you."

I snarled with amused contempt. "What will you do? Try to stop me? I will obliterate all your accomplishments—your school, your students, everything. I slaughtered your beloved and will find and destroy your daughter too."

A loud crash from the hallway caught my attention. I

looked past Mathias and his dead wife to see flaming timbers strewn across the floor.

Damn Amir! He set a blaze to this place!

Mathias crawled across the floor and grabbed my ankles. "Why are you so hell-bent on destroying me?"

"You ruined my life," I spat. "Sent the Timehunters to murder my children. Killed Zara. You hide behind a mask of being a good man, but you're as evil as they come."

"I did not kill your children!" Mathias yelled.

The fire blazed through the hall with alarming intensity. Sparks of orange and yellow rained from the ceiling. Smoke poured from every orifice, billowing upward in an ominous cloud. And it was heading in our direction.

"I'm going to make you suffer!" I roared. "Watch your world burn to the ground, trapped in complete darkness and hopelessness. I will be the master of this dark realm. I shall rule everything!"

The hallway was engulfed in flames, creating a scene of chaotic destruction. Fire licked at the doorframe.

"Think again," Mathias said, releasing my feet from his grip. He tried to heave himself upward by clawing at my legs. "We'll see who finishes last."

One sharp kick was all it took to stop his clawing hands. I grabbed him by both legs and dragged him across the floor until we reached the doorway. With one mighty heave, I flung him into the fire.

Mathias' shrieks filled the air. Flames consumed his clothing, his hair, his skin, everything.

I gave one last satisfied look before blurring into a black cloud of darkness.

My next stop? Find his loathsome child.

Revenge would be mine.

CHAPTER TWO

ALINA

Florence, Italy 1540

Francesco crashed into me, pinning my body against the hay. Ecstasy and lust flooded his veins as he whispered in my ear, "I love you, Alina. I want to be with you forever!"

I clung to his back, scratching my fingernails against his skin, and threw my head back with forced pleasure while I cried out, "Yes, Francesco! Let us stay together forever!"

I never meant what I said, not one word of it. All I wanted was for the moment to end and for Francesco to be finished.

When he finally reached his peak and released a soft grunt, I couldn't help but roll my eyes in annoyance.

My body was being crushed beneath his weight, making it difficult to breathe. I struggled to find my voice, barely managing a whisper as I gasped for air. "Please," I begged in a shaky voice. But Francesco remained absorbed in his pleasure, not even bothering to look at me. Desperate for some response, I forced myself to lie and tell him it was amazing, pushing against his unyielding body.

He remained unmoving, so I put more effort into my shove until he finally rolled away from me onto the scratchy haystack.

Francesco's voice shook as he said, "I love you and want to marry you when the time comes. But I'm a stable boy, and your father won't accept me."

"I would love to marry you, my dear," I lied. "I'll talk to my father and plead your case."

"Oh, would you, *amore*?" He propped his head onto his hand and smiled softly at me. "I will do anything for you. I'll find a way to provide for you, I promise."

A loud male voice called from outside. "Francesco! Where are you?"

"It's the groomsman. I'd better be off," Francesco whispered. "I shall await word from you. May your talk with your father prove fruitful."

He gave me a quick kiss on the lips and donned his clothes. Then, he scrambled down the ladder and shouted to the groomsman, "I'm on my way!"

I waited in the hayloft until the voices in the barn became a distant whisper. Then, I dug my nails into my flesh, drawing thick lines of crimson across my pallid skin until a stinging pain spread through me like wildfire. With a trembling hand, I clawed my fingernails over my cheeks and breasts, biting my lip to muffle the scream of pain that threatened to escape. With my other hand, I yanked at the fabric of my skirt until long tears appeared. I messed up my hair to give myself a more wild and disheveled appearance. I would appear defeated and defiled when I returned home.

I scurried down the ladder, my breath heaving in short gasps. I looked right and left, searching for any of Papa's hired hands. Spying no one, I inhaled deeply and quickened my pace as I rushed toward the house. The night was cool and still, and the smell of damp grass filled the air.

Just as I was about to dash across the yard, the shuffling of feet and the low murmur of voices came from the far side of the house. I shrank back into the darkness and waited, my heart pounding. The voices faded away. I cautiously emerged from my hiding spot and darted across the yard, eager to reach my destination without notice.

Before hurrying into the house, I pulled my hair like a madwoman until the resulting pain brought tears to my eyes.

I had to convince Papa that I'd been defiled.

I staggered through the door, panting like I had been running for hours.

"Papa!" I shouted in despair, my voice raw and desperate. "Oh, Papa!"

"Lady Tocino!" Beatrice, the housekeeper, cried out, her tones echoing my anguish. "What has happened to you?"

"Where is my father?" I sobbed, clutching at her sleeve. "Something awful has happened!"

"He's in the drawing room, sipping brandy. Come with me!" She seized my hand and dragged me across the carpeted floor.

High vaulted arches decorated with gilded foliage in the drawing room reached for the heavens. Each arch was adorned with a painting depicting a Biblical scene, evoking feelings of holiness and reverence.

The walls had been covered in a luxurious velvet fabric strewn with ornate patterns and intricate embroidery. Candle sconces held a bright, flickering flame every few meters, providing a soft light illuminating the room.

A large hearth, built from limestone and intricately carved with the Tocino coat of arms, stood at the center of the drawing room. A fire flickered within, providing comfort and the faint smell of burning oak.

The floor was covered in an ornate rug woven with the family crest, and the furniture was of the finest quality. Chairs and benches were upholstered in rich brocade. The tables and cabinets were made from mahogany, intricately carved with pastoral scenes.

Above the mantel, a large portrait of Papa watched over the room. He was depicted in the traditional Renaissance style but with a regal bearing that spoke of his wealth and power.

On the far side of the room, a large window overlooked the fields and gardens. From this vantage point, one could see the distant rooftops of the many homes and businesses that made up the city of Florence.

A small harpsichord sat in the corner of the room, its keys gleaming in the candlelight. The instrument had been crafted from the most exotic woods and decorated with ornate ivory, brass, and gold inlays.

The room was filled with peace and serenity, and the atmosphere was heavy with a feeling of luxury.

Given the lies I was about to tell, my presence in this stately room seemed like an abomination.

Papa's face screwed up in astonishment when he saw me.

"My child!" he said, his voice full of thunder.

"Oh, Papa!" I sobbed, throwing myself into his arms.

He held me tight against him, the heat of his emotion radiating from his body. "What happened to you? Speak quickly!"

"Make her go away!" I screamed, pointing at Beatrice with a trembling finger. "So, I can tell you in private!"

"Beatrice! Leave us now!" he said, veins standing out in his neck.

Once she'd scurried away, Papa gripped my upper arms and looked into my eyes.

"Tell me what has happened, child. At once!"

I gulped, not daring to look at my father's stern face. "Oh, Papa! It was awful. I was out for a walk. You know how much I enjoy the cool night air. I was out in the field when someone grabbed me and pushed me to the ground. It was Francesco! The stable boy! And he, he…"

I took a deep, shuddering breath. Did I really want to do this to Francesco? He was a good lad and had always been kind to me. But what choice did I have? Francesco was becoming too clingy.

"He tried to kiss me, and I fought back, but he was too strong!" I said. "Then, he…"

I pictured Francesco's kind eyes. I couldn't do it. I couldn't go through with this.

Papa's face was like a storm cloud, and his voice was low and piercing. "Did this boy harm you?"

I shivered as I said, "Yes, Papa. He *defiled* me."

I added a wail for emphasis.

Papa's grip softened, and he released me.

"That's horrible. Then I must demand the presence of Francesco's father this evening," he said.

"No, Papa! He's too far away. We must handle this quickly!" I lied through gritted teeth, laughing inwardly at my growing skill in deception.

"Then let's take care of this right away." He eyed me suspiciously before wrapping an arm around me in a comforting embrace. "You did well, my brave girl. I'm so proud of you."

My heart thundered as Papa left the room, leaving me with guilt and dread. What had I done? What would Francesco's punishment be?

Time passed like cold molasses as I waited for Papa to return with Francesco.

Francesco's face was a mask of terror as he saw me huddled on the sofa, appearing bereft. His eyes implored me with desperation and hope as he asked, "Did you tell him? Did you tell your Papa that I want to marry you?"

Papa's face twisted in rage. "You dare lay claim to my daughter after defiling her? You are nothing more than a filth-stained rat!"

Francesco fell to his knees, his voice ragged with tears. "No, sir, that's not what happened! It was consensual! We love each other!"

But Papa would have none of it. With a fierce growl, he grabbed Francesco by the collar and threw him out of the house, screaming obscenities until his voice grew hoarse.

The air hummed with the moment's intensity as I watched Francesco retreat into the darkness beyond the barn outside. The atmosphere hung low and heavy in the drawing room, a mix of smoke from the fire and my deceit. A cloud of questions swirled in my head, fear spilling into my heart.

"What will happen to him, Papa?" I asked.

He stared at me, his gaze firm yet compassionate. Then, finally, he answered, "The groomsman is awaiting him. Francesco will be whipped in the morning."

Inside, I felt cold, frozen in time, unable to move or speak. But I forced out the words through sobbing tears, "Oh, thank you, Papa. Thank you for protecting my innocence!"

My father pulled me close and hugged me.

The morning sun was inching its way across the sky the following day when I tiptoed out of the house, my heart fluttering like a million caged birds. As Francesco was hauled outside and strapped to a tree, I crept across the grounds and hid behind the barn.

The groomsman stood ready behind him with a long, braided whip in his hands.

Francesco's face was stoic, but I could feel his terror from where I stood.

The groomsman began to whip Francesco's back, each stroke drawing a bright line of crimson across his skin.

I had to bite my lip hard to keep from screaming, tears streaming down my cheeks.

Time seemed to stand still as the groomsman continued his brutal punishment, and finally, he stepped away.

My body trembled with fear and disbelief as the groomsman untied Francesco's bonds and walked away without saying a word.

Francesco collapsed onto the ground, his body wracked with pain. He did not move for a long time. Blood seeped from every angry line on his back. Finally, he staggered to his feet. He caught my eye and stumbled toward me. He bore down on me, his eyes burning with hatred. His lips curled as he cursed me. "Your lies will never go unpunished. You'll burn in the everlasting flames of hell!"

A spray of spittle flew from his mouth and landed at my feet.

I stumbled back, icy fear squeezing my guts tight like a vice.

Francesco gingerly straightened his beat-up back and returned to the barn with a dignity that belied his suffering.

I raced into the house, crying. Once upstairs, I sat on my bed and looked up at the ceiling, sobbing. I had done an unforgivable thing. Francesco's face, pale and emotionless, kept flashing through my mind.

I had deliberately and callously inflicted pain upon him, reveling in the twisted satisfaction it brought me. The guilt of my actions weighed heavily on my conscience as I realized the depth of hurt I had caused. In my cramped, suffocating room, I was consumed by shame and regret, knowing there was no way to undo the damage I had wrought.

That evening, I left the house to meet my other lover, Tomaso. Though I was young and inexperienced, I had grown smitten with him. He was much older than me, twenty-eight to my sixteen. I found him suave and worldly. The way he talked about politics and literature made me feel intelligent and alluring.

I rapped on the door to his home and let myself inside.

"Alina!" he said as he approached me from the drawing room, wrapping me in his arms. "I've missed you, my darling!"

A faint scent of pomade was evident in the brushed ebony of his gleaming hair.

I melted into his embrace, sobbing softly as the morning's events came flooding back to me.

"Oh, Tomaso," I said between tears. "Last night, I was molested and attacked by the stable boy. It was so awful!"

Tomaso's jaw dropped. "Oh, my dear! That's horrible! Did anyone see it? Did anyone help you? Are you all right?"

He held me tighter to him.

I sniffled and shook my head. "No one saw or heard anything, thank goodness. But it was horrible… Last night, when Father confronted him about it, Francesco lied and said he loved me and wanted to marry me!"

My voice trailed off into soft weeping again, and Tomaso rubbed soothing circles on my back while murmuring words of comfort in my ear.

"Please sit," he said, guiding me into his drawing room. "You must be drained from such duress."

In Tomaso's entertainment room, the walls were covered

in richly colored Venetian plaster, which gave the room an elegant background.

In the center of the room stood a large, dark wooden table with intricate carvings along its edges. Several velvet-covered chairs and a luxurious sofa surrounded the table. The chairs had high backs and curved arms and were upholstered in a deep crimson fabric that matched the drapes framing the windows. On either side of the room were two large, intricately carved wooden chests, each with a unique design.

The walls were adorned with various pieces of artwork, including a few large oil paintings and some tapestries. The oil paintings depicted various scenes, ranging from grand landscapes to portraits of notable figures, while the tapestries depicted a combination of mythical creatures and religious figures.

In the corner of the room stood a large stone fireplace with a roaring fire that provided warmth and comfort. Above the fireplace hung a large mirror with an ornate frame that perfectly reflected the room. On either side of the fireplace were two large armchairs upholstered in soft, cream-colored fabric.

The sofa was the main attraction in the room, however. It was a beautiful, curved piece of furniture with a mahogany finish. The deep blue-green fabric upholstery complimented the table and the chairs. The back of the sofa was adorned with intricate designs and carvings, evoking a sense of grandeur and luxury. The seat cushions were filled with soft, fluffy feathers, providing a comfortable seating experience.

I floated to his couch and settled upon it like a falling leaf.

Tomaso sat beside me and held me.

Finally, after a few minutes, he spoke again, leaning away to look at me. "I hope the lad was sufficiently punished for what he did to you. We must find a way to make sure this doesn't happen again."

I held his gaze, my face filled with sorrow. "Yes. He was nearly beaten to death."

"That son of a bitch deserved to die!"

"He got what he had coming," I said, my voice quivering, tears streaming down my cheeks. An icy chill ran through me. The lies and half-truths came easily, like I had been practicing for months. "Please... let's not speak of it anymore. It's too hard to bear."

"It's all right, sweetheart. We won't say another word about it." Tomaso leaned in close, his lips just inches from my ear.

His breath was hot on my neck, and I trembled, barely able to breathe.

"I have something to share with you tonight," he whispered, his voice low and seductive.

"Yes? What is it?" Anticipation built in my stomach as the silence stretched out between us.

"Come with me to a party tomorrow night," he whispered as his warm breath sent shivers down my spine. "Pietro Costa is throwing it."

"Raul's father?" I exclaimed.

"One and the same, and I guarantee you have never experienced anything like it. You have the freedom to do whatever you wish with whomever you please. Of course, I must be included in your escapades. What would the night be without me?"

"Of course," I said, giggling.

The Costas were an intriguing family. They were among Florence's most wealthy, and I'd heard rumors of some of their activities, including creating poisons. What they did with such substances was anyone's guess.

"So," Tomaso said, looking at me earnestly, "will you join me?"

"I wouldn't miss it for the world!" I nearly squealed with delight.

From my window, I saw a shadowy figure standing in the courtyard. His piercing gaze seemed to beckon me toward him like a powerful magnet pulling me closer.

But as I stared at him, an uneasiness settled in my gut. Something about him made my heart race and my palms sweat. Was it his unwavering confidence or the air of untouchable strength that radiated from him?

I wanted to resist his summons, to stay faithful to Tomaso, but I couldn't shake off the curiosity and excitement that bubbled inside me. Yet, there was also a deep-rooted fear gnawing at me, reminding me of the curse my former lover had put on me.

My mind and heart were torn between eagerness and terror as I watched the mysterious man outside my window. What would meeting him mean for my life? And more importantly, what hidden consequences could it bring?

I had no idea what was in store, and I was terrified.

CHAPTER THREE

ALINA

I awoke the following morning with cheer in my heart. I was going to Pietro Costa's masquerade ball tonight. I was already eager to make the most of my first luxurious evening.

I stretched beneath the linen sheets and rolled out of bed, allowing the morning sunlight to dance across my face as I slipped into my robe.

Before heading downstairs, I tiptoed into Mammina's room and rummaged through her luxurious gowns.

Mammina had impeccable taste, and all her clothes were custom-made. Since we were nearly the same size, I took one of her gowns, made of pale white silk, the color of moonlight, and squirreled it away in my armoire. Then, I went down the spiral staircase to the dining room, where breakfast awaited me.

"Good morning, Papa," I said, kissing his grizzled jaw.

He grunted but kept his eyes pinned to his news sheet.

"Good morning, Mammina," I said as I rounded the table to kiss my mother's soft cheek.

"Good morning, Fragolina," Mama said, tipping her cheek.

She often called me "Fragolina," which meant "little strawberry." The endearment gave me a warm, fluttery feeling.

"Eat, eat," she said, gesturing to the cook's feast of prepared treats.

The air was fragrant with freshly baked pastries and a hint of citrus from the marmalade, which I smeared over a warm scone. As I ate, a wave of giddiness washed over me. I watched out of the window, and my heart fluttered as the sun slowly rose, illuminating the sky with its golden rays. Tonight would be full of possibilities. I hadn't ever been to a party of such magnitude.

Mama broke the shell of her soft-boiled egg and scooped out a bit of golden yolk. "What has you in such good spirits today, my child?"

"Tomaso has invited me to his masquerade ball at Pietro Costa's, and I'm going!"

Mama and Papa stared back at me with cold eyes.

"Absolutely not!" Mama said.

"Your mother and I are the only two adults in this house attending that party," Papa said. "It's final!"

"No! You can't do this to me!" I shrieked, slamming my fists on the table. I rose to my feet, taking a deep breath as I steadied myself against the wave of defiance rising within me. "You can't stop me!"

"Watch me!" Papa shot from his seat, seized my arm, and dragged me out of the dining room.

I yelled and screamed as he hauled me to my room.

"I'm doing this for your own good, daughter," he said, his face conflicted as he shoved me backward onto the bed. "It's one thing to defend your innocence. But it's another to allow you to attend a ball of such debauchery."

He stood in the doorway, tall and imposing, as he glared at me.

"I'm an adult, too!" I whined.

"You're sixteen," Papa said, a bit gentler. "You know nothing of the ways of this world. Cherish the time you have before you assume the responsibilities of the world. There will be time enough to spread your wings and fly, my *piccolo uccello*."

Papa's face creased with sadness, his gaze softening as he looked into my eyes. His lips quivered as if he wanted to say something but couldn't find the right words.

I pounced on his moment of vulnerability, my words a sharp blade that cut through the air. "The neighbor's daughter got married at age fifteen. I'm already much more mature than she ever was."

Papa's features tightened with resolve. "No, my child, you're not. My decision is final."

Without another look, he whirled and slammed the door.

The snick of my lock followed.

I wriggled and convulsed in the sea of luxurious linens, desperately searching for an escape from the suffocating embrace. I ripped myself free and lunged toward the side table, snatching the heavy metal candlestick. With all my strength, I hurled it across the room. It gave a deafening crash as it crashed against the wall.

Every fiber of my being seethed with rage over the injustice of being forbidden to attend the party tonight. I lunged for the door with a primal moan, only to find it locked shut. Desperate, I hammered against it with balled fists, screaming my frustrations. When there was no response, I dropped to the floor, broken, and defeated.

Yet something inside me shifted at that moment, and I rose again to my feet. I stumbled toward the armoire, eyes drawn to the shimmering white dress like a magnet. I stepped into it and twirled before my full-length mirror.

It fit me perfectly. No one would ever suspect it had not been made specifically for me.

I carefully removed the gown and hung it up. Softly, as if someone would hear me and come running, I closed the dark oak door and wandered toward my window.

Outside, the sun shone upon the vineyards.

Francesco limped around in the vineyard outside my window. I winced and cast my gaze toward Costa's house. I wasn't going to miss that party.

Could I climb out of here unnoticed and sneak to my friend Raul's house? Maybe. It was worth a try. Perhaps I could procure some poison from Raul to make my parents sick. Then, they wouldn't know I'd escaped to attend the masquerade ball.

As I gazed out the window at the pitched angle of the roof, fear crawled into my belly and bit me. This would be harder than I thought—a daring climb onto that steep slate roof—but I would have my chance at freedom if I succeeded.

With a deep breath, I rucked up my long skirt and tucked the edges in my waistband. I had long been a devotee of exciting adventures, and this particular one was no exception. As I knelt on the sill, the warm summer breeze drifted across my face, starkly contrasting the cold stone of the windowsill. I steadied myself before easing open the window sash and climbing onto the slate tiles baking in the sunlight.

It was a beautiful day, and I felt my heart expanding with each step. It was as if the sun had a kind of magic that could clear my mind and give me clarity of purpose as I had never felt before. I told myself I could take on anything, even if it meant a daring escape from my home.

Making my way carefully along the roof, I stopped at the edge overlooking the garden. Dizziness washed through me as I stared at the ground. I crouched and rested my palms on the tile to steady my heart.

Once I'd assumed some control, I peered down at the trellis to ensure it was stable enough to support my weight.

It seems to be securely attached to the building. But I guess I won't know until I put my weight on it.

Glancing around to ensure no one was watching, I rolled on my belly and eased my legs over the edge of the building. I stretched my toes to find the trellis, then, clutching the roof's edge, let my weight sink onto the solid wood. It supported me. I lowered my body, maintaining a steady grip, moving slowly and deliberately.

I progressed toward the lawn, my heart thudding in my chest. When I was a few feet away from the verdant ground, I paused to savor the feeling of freedom before leaping onto the grass below. I landed smoothly on the ground, soft as water. I allowed myself to revel in the thrill, but I had to make haste for Raul, so I forced myself to leave.

I hugged close to the hedges and kept under cover of their branches until I reached the end of the long driveway. Then, with one last look at my parents' house, I ran toward freedom.

I hadn't realized how far away Raul was when I started out from home, and finally, panting, out of breath, and with no energy left me to run, I arrived at his house on foot.

He sat atop his bay horse in the yard. A wicked smile tugged at his lips when he saw me. "What are you doing here? Come to play?"

"Please, Raul," I said. "I need your help!"

He patted the neck of his horse. "Oh, anything for my darling girl."

"I need an elixir to make my parents sick so I can go to the masquerade tonight."

Darkness swept over his face as he scowled at me. "I don't have any of that kind of potion."

"But you do," I said. "I've seen you concoct love potions to ensnare girls in your charms."

Raul's eyes flickered with mischief. "Has it worked on you?"

I stamped my foot, exasperated. "This is serious! The only way I can get to the ball is if they're incapacitated somehow—and you're the only one who can help me."

He laughed. "You are coming then? To the masquerade?"

My heart raced as I nodded fervently. "Yes, only if you help me!"

"Well, maybe I can find something," he said, rubbing his chin. "However, everything comes at a price. I need something in return."

"What can I do for you?" I clasped my hands beneath my chin.

"Since tonight is the masquerade, I want to have a threesome with you and Tomaso."

I stared at him. "You want me to be part of a threesome with Tomaso, your friend?"

Raul nodded. "It's the only way I'll agree to give you the potion. Besides, we can have some fun."

"I don't know..."

Raul gazed at me intently. "Come on, it's just one night. You won't regret it. And you'll get to go to the masquerade!"

I sighed and nodded. It seemed like a small price to pay to be able to go out tonight. "Alright. But after this, we're done."

"Oh, I doubt that. You like me too much to ever to let me go." Raul dismounted and bent down to kiss me lightly on the lips. "Come with me into the house, and I'll see what I can find."

I made my way back home, every step making my heart race faster, and carefully snuck inside. It was well past noon, and the house was quiet—too quiet. Where had everyone gone? The carriage was still outside, so they couldn't be far.

Even though I knew what I was about to do would bring misery to my entire household, I forced myself to continue with my plan. I spread the poison into the duck waiting to be roasted, the vegetables resting in the basket and the bread which had been cooked for the evening meal. For good measure, I even poured some into the wine flagon. Afterward, I crept upstairs, unlocked my bedroom door, and let myself in.

If Raul was right and the poison was fast-acting, Papa wouldn't bother checking the lock.

As the clock struck dinner time, I crept toward the dining room, my heart racing with anticipation. Hidden in the shadows of the stairwell, I strained to hear every word spoken inside. The poison had done its job, its lethal effects taking hold swiftly and mercilessly. The once peaceful room was now filled with agonized cries and gut-wrenching heaves, a haunting symphony of suffering. My vengeance was complete, and I reveled in the chaos and destruction I had caused.

I tiptoed from my hiding spot and hastened up the stairs.

Footsteps tromped from the dining room, accompanied by moans and more retching.

I threw myself beneath the covers and feigned sickness.

My father opened my door to find me writhing on the bed, moaning. His face was pale as the sheets on the clothes-line, and drops of sweat clung to his skin.

"So, you have it too?" he gasped, dabbing at his face with a sodden handkerchief.

"I don't know what 'it' is, but I'm as sick as a dog," I said.

"We've all got it. Every single member of this household. Your mother is the worst. I've ordered everyone to bed." He shuddered, and his complexion turned green. "Excuse me."

He slammed the door, and his footsteps thudded down the hall.

I let out a quiet laugh. My plan was working perfectly. Raul had said they would be ill for a day or longer.

The house grew silent as a tomb with intermittent bouts of heaving. I endured the silence and the disgusting sounds all day until the light outside the window began to wane.

Moving as stealthily as a barn cat, I donned my attire. First came the silk knickers, the chemise, and the petticoat. Next, a tight-fitting corset accentuated my slender waistline. My mother's moonlight-white silk gown with long sleeves adorned with intricate lacework came next. I fastened the moonstone and ruby necklace around my neck, which Mammina and Papa gifted me for my sixteenth birthday. Matching earrings clasped my ears.

Before adding a short veil, I styled my strawberry-blond hair in an elaborate updo adorned with jewels and ribbons. Fine leather decorated with jewels trimmed my feet.

I studied myself in the full-length mirror, grabbed a small bag and threw a few essentials inside.

The clock ticked louder as I paced around the room, searching for anything I might have forgotten. I didn't have much time left. In a final, desperate gesture, I grabbed the small silver locket my mother had gifted me when I was a child and slipped it around my neck. Lastly, I grabbed the lacy mask Mammina had intended to wear tonight.

Holding my breath, I opened the bedroom door and entered the hallway. This was it—my one chance at freedom.

I couldn't risk my parents hearing Tomaso arrive, so I would meet him along the tree-lined driveway. The horrible smell of sick wafted into my nose as I walked through the house.

The front door let out a loud squeak, and I stilled, my heart hammering in my chest. I waited until I was sure no one in the house moved. Then, I stepped out onto the landing and slowly closed the door.

I crept down the stone stairs, along the stone walkway, and past the fountain. Once I reached the end of the circular driveway, I ran as fast as my delicate shoes would allow.

Ahead, the steady grind of carriage wheels against dirt met my ears. I waved my arms, alerting the carriage driver as to my whereabouts.

As the sleek black horses stopped, I quickly climbed into Tomaso's carriage. He greeted me with a wicked grin, his dark hair tousled and framing his handsome face.

"Alina," he purred, "you're positively enchanting."

A surge of exhilaration swept through me as I realized I had finally escaped my suffocating family home. The night was ours for the taking, and I felt like a powerful witch ready to cast spells and wreak havoc.

CHAPTER FOUR

ALINA

T he carriage pulled up to the entrance of the Costas' estate, and Tomaso exited first, striding around to open my door.

He helped me out of the carriage and twirled me in a circle.

"You look stunning, my lady," he said.

My white dress glinted in the torchlight.

"Thank you, my lord." I cooed, my face flushing.

Tomaso looked handsome in a doublet of luxurious gold velvet decorated with intricate beading. A pair of charcoal-colored breeches that reached just below the knee and silk stockings adorned his powerful legs. His leather shoes had a pointed toe and a high heel, while a large, elaborate lace collar hugged his neck. A black silk and leather cap decorated with feathers and jewels completed his ensemble.

He leaned over to kiss me, then eased back and procured his black mask. "Shall we?"

I slid my lacy mask from my small purse. "We shall."

The night was alive with revelers' sounds, and the

atmosphere was electrifying. Everywhere I looked, there was a visual feast of jewels, masks, and silks.

When we entered the foyer, every man looked at me with admiration and desire.

I felt my skin heat with a thrill of eroticism. I was entranced by the atmosphere and the figures in the colorful costumes. A group of gentlemen wearing Pierrot costumes and masks, their eyes covered in white painted porcelain, smiled at me. A pair of women wearing ornate feathered masks swayed to the music with their arms around each other's waists.

As I stepped through the ornate double doors of the mansion, my senses were assaulted by a symphony of decadence. Women in flowing gowns sipped champagne, their bodies pressed against men in tailored suits. In one corner, a couple passionately kissed under the dim light of a chandelier. On the dance floor, bodies moved in sync with the pulsing music, hands roaming freely over each other's curves and muscles. The air was thick with the scent of perfume and sweat, mingling in a heady aroma that only heightened the atmosphere of hedonism.

Tomaso whispered, "Now that you're here and masked, you can do anything. But you must do everything with me."

"Of course," I said, a smile on my lips.

Tomaso took me farther into the manor.

I kept scanning for Raul and finally found him.

Like Tomaso, he wore a black mask and was surrounded by several masked women. But there was no mistaking his muscular body and long, wavy hair.

I shivered and clung to Tomaso's elbow.

"See someone you fancy playing with?" Tomaso said.

"Why, yes. I do."

When Raul saw me, his eyes lit up with pleasure, and he approached me.

"Raul?" Tomaso said, a note of surprise in his voice.

"Yes, Raul," I said. "I should like to share you both."

Tomaso stepped to one side as Raul and I embraced.

Then, Raul kissed me right there in front of Tomaso.

Raul was only four years older than me. Unlike Tomaso, he lacked the finesse of an experienced lover. But what he lacked in experience, he made up in passion as his tongue tangled with mine.

How is Tomaso taking this? He can be so jealous of others' attention. A quick side-eye in his direction showed me he was interested.

His eyes glittered as he watched us, and an evident bulge formed beneath his breeches.

Encouraged, I melted into Raul. As Raul's hands stroked my back and shoulders, my body quivered with heat and lust.

Finally, we drew apart.

"It's good to see you, Raul," I said, smiling impishly.

"Likewise," he said, grinning.

Then, he turned to Tomaso.

"Tomaso," he said, reaching out his hand.

The two men shook hands, both smirking.

Without another word, we rushed upstairs and found an empty bedroom.

My desire burned hotter than ever as the two men caressed me, exploring my body with their hands and tongues.

Tomaso moved behind me and unlaced my whalebone corset, kissing and biting my neck.

When the corset fell to the floor, Raul unbuttoned the many small pearl buttons, cinching my long-sleeved dress together in the front, starting from the bottom. His eyes grew dark with desire.

When the top button was unfastened, the crimson garment fell from my body and puddled on the floor.

Heady with desire, I let my head fall back against Tomaso as he sucked and licked my neck.

Laughter and music filled the hall through the open door, courtiers chattered, and couples danced together. The smell of perfume and cologne emanating from the guests wafted in the air.

Raul untied each ribbon affixed to the whalebone hoop at the waistband of my petticoat.

Once it was free, I stepped out of it.

He removed my petticoat, lifted my chemise, and began sucking my nipples, first one, then the other. I moaned with the sharp, aching sensations flooding my body. Tomaso laced our fingers together and tugged me. A possessive glint shone in his eyes.

"Let's get comfortable," he said, inclining his head toward the large, four-poster bed.

"Let's," I said, taking Raul's hand and following Tomaso.

Lying on the sumptuous bed, I lay back against the plump silk pillows. "Undress yourselves, my lovers."

Tomaso and Raul stood on opposite sides of the bed, removing their clothes. Their eyes stayed pinned on me as their attire fell away.

My attention was drawn toward one, then the other.

They were each so different. Raul's body was slender yet muscled. His long cock bobbed proudly between his legs once his garments had been dropped to the floor.

I recalled the taste of his cock and the thrill of licking the semen droplets from his sensitive head.

Tomaso, equally as muscled, possessed a stockier build.

His thick erection was slowly engorging yet equally as impressive.

I thought about how it felt to wrap my small hand around his shaft, the fingers barely touching. And Tomaso tasted of earth and musk, a manly taste that spoke to his age and wisdom.

Tomaso crawled onto the bed and leaned in to kiss me, his lips soft and inviting. His stubble scraped against my cheeks as our mouths ground together. As we kissed, the world around us disappeared, leaving us in an isolated world of our own.

The air around us crackled with electricity as Tomaso pulled me closer, our mouths devouring each other. Intense pleasure thrummed through me as he explored my mouth with his tongue. I could taste his desperation and need to be close, sending a feverish heat through my veins.

My legs were shoved apart. I opened my eyes, looking up to find Raul standing over me. His lips curled into a feral grin; his desire palpable.

I kept kissing Tomaso as Raul's tongue slid up my folds. He licked in circles around the entrance to my core, teasing me before finally pushing his tongue inside. I gasped, arching my back, reaching beside me to pull Tomaso closer.

Tomaso pressed his cock to my hip, the pre-cum allowing him to slide along my tender skin. The pressure was delicious, and I moaned loudly.

Raul increased the intensity of his licks, pushing two fingers inside me as he continued to flick his tongue against my sensitive bud. The feeling of two men loving me was almost too much to bear. My body rocked into Raul's tongue as he flicked it against my clit. I moaned louder, pushing my hips up into their combined pleasure.

Tomaso pressed his hard, pulsing cock to my hip, a slick

layer of pre-cum gliding along my skin like a lightning bolt. Raul flicked and swirled his tongue over my clit, until I felt myself hovering on the edge of orgasm. Tomaso kept his mouth fused to mine as he massaged and fondled one of my breasts, tugging at my nipple with each stroke.

I finally wrenched my mouth from Tomaso's.

"Raul! Don't stop! I'm right there!" I reached down and grabbed hold of Tomaso's rigid prow of flesh, thick with anticipation, as I tipped over the edge into a shattering eruption of bliss that seemed to rip me apart.

Tomaso and Raul moved together effortlessly as if they had been engaged in this dance for centuries. Sweat beaded their foreheads, and the air was heavy with the scent of arousal. Tomaso's lips were rosy and swollen from passionate kisses. Raul's hand rested possessively on my hip, his fingertips digging into the flesh.

The only sound in the room was the sound of their breathing, its intensity growing as their pleasure deepened. Tomaso gasped with pure delight as my hand moved lower, exploring the contours of his body with tender reverence. I trailed my other hand across Tomaso's chest and curled my fingers around his neck, digging my nails into his flesh.

Both men gripped their cocks, stroking them wildly.

Tomaso tilted his head back in surrender, eyes closed in absolute rapture.

Tomaso and then Raul roared their release, filling the room with their husky moans of pleasure.

I threw my arms overhead and undulated against the luxurious bedding, lost in the moment's passion.

Raul rolled to my other side, and we lay there, unmoving, silent, blissful. At that moment, we were connected on a level deeper than love. We were joined by the power of our passion.

A noise caught my attention, and I looked up to see the women who had been with Raul earlier.

Raul noticed them, too, and beckoned them closer.

Tomaso whispered in my ear as they sashayed across the richly appointed room, "Let's go somewhere private where I can have you to myself."

His possessiveness gave me a thrill. I rolled away from Raul, leaving a void that would soon be replaced by a buxom redhead, a sassy blonde, and a plump brunette.

Kicking our clothes in the corner for later retrieval, I said, "Where shall we head?"

"Outside," Tomaso said, his eyes glittering with lust. His erection hung at half-mast between his legs, but I was confident I could make it hard again.

I was still aroused, stirred by all the other couples and pairings throughout the house and our own erotic interlude. My body buzzed with electricity.

Naked, I followed Tomaso down the stairs, pushing past the people who freely familiarized themselves with their partners' bodies.

We stepped outside into the sultry evening.

"This way," Tomaso said, taking my hand. He drew my fingers to his lips and kissed them.

As we moved across the yard, heading for the outbuildings, a dark figure watched me from the shadows. The moonlight shone just enough for me to make out a man with a wicked grin. *It's him—the man who beckoned to me before!*

A chill of fear washed over me, and my excitement began to dissipate.

The man looked like Lucifer himself, and I was eager to put some distance between us.

The figure disappeared, sliding into the darkness, and a

wave of anxiety replaced the fear. I glanced in every direction, searching for the mysterious man.

He was nowhere to be found.

Tomaso said, "Let's enter the barn for some privacy. I want you all to myself, dear Alina."

The idea of having sex on a hay pile turned my stomach. It reminded me too much of Francesco. The images of his raw, whipped skin killed my desire.

Reluctantly, I agreed and let Tomaso pull me toward the hayloft. Once inside the barn, Tomaso took me in his arms and kissed me without reserve.

My desire roared back to life, and my core grew wet with need.

"I'm going to fuck you… hard," Tomaso said, his eyelids heavy with lust.

"Oh, yes!" I cried out.

Before I knew it, he was inside me, fucking me against the stone walls of Pietro Costa's horse barn with the horses nickering quietly in their stalls.

Just as we were about to climax, a woman appeared in the doorway. Without warning, she drew a dagger and plunged it into Tomaso's back.

I screamed in shock and horror.

The woman disappeared into the night.

As I screamed in horror, Tomaso's limp body lay splayed on the ground, his once-vibrant eyes now empty and lifeless. Blood pooled around him, staining the hay beneath him crimson. Was this truly the curse of the stable boy coming to fruition? Francesco's warning echoed in my mind as I struggled to comprehend what had happened.

My entire being shook with shock and despair as I knelt beside Tomaso, unable to tear my gaze away from his lifeless form. The commotion of people rushing into the barn swirled around me. Women wailed, and men shouted in disbelief. Some tried to comfort me, but I was too consumed by grief to register their presence.

In the chaos, a kind woman draped a blanket over my naked body and led me out into the moonlit courtyard. She wrapped her arm around my trembling frame, attempting to offer solace, but I couldn't be comforted. I needed answers. I needed to know why someone would do this to my beloved Tomaso.

Determined to find the culprit and make them pay for their heinous act, I pushed past the concerned crowd and raced through the courtyard, my heart heavy with sorrow and vengeance. The hunt for justice had begun.

CHAPTER FIVE

ALINA

The chill air of the night seeped into my bones as I lurched toward the gardens, naked, wrapped in a blanket, utterly horrified at the brutal murder of Tomaso. Around me, the night seemed to wrap its suffocating embrace.

Where could the killer be? Where could she have disappeared?

I stumbled farther into the fields surrounding Count Costa's estate. The stillness of the shadows was broken only by the occasional rustle of a breeze and, from somewhere afar, the faint sound of voices.

Finding no one, I turned back toward the scene of the crime.

The barn was stuffed with onlookers muttering and shrieking over Tomaso's fallen form. People swarmed from the party like bees to honey, eager for a view of the macabre to top off the night's depraved festivities.

"He was such a good fellow," a woman said through her wails. Her voice sounded far away, yet it was only a few meters.

"Kindest lad I ever knew," said another.

I sobbed. Tomaso was indeed a good man, too good for me if I was honest with myself.

I continued my quest for the killer, heading toward a copse of trees.

The night's tension seemed alive as if something was lurking in the shadows waiting to be uncovered. A tremor of fear coursed through my body as I staggered along the dirt surrounding the barn, my every step echoing in the darkness.

A pungent mix of fear and seething determination engulfed my heart as I scoured the deserted outbuildings for any trace of Tomaso's killer. My eyes darted back and forth, scanning for even the slightest movement. Every fiber of my being burned with a desperate need to find her and exact my merciless revenge. In the shadows, mysterious figures seemed to lurk, taunting me with their elusive presence. But just as quickly as they appeared, they vanished into the inky blackness, leaving me alone with my simmering rage.

The full moon cast its pale light on the landscape, creating an eerie backdrop to my quest. The shadows seemed to dance around me as I searched, the darkness growing more oppressive.

The presence of something dark and powerful in the night pricked my awareness. It was a force that seemed to be watching my every move. I had to fight the urge to turn around and run, but instead, I kept walking, searching the estate's perimeter.

I had to strain my eyes to make out anything in the gloom.

A figure shrouded in darkness leaned against a shed wall, clutching a dagger.

She lurched out of the shadows and fixed a menacing leer on me. She wanted to kill me next.

I stumbled backward, my heart pounding in my chest.

Who is this horrible woman?

Someone else slid from the darkness—a man.

This mysterious stranger stood at the garden's edge, his dark hair wild in the wind and his icy-blue eyes flashing in the moonlight. His presence was palpable in the sudden stillness of the night air. He moved like a shadow, and I was captivated by his mesmerizing, hypnotic aura.

His handsome face and commanding presence seemed like a vision out of a fairy tale. His beauty was undeniable, and his gaze seemed to draw me in like a predator hunting for prey. He walked gracefully and effortlessly, cloaked in an air of danger and intrigue, his dark clothing flowing around him like a cape.

The woman wielding the dagger seemed unable to move as her gaze fixed on him.

I stood still as a statue, waiting to see what he would do.

He stalked toward Tomaso's killer, a dark glint in his eye. His hand moved quicker than thought could follow as he drew a blade from his pocket and plunged it into the woman's chest.

She collapsed onto the ground, her life fading away with every rapid breath. A wild cackle ripped through the air as her body dissolved into nothingness before my eyes. My heart raced, almost like I had been part of the act.

The man turned his attention to me. His eyes glittered with mystery and a hint of something dangerous.

I could feel his energy consuming my soul, corrupting me into something I was not. I knew he was not of this world. Power radiated out of him, filling me with cold, paralyzing fear.

"Forgive me," he said in a throaty whisper.

"Who are you?" I replied. "And what have you done to that woman?"

"Nothing that she didn't deserve," he said, his voice gentling into a purr.

He was no longer standing in front of me. His strong arms circled me from behind in the darkness of the night. My heart pounded as a strange rush of pleasure shot through my veins. His warm breath landed on my neck, his strong hands gripping my waist as he pulled me close.

I felt possessed, as though all the love I had kept locked away in my heart was unleashed. I wanted nothing more than to remain in this moment forever.

I wriggled in his grip, turning to face him. The blanket fell from my shoulders. I stood naked with this stranger, whom I felt sure I knew.

His eyes grew black with desire as he gazed down at my body.

Then, on impulse, I pulled him down for a kiss.

I had never felt so alive as I did when his lips met mine. His kiss was wild and passionate, full of love, longing, and desperation. His hands tangled in my hair, his lips pressing hard against mine as if he was trying to consume my entire being in a single moment. With each breath, I felt myself grow closer to him, my heart racing, my blood boiling with desire and emotion.

I could sense the fire in his soul, the intensity beneath his cold exterior. He was devouring me, and I wanted to be devoured. I wanted to be consumed completely, my soul merging with his. Every ounce of my being wanted nothing more than to drown in the sea of his love, to sink into its depths and never resurface.

After an endless eternity, the man pulled away, leaving me breathless and trembling. Our eyes met and I saw something new in him—something intoxicating. The warmth ignited a fire in my soul that I had never felt before our kiss.

Then, my terror resurfaced. *What did I just do? I kissed a complete stranger.*

"I'm so sorry," I said, my voice trembling. "I didn't mean to kiss you."

"No," he said, his voice strong and sure, "I am to blame. I'm a gentleman, and I shouldn't have taken advantage. My name is Lord Balthazar."

He bowed low. When he stood, the moonlight danced across his face.

"I am Lady Alina Tocino," I said, barely above a whisper. "It's truly my fault, Lord Balthazar. I don't know what came over me."

He smiled, the moon's luminescence glinting off his teeth.

"We all make mistakes in the heat of the moment," he said. "It was my pleasure to meet you."

He bowed again and stepped back.

I stood there for a moment, my mind spinning. *Who is this mysterious man? What does he want from me? Is he a gentleman or a cad?*

I wanted to learn more but was terrified of what I would find.

His presence sent chills through every fiber of my body. I could feel his will pressing against me. I inched back, ready to run, but I was held in place by Lord Balthazar's power, unable to move or look away from him.

He closed the gap between us, his eyes never leaving mine. Darkness radiated off him.

"I finally have you," he whispered.

An earthquake of a shudder rocked me.

"You finally *what*?" I said under my breath.

Balthazar shook his head as if freeing a fly from his hair. "My blood ran cold as I watched that woman raise her hand to hurt you. Rage and adrenaline surged through my veins like molten lava, and I was ready to take whatever action necessary to protect you. Now the weight of my obligation to defend you sits heavy on my shoulders. I am destined to care for you forever."

His words filled me with fear and dread, yet simultaneously, I felt a strange pull toward him. I knew I should be running, but instead, I stood in rapt attention, mesmerized by Balthazar's presence.

"You want to care for me?" I said, enraptured.

"Yes, dearest Alina." He brushed his fingertip across my jaw.

The crowd spilled out of the barn, chattering like hens. I watched from the garden's edge, my heart racing with a strange mixture of fear and anticipation.

As the sounds of the gathering grew louder and more intense, I could feel the eyes of the partygoers turning toward me.

I stood there, frozen in place, unable to move or breathe.

Several men emerged from the barn carrying something in their arms. It was Tomaso—his lifeless body and unblinking eyes staring at heaven. A sudden pain overwhelmed my heart, and as my vision blurred, I thought I might faint. Tears streamed down my cheeks, and the weight of this grief was unbearable. I had lost two lovers in just as many days.

The crowd murmured and exchanged looks of sympathy and suspicion. I was sure they knew the truth—Francesco's curse of me had been right. I was doomed to pay for my mistakes.

A voice came from the center of the crowd. It was a woman—Maria, Tomaso's mother. She looked at me, her eyes filled with anger and sorrow.

"You have sinned," she said. "You have brought this curse

upon yourself, and now Tomaso is dead. You must atone for your sins, you filthy whore."

As the others nodded, their glaring eyes felt like an impenetrable wall of judgment and condemnation closing in on me. Desperately, I scanned the onlookers for a sympathetic face, but all I saw were cold stares and turned heads. My chest tightened with intense sorrow, and my head felt heavy, as if I was trapped in a trance. I could not think or speak or act. All I wanted to do was lay beside Tomaso and die with him.

Then Balthazar wrapped his arms around me, turning me away from the onlookers.

His voice sent a shiver down my spine as he leaned close and whispered, "Let me take you home. I won't let anyone hurt you again. I will protect you. I will take care of you. Let us be lovers for eternity."

"Eternity is a very long time." My voice trembled as I glanced at the onlookers.

He grasped my face gently in his hands, his blazing gaze reaching into my soul. "Yes. I'll care for you as long as I have breath in my lungs. You and me, bound together through the ages."

His touch was like a furnace on my skin, burning away all fear with an unbreakable promise. His carriage stood waiting for us, a haven in the night. He bundled me inside, tucking a wrap around me, whispering soothing words of protection and care. He held me close as if to say that nothing would ever come between us now—not now, nor throughout time. We would be together forever.

The carriage pulled up to my dark home. No lights shone from the windows indicating life stirred beneath the roof.

Had they all died? Had the poison I dosed them with been too strong?

I sat on the edge of my seat, my gaze fixated on Lord Balthazar. I let out a heavy breath as I said goodbye, desperately wishing to be by his side.

"Goodbye for now," he murmured, cupping my hands. He clung to me as if he never wanted to let go. Our fingers intertwined for an eternity before he released me with one final lingering kiss.

I cautiously entered my house, dreading the sounds of retching I was sure to hear. Instead, there was only silence. As I crept up the stairs, I was relieved to hear snores from my parents' room.

Entering my bedroom, I closed the door firmly, the sound resonating in the quiet house. I discerned Balthazar beneath my window in the dimness, bathed in the pale moonlight. His intense stare felt like a scorching brand, sending a ripple of shivers down my spine.

My heart quickened, and I found myself immobilized. Was it captivation or dread flowing through my veins? What I understood was an undeniable urge to be close to him, my soul yearning for his touch. An urgent longing engulfed me, and I could no longer resist its magnetic force.

CHAPTER SIX

BALTHAZAR

As the carriage and driver faded into the night on their way to the stables, I stood before my estate. I took a deep breath, inhaling the sweet fragrance of summer roses in the night air and feeling the evening breeze whisper against my skin.

It had been a long time since I'd been back here, and I faced an unexpected dilemma—Lady Tocino—*Alina*—was so different than I expected. I'd arrived to kill her. Instead, I found a stunning creature whose villain ways were only beginning to reveal themselves. She utterly captivated me. I longed to take her further into my wicked world. She was a ripe fruit, ready for the taking.

I suppressed a shudder at the arousing thought.

The stone pillars of the grand entrance of my driveway were still as strong as ever. The wrought iron gates were heavy with age but opened automatically as I approached. The night was quiet save for the rustling of the grass beneath my booted feet. I felt more alive than ever in all my centuries of existence. And it was all due to Alina.

My boots echoed on the marble floors as I entered the

grand foyer, my cloak billowing behind me. Through the tall windows, I caught a glimpse of the sprawling gardens that surrounded the estate. The scent of blooming roses filled the air.

Gardeners had kept the grounds immaculate in my absence. The bright flowers in the beds billowed in the night breeze, marbled paths weaving between them. A delicate topiary stretched before me, still perfectly crafted since its creation a century ago. Beyond the gardens, the villa loomed in its grandeur, its stone walls cast in pale light from the moon overhead.

I stepped closer, gazing at the tall windows and balconies and the intricate stonework that adorned them. Despite the darkness, I could still make out the sprawling frescoes on the exterior and the marble columns that flanked the doorway. Everything seemed so vivid since meeting Alina, as if the world had come alive.

As I stepped through the doorway, a cloud of dust kicked up and filled my nostrils, making me cough. The space was dark and dimly lit, with abandoned furniture covered in white sheets. The musty scent of neglect hung thick in the air.

I've got to get this place cleaned up. I've let everything go since taking over the Coven of Shadows. I've been working like a madman, waiting for the day I'd find Alina and exact my revenge. But life has taken a twist, it seems. Instead of taking her life, I only want to take her—*to take her into my bed as my own.*

I received notice of Alina's whereabouts from the darkness known as Valentina. I'd been searching for Alina since her mother time-traveled her away from me. I'd eagerly destroyed Mathias' legacy, tearing down the once-grand Coven of Shadows with maniacal fervor. Now, all that remained was an eerie landscape of rubble and wreckage, a grim reminder of the darkness that once lurked in that joke of a school.

The school lay in ruins, students scattered and gone or dead. I had systematically dismantled his life, destroying all he held dear, and only one final act remained: the death of his beloved Alina.

Valentina, one of the few surviving darknesses from the school, had traveled with me. We journeyed to 1540 A.D. Florence a fortnight ago on a so-called "romantic getaway."

"So, when we get to Italy, my pet," I'd told Valentina. "Look for a young woman wearing a moonstone necklace."

"Why should I, Lord Balthazar, when you have me?" she'd said, draping herself around my neck like a heavy blanket.

"I don't intend to bed her, Valentina." I nuzzled her creamy neck. "I intend to kill her."

Valentina lit up at that idea.

However, I'd been the one to find Alina in the village marketplace, with a dark-haired fool following her like a puppy. One look at Alina and my plans had changed. She was exquisite, a copper-haired beauty with a bewitching aura. The moonstone and ruby necklace glistened around her slender neck, drawing me in. I started to approach her, but Valentina interrupted me, her voice laced with a hint of malice. "You've found her," she'd said. "It seems like I've been leading you to her all this time."

"You? Ha!" I turned to her, a cruel sneer on my face. "Who is the one who discovered her, hmm? It was me."

"But I led you to her," Valentina hissed.

Valentina had wanted me to reward her for finding Alina. It was a small price to pay for finding the source of my obsession, but it seemed like far too much.

I turned to Valentina and narrowed my eyes. "What do you want?"

Valentina smiled, her eyes glinting with mischief.

"I want you to show me you appreciate my help," she said. "I want you as my exclusive lover."

My heart had filled with rage. I had no intention of giving Valentina anything. I wanted her gone from my sight. But I went along with her ideas, taking her to Lord Costa's party with the promise of exclusivity, which I did not intend to grant. I was consumed with thoughts of Alina.

"I saw your bitch and her lover go into the barn together," Valentina said as we danced in the grand ballroom.

I hesitated, but then I made my decision.

"Very well," I said coldly. "Kill her lover."

I couldn't stand the thought of Alina with another man.

Valentina smiled, a look of satisfaction on her face. She turned on her heel and headed for the barn, leaving me alone with my thoughts.

After Alina's lover had uttered a gurgling yell inside the outbuilding, Valentina slid from the barn. She approached me, satisfaction evident in her eyes. "It is done, my lord."

Alina stumbled out of the barn, her body trembling with terror. Her face was drained of color, a ghostly pale that only accentuated her expression of pure fear.

My heart clenched in agony for her. Perhaps, in my haste, I'd gone too far.

"What have you done?" I snarled at Valentina, my voice dripping with rage and disgust for her actions.

Valentina begged me to forgive her, telling me she'd only done what I wanted to be closer to me. I'd shoved her away from me.

Then she'd gone after Alina. I'd had no choice but to destroy her.

I shook myself free of my memories.

The hall of my house was still decorated in the same manner as when I'd left it, with portrait paintings lined up on the walls, their eyes seeming to follow me as I passed. I moved through the house. The exquisite furniture was now slightly faded, and the draperies and carpets looked somewhat worn. I beheld the grand ballroom, its chandeliers still shining and the intricate tapestries still hanging, feeling like a stranger in my home. I had much to do to prepare it for Alina.

I headed upstairs. Thoughts of revenge, power, love, passion, and greed all swirled around me. I felt invincible, with the darkness of the night closing in on me, the air heavy with the promise of something sinister yet to come.

I dropped to the bed and stared at the ceiling. I had been speechless when I'd found Alina, struck by the beauty of her face and the darkness in her soul. She was unlike anyone I had ever known, captivating me in ways I had never been drawn to before. I wanted to know her, to unravel her secrets, and to feel her warmth.

As I lay there, I recalled the kiss she'd bestowed upon me and how it had felt like I was melting into the darkness of her embrace. I touched my lips, which still tingled, and recalled how her skin had felt as I traced my hands over her neck, back, and waist. Even the slightest movements, like the subtle arch of her back as our bodies pressed together, conveyed a world of emotion and intimacy.

I felt a stirring in my chest and a warmth running down to my toes, a feeling I had never experienced before. I could still smell the scent of Alina's perfume, a delicate floral fragrance that seemed to linger in my bedroom as if her presence was nearby.

Alina and I were beautiful together, and a wave of love and longing washed over me. Pleasure filled me as I imagined what it must feel like to have her in my bed. I thrust my hand beneath my culottes and allowed myself a moment of erotic satisfaction as I thought of her. But my pleasure was momentary, a nothing-much in the scheme of so-much-more. And that so much more would only be satisfied with Alina.

I had to have her *now.*

I strode to the open window and stared into the night sky. The wind brushed against my cold skin. I drew in the night's energy until I was filled to bursting. Then, with a sudden blast of energy, I faded from sight.

Many kilometers away, I reappeared at Alina's house in an open field surrounded by trees. I surveyed the field and the trees. I could sense the power of the land around me, the energy of the trees, grass, and dirt beneath my feet.

The soft glow of candlelight shone from an upstairs window at Alina's house. I knew it was *her* room, and my cock grew hard. With a sudden surge of energy, I disappeared again, leaving nothing but a faint trace of my presence. I reappeared in Alina's boudoir behind her, staring at her as she gazed at our reflection in the mirror.

Alina didn't seem startled or even surprised to see me, as if she'd been expecting me. This was unusual as I appeared to terrify most people. She held a finely-crafted bone brush in her hand and used it to stroke her long, reddish hair. A loose, robe-like garment made of silk sheathed her body, draping to the floor. Delicate floral embroidery adorned the low-cut neckline that revealed her luscious breasts.

I seized her hips and spun her on her stool to face me, removed the brush from her hand, and tossed it on her dressing table. It landed with a noisy clatter. I gathered her hair in my fist, pulling her head back to expose her beautiful neck. "Are you happy to see me?"

"Yes," she breathed, straining against my grasp.

I slowly licked her neck from shoulder to jawline, then urged her to stand with a tug on her hair.

She winced but rose.

I inclined her head back further and ran my teeth across her neck before releasing her.

She shuddered and wiped my spit from her skin.

I scanned the room as if it were mine to command, and Alina trembled.

The only sound in the room was her heart thundering in her chest. It boomed like thunder in my ears, and my cock twitched with desire.

I reached out, tracing my long fingers over her jawline. Alina shivered as I leaned in.

"You're so beautiful," I murmured, my voice low and husky.

Alina blushed, but she couldn't seem to speak.

I smiled, amused by her reaction, and stepped closer, my body pressing against hers. She gasped as my hands found her waist, pulling her close.

"Do you want me to take you?" I asked. "Shall I *fuck* you long and hard?"

"Yes," she whispered, her voice barely audible.

Her skin flushed with desire as I leaned in to kiss her. My lips were demanding, possessing her completely, and she melted beneath my touch.

Without another word, I swept her up in my strong arms. I backed her across the room, pushing her against the wall.

I grabbed her hips, urging her against me as I kissed her deeply. My tongue ravaged her mouth, and my hands explored her body, teasing her and driving her mad with need. With a sudden urgency, I shoved harder against her, my body begging for release.

My mouth never left hers. My hands worked Alina's body in perfect synchronicity.

Soon, she was lost in pleasure, her body trembling with every passionate stroke.

I stepped away when she began to shake, her body burning with pleasure and desire. I could read her passionate desire for me—it was written all over her face. But I had no intention of just giving her what she wanted. I wanted her to *beg*.

"What are you doing?" she asked, her voice feverish with yearning. Her breath came hot and heavy.

"How much do you want me…want this?" I waggled my finger between us.

"Desperately. Can't you *feel* my desire for you?" She tried to reach for me, but I batted her arms away.

"There are certain conditions," I said.

"Tell me. I'll do anything you ask of me," she said. "Please, Lord Balthazar, I'm yours for the taking."

She clasped her hands beneath her chin.

Oh, this will be good. I like it when Alina begs.

"You can be my lover," I said with a satisfied smirk. "I travel a lot, so you can take another lover while I'm gone to satisfy your needs."

I paused to gauge her reaction, but her expression was unreadable.

"When I am home, however," I said, "you must remember that I am your *only* lover. I will come to you. You must forsake all others and devote your heart and body to me alone. If you don't, there will be hell to pay."

I watched as the words sank in.

Conflicted emotions played across her face.

"Tell no one," I said, my voice deep and steady. "I'm your secret."

She looked up at me, searching my face for any hint of deception.

"Okay," she whispered finally, her lips barely parting as she spoke.

I smiled and placed my hand on her shoulder, using my thumb to caress her creamy neck. We just sat there, looking into each other's eyes in silent understanding. I knew that she wouldn't tell anyone about our arrangement.

I leaned forward, my eyes never leaving hers, and brushed my lips against hers.

She remained stiff and unmoving, afraid to yield to our potent connection. Then, she nipped my lip with her teeth.

I yanked back my head and studied her face, grinning. *So, there's a wild streak in her, is there?* I wiped the blood from my lip with my thumb and spread it on her lips.

Alina hissed and sucked my thumb into her mouth.

I kissed her again, more passionately this time, and was rewarded with a soft moan. I caressed her face and then moved my hands to her neck, feeling the warmth of her skin beneath my touch. With my lips, I traced a path along her jaw and down her neck, and as my mouth found her earlobe, her body trembled beneath my touch, her breathing more rapid.

I drew back, took her hand, and led her to the bed.

As she sat on the edge of the feather and herb-stuffed mattress encased in silk, I removed her dressing gown, her eyes never leaving mine. I hung it on the back of the chair in the corner and stepped closer to her. I ran my fingers through her hair and down her neck, and she closed her eyes, leaning into my touch. Her skin was softer than silk, and I couldn't help but linger at her neck and shoulder.

I growled at my tender regard for her. I wanted to *possess* her, not woo her like a simpering schoolboy.

My own clothes were discarded quickly, and I returned to

the bed where she lay. I had never wanted someone as badly as I wanted Alina. With her curves and angelic looks, she perfectly embodied everything I wanted in a lover. But what excited me more was taking her and controlling her completely.

She trembled beneath my gaze, which only heightened my desire for her.

My eyes glittered with lust in the dim light, and I was delighted when she seemed to shrink before me. My tall frame towered over her, and she appeared small and powerless in my presence.

I smiled and licked my lips. My seduction proceeded flawlessly.

I leaned down, my lips just inches from her ear. My hot breath tickled her skin, and she shivered.

"Do you want to be *mine*?" I asked in a low, rough voice.

Alina nodded weakly in response.

"How much?"

"With all my heart and soul," she said.

"Show me." I crawled onto the bed and pressed my naked body against hers. My rough hand grasped her hips, pulling her closer. I raked my fingers down her body, exploring every inch of her curves.

She arched her back, wanting more of my touch. I smiled against her ear, pleased with her response, and my lips found her neck, kissing and exploring the delicate skin. Then, I bit down, hard, on her tender juncture between neck and shoulder.

She whimpered and lay stock still, unsure of what I might do.

I clamped my teeth against her neck, sucking and tasting blood. But Alina didn't move.

Good girl. She's submitting to me nicely.

As I released my grip on her, she let out a soft moan of pleasure. My lips left a trail of heat as I moved down her body, reveling in the smoothness of her skin. My hands roamed over her thighs, squeezing and caressing every inch as I made my way to her inner thighs. With slow, deliberate movements, I teased and licked at her clit until she couldn't hold back her moans any longer. As she writhed beneath me, I pulled away with a devilish smirk. Crawling off the bed, I left her wanting more.

"Where are you going?" she said, her eyes wide and wild.

"Wherever I want." I smirked.

"Don't you want *me*? Am I not pleasing you?" She covered her naked form with her arms.

"Don't do that. Don't cover yourself up," I said.

She shook her head and curled into a ball.

"I said, *don't do that*," I commanded, my words echoing around the room. "Lay back, and let me look at you."

Trembling, she unfurled, and I grasped my rigid erection, stroking myself.

I wanted to come all over her, to mark and claim her, but I held myself in check. "You're gorgeous."

She lay still, panting like a frightened rabbit.

As I sat on the edge of the bed, my hands roamed up her body with purpose. One hand cupped her breast, teasing and tweaking her nipple until she gasped in pleasure. My other hand ventured down between her thighs, caressing and exploring every inch until she arched her back and moaned beneath me.

"You are *mine*, Alina," I growled. "Do you understand?"

She nodded, her beautiful eyes luminescent in the candlelight.

"And someday, I shall take you away from everything you know. We shall be together from that day forth." My lips found hers, and I could sense her need. I grabbed her wrists, forcing them above her head as I kissed her more deeply.

Alina continued to tremble beneath me. She was mine for the taking, supple and compliant, just as I wanted her to be.

I moved my body against hers, exploring and teasing her until she was moaning and begging for more. I smiled against her lips.

She gasped, arching her hips against mine.

I yanked a corner of the bedding free and wound it around her arms, binding them over her head.

She writhed beneath me, unable to control her response to my touch.

I grasped my cock and fit it inside her, giving her time to adjust to my generous size.

She winced and scrunched up her face.

I seized her jaw and forced her to look at me. "Take me in, Alina. All of me."

She nodded obediently.

I traced the curves of her body with my fingertips as I thrust into her, savoring every gasp and moan that escaped her lips. My hands danced along her skin, finding every sensitive spot and causing her to arch beneath me. Each movement was deliberate and calculated, driving us both toward ecstasy.

"I'm on fire for you," Alina breathed. "Fuck me deeper."

Good girl.

I pushed her limits faster and harder, and Alina cried out in pleasure.

Then, when I felt her body quivering, approaching its release, I stopped and slid out of her.

"Balthazar!" she cried out. "You're torturing me! Get back inside me!"

"Not yet," I said, smiling as I toyed with her nipple.

She let out an animalistic groan. "Take me, Balthazar. Fuck me, *please.*"

The desperation in her voice was such a turn-on.

"Who do you belong to?" I said, lowering my lips to within kissing distance.

"I belong to you," she said.

"Say it again," I commanded, breathing against her mouth.

"I'm yours, Balthazar," she said, her voice strained with pleasure. "Yours, yours, only yours."

I grinned wickedly, grabbed my cock, and thrust into her again, pushing her closer and closer to the edge. I drove into her unrelentingly, and she took all I gave her.

Finally, she screamed out my name as her body shook with pleasure. I followed soon after and collapsed against her in exhaustion.

I reached up to unbind her wrists. Her hands flew to my back, clawing down my skin and leaving marks. I chuckled.

So, my submissive little kitten still has claws. I can work with that.

I brought my hand down to her sated core.

"Don't start another fire if you aren't ready for another fucking," I said.

"Who says I'm not ready?" she purred.

"Oh, you wicked little vixen," I said, hardening again. This time I rolled on top without preamble and fucked her fast and furious.

She practically came on contact. I roared my release, pumping into her with unbridled passion, hot and dirty.

When I had finished, we lay together in the afterglow, completely sated.

Everything else faded from my thoughts as I felt the warmth of Alina's body against mine. I took a deep breath and let her sweet scent fill me up. I could feel her energy coursing through me, and I let my energy snake inside her body.

Alina's veins pulsed with darkness, a legacy left by Mathias. But I knew she was unaware of what she held inside.

I eyed her knowingly and spoke with a honeyed voice dripping with malice. "I can sense your desire to unleash the darkness inside you."

I inhaled deeply as if the scent of her darkness was a love potion.

Alina shook her head, her long hair tangling in the silken bedding. "I don't know what you're talking about."

"Oh, yes, you do. Don't fight it. I saw what you did to your parents, how you poisoned them, and what you did to that stable boy."

Alina froze, unable to speak as I laid bare her secrets.

"Don't be afraid of your dark and villainous ways," I said. "Your secret is safe with me."

Inwardly, I smiled. I would fan the flames of Alina's darkness until it consumed her entirely.

In the distance, a howl pierced the air, a sound both ethereal and primal. The hairs on my arms stood up, and my spine tingled with excitement. As the howling continued, something stirred inside me, a feeling that was both familiar and strange. A sense of power and strength seemed to radiate within me, and I realized its source: my darkness combined with hers.

Alina's darkness was potent, and I laughed as I coaxed it to life. I embraced its power, feeling both liberated and fearless. Something magical was in the air, a mysterious force hidden in the shadows.

The howling stopped, and the night descended into silent stillness.

We stayed like that for an eternity, our energies entwined. And when I finally felt sated, I summoned my energy and faded from the room. I left her with a smile on her lips, contented and at peace. I had finally found what I'd been missing—that little bit of pleasure shared between two people, the essence of life.

And I was determined never to let go. Unless, of course, I decided to kill her.

Time would only tell.

CHAPTER SEVEN

ALINA

Balthazar arrived at my door at the stroke of midnight. He wore a shiny ebony jacket, a leather sash around his neck, and an extravagant silver clasp. He looked wild and untamed, his unruly hair cascading around his face like a lion's mane, his ice-blue eyes smoldering with an intensity that made my heart race.

I opened the door, and he stepped inside without saying a word. His gaze met mine, and I felt an irresistible urge to follow him wherever he would lead. It had been like this for five years—secret trysts in the dead of night—and the intensity between us never waned.

He held out his hand, and I took it without hesitation. It felt solid and firm, and my skin tingled with anticipation. He pulled me toward him, and as I stood in his arms, a wave of warmth washed over me. His heart pounded against my breasts, and I could sense the strength of his love.

"Come with me," he said softly.

Our eyes met, and I knew what he meant. He offered me a chance to escape my mundane life, filled with my parents' social events and my tedious education, learning social arts and etiquette, music, and domestic skills, all of which I never intended to use. When I was with Balthazar, I could live a wild and free life driven by love and darkness.

My love for him had grown stronger with each passing moment, but I never dared to ask him if he felt the same. We connected in a way I had never felt before. The sex was always so passionate and intense, regardless of our moods. Sometimes we fucked like animals, and other times we would make love, and I would feel like our souls and bodies were married to one another.

Once, we escaped during the day, sitting side-by-side on the banks of the river, our bare feet dangling in the cool, clear water. We had sneaked away from the bustling city to this secluded spot, a hidden gem known only to a select few. The sun was setting, casting a warm orange glow over the surrounding landscape. The air was thick with the earthy scent of wet grass and crickets chirping in the distance.

As we gazed out at the rippling water, I couldn't help but feel a sense of contentment wash over me. This was my safe haven, my escape from the world's chaos. And sitting here with Balthazar, I felt more at peace than ever.

We didn't need to speak to understand each other. We communicated through glances, touches, and shared silences. Balthazar reached out and took my hand in his, intertwining our fingers. I smiled, leaning my head against his shoulder.

Together, we watched as a family of ducks waddled by, the ducklings peeping and splashing in the water. I couldn't help but feel a twinge of envy for their simple, carefree existence. When was this forever he promised? I still had to endure a miserable life with my family.

Balthazar leaned in and whispered, "I love moments like this when it's just the two of us, and the world disappears."

I turned to look at him, my heart swelling with affection. I pressed my lips to his mouth, savoring the taste of his sweetness. We stayed like that for a while, lost in our own little world.

As the last rays of sunlight disappeared behind the horizon, we knew it was time to return to reality. But for now, in this peaceful moment, we cherished the passion and companionship we shared.

But when I wasn't with him, I was often plagued by insecurity. As much as I wanted to believe that he would never leave me or hurt me, I couldn't get rid of my deepest fear that one day it could all go wrong, and he could turn his back on me. Even though we shared an unconditional bond, I knew that nothing was promised to me, and no matter how scared I was of losing him, I could do nothing but hope and keep loving him.

But then he'd appear on my doorstep, appearing more handsome than ever and whisking away my fears.

When he arrived one night, I had experienced a dreadful day, plagued by fear.

"Hello, Balthazar," I whispered, holding the door wide.

He stood on the stoop in the moonlight. "Are you coming with me?" he said, nudging me away from my fearful thoughts.

"Where are we going tonight?"

"Into the city. There's no one about."

I paused, considering. I wanted more—so much more. But if snatched moments were all I got, I'd take them.

He smiled, a gentle upturn of the lips, and before I had time to think it through, I gave an eager nod. He stepped closer, wrapping me in his warm embrace.

"I will never let you go," he murmured against my hair.

"Nor I, you," I breathed.

We rode horseback into the city with me behind him,

pressed to his strong back. Once we arrived in town, we tied up the horse and began our exploration, with no witnesses to cast judgment or issue warnings. My heart raced with anticipation as we sprinted down empty streets, our feet pounding against the pavement. The wind whipped through my hair, and I couldn't help but let out a wild laugh. This was the freedom I craved, and I held on tight to him, never wanting this moment to end.

We reached a clearing at the edge of town, and he pulled me down to the grassy ground.

The moonlight glowed around us, and the blood surged in my veins as I looked into his eyes.

My entire being shivered with anticipation as his body pressed close to mine. I felt like I had been waiting for this moment my whole life. It was always like this between us— forever new, forever as if the first time we made love.

The heat of his skin against mine sent an intense wave of pleasure coursing through my veins.

His strong hands tangled in my messy hair, pulling me closer as our lips met in a fiery embrace. My body tingled with heat and pleasure as his skilled touch sent me into uncharted realms of ecstasy. Our desire burned hot, and we gave in to each other without hesitation, exploring every inch of each other's bodies with reckless abandon.

Under the twinkling stars, he whispered sweet nothings that made my heart flutter and my soul soar. Together, we reached new heights of passion and love, lost in a world where inhibitions held no power over us.

As the night wore on, I knew that this love was something I never wanted to let go of. I wanted to spend eternity in Balthazar's arms and live this wild, free life of passion.

But when the sun rose and the night ended, I had a life to lead. My parents still hoped I would take the traditional route, get married, and have children. The idea made my skin crawl. I dreamed of a life with Balthazar, only him. Whenever my parents suggested motherhood to me, I loathed the idea.

My heart pounded as I tore across the grassy field and burst into the back of the house. Without pausing for breath, I stormed through the kitchen. The shadows from my fierce gaze made the cook step back, her face paling. I'd warned her of dire consequences if she ever revealed what she knew about my trysts with Balthazar.

I crept upstairs, wary of rousing my parents from their slumber. The wooden door protested with a loud creak as I cautiously pushed it open, my heart thumping in fear of being caught. The room was silent except for the soft rustling of blankets and the occasional snore. With bated breath, I carefully closed the door and crept toward my bed, careful not to make any noise that could give me away.

I fell back on my bed and quietly laughed. A surge of victory about my deceit swept through me. I'd been getting away with my wanton behavior for five years, sneaking out at night to see my lover, with no one the wiser. I lay there, my veins pulsing with an unfettered force unleashed since I became Balthazar's lover. An electrifying energy surged through me that could only be described as delicious chaos, awakening a seething darkness within me that was eager for release.

I reached for my journal and pen and ink, rolled on my stomach, and began to scribe.

Dear Journal, I've been with Balthazar for many years. He is as fascinating as he is mysterious. I feel as if I will never fully understand who he is, but I want to know him intimately.

I continued to write, adding to the chronicles of my time with Balthazar until my ink well ran dry. Then, I rose, performed my daily ablutions, dressed, and headed downstairs to breakfast.

The sun had just begun to peek over the horizon as the first rays crept through the windows of our opulent home. A feast had been laid out on a long mahogany table in the dining room. The table was lined with plates of freshly baked bread, still warm to the touch. Jars of homemade jams and bowls of vibrant fruits glistened in the morning sun, each bursting with flavor and color. As if on cue, the smell of freshly roasted coffee beans wafted through the air, mingling with the sweet scents of fruit and bread. It was a feast for the senses, a perfect start to the day.

A fire roared in the stone hearth while beautiful tapestries adorned the walls and priceless paintings hung above the mantel. An array of candelabras filled the room with a warm glow, and silver chandeliers hung from the ceiling, glinting in the morning light.

Our servant, Matilda, bustled around the room, setting out fine China and napkins and checking the temperature of the dishes.

It was a beautiful start to a perfect day, and the sun seemed to shine a little brighter as I recalled the bliss I'd shared with Balthazar a short time ago.

Mother and Father sat in their seats, focused on the morning news sheet.

"Good morning, Papa," I said, kissing his cheek.

"Good morning, Mammina," I said, rounding the table to kiss her soft temple.

"Good morning, dear," Mother replied, not looking up.

Papa lifted his gaze to regard me. His eyes bore into mine, and my heart skipped a beat.

"You look cheerful," he said, his voice laced with suspicion. His tone was almost accusatory, as if he knew about my secret tryst. "Is it the picnic outing you're going on with Lord Amato that's got you so happy? Or is it something else?"

My stomach turned at the mention of Davide Amato's name. I had pushed him to the back of my mind, but now he was front and center again. The thought of spending time alone with him made me uneasy, but I couldn't let Papa know that.

"It'll be nice," I said lamely, trying to sound excited. But all I could think about was how much I wished I could get out of it and return to Balthazar's arms.

Davide was nice enough but so ordinary compared to my true love. Davide was commanding, standing tall with a well-built frame that exuded confidence. He had dark, wavy hair that fell just above his shoulders and a neatly trimmed beard. His piercing eyes, often filled with ambition, were a shade of deep brown that seemed to hide a hint of roguery. He paid attention to his appearance, dressing in fashionable garments that reflected his status and enhanced his charismatic aura.

But I saw through his charm and recognized his manipulative nature. Davide was selfish and driven solely by his own interests. I resented the hold Davide had over my parents. They were blind to his true character.

"When are you leaving?" Mammina asked, her eyes burning into mine like fire.

"This afternoon," I replied, my voice trembling with anger. "His carriage is set to arrive in precisely six hours."

"Be sure to dress appropriately," she said, her words dripping with disdain.

"What does that mean?" I spat out, my patience thinning at the edges.

Mother's gaze intensified as she looked at me. "Something pretty, dear. Something that reflects your station in life —impeccably."

A boiling rage simmered inside as I stared at my parents. They constantly interfered in my life, snooping around where they had no right to be. I was angry that they pushed me to get married and start a family when I wasn't ready. Yet, despite my anger, I knew their intentions came from a place of love.

With a sigh, I allowed my shoulders to drop.

"Of course, Mammina," I said demurely. "I will dress in my finest picnic attire."

At two o'clock on the dot, I flounced down the stairs, wearing an emerald-green silk dress with a low-cut bodice that accentuated my waistline and created a graceful silhouette. My outfit was complete with fashionable, puffy sleeves adorned with embroidered flowers. My head was topped with a wide-brimmed hat decorated with ribbons to add a touch of style. Delicate gold chains hung from my neck, and my feet were comfortably clad in low-heeled leather shoes.

Davide was already poised in the front parlor, his intentions clear as he chatted with my parents.

Standing on the bottom step, I froze like ice when I heard him say, "Ask for your daughter's hand in marriage."

My stomach churned with dread and anger. I could not accept Davide's proposal.

Papa muttered something about what an upstanding young man Davide was, and could he care for me the way I deserved?

"Naturally," Davide said with a smug smile. "My career in banking is quite lucrative."

I was terrified as I stood out of sight on the parquet floor.

To my left, my parents and Davide were waiting for me through the archway. I could run out the door to my right and make a break for freedom. My heart raced as I considered my options. I knew I had to face them, so I tried acting cheerful and entered the room.

"Why, hello, Lord Amato!" I said as I swept into the parlor.

Davide bolted to his feet.

"Lady Tocino," he said, his eyes glittering. "You look splendid."

He reached for me, drawing my hand to his lips and kissing my knuckles.

"Thank you," I said coyly, fluttering my lashes. All the while, my mind raced to find a solution to this dilemma. There was no way in hell I would marry Davide Amato.

My parents clucked and chirped around me, their words a never-ending drone of admonishments aimed in my direction. The tension was unbearable until we finally broke free from the suffocating scrutiny of my parents' gaze. I knew in their hearts they thought today would be the big send-off, the moment they'd been waiting for. Their beloved daughter would finally be betrothed.

I had other plans.

We bade my parents goodbye. Their eyes sparkled, and Mammina sniffled as I tucked my hand in the crook of Davide's arm. She was probably already planning my wedding feast.

Davide escorted me outside and led me to his glossy black carriage, a four-wheeled box-like structure with a fold-down roof called a calèche. As the day was warm, the calèche had been pulled back and fastened to the sides.

I lost my footing and lurched forward.

The two snow-white Andalusian horses harnessed to the

cart quivered at my actions, the whites of their eyes flashing in terror. Their nostrils flared, and their manes whipped wildly as they tried to pull back from the carriage.

Davide stepped forward, shouting in a thunderous voice, "Ivory Moon! Frostfire! Whoa!"

He wrenched on the harness, trying to steady them as they stamped and snorted in fear.

When he finally managed to calm them, he helped me into the seat, muttering, "I don't know what got into them. They're generally well-behaved."

"Perhaps they saw something that spooked them," I said, smiling sweetly as I settled onto the plush leather.

"Perhaps. But I don't want you to be alarmed," he said, climbing beside me. "I would never put you in harm's way."

He made a sharp clucking sound and tapped the reins hard against the horses' rumps, urging them to move faster to get away from whatever it was that had frightened them.

I didn't understand why the horses reacted to me, but a plan began to form to eliminate Davide from my life.

And from everyone's life, I thought with a sly grin. I would find a way to scare the horses deliberately. I didn't know how to do that, so Davide was harmed. But I was a clever, resourceful girl.

We trotted along the dusty road before finally stopping near a lovely creek lined by grasses.

Davide reined his steeds to a halt and climbed from the seat. He rounded to my side, reached up, and grabbed me around the waist to help me down.

My skin prickled at his touch.

Instead of placing me on the ground, he whirled me in a circle, his face alight with joy. "Oh, my beautiful, Alina."

I forced a smile through this dizzying display of affection. As soon as my toes touched the ground,

Davide launched himself forward for what he thought would be a kiss. But I wasn't in the mood for that, so I dodged his attempt and stepped back out of his reach. His head tilted to one side as if he didn't understand why I avoided him.

"What's going on? Is something wrong?" he asked. "Is my wildcat lover suddenly shy?"

I'd gone against modern propriety with Davide, as I had with all my lovers. But this relationship had taken a turn for the worse—Davide thought I loved him in the way a man ought to love a wife.

"Of course not, darling. I wish to enjoy the beauty of this land before we get lost in each other's arms."

I stepped closer and brushed my hand against his smooth-shaven jaw.

His expression brightened. He probably thought I was playing hard to get. "Of course, my sweet. Let me settle you, and I'll see to the horses."

He strode to the back of the carriage and procured a wicker picnic basket. He found a grassy place he deemed suitable for our tryst, not considering my desires. Everything with Davide was always on *his* terms.

He spread the picnic blanket and set out food and wine. "My darling, Alina. Would you care to join me?"

"Aren't you going to turn out the horses in the grass?" I smiled sweetly at him. "You don't expect them to inhale road dust all afternoon, do you?"

He stared blankly at the Andalusians. "You're right, my dear. I lost my head for a moment."

As Davide fussed with the horses' reins and harnesses, I screamed and clapped my hands. The horses grew increasingly agitated, whinnying and stomping with their powerful hooves. Fear seeped into their eyes until they bulged with terror, their shrieks piercing the sky as they tugged at their restraints.

"Alina! Stop this foolish behavior at once!" Davide cried out.

I did no such thing. I continued to yell and stomp about.

Davide bellowed for the horses to stop, but his words were useless against their prey instincts. They reared up, then dropped to the ground, kicking out. Their hooves collided with Davide's skull, sending him tumbling end over end through the air until he lay in a lifeless heap on the ground.

I laughed and ceased my frenetic movements, uttering soothing words to Ivory Moon and Frostfire. The horses glanced at me with wide, fearful eyes.

Now what? I hadn't thought this through.

I strolled toward the feast, plucked a ripe pear from the basket, and munched it thoughtfully. Its sweet juices dribbled down my chin. When finished, I pitched the core away, watching it disappear in the grass.

I stalked toward Davide and crouched by his side. I shook his shoulder. "Davide?"

No response.

"Are you alive, my dear?" Still, no answer save for the blood that seeped from his skull.

I rose to my feet, propped my hands on my hips, and looked around. We were far from anywhere.

"Well, I guess it's up to me to gather help." I knew my way around a harness, so I loosened the traces, removed the reins, and undid the breast collar and backband.

The horses quivered and nickered as I moved around them.

I took several deep, calming breaths and continued my tasks until the horses were free of the carriage. I removed the bridle and bit from one of the steeds and slapped him on the rump. He tossed his head and galloped a few meters away from me toward the grassy knoll.

"I know, I know," I said to the horse whose reins I gripped. You want to join your friend, but you have a job to do."

I roughly tousled my hair with my free hand before grabbing a handful of the horse's mane. In one swift motion, I pulled myself onto his back and kicked him into a frenzied gallop. With every stride toward home, I summoned more emotion—fear, uncertainty, and despair—building on the deception I had mastered since that fateful day with Francesco.

When I arrived at my house, I threw myself off the horse's back and ran into the house, crying. "Papa, come quick! Something's happened to Davide!"

Papa burst from his study. "What is it, Alina?"

"The horses... They panicked, and one of them kicked Davide. He wasn't moving when I left him." I wrung my hands. "Oh, Papa, I fear he's gone to his maker."

My father's eyes narrowed as he regarded me. "Why is it that something tragic happens to each man who courts you?"

I feigned shock. "Papa, I don't know what you're talking about!"

"Don't you, Alina? It's time to set things right. We need to clean up this mess and talk while we're at it. You have to come with me." He marched toward the front door with a stern expression.

"No, Papa!" I exclaimed, my voice shaking with fury. "I can't take it anymore! I saw Davide's lifeless body, and if you make me relive this again, I swear I'll break down!"

Tears streamed down my contorted face as a raging fire of emotion burned within me.

Papa glanced at me, and confusion and disappointment

flickered across his face. "It doesn't matter what I want or don't want. What matters is that we fix this so it doesn't happen again. Now, *come*!"

Outside, Papa harnessed Davide's horse and one of his own to our carriage, and we set off. I sat glumly on the seat beside him, my mouth turned down in a frown, and my arms crossed over my chest.

"People are starting to talk, Alina. They're fearful of letting their sons court you," he said.

Stupid birds chirped around us as if taking glee in the scolding I was about to get.

"I can't help it if their sons are careless or take me for a ride with willful, unruly horses. You should have seen their behavior," I said. "Did you see how they acted out when I approached the carriage?"

Papa sighed. "Yes, I saw. But it seems like bad things follow you around. When we found you, this wasn't the life your mother and I envisioned for you."

He clucked to the horses, hastening their pace.

"Wait, what? What do you mean you *found* me?"

Papa remained silent before saying, "My beloved daughter, you're adopted. Your mother and I were strolling in the park one day when we saw you nestled in a basket with a note requesting that whoever found you take care of you. The message was impossible to ignore, especially for your mother and I, who had faced countless struggles in trying to conceive a child. So, we took you home with us. We gave your dagger to Giovanni, who told us you were a Timeborne, not from this time. You were brought to us through adoption."

I stared at him, my emotions reeling. "You mean...my biological parents didn't want me? And what's this about being a Timeborne and a dagger? What does that even mean?"

Papa swallowed hard. Finally, as we rounded a bend in the road, he spoke. His voice was soft, his tone gentle. "It means, my dear, that you can travel through time. You were born with a mystical dagger by your side. We gave the dagger to our close friend Giovanni, who told us of your abilities. We didn't want to tell you until you were ready to hear it. Since you are here, it seems that now is the time."

I sat there, reeling in shock as we trotted through the Italian countryside. The news that I could travel through time was impossible to process. I felt like I was dreaming... as if the world had suddenly shifted and I was no longer in control. What did this mean for me, for my future? Would I be able to travel to the past and the future? Would I be able to change the course of history? All these questions raced through my mind as Papa watched me.

And then another, more disturbing thought entered my mind.

Did Balthazar know I was a Timeborne? Can he travel through time?

Through all these years, I should have learned *everything* about Balthazar. But I knew very little. He was a mysterious man who came and went. He encouraged me to take lovers when he was gone but demanded exclusivity when we were together. He'd even been the one to murder a few of my lovers. When I asked him about his travels, he brushed me off with comments like, "Let's speak of other things, my love. Where I go is of no concern to you."

"There's something else we need to discuss," Papa said slowly, his voice tinged with worry.

I swallowed hard, wanting nothing more than to disappear into the earth.

My throat tightened as my father's words hit me like a wave. The rumors about me and Lord Balthazar were not just whispers anymore. They had reached my own father's ears. His accusing eyes bore into mine, and I could see the sadness behind them. But how could he accuse me of something so untrue? I knew the unsavory rumors about Lord Balthazar, but I also knew I loved him with all my heart. My father may have raised me, but he was not my real father. And now, in this moment of conflict between us, I couldn't help but wonder if he ever truly knew me.

The color drained from Papa's face. "Darling girl, he's not right for you. He's too dangerous. And there are whispers that he's a murderer. He'll kill you, too."

My lips curled into an angry sneer. "I don't care. I'm going to be with Lord Balthazar no matter what!"

My father's mouth pressed into a stiff, unyielding line, and we silently continued our journey.

I sat next to him, fuming. I had spent the last five years manipulating and torturing my lovers, who wanted to please me more than anything else. Yet, none of them had been able to satisfy me. And then there was Lord Balthazar, who had entered my life like a storm. I did not trust him—not because of the rumors that followed him wherever he went, but because I could never quite make out his intentions.

I was intrigued by Balthazar and in love with him. Yet I was also scared. How could this man be so powerful? What secrets did he hold? How could I ever hope to understand him?

I was determined to find out who Balthazar was and control him. I wanted to take all his secrets, desires, thoughts, and dreams and use them against him so that he would never be able to replace me. But how could I do that?

I had no idea yet but was determined to figure him out.

CHAPTER EIGHT
BALTHAZAR

S weet orange and musky incense smells were heavy in the late afternoon air. The sound of laughter and fountains provided an irritating backdrop as the sun sank lower in the sky. The streets were a maze of cobblestones, twisting and turning through vibrant markets filled with stalls overflowing with colorful goods. Street performers gathered around plazas, serenading the citizens with music and laughter. Merchants hawked their wares along the streets.

The entire scene disgusted me. It was too cheerful, too jolly, too *everything*. Glowering, I strode through the marketplace, Alina by my side.

Men sauntered past us, openly ogling Alina, regardless of my obvious claim on her. She'd tucked her hand into the crook of my elbow on our lover's stroll but kept glancing at the lusty men. Her beauty, grace, and power entranced them, and they seemed ready to do anything for her. And she got off on their attention.

The two men currently passing by pushed and shoved one another, ready to get into fisticuffs over my lover.

Annoyance shot through me like an arrow, and I sneered.

Alina laughed at the display of machismo before turning back to me.

My chest tightened as her eyes met mine.

"Why the angry face, my love?" she said teasingly. She wore a dress of gossamer green silk, fitted at the bodice with a wide skirt. The modestly curved neckline afforded the barest glimpse of her beautiful breasts.

She carried herself with an air of dominance, and I did not like it. Whenever she walked into a room, heads would turn, and conversations would pause. *I* wanted the upper hand in the relationship. I wanted her to desire *me*. But I feared I was losing her attraction.

"I'm famished," I said, quickening to hurry her along. "Let's find a place to eat."

I was filled with a complex mix of love and jealousy and was desperate to regain control of the relationship. She was *mine.*

I don't want to share Alina any longer. I want exclusive rights.

I had no idea how to assert my claim over her. She was an enigma, unlike anyone else I'd ever screwed. I was afraid it might push her away if I tried to be possessive of her. I was terrified that if I showed too much jealousy, it could ruin our relationship. I wanted to keep my desire for her but also to be able to trust her. I knew I had to take control of the situation, but I wasn't sure how to do that without making her feel like I was trying to dominate her.

And all these feelings made me feel weak. I *despised* weakness in anyone, but especially in me.

A sinister grin spread across my face. With a cold, calculating gaze, I plotted my next move. I would reveal my true nature and brutally take someone's life in front of her. She'd seen me kill before, but this time would be different. This time, Alina would see me as a monster and submit to my power.

I turned to her and said, "I have a surprise for you."

"A surprise?" she said, pleased.

I couldn't take my eyes off Alina as we stood in the town square illuminated by the oncoming sunset. I was drawn to her like she was a lodestone, and I was a needle. I wanted the whole world to know that she was mine.

I moved closer, pressed my hands to either side of her face, and kissed her madly and passionately right in the middle of the square. Pulling her close, I reveled in her moan, grinding my bulging erection against her. I thrust my tongue into her mouth, and she responded by sucking it and twirling her tongue around mine.

I glanced out of the corner of my eye.

People gawked and stared. No one displayed public affection in this town. I didn't care. I was in lust; Alina was mine, and I wanted the world to know.

Alina's eyes glittered with desire. Her cheeks were flushed, and her breasts heaved.

"Was that the surprise?" she said, brushing her swollen lips with her fingertip.

I shook my head. Without a word, I grabbed her hand and left the square behind.

We found a quiet cafe, and I bade her to sit at one of the outdoor tables.

She sat, still stunned by the brutal kiss.

The outdoor area was lit by torches held aloft by intricately designed iron poles. The warm glow of the flames cast a golden light onto the surrounding cobblestone walls, leaving behind a gentle, amber hue.

The seating area consisted of comfortable chairs, tables with fine Italian linen draped over them, and a few sets of benches. Thick, red, and blue blankets hanging over some of the chairs and benches made the atmosphere even warmer, adding a cozy, inviting touch.

I ordered two glasses of Valpolicella, a red wine produced in the Veneto region of northern Italy. The wine was a medium-bodied favorite of mine, with flavors of cherries, berries, and a hint of spice.

As we waited for the Valpolicella, I reached across the round table and stroked Alina's hand. "You look breathtaking, as usual, *cara mia*."

"Thank you." Alina lowered her head and gazed up at me through her lashes. "Is *this* the surprise?"

"Just wait."

When the vino arrived, we sipped it and conversed flirtatiously about nothing as the sky darkened to a star-filled black.

As the buzz of alcohol filled my limbs with languor, I eyed Alina. Her hair was an auburn curtain around her face, but all I could see were her big eyes sparkling like stars in the night sky.

My arousal for her grew like a tempestuous storm. The thought of killing someone in front of her thrilled me to no end. Soon, Alina would be my submissive angel, and I would possess exclusive rights.

Other couples joined us as we sat there, and the atmosphere became a heady mixture of sexual tension and desire. I felt certain everyone fed off the delicious vibes between Alina and me.

I scooted my chair around the table, lifted Alina's hair from her neck, and nuzzled her. "You're everything to me, *cara mia*."

"As are you," Alina breathed, arching her head back and baring her slender neck. She slid her hand around my face and stroked my stubble-covered jaw. "You please me to no end."

"I strive to satisfy," I said. I glanced around, noting eyes darting in our direction and back to their paramours.

One man brushed his fingers across the top of his partner's breasts while whispering in her ear.

A woman had her hand beneath the table and stroked her lover's rigid flesh, thinking no one could see. I could see everything from my vantage point, including her long, pointed fingernails.

Aroused, I crashed my lips against Alina's, devouring her hungrily as I let my tongue explore her mouth. She gasped, and the sharp sting of her nails dug into my back. The hunger rose in me like a heatwave, and I curved my hand around her core, pushing through the fabric of her silk dress. Her body shuddered with pleasure as she melted beneath my touch.

"I need you *now*, Alina. Don't make me wait any longer," I growled in her ear.

"Yes, take me," she replied huskily, her eyes burning with desire.

My eyes darted around the plaza, searching for my next victim. A mousy looking woman scurried along the darkened walkway, head down. *That's her. She's weak. Inconsequential. No one will miss her. She'll do nicely.* "I'll take the path to the alleyway first. Meet me there in five minutes with no hesitation. I have an insatiable appetite that must be fed."

My tone was raw and primal as I spoke.

Alina quivered with anticipation. "Hurry, my love."

On the way to the alley, I seized the lone woman, clamping my hand over her mouth to stifle any cries for help. I had chosen my victim carefully, favoring her slight frame and the promise of acquiescence.

I pushed the woman into the shadows of the corridor. She

gasped, struggling to free herself, but I held her firmly in place, my hands like iron bands from which she could not escape. In the darkness, I could feel her terror; her body was trembling, and her eyes wide with fear.

Alina appeared at the entrance to the alley and paused.

In one swift motion, I unsheathed my knife and drove it into the stranger's neck, feeling the rush of life leaving her body and the warmth of her blood splattering against my face. She gurgled and died, her limbs limp beneath me. I stepped away, wiping the blood off my hands and the knife with a handkerchief.

Alina watched me, her face emotionless, as if what she had just witnessed was not even worth a flicker of surprise. Her brazenness both shocked and intrigued me. If I were a different man, I would be disgusted, but instead, I felt something else—a strange, powerful attraction.

With one swift movement, she came closer to me and licked the remaining blood from my fingers, astounding me with her courage and boldness.

She lacked any fear of me, and this made her even more attractive. We stared at each other for an eternity before she finally broke the silence.

"Tell me, my beloved," she purred, "why did you kill her?"

She looked up at me with her burning gaze, expecting me to answer.

I wished I could, but the truth was, I didn't know. I thought I'd done it to earn Alina's fear, but now I was baffled. I was lost in a fog, filled with rage, excitement, and confusion.

Alina seemed to understand me and my cravings for violence. Instead of pressing me further, she simply brought her mouth to my cheeks, lapping the tiny drops of blood that clung to my skin. As she did so, a strange comfort washed over me, and my body relaxed.

"Did she hurt you?" Alina asked, her voice still so mellifluous that it unexpectedly aroused me.

I shook my head slowly, though I wasn't sure if I was responding to her question or simply marveling at her ability to soothe me. I didn't know if she could even sense it, but her presence was like a balm, helping to ease the pain and confusion that had taken over my mind.

Then I became enraged. This hadn't gone the way I'd planned. Alina was still a dominant force in my life. And I needed—no, *demanded*—to be in control. I whirled and seized her neck in my powerful grip, bending her over the dead body at my feet.

The air around us was tense, barely held in check by a fragile cord of fear. I towered over the petite figure of Alina, her long auburn curls cascading down her shoulders and her eyes wide with terror as my grasp around her neck tightened.

"What are you playing at?" I asked, my voice low and threatening. "You think you can tease me like this? You should fear me."

I leaned in closer, pressing my face against hers, my lips grazing her cheek. "I'm dangerous. I killed a woman like a brute. I'm a monster. Yet now you're sucking my fingers?"

My grip tightened as I spoke, and Alina tried to form words but only managed a choked rasp. My eyes bored into her until I finally relented and let go, allowing her to take a deep breath and regain her composure.

She stumbled away from the corpse, her long skirt dragging through the blood.

"You need to stop tormenting me," I said, still gruff. "Your games will get you nowhere. Remember who's in charge here."

I stepped back, and my expression softened slightly. I wiped my face, weary. "Alina, you're driving me crazy."

Alina grinned. "You're so powerful when you unleash your monstrous self, Balthazar. It takes my breath away."

The air between us seemed to crackle with static electricity, and I could feel her heat, like a tangible force drawing me in. I expected her to look away, to shy away from her own boldness, but instead, I found her looking back at me with a craving deep in her eyes.

I was hard now, and she seemed to sense it. Her cheeks flushed, and she melted into me like she was ready to accept my dark capabilities, the same capabilities that she inherited from her father. Only my abilities were far worse. I knew then that I had to whisk her away to someplace private where we could explore this newfound attraction without scrutiny or judgment.

With a powerful gesture, I ripped open a swirling vortex of darkness and beckoned her inside. She shrieked in terror as she was carried by the wind, suspended in an otherworldly embrace. In a blink, we materialized at my sprawling estate, stepping out from the suffocating clouds of blackness. As she gazed up at me, trembling with adrenaline and shock, I reveled in the exhilaration of our journey. And as she crumpled into my arms, exhausted and overwhelmed by the intensity of our encounter, I knew she would never be the same again.

CHAPTER NINE
ALINA

My heart crashed wildly in my ribcage as I awoke in an unfamiliar setting. Balthazar was nowhere to be seen.

I stood on the threshold of a lavish estate. The sprawling grounds were a spectacle of beauty. Everywhere, tall cypress trees swayed in the warm summer's night breeze, their dark-green foliage barely visible in the mystery of the gloaming. The air was heavy with the scent of jasmine and the earthy aroma of olives.

In the distance, a crystal-clear river ran through the grounds, the moon glinting on its surface. In the center, a majestic estate stood proudly, its white marble facade sparkling in the moonlight.

As I stepped closer, I noticed the intricate details of the structure—the delicately-carved columns, the elegant arches, and the fine masonry work. The entrance to the estate was a majestic pair of double doors, each adorned with heavy iron handles and panels of glass stained with dancing images of the gods and goddesses of ancient mythology. A gilded placard had been placed next to the door, with the words

"*Lord Balthazar*" written in a flowing script. The doors hung open in invitation, and I couldn't resist.

A sense of awe swept over me as I crossed the threshold and stepped into the massive dwelling. But all wonder ceased. I turned to look over my shoulder. *How did I get here? Had I fainted, and Balthazar carried me here? And where did he go?*

I stepped cautiously through the foyer, my heart still pounding. It was much darker than I had expected—even with the dim light from the torches on the wall, the space felt oppressively shrouded in gloom. A chill ran down my spine as I looked around the circular stone chamber, taking in the stacks of books and scrolls, the various strange artifacts, and the iron-barred door leading to an even deeper darkness.

My skin prickled, and my heart raced as I explored Balthazar's hidden chamber. The air was thick with an eerie stillness, broken only by the soft flicker of candlelight. As I gazed around the room, my eyes fell upon a collection of strange objects and artifacts, each one seemingly more mysterious than the last. Despite the overwhelming sense of dread that washed over me, I couldn't resist the pull to explore further.

I moved cautiously through the shadows, my hand grazing along ancient scrolls and peculiar trinkets. Every step I took felt like a journey deeper into the enigmatic mind of Balthazar. My fear urged me to turn back, but my curiosity drove me on, pushing me to uncover the secrets that lay within this place and within my lover himself.

Balthazar appeared out of nowhere, looking threatening and insane.

I gasped in surprise and stepped back. "Where did you come from? And how did we get here? To your home, I mean."

He didn't answer me. Instead, he seized my arm and hauled me up an elaborately curved staircase.

"Stop!" I cried, clawing at his hand. "Where are you taking me?"

"To bed," he snarled.

The exhilaration I'd experienced over seeing him brutally murder that woman vanished as he forced me up the stairs. I stumbled as I ascended.

Upstairs, it was dark, and the only light came from a room at the end of the hallway.

His sleeping chamber?

My mind raced with a thousand horrifying possibilities of what would happen next.

What kind of man was Balthazar? Tonight, I'd glimpsed his depravity, enacted, it seemed, for my benefit. What did he want from me? Would he hurt me?

My feet dragged, my body refusing to move closer to my lover's chamber. With every step, my fear grew, and I was more and more convinced that I would be devoured alive. I could feel the hot breath on the back of my neck, could almost feel his nails clawing their way into my flesh, and I wanted nothing more than to turn around and run away.

But I knew that was impossible. There was no escape from this. I was in Balthazar's grasp, and there was nothing I could do but move forward, step by step. The closer I got to the bedroom, the more I felt like I would faint from fear. I wished I had the courage to yell, scream, and fight, but I was too paralyzed by fear to even move my lips.

Finally, we reached the bedroom door. Balthazar pushed me through the entrance.

My fearsome lover's bedroom was filled with a dizzying array of strange and exotic items. I was taken aback by its sheer opulence and grandeur. The sights and smells hit me like a wave: the lush fabrics that hung from the walls, the heavy perfume of incense and burning wax, and the glint of gold everywhere in the room.

It was almost like walking into a small palace with its high ceilings and tall windows. Everything was perfectly symmetrical, with each piece of furniture in its place. An ornate four-poster canopy bed was centered in the room, draped with deep red velvet curtains. On the walls hung beautiful paintings depicting scenes of mythical creatures and battles.

The floors were covered in a thick, intricate dark-green and black rug with gold trim. There were several other pieces of furniture, such as a large armoire, a writing desk, and even a small chaise lounge.

The room was lit by large candelabras, providing a warm, flickering glow. Moonlight shone through the tall windows, illuminating the room, and giving it a mysterious air. It was a place of secrets and power, the perfect place for a madman to reside.

Balthazar picked me up as if I weighed nothing and threw me on the bed. He climbed on top of me and pinned my arms over my head.

"What are you playing at, Alina?" he snarled.

I lay on the bed, writhing beneath his looming presence, his arms securing my wrists to the bed. He was testing me, gauging my response to his depravity and power. I embraced it, despite my fear.

I knew, deep down, that my morbid fascination with watching him kill was wrong. It was twisted and sick in its own way. But to me, it felt like a game. I told myself that by watching him kill, I somehow felt closer to him, making me want him more.

The way he'd killed that woman had been intentional and

savage. He'd acted without guilt or remorse. I always made my killings look like an accident, like some freakish event that sprang out of nowhere, like a sudden flood or forest fire. And afterward, I would be seized by shame and self-loathing at my actions. But Balthazar had simply drawn his weapon and plunged it into the young woman's neck. Deed done.

Who, exactly, was Balthazar? What did he want from me? After many years of passion, I had no idea who this man was, yet I was trying to capture him and make him mine. He seemed both a predator and a friend, an angel, and a devil, all at once. I felt drawn to him and scared of him at the same time.

All I knew was he seemed like the one with all the power. He could take or leave me, and it scared me to think I had no control over him. I was in his hands, and I knew that if he wanted, he could kill me in an instant.

His intense gaze bore into me, sending shivers down my spine. My heart raced with fear, but I couldn't look away. It was as if a magnetic force was drawing me toward him.

My mind was consumed with thoughts of him, and a primal need to possess him overtook all rational thought. I could almost taste his love on my tongue, the desire burning within me like a raging fire.

As he loomed over me, I was scared and entranced by his presence. The energy between us crackled and pulsed with every passing moment. I closed my eyes, trying to make sense of my conflicting emotions.

A heavy pressure filled the air, making it hard for me to breathe. When I opened my eyes again, Balthazar's face was outlined by the moonlight and flickering candles. All my fears melted away in that moment as I surrendered to the raw passion between us.

He was no longer the composed, regal figure I was used

to seeing. Instead, his expression was wild and feral, and he had unleashed his inner darkness. His face was a rugged terrain of contorted features, like a monster pulled from the bowels of hell. His eyes blazed with an inferno of white-hot intensity that seemed to reach into my soul and burn me alive. I could feel the immense power radiating off him like waves of heat, making even the air around us tremble.

I watched in silent fascination as Balthazar continued to transform. His typically brilliant-blue eyes caught the light as if they were made of black diamonds, his hair tumbling down his shoulders like a storm cloud. His muscles seemed to swell with unmatched power, making him look enormous. This was the beast within him, and I was surprisingly unafraid. I welcomed it and allowed myself to be carried away on its wings.

He touched my face, his fingers like electricity against my skin. He stared at me before finally speaking: "Tonight, I will show you a glimpse of who I really am."

"Oh, yes, Balthazar, show me." My core flooded with juicy wetness. I burned with longing to have him inside me.

Balthazar grasped my wrists between his strong fingers while his other hand brushed my cheek. He was beautiful even in his monstrous form as he slowly ground his hips into me.

"What do you have in store for me?" he asked, his voice soft and gritty. "What schemes are you up to, my sinful angel?"

"Nothing you don't already crave, *my lord*," I said.

His face contorted in agony. "Don't call me that. Only my subjects use that term with me."

The slow, insistent push of his erection against my core drove me to madness, even with the fabric between us.

"What shall I call you, then?" I breathed, matching his grinding rhythm.

"Yours," he snarled, baring his teeth.

"Mine," I said.

"And you are *exclusively* mine." He brought his lips to mine in a feral, bruising kiss. When he withdrew, we were both breathless. His darkly hooded gaze bore into me. "I forbid you to take lovers when I am away."

The thought of belonging to Balthazar thrilled me. And it also gave me pause. He would be gone for days, sometimes weeks, when he left on his mysterious sojourns. Once, he had left me for months. I became bored when he was away. It seemed only fitting to take lovers to fill the time.

But another thought, more insidious, intrigued me. *Is Balthazar developing feelings for me?*

I felt a sudden urge to exploit this weakness.

Balthazar stared into my eyes. "Why weren't you scared when I slaughtered that woman? Why did you lick the blood from my face?"

I attempted to stand up for his actions. "You had no other choice. That whore must have done something unforgivable to deserve it."

"Yes," he said. "She killed her own children."

I leveled him with my gaze. I knew he was lying. Without flinching, I replied, "You were too merciful then. The murderous woman deserved more pain."

"Do you really think that?" he said, narrowing his eyes.

"Yes, my…" I bit my lip. "Yes, Balthazar."

The air in the room became still and oppressive.

"But am I going to suffer the same fate someday? Will you similarly murder me?" I tried to sound as if I were joking.

His expression didn't change, but his voice was curt and

unforgiving. "Never. You will always be safe and loved by me."

I swallowed hard, my heart racing as I gazed up at him. The heat in the air around me felt suffocating, and desire pulsed through my veins. I took a deep breath, steeling myself for whatever was about to happen.

Balthazar released my wrists and watched me as he slowly unbuttoned his dark silk doublet, his gaze never leaving mine. He tossed his clothes aside, slid out of his hose, and hammered silver codpiece, adding them to the pile on the floor. Then, he crawled toward me, his bare chest gleaming in the candlelight. In his monstrous form, his presence was overwhelming yet somehow comforting.

His warm, calloused hand lightly grazed my cheek, electrifying my skin with tingles of pleasure. As his fingers combed through my hair, I felt a delicate pressure on the back of my neck, sending chills down my spine. With his lips hovering just inches from mine, I could feel the heat of his breath and the anticipation building between us. I closed my eyes as his mouth came down on mine, his kiss passionate and hungry. His lips were full and velvety, and my whole body melted from the touch.

I slid my hands to his chest, feeling the chiseled muscles beneath. He groaned in pleasure, delving his hand further into my hair as he deepened the kiss. I gasped as his tongue explored my mouth, tasting and taunting me.

Balthazar leaned away, a sly smile spreading across his lips. His eyes sparkled as they scanned me, setting me ablaze with heat as their gaze lingered.

"Let's remove these garments," he suggested, helping me sit up. He unfastened my bodice and peeled it from my form. He slowly and deliberately removed each layer: my skirt, chemise, corset, stockings, and other adornments until I was left only in my jewelry.

"Now, we begin to play," he declared, his voice commanding and deep.

My legs trembled with anticipation. I gasped as Balthazar's hands caressed my hips and stomach, igniting sparks of pleasure within me. He guided me back onto the bed and hovered above me. With his touch, I was electrified and consumed by waves of pleasure.

He crawled lower, teasing my inner thighs with soft kisses. My moans grew louder as his tongue traced fiery trails along my skin while his hands explored my hips. He tantalized every inch of my sensitive skin with gentle touches and tickles until he reached my navel.

He pulled me closer as he pressed his lips to my clit. I cried out in pleasure as he licked and sucked me, his tongue exploring every inch of my slick canal. His mouth moved in perfect time with my body, his touch igniting a fire I had never known before. My arousal grew in guilt-laden pleasure as the memory of Balthazar plunging a dagger into that woman's neck shot through my brain.

He moved quicker, his fingers teasing me as he worked my body into a frenzy. I groaned as he increased the pressure, pleasure radiating through my body. He paused, his lips still near my core as he looked up at me. His gaze was intense, and my body trembled beneath his.

He smiled, a wicked glint in his eyes. Then he dipped his head down and started to pleasure me with his mouth again. His touch brought me to a new level of pleasure, my body shaking with each lapping movement of his tongue.

My climax built, the intensity increasing until it felt like my body was on fire. I orgasmed like a dragon's breath consumed me, the flames of pleasure burning away my flesh, leaving behind my scorched soul. I cried out his name, the pleasure overwhelming me. He drank it in, my body shuddering beneath him.

As the moment ended, he seized me in a fierce embrace, crushing my body against his with an urgency that both thrilled and terrified me. His kiss was wild and possessive, leaving trails of fire across my skin. When he finally pulled away, his eyes smoldered with desire and something darker.

"You are pure temptation, my sinful angel," he breathed, his voice husky with longing as he wrapped himself around me once more, claiming me completely.

My heart swelled. Yet, simultaneously, the machinations of my mind continued to plot and scheme. Balthazar was falling for me—I just knew it. And I planned on using this knowledge to my advantage.

The candles sputtered and burned out, leaving us in darkness. We lay there in silence, our bodies intertwined, the air still thick with the scent of sex and desire.

"I've got to go," I whispered.

Balthazar didn't respond. His breath was slow and heavy as if he was fast asleep.

"Balthazar, I've got to go," I repeated, my voice still soft.

No response.

"My father's going to kill me if I'm not back by morning," I whispered.

Balthazar groaned and rolled on his back, throwing his arm over his head.

I slid free from his side, donned my clothing, and headed out into the night. I borrowed one of his horses and rode it hard and fast to my home. Once there, I slapped its rump, sending it home. Then, I sneaked into my dark house.

I was almost on the stairs, only a few steps away from safety when a candle flickered in the darkness. I yelped in surprise. My father stood in the shadows, ready to confront me. He held the light aloft, and his expression was a mix of rage and disappointment.

"Papa!" I said. "What a fright you gave me."

"You've been seeing Balthazar, haven't you?" he growled, though it seemed he already knew the answer.

"Yes, Papa," I said, standing tall, my eyes blazing with defiance. "I have, and I shall continue to do so."

An angry slap smacked my cheek. I stared at my father, outraged. He had never lifted a hand against me in all my rebellion.

I placed my palm on my smarting flesh, and my lip curled in disdain. "What have you done to me?"

"You need to get married and settle down," he said firmly.

I clenched my fists and stared at him, jaw tight with the effort of holding back tears. His condescending tone reignited all my frustrations with how he treated me like a possession instead of an individual, all the times he resisted my dreams of independence and self-fulfillment. He wanted me to leave Balthazar, find a suitable husband, and forget who I was.

"Go to Giovanni Zampa's house and learn the truth of who you are," he said.

"Why should I?" I shot back.

I wanted to defy him, but deep down, part of me knew that maybe this was an opportunity to learn something about myself.

"Because it's time you discovered the truth about who you are."

"I won't do it! I hate you!" I screamed. "You're not my father!"

Without hesitation, I turned and marched up the stairs.

Upstairs in my room, I thought about the evening's

events. I didn't know who I was or who Balthazar was. It felt as if something evil lurked inside me, begging for release.

Does Signor Zampa really know the answer?

My heart thundered in my chest as visions of over-throwing my father and overpowering Balthazar clouded my thoughts. I decided to head to Signor Zampa's at first light, determined to discover the secrets of my identity. I had to know who I was; this might be my only chance to find out.

CHAPTER TEN

ALINA

I stood in front of Giovanni Zampa's house, a tall, imposing structure that seemed to own the street. Dawn was just beginning to make its presence known, the first streaks of pink and gold washing over the dark sky.

Giovanni Zampa opened the door before I had the chance to knock. He was a small, wizened man with an air of wisdom and knowledge that seemed to fill the foyer. His eyes were bright and inquisitive, his gaze focused on me.

"*Egregio* Signor Zampa. My father told me to come to you and find out what a Timeborne is," I said, my words spilling out in a nervous rush.

"Don't talk about this outside," he said, glancing left and right. "Come inside."

He opened the door and stepped to the side, motioning for me to enter. As I crossed the threshold, my heart fluttered with excitement and anxiety.

Signor Zampa led me down the hallway and into a dimly lit room. In the center of the room, he gestured at an ornately carved wooden table with an aged object resting on top. It was a dagger, its hilt glimmering in the light.

"This arrived with you as a baby," he said quietly and thoughtfully. "Along with a note. That was it."

I stepped closer to the dagger, feeling its odd energy tingle.

"You can use the sacred words and travel during the full moon," he said. "You can visit different places, different eras."

I stared in disbelief at Signor Zampa.

At first, my mind couldn't process the information: it felt like I was standing in a dream, my body heavy and disconnected from the reality unfolding before me. But then, as the news sunk in, a million different feelings began to swirl within me. Excitement and fear, awe and apprehension all vied for control as I tried to make sense of the implications of what Zampa had just told me.

Was this really happening? Could I really travel through time? I wasn't sure, but as my anxiety and trepidation faded, I realized that I was also inexplicably, headily, alive with anticipation. What wonders could I discover if I could unlock the secrets of time?

My excitement bubbled up, and I couldn't help but smile. Here was something that could give me answers, a way to explore the world beyond my small Italian village.

"Tell me more, Signor," I said. "Can I just leave Florence, Italy, and travel to another time?"

"Please," Signor Zampa said, gesturing to his drawing room. "Let us sit, and I shall tell you more."

I swept past him and settled on one of the intricately-carved, velvet-cushioned settees arranged around a low table.

Signor Zampa's salon was a spacious chamber featuring ornate architectural details and decorative elements. The walls were adorned with tapestries, paintings, and frescoes depicting scenes from mythology and landscapes. Intricate plasterwork covered the ceiling.

Once we'd both settled in our respective seats, the room was still, save for the gentle thumping of Signor Zampa's finger tapping the armrest of his chair. He had been silent for a while, and I wondered if he had forgotten why I was there. But then, finally, he spoke.

"Yes, you can travel to other eras, other places," he said. A bruised expression washed over his face. "But your travels will only make the darkness stronger."

A chill ran down my spine. I had only just begun to consider the possibility of time travel—but the prospect of it being dangerous made me reconsider.

"What do you mean?" I asked.

"Time travel is a power that can be tapped into," Signor Zampa said. "For those who understand it, it can give access to great knowledge and even greater power. But it comes at a price. You must be aware of the darkness, potential danger, and corruption. It is a power that must be respected."

I remained silent, letting the words sink in. I had heard tales of time travel but never before had the possibility of it being so real, so within reach occurred to me. I felt a strange combination of trepidation and excitement—a feeling I could not ignore.

But still, I had many questions. "You haven't told me what the darkness is, Signor. And how is it dangerous?"

Signor Zampa's eyes looked like hollowed-out caves as he spoke. "The darkness isn't a *what*. It's a *who*. And there are many. The darkness is created when you are born and lives inside your dagger. Have you heard of a genie in a bottle?"

"That old fairy tale?" I said with a swish of my hand. "Of course."

SARA SAMUELS

"Don't play coy, Lady Tocino. This is serious." A brooding expression crossed his face.

"What do you mean?" I said, my hackles bristling as I feigned a nonchalance I did not feel. Inside, I was terrified at everything he said to me.

"When you time traveled at one month of age, your darkness was created. I suspect its roaming around Italy, trying to kill you."

I snorted in a most unladylike manner. I couldn't help it. "This story is preposterous."

"Think so?" Signor Zampa cast a chilling glare at me. "Your lover, Lord Balthazar, is one of the darkest of the dark."

I shuddered despite being wrapped inside my thick crimson mantle. "And how do you know of my associations with Lord Balthazar?"

Signor Zampa's lips parted with a mirthless laugh. "Child, I make it my policy to know about Timebornes and their activities. Your acquaintance with Lord Balthazar is, shall we say, common knowledge in certain circles of which I am a part."

A chill overtook me, and I pulled my velvet cloak closer around me. I didn't like the thought that people knew or kept track of my actions, which I'd considered so secret and private. I drew myself up haughtily, jutting out my chin. I wanted Signor Zampa to know I wasn't afraid and was in control.

"So what do you think you know about me, Signor, or any activity I conduct in my private time?"

The drawing room became unbearably quiet as I waited for his answer.

Signor Zampa eyed me carefully, and a sly smile played on his lips.

"I know Balthazar wants to kill you," he said, his voice low but clear.

My heart sank into my stomach. I had no idea what Signor Zampa was trying to insinuate, but it was clear he knew far more than he was letting on.

I took a deep breath and steadied my nerves. "How do you know this?"

Signor Zampa shrugged. "I told you. I make it my business to monitor Timebornes. I monitor darknesses."

"Wait a minute," I said, leaning forward. "Are you saying that Balthazar came into existence at the same time I was born, like some sort of evil spirit?"

Signor Zampa scoffed. "Oh, no, child. He is older than time itself."

I stared at Signor Zampa in his drawing room, my mind spinning with confusion and distrust. He was a mysterious figure with the bearing of one accustomed to power. He knew more than he was letting on.

"Lord Balthazar will grow tired of you, my child," he said with a knowing smirk. "He always grows tired of his lovers."

A wave of intense and unexpected jealousy surged through my body. I never wanted any other woman to have Balthazar or look at him.

Is that what he does when he's away from me? Does he take lovers, too?

Signor Zampa must have sensed my distress, for he leaned forward and patted my shoulder.

"My dear," he said, his voice softer now, "he is a fickle man, but you are young, beautiful, and have much to offer. Don't be too hard on yourself."

I said nothing but held his gaze, silently conveying my confusion and mistrust.

He seemed to understand, for he gave me a warm smile. "Come, let me show you something."

He led me deeper into the room, where we stopped in front of a large, ornate mirror. He gestured to it, and I stepped over to look closer. As I gazed at my reflection in the antique mirror, the warm light from the setting sun cast a golden glow on my features. I ran my fingers through my hair, admiring how it caught the light and framed my face. But beneath the surface, a soft light pulsed and flickered like a million tiny stars all calling to me. My eyes widened in surprise and awe.

"This," he said, his voice barely above a whisper. "Look at yourself. Look at all the power you wield. It will never waver or dim. Always remember that."

I recalled Balthazar's magnificent estate, the stacks of books and scrolls, the various strange artifacts, and that feeling I had that I was journeying into his deepest secrets by exploring his private dwelling.

As I gazed at my reflection, I realized something: I, too, was powerful. I had my own secrets, strengths, and knowledge and wanted to be Balthazar's equal. However, I didn't want him to know what I knew; I wanted to reveal his secrets. I thought of Balthazar's handsome face, our strong bond, and how I wanted to be with him forever. I longed to exploit his vulnerabilities and move through life together as king and queen.

"I think you're wrong, Signor Zampa," I said. "Balthazar is complicated but good to me."

Signor Zampa sighed heavily and turned me to face him. His eyes, dark and intense, met mine.

"Listen to me," he said. "He's only good to you because you're giving him what he wants."

I was tired of hearing about how horrible Balthazar was, so I turned away, my heart pounding. I knew Signor Zampa was speaking out of care, but his words made me feel exposed and vulnerable. I didn't want to believe that Balthazar could be anything less than perfect.

"Thank you for your warning," I said coolly. "I'll keep it in mind."

I readied myself to depart, pivoting with a flourish, but Signor Zampa caught my arm.

"Balthazar isn't your only problem," Signor Zampa said. "There are also Timehunters. The Timehunters have taken it upon themselves to rid the world of all time travelers. I suggest you depart to some distant time and place and leave all this behind. The Timehunters are slow to find their victims."

I stared at his fingers, which clutched my arm. "Unhand me, Signor. I don't believe you. You're only trying to scare me. I've heard enough, and now I shall take my leave."

His face was filled with understanding and sadness. He released me and accompanied me to the door.

"Take care, Lady Tocino," he said, his hand on the polished brass doorknob as I swept across the threshold. "And be careful."

Outside, a groomsman helped me onto my horse. I eschewed modern convention and swung my leg over the saddle, refusing to ride side-saddle. The groomsman kept sneaking lust-filled looks at me as he secured my flowing skirts to the sides of the saddle with a leather strap, allowing my legs to be positioned comfortably and securely in the stirrups. With my gloved hands firmly grasping the reins, I urged the horse forward with a gentle kick of my leg, setting off at a steady canter. The sun's heat radiated down on me as I rode along the driveway comfortably.

I felt frustrated, bewildered, and confused. These last two

days had been both insightful and alarming. There was too much information to comprehend.

My foot faltered as I crossed the threshold into our opulent home. It was silent, too silent for comfort. A sudden chill ripped through my body, making me shiver uncontrollably as I cautiously approached the living room.

The scene that greeted me was like something out of a nightmare. My family lay motionless on the floor, their bodies twisted and contorted in unnatural positions. Blood pooled beneath them, staining the expensive carpet with dark red blotches. Bile rose in my throat as I stumbled backward, trying to make sense of the horrifying sight before me. The silence was deafening, broken only by the sound of my own ragged breaths as I realized that my worst fears had become a gruesome reality.

The couch cushions, once plush and comforting, were now stained with dark-red splatters. The expensive rug, a relative's gift, was soaked with a crimson liquid that glistened in the light like an evil omen.

The remains of my loved ones were strewn around the room like broken dolls, and I could not hold back my tears. I had lost everything dear to me in an instant, and the reality of the horror sank in like a heavy stone.

Who could have done such a thing?

The numbness spread from the tips of my fingers to my core, and I crumbled to the floor in a heap. My mind was a blur of disbelief and confusion, unable to process what had just happened. But as I lay there on the cold tile, my thoughts drifted to everything that would change now that this had occurred. And surprisingly, a sense of peaceful acceptance washed over me, like a lighthouse guiding me through the stormy sea of emotions. No one was there to judge me. No one was there to tell me what I could and couldn't do. I had complete freedom. A surge of energy and adrenaline rushed through my veins. At the sound of a clatter from upstairs, I pulled myself free from my thoughts and ran up the steps.

I stood motionless on the threshold of my bedroom. My eyes were wide with shock and anguish as I beheld the horrific scene before me. The room was drenched in a pool of bright red, the walls and floor spattered with spots of crimson. Balthazar, my beloved, held a bloody dagger in one hand. Across from him stood my sister, whose eyes were dull yet still held a trace of fear and betrayal. The reality of the situation crashed over me like a tidal wave.

Balthazar turned to face me, and all the passion he once held for me had vanished from his gaze. He stared at me and the dagger in his hand as if trying to understand how it had all come to this.

My sister's limp body lay sprawled on the ground, a stark contrast to the gleaming dagger held triumphantly in Balthazar's hand. The sunlight glinted off the blade, casting a macabre glow over the scene. Instead of feeling sorrow and anguish, I was filled with euphoria as I gazed at Balthazar. With this act, we could be together forever, bound by blood and death. My twisted smile mirrored his as we reveled in our victory and newfound eternal companionship. With my wretched family out of the way, anything was possible.

CHAPTER ELEVEN

BALTHAZAR

I stood still in the upstairs bedroom of Alina's house, my eyes trained on her sister's body, whom I had just killed. My hands were still trembling from the adrenaline of the act, and my insides were roiling with a strange mixture of elation and dread. I'd just slaughtered everyone in the household—*everyone.*

I thought killing Alina's adopted father would be satisfying, but it had not been. The man had pleaded for his life, and there had been something about his pleading that had made me feel almost remorseful.

But I wanted to see Alina's reaction when she saw that I had killed her entire family. Now, she stood in the doorway, smiling at me. She was *smiling* at me. I couldn't tell if her lack of fear was a facade to demonstrate her poise or if she genuinely had great bravery during peril. As I studied her, I could see the echoes of her father, Mathias, in her. This both disturbed and intrigued me. To others, Alina appeared to be nothing more than a naive young woman, but I knew there was a sinister side to her. She carried herself with an air of innocence, but I suspected no one knew about her wickedness.

With me, she appeared dominating and superior. And her reaction to me killing a stranger had been alarming. But here, in her house, with the bloody remains of family and servants strewn around the house, she seemed exhilarated.

Then, her lip curled in disgust. "What did you do to my family?"

She rushed forward, seized the knife from my hands, and tried to slash my neck. I wrestled the knife from her and pushed her aside.

Had she been bluffing? Perhaps. There was a gleam in her eyes that belied her anger.

"I killed them," I said evenly. I licked the blade clean before sliding it into its sheath at my waist. "Savagely and brutally. I enjoyed their cries of terror and their pleas for me to stop."

I wanted to test Alina. To prove that her heart was as wicked and dark as mine.

"Are you displeased with me now that you can see what a monster I am?" I asked.

She stood silently, framed by the window with the sun shining, making her hair appear like flames.

The room was awash in a violent hue of red, her white sheets and floor covered in a layer of dried blood. A pile of broken furniture and shattered glass littered the floor, evidence of my struggle with her feisty sister. Sunlight streamed through the window, making the carnage seem even more surreal.

Alina closed her eyes and took a deep breath.

"Answer me!" I demanded. "I have let you witness my dark side, the same side I sought to shield you from all these years. How does it make you feel?"

She opened her eyes as a slow smile spread across her face. She untied the cloak at her neck and let it fall into a pool of blood. Alina, her large eyes shining with adoration, stepped closer to me.

"Alina! Don't you fear me now that you know I'm a monster?"

"I'm happy you killed them, my lord," she said, her voice soft and trembling.

I ignored her use of the term "my lord" and held her gaze. She sauntered toward me, her lips parted slightly.

"I'm proud of my dark, wicked monster," she said, her voice a low whisper. "I despised my adopted parents and their whimpering whelps, and now you've rid me of them."

Her small, delicate fingers grazed the crisp fabric of my collar, eliciting a shiver down my spine. I could practically taste her desire for the darkness within me, the thrill of danger that pulsed through my veins.

"You crave a monster," I growled, gently gripping her chin. "Someone who kills."

Alina's heart pounded like a war drum against her chest, but her expression remained stoic. Yet, the heat radiating off her body and the longing in her eyes betrayed her true desires. She longed to be consumed by my darkness, enveloped in my strength, and loved by the monster I had always been.

"I don't fear you," she said with conviction in her soft yet powerful voice. "I embrace you. Finally, I feel liberated, like a weight has been lifted from my shoulders. And it's all because of you."

"Fuck, Alina. What are you doing to me?" My voice was low and full of need.

Without saying a word, she touched my face, her fingertips tracing the curves of my features.

I let my hand drift lower until I gripped her waist.

She gasped, and I felt her shudder. Then she burrowed her hand inside my breeches, grabbed hold of my erection firmly and confidently, and said, "Watching you kill makes me wet with need."

I couldn't believe it. I had never met anyone like this, my wicked lover.

Without hesitation, she hiked up her skirt and underclothing, put her fingers to her core, and began playing with herself. I couldn't believe what I saw, and her pleasure sent a wave of lust through me.

Unable to take it anymore, I threw her onto the bed and climbed on top, straining against her.

"I want you to fuck me like an animal," she said, her voice low and feral.

I pushed myself into her. "I'm going to make you my queen forever. I shall make you darker and more wicked. I shall make you as dark as me."

I had never felt so alive, so connected to another person in all my life.

I was taken aback by the sentiment. I had adored Zara and the children more than anything else. But then Zara betrayed me, and my babies were haunting my dreams from the underworld. Desperately, I forced every thought of her and our past relationship out of my mind.

I stared deeply into Alina's eyes, feeling the electricity between us as if it were a physical force. Then, I caught sight of something disturbing deep in her soul, glimmering just beyond the surface. Alina was darker than I had given her credit for.

Would she become too wicked to be trusted?

CHAPTER TWELVE

ALINA

I nvigorated from our lovemaking, I felt like a boulder had been lifted off my chest. Filled with glee, I waltzed through the house, stepping over my family's dead bodies. No longer were my parents' oppressive, conservative values weighing me down. I was free—free to live my life the way I wanted. The man responsible for this change—my lover, Balthazar—was wickedly powerful. And yet I felt safe with him, even though I knew of his evil ways.

"I've never seen you so cheerful," Balthazar said, standing in the doorway to the drawing room, his arms folded over his chest.

His breeches hung open, and his shirt was rather crumpled. Coupled with the long, messy hair I'd raked my hands through minutes ago, he bore a savage appearance. He began to smooth his clothing, tucking the shirt inside his waistband and fastening the buttons at the waist. His expression was bemused and concerned, like maybe I'd gone over the edge of sanity.

Maybe I had, but I felt so exhilarated at today's events.

When Balthazar killed another, it aroused me. It was like a call of the wild was being answered.

I felt a peace in my heart that I had never known before. I could not help but love Balthazar deeply for giving me this newfound freedom.

I no longer had to pretend to be something I was not. Every move I made from this point on would be a dance to my own tune, and Balthazar was the conductor. I could feel the energy radiating off him, making *me* feel alive and powerful. For the first time in my life, anything was possible, and I was determined to explore and seize every opportunity that came my way.

"Would it be possible for you to cease your frolicking and kiss me farewell, *amore mio*?" Balthazar said, preening in the blood-spattered mirror on the wall.

I turned to face him. "Where are you going?"

"I have things to take care of," he said smoothly.

"What kind of things?" A stab of annoyance popped into my good mood.

"This and that." He waved his hand before raking his hair into submission with his fingers.

"Why won't you tell me?" I sashayed toward him and stroked his jaw.

He didn't answer. Instead, he seized my jaw and kissed me roughly, possessively.

I squirmed to get away from his manhandling, my hand poised to slap him. But when I swung my arm, it met nothing but a wisp of blackness.

He'd faded from sight.

"Damn you, Balthazar!" I screamed.

I swore I could hear his answering chuckle. I stormed across the drawing room, kicking my father's head when I passed. But then I stopped. Balthazar was always testing me. *Always*.

It was time I pushed him back.

I stood alone in the creepy stillness of the house, dead bodies everywhere. My heart pounded with fear. I rubbed my mouth back and forth as I schemed.

What will happen to Balthazar if I disappear? Will he miss me? Will he search for me?

I assumed that my arousal over his killing would make us equals, but deep down, I knew it wasn't true.

I looked around the room, taking in the lifeless bodies of the people who had been living here, my so-called family. Now, they were nothing but meat bags bleeding all over the floor. A thought occurred to me.

What will people think when they find out I'm the only one alive? Surely, they'll assume I had something to do with the deaths.

I needed to leave—and *fast*.

Taking a deep breath, I made a split-second decision. *I'll go to Signor Zampa's house and tell him the truth—that I was in danger. Balthazar killed my entire family, and he would kill me, too.*

I would do whatever it took to make him believe me, even if it meant tricking him into thinking I was innocent.

And then I'll beg him to teach me how to time travel.

I gathered my belongings and went to the door with a renewed sense of purpose. I prayed that my plan would work and I could put my scheme in motion.

I flung myself from my horse's back and burst into Signor Zampa's estate, wailing. "Something awful has happened, Signor Zampa! Balthazar has killed my entire family!"

Sitting in his armchair reading a dusty book, Zampa looked up with a start. He slammed the book shut and leaped to his feet. As I sagged in the doorway, sobbing, he rushed to meet me and put a comforting arm around my shoulders.

"Good lord, child! Are you certain?" he asked in his soft and urgent voice.

"Yes," I cried out, forcing tears. "I'm scared for my life!"

Signor Zampa held me close and stroked my hair. "It's alright. You don't have to be scared. Come now, tell me everything that happened."

Shaking uncontrollably, I recounted how Balthazar had killed my family one by one. I added details of the slaughter, embellishing as I told the tale. When I finished, Signor Zampa was scowling deeply.

"This is terrible news," he murmured, his face grave. "But you don't have to worry any longer. I'm here, and I will help you. We'll find a way to get justice for your family."

I forced a sob from my throat. "Oh, Signor Zampa! You don't understand. Justice will not solve anything! I am in danger."

"Yes, you are," he said. "You've got to get away. Balthazar is like a king in his own way. He gets away with everything. You can time travel and start over. The full moon is six days away. You can only time travel during the full moon. You must memorize the scripture."

Signor Zampa's words simultaneously excited and mystified me. At last, I'd get to experience time travel.

His intense stare focused on me as if waiting for a reaction. I took a deep breath and nodded slowly, unsure what to say.

"You must leave in six days, or you'll never escape," he said. "Balthazar will find you wherever you go. He has eyes everywhere. He knows when you're coming and going. Make sure you have a plan."

I nodded, still unsure of what course of action to take, but determined to find out. I was going to time travel. I was going to start over.

Signor Zampa said, "You must stay with me so Balthazar can't find you. I will protect you."

As I looked into his determined face, gratitude and relief swept over me. Signor Zampa didn't really know me, and he didn't owe me anything, yet here he was, offering me a place of refuge. A little spark of hope lit up inside me. Maybe, just maybe, I could pull off my plan. I opened my mouth to thank him, but his expression changed before I could say a word.

His kind face hardened into a mask of determination, and he said, "This is serious, Lady Tocino. You must do as I say for the next six days. I can't let you out of my sight."

I nodded, then ducked my head. I could not suppress the longing for Balthazar that rose up within me. We could never stay away from one another for long. Already, I ached for his touch, his presence, and the connection that seemed to exist solely between us.

The longing painted a picture in my mind. I imagined us curled up together on a window seat, our fingers entwined, looking out at a vibrant sunset. Or strolling through an old cemetery, shadows of the past all around us, while we were completely immersed in each other.

The memories, relentless reminders of the past, kept flooding back. Years of romantic trysts in the city or sitting by a river, laughing and talking. And then there were the murders. These memories filled me with a sick fascination that pooled in my belly like lust. I was swept away with desire, wanting nothing more than to be in Balthazar's embrace and feel our connection again. But this was a dangerous game. I had to follow through with Signor

Zampa's plan. I needed to even the score between Balthazar and me.

After getting me settled in a bedroom in his estate, Signor Zampa stood in the doorway and said, "I'm going to gather some men and take care of the bodies of your loved ones. Under no circumstance are you to leave this house."

I nodded demurely, but inside I was desperate to see Balthazar again. To touch him. To feel him inside me. To clench my core around his big cock as he drove it into me with a fury.

Signor Zampa shut the door behind him. Then I heard the distinct snick of a lock. I growled, feeling trapped like my fake father had locked me in my room years ago.

"Oh, well," I muttered. "In less than a week, I shall be elsewhere. I wish I could see Balthazar's face when he discovers I've gone missing."

I let out a hearty laugh, one unbecoming for a lady, but who cared? Everyone who would wish to heel me was dead.

The following day, Signor Zampa informed me the community had been told of the brutal murders of the Tocino family, sending a ripple of fear throughout the city. Everyone wondered who had done such a horrible deed.

"I let the Balìa know who is to blame," he said as he prepared our supper. "I will let them deal with the savagery. I'm so glad you came to me, Lady Tocino. This is a terrible tragedy, and I wish you to get to safety as soon as the moon is at its fullest."

"Thank you, Signor. I don't know what I would have done if it wasn't for you." A tear rolled down my cheek, and I dabbed it away with a handkerchief. I hated putting on this show of emotions, but it had become part of my routine. I was growing more proficient at feigning sentiments that weren't real.

Two days later, I slunk in the shadows, dodging behind buildings and hiding in the trees, watching the funeral procession out of sight, dressed in my black mourning attire.

I couldn't afford to be seen. Horrible rumors about my involvement in the gruesome slayings had spread like wildfire, leaving me living on borrowed time. People threatened to take my life if I was ever seen again. My heart raced as the whispers of my involvement in the murders echoed in my ears.

The funeral was a grand and elaborate parade of mourners, priests, and two holy friars draped in black gliding through Florence. The priests gripped gold crosses and religious icons while intoning prayers for the Tocino family and their loyal staff. Somber music played on trumpets, flutes, and drums accompanied the procession. They performed ghastly dirges and hymns, contributing to the solemn atmosphere.

The heavy wooden coffins were laden with wreaths and mementos of love, a dull reminder of lives lost too soon. Glistening black horses pulled the carts through the graveyard as I hid in the shadows in my long black gown, its high neckline constricting my chest as if to prevent any emotion from escaping. A breeze would pass with every step, pressing my sheer black mantilla against my face as if to form an invisible cage around me. My rosary felt icy cold against my skin.

Seeking some form of absolution for my sins, I murmured prayers almost absently, knowing that no repentance could save me from the depths of hell. The wooden cross dangling from my bracelet of beads seemed to burn with an infernal flame.

The wind blew a chill on my sweaty skin. The funeral procession moved forward, and I couldn't help but feel the weight of sorrow pressing down on me, causing tears to well up in my eyes.

I felt Balthazar's presence. He was out there somewhere, waiting and watching me. Would he prevent me from heading back to Signor Zampa's? I bowed my head and glanced left and right, searching for him, but he did not reveal himself like the predator he was.

I couldn't wait for the funeral to end so I could go home with Signor Zampa. The priest went on and on, intoning scriptures and prayers for justice. When he finished, I looked around for Signor Zampa, eager to be whisked home under his protection.

Another priest stepped toward the mausoleum where the Tocino coffins would be laid to rest and prayed fervently. "Almighty and merciful God, we gather here today to commend the souls of our dear departed Tocino family into your loving and forgiving hands. We stand before you with heavy hearts, for they have met a tragic end through an act of violence. We mourn the loss of lives cut short, the pain and anguish caused by this heinous act."

I rolled my eyes behind the privacy of my mantilla.

"Lord, we pray for justice to be served," he said, "that those responsible for this crime may be brought to account. Give wisdom and strength to those involved in the pursuit of truth and the administration of justice, that they may uncover the fullness of the truth and ensure that the guilty do not go unpunished."

Come on, come on.

"We also pray for the family and loved ones of the Tocino family. Comfort them in their grief, O Lord. Surround them with your tender embrace and grant them solace in knowing they are now in your eternal care. Ease their burden of sorrow and grant them the strength to face the difficult days ahead."

Goodness, enough already.

"We beseech you, Lord," the priest said, "to bring healing to our community. In the face of violence and unrest, instill a spirit of forgiveness and reconciliation within us. Help us to find ways to prevent such tragedies from occurring in the future. Guide us toward a world where love, compassion, and justice prevail."

His words swarmed around my ears like insects, biting and nipping me. I wanted it to be *over.*

"Lastly, O God, we pray for the soul of the Tocinos. May they find peace and rest in your everlasting presence. Look upon them with mercy, and grant them the reward of eternal life in your heavenly kingdom. May their suffering be transformed into glory, and may they know your eternal love and forgiveness."

I was ready to commit, *colpo alla gola per spezzare la voce*—a strike to the throat—to silence the fucking priest.

Finally, he said, "We offer these prayers in the name of your son, our savior Jesus Christ, who conquered death and offers us hope. Amen."

"Amen," I whispered, hidden behind a statue of Jesus.

I jolted as a firm hand clamped onto my shoulder, and I turned to see Signor Zampa standing next to me. His dark eyes were fixed on mine with a look of concern. His face was stern and resolute. "I've been looking for you all day. Lady Tocino, you need rest. Let us be away at once."

Through tears streaming down my face and a hollow voice that quaked with feigned emotion, I begged him in between sobs, "Please...please take me home."

He grabbed me by the arm and dragged me to his carriage

with a growing sense of urgency. His gaze darted around like a frightened animal, and I wondered if Balthazar would appear and tear us apart at any moment. He almost shoved me inside the carriage before vaulting into the driver's seat and whipping the horses until they galloped across the terrain. Sheer luck kept us safe as we pulled up to his estate.

My feet flew up the stairs two at a time before I slammed the door shut behind me, desperate for respite from the funeral's cruel judgment and this wretched little town. I would be free if I could make it through three more days.

The following day, Signor Zampa lurked at the bottom of the stairs, his eyes heavy and harsh.

"Lady Tocino, there is no time to spare," he said. "We must begin our studies of the sacred scriptures now."

His voice echoed like thunder as he spoke, revealing a hint of zealotry beneath his words.

I was taken aback. "Might I have breakfast first?"

"Go, go! Time is of the essence. I'll await you in my study." He sprinted down the hall.

My heart raced like a wild horse. What had happened to cause such urgency? I gobbled down my breakfast and ran for Zampa's study with trepidation, not knowing what lay ahead.

Signor Zampa produced a worn-looking parchment and smoothed the frail paper on his desk. He slammed his hand down onto the wood, and I jumped.

His eyes blazed with anger. "Memorize this, now!"

I trembled at the prospect of failing him and quickly began reciting, *"Ya hamiat alqamar fi allayl, 'adeuk litutliq aleinan lilnuwr waturshiduni khilal alzalami. Dae alshams aleazimat tarqus min hawlik bialhubi walmawadati."*

Signor Zampa barked out corrections like a cruel warden demanding perfection from his prisoners. Every mistake was met with another blistering rebuke until I finally mastered the text to his exacting standards.

He slumped back in his chair, exhausted from his teaching. "I know it's harsh to speak to you this way, Lady Tocino, but I *saw* Lord Balthazar lurking in the shadows at the funeral. When I couldn't find you, I feared the worst. He's waiting and watching, and I won't let him hurt you."

My breath caught in my throat as I watched him clench his fist, knuckles turning white. My heart raced with a mix of fear and excitement, knowing that Balthazar was close by. The thought of seeing him again filled me with a strange concoction of dread and desire, bubbling up inside me until it threatened to consume me entirely. With each passing second, the anticipation only grew stronger, pulling me closer to the edge of reason.

"May I be excused?" I said sweetly, trying to still my beating heart.

"Of course." Signor Zampa dabbed at his brow with his handkerchief. "Keep practicing. I'll test you on the scripture tomorrow."

I crossed the room and kissed him on the cheek. "Thank you for your kindness, signor."

His gaze hardened with determination. "I will do anything to keep you safe until you can time travel. But first, fetch me my whiskey before you depart."

"Yes, of course," I replied.

Signor Zampa must be terribly afraid if he needed whiskey before noon. But then, so was I.

I swiftly grabbed a tall bottle of amber liquid in the elegant drawing room and took a deep swig. The fiery burn spread through my throat and settled in my stomach, making me feel alive. I hastily went to his study, bringing a delicate crystal tumbler and setting both items on his mahogany desk. With quick footsteps, I raced back upstairs to my bedroom.

Lying in bed, the heat of the liquor seeped into my body, warming me from within. Desire surged as I slipped my hand under my skirts, yearning for release.

I tugged up the volumes of fabric concealing me and slid my fingers into my slick folds. How I wanted Balthazar to be here. My heart ached for him, yet I knew that I had to leave him if I wanted to prove that I was his equal. The thought of being separated from him made me feel sick, but I forced myself to face the truth: there was no other way.

I quickly brought myself to orgasm, but the pleasure was short-lived. Fretful thoughts filled my head. *What would Signor Zampa think if he found out the blood of darkness runs through my veins? What if Balthazar can't find me? Worse, what if he never looks for me?*

Unable to quiet my mind, I burst from my bedroom, searching for Signor Zampa.

He sprawled on the sofa in the drawing room like a fly caught in a web of blissful drunkenness. The side table held a half-full whiskey bottle, and his limp hands clasped an empty tumbler to his chest. His bleary eyes glinted when he saw me, and he grinned crookedly.

"What can I do for you, Lady Tocino?" he slurred.

My voice cracked as I spoke. "Will Lord Balthazar be able to find me once I've time traveled?"

Signor Zampa slowly pulled himself up on the sofa. "No, he won't be able to figure out which time you're in unless there's a group of time travelers traveling together. You don't have anything to worry about."

I couldn't help but feel a tinge of fear wash over me for an entirely different reason than what Signor Zampa assumed. I *wanted* Balthazar to find me. I craved it.

"I don't know if I can do this," I said. "What if I end up in the wrong era?"

Signor Zampa let out a drunken chuckle and patted the seat beside him. "Oh, my dear. You worry too much. Just think where you want to go, and the dagger will guide you there."

I hesitated before taking a seat beside him. The fabric felt cold and unwelcoming against my skin.

"What if I can't do it?" I asked, struggling to keep my voice steady.

Signor Zampa's smile faltered before he took another swig from his bottle and placed it back beside him.

"Don't worry about that, my dear. Enjoy the journey and the safety you will find away from Lord Balthazar."

The words did little to calm my nerves. Lightning struck in my mind as I had a brilliant idea. I thanked Signor Zampa for his kind words and returned to my room.

Finding a pen and paper, I scribbled down the random era I desired to travel to—1666. It was a gamble leaving it for Balthazar to find, but there was no other choice. I just had to hope that it would work.

The night of the full moon was especially dark, and I was filled with anxious energy as I followed Signor Zampa through town. We were searching for a secret place to hold our rendezvous, but my heart felt like it was pulling me somewhere else—back to Balthazar's side. I was both filled with joy and dread when we eventually ended up at the park where Balthazar and I had shared so many clandestine meetings.

I clutched the paper on which I'd written the date in my neat, flowery handwriting.

Signor Zampa led me to a shadowy corner and showed me the dagger. I stared at it with awe and fear as its glistening steel and golden handle promised the power to transport me to faraway lands. Its curved blade had a life of its own, reflecting my determination as I paused to consider what destiny lay ahead.

Signor Zampa grabbed my chin like a vice and gazed into my eyes. His voice was deadly calm when he asked me, "Are you ready, child?"

"Yes," I whispered.

He gripped the knife. "I must cut open your hand with this blade as you repeat the sacred words. Remember—there must not be any mistakes!"

His hard gaze pierced through me.

My heart raced as I recited the scripture under my breath. Signor Zampa raised the blade and sliced it across my palm with one precise motion. I screamed in agony as the sharp steel bit into my skin and then continued to chant the words of power.

He placed the dagger's hilt in my palm and curled my fingers around it. As I murmured the words, the knife illuminated the darkness with an eerie glow. As I gripped the ancient blade, a jolt of electricity coursed through my body. My hands shook with excitement and fear as I prepared to wield its magic. It was a weapon unlike any other, capable of great destruction if not used carefully. But I knew I had no choice but to harness its power in this moment of desperation. The blade seemed alive with energy, almost as if it had been waiting for me.

The world around me slowly dissolved into oblivion. I clumsily groped for the paper in my pocket, feeling the edges of time slipping away. Finally, I released the paper from my clenched fist. I watched it dance on the wind down to the ground, a delicate reminder of my fleeting existence and a beckoning to the man I loved.

I felt a strange sensation as I faded from one era to another. I was being pulled in two different directions at once. My body felt heavy and light all at the same time. My heart raced as the memories of the past and hopes of the future seemed to crash together in my mind, all in a single moment.

The air around me felt thick and dense like a fog, yet strangely ethereal, as if I was being swept away by a breeze. I could feel the time around me shift and bend as if it was wrapping itself around me like a blanket.

Then, it was gone, and I was no longer standing in the park with Signor Zampa.

CHAPTER THIRTEEN
BALTHAZAR

I remained motionless in my chair, fuming in my candle-lit study. As I stared ahead, the shadows on the walls seemed to move and whisper.

Alina had disappeared. The last time I had seen her was a couple of days ago, skirting the edges of the funeral procession. Everywhere I went to find her, I only received dead ends. The rumors whispered in taverns and among the gossip-mongers infuriated me. Some said Alina had murdered her family. Others said she was running away from me, frightened because I slaughtered her family, and had departed for other lands.

A loud knock from the entrance shook me out of my trance. I flew toward the door and yanked it open with seething rage, ready to bellow a tirade.

Before me stood Medici's men, the Bargello, with their weapons drawn. I narrowed my eyes.

The three Bargello henchmen of the Medici family were clad in dark, almost black leather doublets. Their weapons of choice were daggers and maces, tools of intimidation that glinted in the lamplight and that they brandished with confidence. Their faces were hard and unyielding, and their features seemed set in a perpetual expression of threat.

Their hats were tall and black with a feather plume that curved upward, and their cloaks were heavy. They wore high boots and gauntlets. These men were a powerful representation of the Medici family and all its might.

They didn't scare me in the least. I was a patron of the Medici family, generously donating to the Gonfalonier, the powerful individuals the Medicis had hired to oversee law enforcement. The Gonfalonier had assembled the Bargello to patrol the streets, apprehend criminals, and maintain public order.

"How may I be of service, gentlemen?" I asked politely.

"You can come with us, Lord Balthazar," the largest man said. "You're wanted for murder."

"Is that so?" I said without emotion. "What is your evidence?"

They rattled off a few facts about the Tocino family found murdered and the details of the assault. I paid them no mind until "Lady Tocino" was uttered.

"What did you say?" I said to the tallest of the three men.

A smirk spread across his face like he'd caught the cat with the mouse in his mouth. "I said, Lady Tocino has given her eyewitness description of the horrific events. She said she caught you red-handed with a knife in her sister's neck. Said she saw you drinking the blood like a vampire. Are you a vampire, Lord Balthazar?"

He leered at me.

That little bitch. What is she playing at telling all those fabrications of the truth?

"I assure you, fine gentlemen, I am no vampire." I bared my teeth. "See? No fangs. And I've heard Lady Tocino is prone to delusions and fanciful tales of her own device."

"Is she now?" the Bargello henchman spat, his booted feet as still as stone. His piercing gaze whipped back and forth between the men at his side.

"She is a liar—I've heard her lies before." I forced myself to remain calm, but my heart pounded against my ribs. "Did Giovanni di Lorenzo de' Medici personally command you to bring me in?"

Giovanni, the second son of the powerful and esteemed Lorenzo the Magnificent, along with the Signoria, had much authority over Florence and its people.

The tall Bargello fixed me with an icy stare. "We act on his and his brother's behalf."

"Does that mean he commanded you personally to apprehend me?" I asked again. "Did he say you are to apprehend Lord Balthazar?"

"We follow their orders. We serve them both," he said.

"So, then," I said, clutching my golden doorknob, "the answer to my question is no. Neither Giovanni, his brother Giuliano, nor the Signoria personally contacted you to apprehend me. And, since I am a patron of considerable esteem of the Medicis, I'll kindly ask you to leave at once. Without evidence other than the fanciful tales of Lady Tocino, you have nothing to pin your accusations on."

I paused, then, added, "I think that Lady Tocino killed her family. I think she is guilty, because no one has seen her for a week since the murders happened. If I'm guilty, I would have fled. But seems to me she's the one who has disappeared, gentlemen. I think you should be looking for her, not me."

The three Bargello trembled with fear as they faced me.

But the tallest one mustered every ounce of courage and said, "We'll be back. I guarantee it. I doubt a beauty like Lady Tocino would ever commit murder. Especially her parents…"

SARA SAMUELS

"Do your best to arrest me, but I doubt you'll find any evidence. You'd be surprised what Alina is capable of."

In a single thunderous roar, my body burst into flames and loomed before them as a creature of pure terror. My infernal form burned with an unquenchable rage that sent the three men fleeing into the night. I was certain their minds had been forever burned by the sight of my monstrous transformation.

Back in my human form, I stalked through my home, outraged at what Alina had done. She'd gone to the authorities to have me apprehended! After all I'd done for her! I'd find her, by God, and make her pay.

Unable to stand being indoors, I threw on my coat and stalked out into the night. My anger, once simmering, began to boil as I walked the streets, searching for any trace of Alina. I attended every party in town, but no one had any information about her whereabouts. I clenched my fists as I imagined her with another man, or worse, far away from me. Every step I took ground in the betrayal. Alina had abandoned me without a second thought, without hesitation.

I wanted to scream and tear apart the city, to kill without mercy or thought, but instead, I forced myself to breathe. Alina was out there somewhere, and I was determined to find her. I silently vowed never to stop hunting for her. No matter how long it took or how far I had to go, I would find her.

The night of the full moon hung heavy in the cloud-filled sky. I searched desperately for a sign of my beloved Alina everywhere I went. A shiver ran down my spine as I reached our trysting place in the shadows of a secluded park.

My heart raced as I discovered the note hanging from a tree leaf, its surface still damp with the morning dew. I struggled to make out the thin strokes of Alina's handwriting that read 1666.

The words seemed to mock me as they demanded my attention, taunting me to participate in my beautiful monster's game. With a determination that pushed away any doubt, I knew I had to be ready when the next full moon arrived.

The days dragged on endlessly as I impatiently awaited when the moon would be at its fullest. The feeling of being deprived of her was like a drug addict going through withdrawal. As my temper grew, I killed more than necessary. My presence filled those around me with fear everywhere I went as I stormed and raged through the city streets.

I vowed to make Alina pay for leaving me in such agony.

Finally, the night had come. As I stood in the eerie light of the full moon, I had no idea if I would be heading to the right era. I questioned whether having trusted Alina and the note she left was a mistake. She was a cunning creature. No matter what, though, I knew I would persist in my search for her, even if centuries passed. I would find the bitch and make her pay. I repeated the sacred scripture and slit my hand as an offering to the night sky.

I was transported to a lush place. Rolling hills dotted with sheep and bordered by stone fences stretched as far as the eye could see. Could this be Ireland? I'd heard tales of such a place, spoken by shopkeepers or their patrons. Everywhere I looked, the unfamiliar landscape filled me with a sense of otherworldliness: a strange language, a foreign smell, and too much blinding light. Despite the fear that threatened to overwhelm me, I drank it all in, taking a risk in the hopes that I might find her.

I spotted a group of men huddled together, speaking in a

language I didn't understand. One of them caught my eye, and I approached, my heart racing with nerves. But as soon as they saw me, their expressions turned dark, and one of them drew out a gun. Without hesitation, I pulled out my trusty dagger and swiftly opened the man's throat. The others backed away in fear, hands held up defensively. Using the chaos to my advantage, I quickly stripped the dead man of his clothes and put them on, blending in with the unfamiliar crowd.

My eyes scanned the faces around me, searching for Alina amidst the chaos and my own thoughts raced with worry for her safety.

She had no skills other than sex and manipulation. How could she survive? I roamed the town, desperate to find her and unsure what to do if our paths crossed.

On the one hand, I desired to safeguard her; on the other, I expected her to be punished for deceiving me. Emotions of hostility, sympathy, and perplexity blended inside my head, and I had no idea how to make them disappear.

As the sun began to set, my footsteps grew heavier, each one taking more effort than the last. The time-traveling had drained me of all energy, and I was desperate for sustenance —something to replenish my soul. Spotting a military encampment on the outskirts of town, I thought it was the perfect opportunity to find a willing prostitute to satisfy my needs before ultimately killing her. But to my frustration, there were no women in sight.

I cursed my luck as I stepped away from the military encampment. It had been a long and difficult day, and all I wanted was to make my way back to town and find solace between a willing female's legs.

But then I saw her, a dark silhouette standing in the shadows of a nearby alleyway. She smiled at me, her eyes twinkling in the moonlight, her blond hair flowing around her shoulders.

"Zara?" I whispered. "Is that you? Why does your spirit haunt me? You're long gone, dead and buried."

I felt drawn to her, a deep and primal instinct rising within me. She wasn't Alina—no one could ever be Alina—but she would restore my strength. I stepped closer, and she welcomed me with open arms, leading me farther into the alleyway.

She touched my face gently and spoke in a low, sultry voice, her words full of promises of pleasure. I surrendered to her, a sensation of pleasure and anticipation flooding me.

We fell onto the cold, damp ground, and I lost myself in her embrace. She was skilled and passionate, and my body melted into hers.

When it was over, an unexpected rage boiled up inside me. My passions had been satisfied, my strength restored, yet something else remained, an emptiness that demanded to be filled. This bitch wasn't *Alina*. And, I would never have fucked her had Alina not left me. In a blind fury, I grabbed a nearby rock and smashed it into her forehead, killing her instantly.

A twisted smile spread across my lips as I stepped back from the gruesome scene. My hands shook with adrenaline and satisfaction, my body trembling with the thrill of release. I turned and strode away, leaving behind the lifeless body of the woman I had just killed in the dark alleyway.

I pushed open the doors to a nearby tavern, and all eyes instantly fell on me. The murmurs and whispers stopped as everyone was drawn to my disheveled appearance. My hands clenched into fists as I spotted Alina perched on a man's lap, her laugh echoing through the room. Fury boiled inside me as I made my way toward them.

How dare she!

I had made it clear that there was to be no other man, yet there she was, flaunting her betrayal in my face.

The stranger had a chiseled jaw, his blue eyes shining in the lamplight. Alina glanced at me and smirked. Then, she reached up and grasped the stranger's neck, pulling his mouth toward hers. She kissed him deeply, her lips pressing against his with fierce determination. She pulled back, then slid her hands down his chest, gripping his shirt and tugging it off.

The stranger shuddered with excitement, heedless of his public display of intimacy. Other men eyed him with envy, hoping to have their turn with Alina next.

A few scantily clad women sashayed down the stairs and approached several men. One of the whores approached me, but I shoved her out of the way as Alina continued to kiss and grope the stranger.

An uncontrollable anger washed over me, paralyzing me in place. The fury I felt was like a raging inferno, consuming my heart and soul. My vision blurred as rage boiled my blood, and all I could hear was the roar of disbelief encircling me.

Alina explored the stranger's body with her hands, casting furtive glances in my direction.

The bitch knew I was watching them. She was taunting me on purpose. She held the man closer, her lips searching for his as they moved rhythmically together.

The stranger leaned back, and Alina gazed into his piercing blue eyes. She ran her fingers over the rough stubble on his jawline, tugging him closer as she brought his lips to hers.

But just as things were heating up, I unleashed my fire powers in a fit of jealousy. The wooden floor sizzled and smoked beneath my feet, creating a charred circle around me.

One of the whores screamed and fled from the man she'd seduced. The others clutched their marks for protection. A few men drew their pistols, pointing them at me.

All eyes watched me as I strode over to Alina and the stranger's table and, without a word, grabbed Alina by the neck and pushed her off the stranger's lap. He jumped up, and fear emanated from his eyes.

Alina clung to me, her body trembling with desire. As she looked up into my eyes, I felt my heart stop at her mischievous grin. The heat of lust surged through me, and my need for her shook me to the core. Oh, I was cursed by Alina's beauty—a fool beyond redemption. My cock strained against the confines of my clothing, desperate to be one with her flesh.

"You finally found me," she said softly. "What took you so long?"

CHAPTER FOURTEEN

ALINA

My heart pounded when I heard heavy footsteps outside the brothel door. Balthazar had come at last. I had been waiting for him for thirty days, my body aching with anticipation. I slid into the lap of the man I'd been flirting with for the past hour—I think his name was Eoin.

The tavern door opened, and an imposing figure strode through the doorway—*Balthazar*. His eyes were like blazing coals, and his features contorted in fury. He seemed larger than life, a demigod capable of destroying entire cities.

As he raged in front of me, I could barely breathe. My skin blazed, and my heart thundered. A rush of desire flooded my body as Eoin's hand grazed my skin. I leaned in and pressed my lips to his, feeling the intensity of our chemistry. At that moment, I imagined him as Balthazar, who had captured my heart. But then, the real Balthazar stormed across the room, his eyes full of fury. As he grabbed my neck and pulled me away from Eoin, a jolt of electricity pulsed through me, and I couldn't help but feel a surge of arousal at the dangerous situation unfolding before me.

As his cock strained in his trousers, begging for release, I knew I had him where I wanted him. I'd bested Lord Balthazar at long last.

He gripped my cheeks with his strong hand. "How many men have you fucked? Tell me!"

"I have not let another man touch the places you have touched, my love," I said, shoving aside his hand. "No man has entered me."

Balthazar bore his eyes into mine, rage boiling in his veins. His lip curled with disdain. "You dare to taunt me with this pitiful man?"

He clutched Eoin against his body.

Eoin whimpered in terror, tears streaming down his cheeks. "Please don't hurt me. I had no idea she was taken."

Balthazar snarled and drew his dagger, slicing deep into Eoin's throat. Blood gushed, and Eoin crumpled to the floor in a lifeless heap.

The other prostitutes screamed. Chaos broke out as the tavern's patrons raced to escape.

An exhilarating glee coursed through my bloodstream. My love had found me! He'd found me, and now we were equals.

Balthazar's normally composed demeanor was replaced with a mix of wrath and fear. His eyes were wild, as he clenched his fists and murmured something through his gritted teeth.

I drew closer, emboldened to connect with him in this moment of fury. I wanted to tell him he was not alone, even in his darkest hours.

"I'm not scared of you," I said, not breaking our eye contact. "I know you're the darkness. I know you can kill me, but I'm not scared. You are my monster, and I love you. I don't care what you are."

Balthazar seemed taken aback by my words, a potent mix of surprise and relief washing over his face. Without a word, he drew me into a fierce embrace, pressing his forehead against mine and finally allowing himself to accept the comfort I offered.

We stayed like that for a while, swaying in the darkness. Finally, Balthazar pulled away and ran his fingers through my hair. He stared longingly into my eyes, a look of contentment overcoming the stress on his face.

"Thank you," he said.

The negative energy that had previously filled the space between us had dissipated, replaced by a new mutual understanding and connection. We were no longer two distinct people but rather two components of something greater, something meant to be inextricably intertwined like two stars in a cosmic dance.

However, the tranquility was dispelled by something else entirely: a feeling of dread and unholiness. Balthazar seized my jaw and pulled me toward him. He kissed me with a savagery I'd never felt before. I wrapped my arms around him and ground my body against his.

Balthazar began to transform, and I pushed away from him. His skin split open like a ripe melon, tearing and ripping to reveal a skeleton of hard bone and tight sinew. Veins and arteries throbbed with blood right before my eyes. His eyes glowed with unholy fire, and his teeth grew sharp and jagged as knives. Even as his body contorted into a beastly shape, he radiated power most people couldn't imagine possessing.

Maggots began to crawl from his flesh as if some ancient force was coming alive beneath his skin. He bellowed a cry like an enraged bull that shook the air around us. My heart pounded madly for Balthazar, and I wished we would forever be intertwined with all my being.

"I love you, Lord Balthazar, with all my wicked heart!" I cried.

"How can you say that? Look at me!" He beat his bloody chest with his fists, spattering blood across the tawdry linens. The heat of his breath on my face scorched my flesh, causing me to arch backward.

I shielded my face from his intense heat with my arm.

"I wish the world were dark," I whispered, thick with emotion. "We're villains in this place, but we could rule it all together."

The air between us crackled with lightning as we moved closer, our eyes locked in a potent dance. Something wild and untamed passed between us, and I knew there was no turning back from the darkness that awaited us.

I scanned the worn wooden walls. The stench of cigar smoke, booze, and sex permeated the empty tavern, and my stomach roiled. I felt Balthazar's gaze following me, but I refused to look at him.

Finally, I stopped and looked at him, my eyes blazing with a fierce intensity.

"We like when people are in pain," I said. "I like that we are who we are. I wish we could make the world in our image."

Balthazar stared at me with glowing eyes and said, "Where have you been all my life? The others always try to please me. All they wanted was my love. You challenge me. You *want* to be with me."

A sense of wonder permeated his words.

Deep warmth filled my chest, and I was truly no longer afraid. I took a step closer to my hideous monster, and he smiled. We stood silently until he finally broke the quietude.

"Come," he said, his voice slithering from his throat like silk. "I must claim you as the darkness you are."

The stairway creaked as he took my hand and led me upstairs. Smells of musk and semen filled my nostrils at the top of the landing, and my heart fluttered in anticipation as Balthazar kicked open the bedroom door. He swept me in his arms and tossed me on the unmade bed. My body sunk into the scratchy mattress as I waited for what would come next.

He stood at the foot of the bed, looking down at me with a mischievous glint and a smirk on his lips. Balthazar's half-human, half-monstrous form was a sight to behold. His body was a play of the grotesque and human perfection. Skin hung from half his side while the other side bulged with muscles. One blue eye probed me while the other stared at me from the bowels of the underworld. I was at once horrified and intoxicated.

His voice was deep and soft as he said, "My wicked temptress."

He crawled on top of me, all power and might. His skin seemed to glow from within, giving off a mysterious and powerful energy. His power, confidence, and desire for me drew me in. He lay beside me, pressing his body against mine. His lips were like fire as they brushed against mine, and my whole being melted into him.

I was overcome with fear and fascination, but I was determined to keep my composure. I wanted him to take me, and he seemed more than willing.

His hands seemed both gentle and powerful as they caressed my body. A thrill of pleasure rushed through me as he touched me, and soon, my clothing was discarded. I hardly registered the coolness of the night air blowing through the window on my exposed flesh, nor did I see the maggots that had begun to fall from Balthazar's form, landing on my skin like a thousand tiny pustules. All I could feel was his cock pushing into me, filling me with inexplicable pleasure and horror.

The squirming larvae undulated across my skin. I cried out and brushed the maggots away from my body in terror while my core still yearned for more. Balthazar seemed to understand this paradox, and he moved his body in a powerful rhythm, pushing me to the brink of pleasure with each thrust.

The walls of the whore's bedroom blurred together by the smoke created by the flickering candles, which cast a red hue across my skin and the cadaverous face of my beloved. His eyes glowed, bearing into me with such intensity that I felt my reality unraveling.

We moved together in a slow and sensual ritual, my monster and I, our limbs weaving in and out of each other in a timeless dance. His cool skin, in stark contrast to the heat rising off his body, felt like a balm against mine. His presence grew increasingly intense with every breath until I was almost drunk on the strange emotions his body evoked.

I looked up at his face, which was always expressionless and yet paradoxically full of emotion. Balthazar's presence radiated something I could not comprehend, something that was both beautiful and deeply disturbing. This experience tipped my mind toward madness; I was fucking a half-corpse, half-human radiating heat like an inferno.

I felt trapped in a dream, unable to move or speak as Balthazar thrust inside me, his fingers tracing my veins. His bloody heart pulsated against me, winding and unwinding as it pushed blood through his arteries. We stayed together like that for hours until the candles melted away, and the room was again filled with darkness.

A strange peace came over me. I had never felt such a deep connection to anyone before. I was adrift in a sea of fire and water. Eventually, the pleasure and terror became too much. I became a cauldron of lava, boiling, churning, ready to explode and spill over the edges of my being. I writhed beneath Balthazar, clutching his bones in one hand and skin-covered muscle in the other.

"I'm about to come, Balthazar. Don't stop."

He bucked into me with relentless fury, unraveling me, taking me to a dangerous place I knew I'd never escape. And then I exploded into a million microorganisms, fragments of my humanity cascading through the stars. I lost consciousness and was sailing through the blackness, vibrating with ecstatic, throbbing impulses.

When I came to, Balthazar was by my side, fully human, propped on one elbow as he stroked my hair the way one might pet a cat.

"You're back," he said with a smile.

"Where did I go?" I frowned, trying to recall. Had Balthazar really transformed into a monster, or was I having delusions?

"Who can say?" he said, caressing my cheek. "How do you feel?"

"I'm not sure." I rolled on my back. The sheets felt scratchy and worn, unlike the fine linens I'd grown accustomed to.

My frown deepened as Balthazar pulled me close and whispered, "Who better to ask than you?"

His powerful leg slid over my slender one, and his half-hard cock pressed against my hip. His gentle strokes and caresses felt so uncertain, so out of place, like a warm breeze on a frosty night.

"That was truly beautiful, my little monster," he said.

The words chilled me to the core, and I struggled to keep

my expression neutral. I didn't want him to see the hurt and anger under the surface.

I wanted to push him away. I wanted to tell him I wasn't his little monster and wasn't something to be possessed or owned. Instead, I stayed still and silent, letting him think he had found what he wanted.

The wind singing through the open window was the only sound in the small room as I lay in tangled sheets, heavy with fear and sorrow. I felt a sudden urge to flee, to get away from this man and this place. I knew I would never find a man like him again. No one would accept my darkness the way Balthazar did. So I stayed there, trembling and silent, until he finally released me, rolling from the hay-filled mattress.

As he donned his clothes, he said, almost casually, "I was meant to slaughter you, Alina. I hunted you, certain I would kill you when I found you. Instead, I fell in love."

The words numbed me like a drug, paralyzing my limbs as I tried to process the meaning of what had just happened. I needed time to sort through the whirlwind these revelations had brought; only then could Balthazar and I decide our fate and future.

CHAPTER FIFTEEN
BALTHAZAR

I'd transformed back to my "normal" looking self as I lay beside Alina, taking in the tawdry room in this brothel. The room was small, the walls speckled with dampness and the air thick with the smell of musty rot. It was sparsely decorated with an old, rickety bed, a plain wooden chair, and a chipped washbasin atop a three-legged stool.

The only light source was a single window framed by faded, threadbare curtains. A weak light filtered in from the street outside through the window, dimly illuminating the small space with a sick, yellow glow. In the corner of the room was a wooden chest filled with the scant possessions of a poor prostitute. A pair of grimy, stained blouses, a dirty brown shawl, a cracked mirror, and a few other meager items comprised the sum of the whore's worldly goods.

The walls were bare, save for a single oil painting of a woman, her hair done up in intricate curls and her face painted a brilliant white. But the beauty of that woman in the picture was in stark contrast to the grubby whore's room in which it hung. It was a room of desperation and despair, a place of shadows and secrets, where anything could happen, and no one would ever know. It had been perfect for revealing my true nature, where regular depravity occurred.

A grim smile stretched my cheeks as I thought of the potent exchange Alina and I had just experienced. I could guarantee no other person who entered this room ever had an experience like Alina and I had. I'd let her see me, truly see me in all my depraved gruesomeness. I was born of decay and darkness. I lived in the shadows, in the places where nightmares were born—never a pretty sight to feast one's eyes upon. I'd learned through the years to cloak myself in a more presentable fashion as a wickedly handsome male. No sense in terrifying all the women I bedded. But with Alina, everything was different.

Everything.

I'd thought I would never find someone who accepted the real me. Zara always loved me because we were the same, both born of darkness. But here she was, my Alina, with a dark past that aligned with mine. My mind reeled with disbelief at Alina's admission. I couldn't believe I'd found a partner again who accepted me completely, even in my monstrous form.

"What are you thinking about?" Alina said, scraping one long, pointed nail across my back.

I sat up and propped one of the dingy, tattered pillows behind me. "About us."

"What about us?" She propped herself up similarly, pressing her naked leg next to mine, and cocked her head to study me. "You're rather disturbing in your true form, by the way. It's a sharp contrast to the way you currently look."

My gaze snagged on her moonstone and ruby necklace, which belonged around Zara's throat. Fury coursed through me like liquid fire, but I managed to keep it locked beneath the facade of my calm demeanor. "Did it bother you?"

She shook her head, pushing her long, tangled hair out of her face.

"Not at all. I found it a total turn-on." A frown marred her features. "Except for the maggots, perhaps. It's hard to say. The whole experience was shockingly outrageous. I'm certainly not opposed to experiencing it again."

A shy smile flashed across her pretty face.

Alina was such a contradiction in extremes. One second, she was willing to let loose into her darkness; the next, she was as vulnerable and innocent as a young schoolgirl.

I stroked her warm thigh. "I suppose it was fated to be this way. When we first met, you were so wild and passionate, yet I couldn't break you as I wanted. You're just like me, a sadistic monster who never lets anyone stand in their way. I slaughtered your parents, yet here you are, lying by my side."

"Tell me more about the darkness," Alina asked, her voice laced with intrigue.

My throat constricted.

"Your father was the first darkness," I said, my voice soft. "He took me under his wing long ago and taught me the ins and outs of the depths of depravity, how to survive in a world of never-ending darkness. He showed me ways I thought unimaginable, and I followed them faithfully, now forever scarred by his malevolent intentions."

Alina was quiet, digesting this information. Then she leaned forward, her face full of questions. "Do you have to kill to survive?"

I met her gaze steadily, unwilling to look away.

"Yes," I replied, my voice barely a whisper. "I do."

"So, my father wanted to turn 'bad' people into 'good' people," Alina said, her eyes wide in amazement.

I nodded. "He wanted to save the world from evil and train us to be the hunters of evil."

Alina frowned. "But why did he want you to kill people like you?"

"Your father thought it was the only way to ensure these criminals wouldn't do more harm," I said. "He felt that if he punished them, they would eventually stop their criminal activities. He believed that society could only be saved by eliminating bad influences."

Alina shook her head in disbelief. "I just don't understand why he wanted you to only take the lives of the depraved. We should be able to kill whom we choose."

I sighed. "Nor did I. It wasn't easy for me either, since I am admittedly the most depraved of all. Yet, at first, I was happy doing what Mathias asked of me. I yearned for his approval. But as time passed, I started having doubts about what we were doing. Who was I, born of darkness, to be killing only those like me? I wanted to go after the good, too —I didn't want to make an exception."

Alina looked at me sympathetically. "You mean my father didn't even know what he was doing, wasn't right?"

I shook my head before continuing my story, telling Alina how Cora had been instrumental in changing Mathias' plan and how Cora had convinced Mathias that training and reha-bilitation could help some of the criminals instead of killing them all outright, which had been his original plan.

"That's when your father designed his training school." I glowered as the memory took command of my mind. "Cora was a sweet, simpering woman with a kindly disposition. I came to loathe her."

"I can see why," Alina said.

I narrowed my eyes. "You can?"

"Yes. I probably would have despised her as well." Her eyes darkened as she spoke. "My adopted parents were equally as tedious, as you know. All their insistent crap about marrying well and meeting the right man was as loathsome as it gets. It was as if the only option for a woman was to get married and bear the man's whelps. *So* not fulfilling. Men get to travel and hunt and build things and increase their knowledge and all the other activities known to *mankind.* I wanted what you have—the freedom to exist as I want."

The intensity of her shadowed eyes took me by surprise, sparking my ardor. My cock began to harden, begging me to cease this conversational quest. I traced seductive circles on her leg, but she seemed preoccupied with questions, endless questions.

"How old are you, Balthazar?" she asked. The question hung between us, heavy and full of implications.

I tried to determine whether I should trust her with the answer or not.

"Very," I finally said, my voice clipped and guarded. "Old enough to know better. And old enough to know which of your questions deserves an answer."

My eyes locked onto hers, daring her to back down. But instead, she stared back with equal intensity, unflinching and determined. The air between us crackled with tension and neither of us was willing to break first.

"Where were you born?" she said, unceasing in her quest to know me.

"The land of the Norseman, many centuries ago," I said. My heart ached with a pain I could never explain, like something inside of me was dead and gone. Thoughts raced through my mind of Zara's sweet laughter, my precious daughters' faces, the memories of my past relentlessly tearing me apart from within. It was a pain that had become an eternal part of me, impossible to forget. I strained and fought with all my might to shove it away…to bury the memories of a lifetime that haunted me. Desperately, I clawed at the abyss of darkness, trying to erase the echoes of time that lingered in my soul.

"Look. I don't wish to speak of where I was born or any of these questions about my origins. None of it matters."

"It does to me," she shot back, appearing wounded.

Without warning, I trapped her with my arm, crushing her throat. A violent surge of fury ripped through my body like lightning, as memories of my past clawed their way into my mind. The phantom sensations of betrayal and despair gnawed at me, threatening to consume me whole. I gritted my teeth and balled my fists, determined not to let the festering rage within me overtake my sanity.

"We're done here, Alina! Not another word about where I come from. Do you hear me?"

She fought me with wild ferocity, her sharp nails clawing at my skin. I could overpower her in an instant but instead chose to press my seething desire into her soft belly as if demonstrating my power over her. She closed her eyes, and she shuddered, her body unable to resist the maddening sensation of my wanton arousal. I grabbed her face with my rough hands, forcing our mouths together. I sucked her lower lip between my teeth and bit down until I tasted the salty tang of her blood. She gasped in pain, but I drank it hungrily, savoring the sweetness of her suffering. As soon as I released her from my grip, I rolled away, creating an achingly empty space between us.

Alina lay beside me, her chest heaving. Her eyes were ablaze with a fire of hunger and desperation.

I grinned wickedly, daring her to ask something that defied the rules I'd so clearly defined.

"What else would you like to know?" I said, my voice dripping with honey-laced innuendos. "What dark secrets do you desire to know apart from the stories of my creation?"

She licked her swollen lip, flashing me a feral, wounded look like a fox caught in a trap. "Tell me more about what my father was like. Say more about Mathias."

The mention of Mathias sent my heart into a tailspin. "He was always more than a friend to me. He was a teacher figure I emulated and respected. When I killed him, it left an irreplaceable void in my soul. But he ultimately betrayed me, so I was glad I ended his life."

"What did he do?" she asked.

I wanted to tell her the truth about her father, yet I couldn't bring myself to do it. I knew that she would be confused and overwhelmed. So, instead of telling her about Mathias, I told her a story about my first love, Zara, and how Mathias had taken her from me. My soul was alight with fire as I spoke of my one true love, every syllable dripping with emotion and inflection. My words grew fierce and pointed, an immense torrent of feelings erupting from within. I knew I had buried my love for Zara, trying to convince myself that Alina was the one I loved. But nothing could be further from the truth. Zara was once the moon to my sun, my reason for existence.

The memories of my once-perfect life flooded back, tearing at my heart with sharp claws. But as I spoke to Alina about Zara, the love of my life, and our precious children, I painted a false picture of indifference. As if she was just another one of Mathias' countless students, instead of the woman who held my heart in her hands until it shattered into a million pieces. "One of his students was a woman—dark, dangerous, and deadly—with whom I shared an unnatural bond. She and I were two sides of the same coin, competing to see which could claim the most kills. She completed me. I told Mathias that she was mine forever, and I was hers."

A low growl left Alina's throat.

I leveled her with a cold glare.

"Where is this lover now? Do I need to kill her?" Alina spat out the words with such venom I nearly laughed in triumph. Alina was jealous of a ghost.

"Your father took care of her," I said.

Alina was practically shaking with envy. "What do you mean?"

I glared at her with eyes like razor blades. My gaze could break through steel.

"I told your father that she was mine, and if there were ways I could have had her again, I would do them. I couldn't let her go. It wasn't a choice. Love made me crazy. It turned my brain into water," I said, each word carving holes through the air between us.

Alina's fists clenched at her sides, and she glared at me. "What is her name?" Her voice trembled with anger and hurt.

I raised my chin defiantly. "That name will never leave my lips." My words were like a sharp gust of arctic wind, freezing the air between us.

Alina's eyes flashed with rage as she clenched her fists in frustration. "You're driving a stake through my heart with this part of your history, and yet I'm expected to remain quiet about your past, which is anything but. Balthazar, you're killing me."

She squeezed her eyes tight. Her words were like daggers flying from her mouth. "I don't want you to bring up the ghost of her. I demand that you solemnly bless us now. We are the killers who are together now—*us*."

A malicious leer spread across my face.

"I'll talk about her if I choose to," I spat out with venom. "Your father was fully aware of my deep love for her, yet he still thought he could claim her as his own—and that's what he did."

Rage made my blood burn hot. "He was also with her but didn't say anything. I found her with Mathias one day. I lost control. God, how I loved her. Yet everything was taken from me."

The room fell silent as my words hung heavy in the air, pulsating with an intense energy that could be felt by anyone within earshot. My mind grew black with the next memory. My hollow-sounding voice emerged from the cracks and the shadows of the past.

"When I saw Mathias with her, I lost control and broke all his rules. I became my true monster self. Mathias imprisoned me and put me in a cell filled with poisons. My mind was engulfed in madness. My lover never came to see me or comfort me when I was imprisoned. Mathias laughed at me and criticized me for being a weak man who lost control of his emotions. Then he said, 'I can't share her either because I love her. I must kill her so we both can be free from her presence.' I didn't think he meant it. "

My voice grew dead, listless. "I was wrong, however. Mathias killed her. He destroyed the love of my life. He plunged his dagger into her throat, wiped the blade clean with his fingertips, and licked the blood from his fingers. All while staring me straight in the eye." I let out a bitter chuckle. "He just wanted to control me. I got away with things unbeknownst to him."

Alina's anguished moans filled the room, but I could only vaguely hear them. My mind was consumed with memories of my heartbreak. As Alina's face twisted in pain, she asked me, "Do you still love her?" Her words stung as I spoke of this woman that still held my heart.

"How can I forget about the woman who gave me love… a home…a sense of belonging? I shared everything with her: body, heart, and soul." My throat tightened as I thought about the woman who had filled my life with passion and warmth. Every memory of her was etched upon my heart, impossible to forget. As my anguish became too much to contain, a guttural howl escaped my lips, shaking the foundations around me with its force.

The moonstone necklace dangling from Alina's throat glimmered and shone, taunting me with its horrible beauty. In a flash of rage, I seized it and crushed it to bits, sending fragments of jewels flying.

With a gasp, Alina touched her throat. "Why did you do that? I loved that necklace!"

An angry red line formed on her delicate skin where the gold chain had bit into her skin as it broke.

"Because *I* gave that to her. *Me*. It was once *hers,* the woman whose name I shall never repeat," I snarled through clenched teeth.

Alina pulled her head back as if repulsed she'd worn that necklace all these years.

I straddled Alina and seized her throat, not enough to restrict her breath but with enough force she'd know I meant business. My tone became deadly. "The worst thing you can ever do to me, Alina, is love another. That is the *only* thing. If you open your legs to another man, I will kill you, Alina. Mark my words. My dark lover betrayed me. She was everything to me...*everything."*

My voice simmered with intensity.

Alina shoved my hand away with uncharacteristic strength. "Then why did you allow me to take lovers at the beginning of our relationship?"

I growled. "I was trying to safeguard my dark heart. Promise me this, Alina. Never betray me. If you ever open your legs to another man again, I'll ensure you won't have a chance to live and tell about it." My voice was low, vibrating with menace. "I will never break your trust—no one can replace your love. Tonight, you have proved that to me. You have seen me as I am, yet you still want me. For that, I demand your utmost loyalty."

Looking deeply into my eyes, she said in a solemn voice, "I will never betray you. No one will ever accept me like you do. That is the past now. We are the future and invincible." She paused before adding, "I am happy you killed my father. If you hadn't killed him, I would." Her soft hands grasped my hard heat and guided it to her slick opening.

She was ready for me, and I growled my approval.

"I hope nothing will ever break us apart. I wanted to make humans evil like me and overpower my teacher. To over-power my master. He backstabbed me. Took away the love of my life." My muscles strained as I knelt above the woman who had become everything to me.

A look of carnal rage darkened Alina's features like she might kill *me* if I kept talking. I closed my mouth around hers and silenced my words with a savage kiss. And then I fucked her with brutal intensity, letting her know she was mine, all mine. And if she ever dared to break her vow, I'd at least warned her what would happen.

And I meant every word.

CHAPTER SIXTEEN

ALINA

Crickets and frogs peeped, calling for mates or their young lost to the dark as the sounds of dawn echoed through the window. The sound was soothing and innocent, drawing me out of the room.

But the moment popped like a bubble, revealing boiling rage at the picture Balthazar had painted of my father and Balthazar's so-called love. Father sounded like nothing but a pious individual, more suited to a life of the cloth than the darkness. But the twist between him, Balthazar, and *that woman* made me livid. I wanted to kill her twice for having left such longing in Balthazar. I wanted to kill *him* for sharing his story with me. How dare he parade a story of such potent love with me? He should have no other love save for ours.

"I should have been allowed to join you in my father's execution," I hissed through clenched teeth.

"It's an honor I had to take with a single hand," Balthazar replied coolly. "And you were but a babe."

"My loathing for him is only overshadowed by my pride that you've eliminated my mother, as well," I spat. "No more mercy for those too sweet."

Balthazar arched an eyebrow at me but said nothing.

I grew weary of this tawdry bedroom, stinking of sex, perspiration, and lust with its faded wallpaper and funky appearance. I rolled out of bed and stormed across the room, snatching up clothing. I threw Balthazar's garments at him. He warded them off with raised arms and a smirk.

"What's got you in such a snit?" he said.

"Everything! My father was a simpering bastard," I said, yanking on my undergarments. "And your former lover…I want to summon her from hell and exact my revenge on her for simply existing."

Balthazar hummed a low tune as he watched me. The sound drove me crazy.

"Your father never wanted you," Balthazar said abruptly. He wanted nothing to do with a daughter. He was determined to forget you ever existed."

I blinked at Balthazar, my face a mix of shock and confusion.

"He ran away from your mother when she gave birth to you," Balthazar said. "He returned when she begged him to, but he'd made himself clear. He never wanted to be a father, and he never wanted to face the responsibility of having a child, of having you."

I looked away, my eyes glistening with unshed tears.

"It's not your fault," Balthazar said softly. "He had his own demons and was never ready to be a father."

I picked up a cheap figurine, probably a gift from the whore's enamored client, and hurled it across the room. It shattered, sending shards of painted porcelain everywhere.

"I'm sick of this room. Do you hear me? Sick of it! I want to go home!" I yanked my dress over my arms and began to fasten the tiny buttons one by one. Only my shaking hands made the task impossible, and I finally gave up, throwing my arms up in frustration.

Balthazar elegantly rolled out of bed, tugged on his clothes unhurriedly, and sauntered before me. He planted a kiss on my nose and began to slowly affix each button. "It doesn't matter what your father did or didn't think about you. He was a selfish man, always looking out for his best interests. Think about it…" He lifted his head, eyed me, and slurped a tear from my face. "If he had been there for you, raised you right, do you think the outcome would have been any differently? Would you have been a different person?"

I hated it when Balthazar became loving and soft. I would almost rather he raged and stormed about than be kind and vulnerable with me. His tenderness made me feel quivery inside, like a leaf about to be torn from the tree by a gentle breeze. I despised that feeling, so I shoved Balthazar away from me. He didn't get angry, though—he simply laughed.

He surged toward me, threw his arms around me, and, together, we faded into the darkness, wrapping ourselves in the shadows and blurring back to his place. And I left all thoughts and hatred of my father and *that woman* back where they belonged—in that wretched whore's bedroom.

Our days settled into mundane pleasures, enjoying each other's companionship, and endlessly screwing. But then Balthazar went on one of his mysterious journeys with no warning. His sudden disappearance left me with a deep sense of unease, but as the days turned into weeks and I received no word from him, my anxiety spiraled into panic. Every night, I would stare at the full moon and feel the urge to leave, to search for him. Finally, I could take it no longer and, in a frenzy, I packed a bag and left a cryptic message for Balthazar in the form of an expensive French perfume bottle. The sharp letters '1411 France' were etched onto the glass, a desperate plea for him to find me. And just like that, I found myself transported to 1411 France, where I awaited Balthazar.

It took him two months to find me. Our reunion was joyous and tempestuous, as usual—but then I took off again. Our cat-and-mouse game continued for a couple of years. I became a master of time travel. I could move through time effortlessly, like a ghost, leaving only the faintest hint of my presence behind. I would disappear at a moment's notice, never giving Balthazar a chance to catch me. I would traverse through time, leaving clues behind but never staying in one place for long. I found the thrill of being pursued and playing hide-and-seek through history exhilarating. Balthazar was endlessly amused and perplexed by my maneuvers.

Each time we were reunited, it was like a brand-new adventure. Balthazar would try to understand my clues and unravel my movements, unable to get enough of my elusive charm. I enjoyed keeping Balthazar on his toes; it helped equalize our dynamic. I never forgot how ruthlessly he had pinned me in the whore's bed, nearly choking me, to make his point. I figured he deserved to have to find me throughout time.

The sex we experienced upon reuniting was always deep, depraved, and satisfying. We were so open to each other, sharing our secrets and hidden desires. We were always consumed in our own private world to the exclusion of all others.

On one occasion, Balthazar stormed into the drawing room, his usually dashing features twisted into a scowl. I sat on the plush velvet sofa, my journal open on my lap, the warm sun streaming in through the large bay window and casting a golden glow on my face. I wore a shimmering emerald-green satin dress that rustled with every movement. He slammed the door shut and I jumped, frantically trying to hide my journal before he saw it.

"Put down that blasted book," he roared, sending a trembling shockwave through my body. "You're always writing in that fucking thing."

He stalked toward me, snatched the journal from my hands, and threw it across the room.

My mouth gaped as my diary thwacked against the wall and fell unceremoniously. Coolly, I sauntered across the room, picked it up, and placed it on the side table near the settee where I lounged.

"Rough day, *my lord*?" I said, using the phrase "my lord" like a weapon.

"I told you never to call me that," he snarled.

"Apologies, my lord," I said, curtsying.

"God damn it, Alina! Stop fucking with me." He rushed toward me, seized my face, and squeezed.

I fought hard not to cry. I blinked, maintained eye contact, and said, "I shall never do it again, my…" I caught myself, then said, "My love."

"That's better." He pulled me toward him until our lips engaged in a punishing kiss. He tugged up my voluminous skirts and wriggled inside my undergarments until he found what he wanted—sweet, silky skin wet with desire. He finger-fucked me until I came, then forced me on my knees to suck him off, which I did with delight.

When he came, he let out a mighty roar. Then, he backed away, tucked himself inside his trousers, and stalked away, humming a tuneless tune. After that, he disappeared again for several days.

Each day, I sat in the drawing room on the striped settee, with its upholstered seat and elaborately carved back, writing in my journal. Fuck Balthazar and his annoyance with my writing. I did it to keep from losing my mind in his absence. He could return from wherever he went in whatever mood he found himself in, but I would not let him take away this one small pleasure I indulged in.

The room of this estate in 19th century England was large and airy but filled with an oppressive atmosphere of the past. Large tapestries hung on the walls, depicting ancient hunting scenes. The colors were muted, but the images retained a hint of grandeur. A heavy velvet curtain hung from a tall window, filtering the light seeping through the thick lace. A grand, mahogany desk sat in the corner, with an ancient typewriter on top, its once shiny keys now tarnished and dull. An aged grandfather clock ticked in the corner, its steady rhythm the only sound in the room.

A loud clatter came from the foyer, startling me. I bolted to my feet and raced to see if Balthazar had arrived home again. I was oh, so eager to see him.

A strange but beautiful man carried Balthazar in his arms, walking across the floor with purposeful strides. He looked up when I slipped through the doorway, and I was met with eyes the color of emeralds.

"Ah, you're home, Lady Tocino. Where might I put him?"

I was shocked he knew my name yet deeply disturbed to see Balthazar hanging limply in his arms.

"Is he dead?" I said, my hands fluttering around my face like birds.

"Balthazar?" the male said, his eyebrows arching. "No. But he's quite ill. He killed the wrong person. He killed a sick person and took on their bad energy. Where might I place him, mademoiselle? He's growing heavier by the second."

I became lost in the stranger's green-eyed and sculpted face as he drew closer. His strong jawline was lined with a day's dark stubble, and his high, prominent cheekbones gave way to a wide forehead that spoke of intelligence and strength. His eyes were almond-shaped and bright, with long, dark eyelashes that danced like a fan when he blinked.

My breath caught in my chest, and my skin flushed with heat. I'd never felt such a physical reaction to anyone before, and the sensation was dizzying.

The stranger smiled at me, his eyes twinkling with mischief and understanding. "Mademoiselle?"

His gaze flitted toward Balthazar, who sagged in the stranger's arms.

"Oh! Of course!" I said, coming out of my reverie. "Bring him into the drawing room, if you please."

I scurried past him, gesturing for him to follow. I removed my diary from the settee and stepped aside for him to place Balthazar there.

He did so as gently as a father placing his child in a cradle.

Balthazar let out a groan.

"You'd best fetch a basin," the stranger said. "He'll be quite ill when he wakes up. Do you have any kind of tincture or draught for gastritis?"

"Gastritis?" I said, my eyebrows stitching together.

"A stomach condition," he explained, his gaze kind.

He perched next to Balthazar and stroked his damp forehead.

"Quick," he said without looking up. "He's burning with fever."

Balthazar curled on his side and drew his legs toward his stomach. Another moan left his mouth.

I hurried out of the room to fetch the supplies this stranger had requested. When I returned, the stranger was gone, and Balthazar was hunched over his stomach, groaning.

He glanced up at me and gestured impatiently with his hand. "Over here with that basin. Quickly!"

I rushed across the floor just in time to get the basin in position beneath Balthazar's heaving throat. Streams of foul-smelling vomit hurled from his stomach, and I wanted to join him in retching. I was not prone to nursemaid activity, but this particular act was horrible. It was all I could do to not hurl the basin across the room and run screaming from the parlor.

When he'd finally finished, Balthazar leaned back against the settee, his face and neck damp with sweat.

"Get me some water," he croaked. "And get that putrid mess out of here."

He gestured impatiently at the basin full of foul-smelling, steaming liquid.

I didn't have to be asked twice. I held my breath as I rushed to the kitchen, opened the back door, and flung the basin and contents into the dusty street.

When I returned bearing a glass of water, Balthazar downed the whole thing in one long gulp. He handed me back the glass, rested his forearms over his thighs, and hung his head.

"Who was that man who brought you here? How did he know my name?" I said, settling beside Balthazar.

"His name is Malik. He's a friend of mine." He heaved his body backward, and his head flopped on the back of the settee. "Good God, what a fucking mistake I made earlier. Sometimes I hate being the darkness. I always have to kill to keep going. I wish I could kill when I felt like it and not because I had to. Get me a cloth to wipe away this sweat, will you? Even my perspiration smells putrid."

I bit my lip to keep from protesting at his constant orders, rose, and did his bidding. When I returned, his eyes were closed, and a sheen of sweat covered his face. I dabbed at his cheeks, jaw, brow, and neck, wrinkling my nose at the stench.

"Perhaps a bath would be soothing," I said.

"Perhaps," he mumbled. "It's so much work to have to kill constantly."

I used my fingertips to gently fold the cloth and place it on the floor. "How did this happen? I've never seen you so ill."

His eyes opened, and he hauled himself up to sitting like his body weighed a ton. "Malik and I were hunting."

I pressed my lips tightly together. *He and this Malik fellow hunt together? How close are they?*

"We came upon a person sick with boils covering his skin. I was famished and not thinking clearly. The man was writhing in pain, and I thought I could put him out of his misery, stop his incessant wails, and restore myself." He dragged his hand through his damp hair. "How wrong I was. Once I sucked in his essence, I took on his illness."

Balthazar slumped to the side, resting his head in my lap.

I jerked from the sudden intrusion and stroked his damp face and hair, somewhat repulsed by the moist, hot feel of him. "How do you know this Malik fellow?"

"I have raised him. Taught him everything he knows," Balthazar murmured, eyes closed. "He's like a son to me."

My stomach clenched. How dare he have a companion, a son-like figure in his life, and not tell me about him!

"I see," I said cautiously, not wanting to cause a fight. "Is there a way you can simply kill for fun?"

"It's funny you should say that. Malik and I were just talking about that before I made that mistake of killing." He burrowed his head against my thighs and inhaled as if restoring himself from my scent.

A pang of jealousy shot through me as he mentioned

Malik, the man who kept my lover company in my absence. I wanted to trust that Balthazar only felt bland interest in him, but the pride and adoration in his tone made me question that belief.

I kept my expression calm and focused on the conversation. But inside, I desperately tried to understand how I could compete with such an emotional connection. Balthazar would never admit it, but this man seemed like a rival for his affections. The knowledge stung, but I refused to let my jealousy overwhelm me.

I smiled and nodded, forcing a lightness into my voice as I said, "And what did you two discuss? Enlighten me."

"Malik contends there is a way to give us a happy ending." He opened his eyes and sneered. "A happy ending for the darkness. Can you believe that?"

"No," I said. "It's a preposterous idea. And why would we want that, anyway? I crave more darkness, not more light."

The room grew still save for the insistent ticking of the grandfather clock. I glanced at Balthazar, wondering if he'd fallen asleep. But he seemed far, far away, riding next to Malik, his son and companion. I wanted to slap him back to the present. He needed to be here in this room with *me*.

"Say more about this happy ending," I prompted.

Balthazar sat up abruptly, still appearing to peer into the past. He turned to look at me, seeming to see me for the first time.

"Malik and his lover, Layla, contend there are two daggers, the sun and the moon dagger, that, when used together, can make us live forever in bliss." His brow furrowed. "But I don't believe him. I don't see how two knives can make a difference."

A chill ran down my spine as I heard Balthazar's words.

"What if this Malik fellow is trying to take advantage of you?" I said hesitantly, unsure of how he would react.

Balthazar growled, his fierce eyes piercing through me. "Nonsense! I raised Malik! Taught him everything. There's no way he would turn on me!" he said, but his voice and posture betrayed a hint of doubt. His eyes widened with incredulity and despair as he said, "I love Malik with every fiber of my being!"

His words were like a thousand knives lacerating my heart. I had to do something to sour Balthazar's affections for Malik.

"You loved my father, too, Balthazar! What did he do to you? He betrayed you! It sounds like Malik is doing the same thing to you. He wants to kill you and overcome the master, don't you see?" I stalked toward the hearth, my malicious intents illuminated by the firelight.

"How can you even consider such a thought?" Balthazar's voice cracked. His words were razor-sharp, slicing through the air like shards of broken glass. "Malik would never betray me. I nurtured him with my hands, giving him more than any father ever could."

His face contorted with agony as he grappled with my heinous suggestion.

"That's exactly what people do," I said, relishing in his pain. "They take advantage of those weaker than them, searching for ways to outmaneuver their teacher. You, Balthazar, assassinated my father to prove your superiority. Now, Malik is simply following in your footsteps."

Balthazar rose from the settee and stalked toward me, his eyes searing with confusion and suspicion. He scrutinized me as if he sensed my deceitful intentions.

"What are you doing?" he said. "Why are you trying to turn me against my own son?"

I tried to hide the rage and hurt inside me, but its flames licked at my skin, begging for release. Balthazar had kept Malik a secret from me all this time. I wanted to expose their bond and burn it until nothing was left.

My voice rose wildly as I exclaimed, "Can't you see? Malik is trying to outwit the master! He'll use any means necessary to get what he wants, and our happiness will be sacrificed in the process. We must stop him from finding these blades. They bring only false promises of joy. We must rid ourselves of Malik and Layla before it's too late!"

CHAPTER SEVENTEEN
BALTHAZAR

Truth began to dawn as I gazed into Alina's eyes, and her words sank in. It made perfect sense—Layla was making Malik soft like Cora with Mathias. She was changing him into someone I didn't recognize; she was transforming him into a *good* person.

My heart raced, and fear rose inside me like a burning rage. I knew what Malik wanted—he wanted to destroy me! In my mind, his figure morphed from one of innocence to something dark and sinister, a creature intent on revenge. I had to act quickly, or he would be my undoing.

I drew Alina close and hugged her hard, rocking her back and forth. "Oh, my beloved Alina. Where would I be in life without your wise counsel? You have pulled the wool from my eyes."

"I'm so glad you're able to see things clearly before it's too late," she said, wrapping her arms around me.

A sudden thought seized my brain. I stiffened and pushed away from her, beseeching her understanding. "I must go speak to Malik alone."

"Yes, yes," she exclaimed, her eyes sparkling with urgency. "You must hurry before it's too late."

With a newfound determination, I quickly made my way to his house on the other side of town.

Malik's elegant estate was situated in a quiet corner of London, its walls and gates towering with impressive grandeur. The manicured gardens surrounding it seemed to expand endlessly, boasting colorful blooms of all shapes and sizes in the lush beds and a billowing fountain at the center of it all. The white house stood majestically at the end of a long path lined with shrubs, its facade decorated with ornate details.

The entrance to Malik's estate was an ornate work of art, thoughtfully carved with detailed filigree and expertly painted in a deep shade of burgundy. The door was made of solid mahogany, with two brass knockers outside. The knockers were shaped like lion heads, with their mouths open in a silent roar. A small metal plaque was set into the door, engraved with an intricate pattern of curlicues and swirls.

Above the door, a large bay window overlooked the street, and a balcony of the same woods and paint stretched out on either side like a pair of welcoming arms. The house was a work of beauty, which matched Malik's aesthetics. He always loved the finer things in life.

He seemed surprised when he opened the door to find me on his stoop. "Balthazar! You've recovered quickly. How fortunate."

"Yes, yes, spare me the sympathy," I said, brushing past him to enter his foyer. I hung my coat and hat on the carved coat rack and turned to face him. "We need to talk."

Standing before him, I desperately wanted to prove Alina wrong. I loved Malik. Adored him. Had groomed and carefully cultivated his darkness. Throughout the years, we'd

gone on killing sprees together, shared whores, shared everything. It deeply wounded me to think he now wanted to
assume dominance over me and betray me.

"Of course," he said, softly closing the door. "Can I get
you anything? A glass of wine or bourbon, perhaps?"

"No, no. I'm fine," I said, holding up my hand. "Where
can we talk?"

Malik led me through his chambers filled with luxurious
furniture and baubles from his travels worldwide. The cloy-
ingly sweet smell of flowers arranged on the coffee and side
tables perfumed the air.

We stopped in his smoking parlor, which smelled of
tobacco and leather—much more to my liking than the scent
of flowers. The smoking parlor was furnished with comfortable leather armchairs and stands for ashtrays and tobacco
accessories. The room was decorated with masculine
elements and rich colors and adorned with artwork consisting
of hounds and men on horseback.

Malik gestured to one of the armchairs. I sat as he crossed
the room and removed a box of the finest cigars from a
humidor lined with Spanish cedar in the corner of the room.
He extended the box to me, and I plucked a cigar and drew it
under my nose, savoring the rich scent of tobacco.

Malik selected a cigar and sat in one of the armchairs.

"Let's light up, shall we?" he asked, reaching for a box of
wooden matches. Casually, he struck a match against the
striker on the side of the box and held it aloft, allowing the
flame to flicker in the smoky air.

I did the same, lighting the tip of my cigar and puffing on
it to bring it to life. Smoke curled around our faces as we
puffed in companionable silence.

Malik finally said, "What do you wish to speak of?"

I rested my cigar in the ashtray, watching a coil of smoke

lazily rise into the air. I met his gaze and said, "I've known you since your inception, have I not?"

It was a rhetorical question, but Malik nodded.

"I've watched you grow up. I've schooled you from a wanton killer to a refined aristocrat who is discriminate in his killing."

"Indeed, you have," he said as cigar smoke spilled from his lips.

"So why is it suddenly that you are seeking a cure from the darkness? Have I steered you in an untoward direction? Led you astray?" I picked up my cigar and took another puff.

"Not at all," he said, resting one ankle on his knee. His lips curled into a tight smile. "I'm telling you, Layla and I have discovered the unthinkable. The original daggers which were born from darkness. The first ones. Can you imagine what it would be like to get our hands on those blades?"

I missed nearly everything he said, stuck on the words, "Layla and I."

I knew it! She's the one putting these foolish ideas in his head.

I bit down on the end of my cigar, filling my mouth with a bitter taste.

"So, this was not your idea…it came from *Layla?*" I spat out.

Malik frowned as he regarded me.

"It was the result of *our* research. Layla knows how unhappy I am being a creature of the darkness." His frown deepened. "Don't you ever want to be normal and not have to kill to survive? Layla's convinced the sun and moon daggers are the answer."

"Have you listened to yourself lately?" I said with a sneer and a wave of my hand, not daring to mention I'd had this very conversation with Alina less than an hour ago. "It's like you think there are these magic daggers that will automatically make all your problems disappear. Doesn't that seem preposterous?"

Malik leaned forward in his chair, eyes burning with hope. "What's preposterous is that you sound so sure that the daggers won't do what we were promised! Layla and I were told that our endless cravings will be silenced if we found them. We can finally have normal lives or even a family. Doesn't that sound divine? I want a family, don't you?"

I'd had a family long ago, and recreating a family held an appeal. But I was scared to relive the past again. It was hard for me to accept that such a thing was possible. I'd certainly enjoyed raising Malik as my own.

Malik's eyes burned with hope. "Just imagine it! We could both find our own happiness, free from the chains of death and destruction. We'd never have to face the brutality of feasting upon another's soul again. I can feel the burden already lifting from my shoulders at just the thought of it."

My body recoiled in agony from recent memories of the wretchedness that had spewed from me so recently.

"I hear you," I said, "but do you know *where* these mystical daggers are? And do you know they're not merely the stuff of legend? They might not even exist."

Malik's next words flew from his mouth like pouncing dogs. "Oh, they exist. We have it on good authority. I trust my sources."

I scrutinized Malik's every word, searching for the slightest hint of untruth. My jaw tensed as I asked, "How did it happen? How did you meet Layla? You better start from the beginning."

Malik scowled at me. "You can't be serious. I've told you a million times."

"No," I said coldly, my eyes drilling into him. "Tell me as if I know nothing."

"It was an experience of a lifetime. I was studying abroad in Anatolia, and when our eyes locked, it was like the universe stood still. Her beauty instantly captivated me, and my admiration for her deepened as I got to know her better. She consumed me, with all my heart and soul surrendering to the love that had just been born." His eyes shone with a passionate intensity. "After that, it felt unjust to shield her from the truth of my existence. I told her everything—how I was darkness. She confessed to being a Timeborne."

"Well, well—it sounds like my story with Alina. She, too, is a Timeborne." I eyed the stub of my cigar, which no longer smoldered.

"It's remarkable how two of the darkest of the darks have met their match among Timebornes," Malik said. "Oh, I can't wait to start a family with Layla!"

His eyes gleamed madly as he envisioned the future that awaited him and his chosen mate. "We have blazed a path to reach this moment and rid ourselves of the tyranny of her father, the Timehunter. There stands no impediment between us and bliss. Balthazar, can you not sense it?"

Layla's father was a Timehunter? The Timehunters were the ones who had destroyed my life and took my family away from me. I couldn't believe her father was a fucking Time-hunter. I was sure they were all working together to destroy me.

Alina's words still rang in my mind, tearing the truth of Malik's words to shreds. *We must stop him from finding these blades; they bring only false promises of joy. We must rid ourselves of Malik and Layla before it's too late!*

I sat back and stroked my jaw, pretending to be deep in thought.

"Your plan holds merit, my son. *If* we can find the daggers." I leaned forward as if about to rise. "Tell you what. I would like to get to know Layla better. I would like to have you and Layla over for dinner to discuss this in more detail. What do you think?"

Malik's eyes lit up. "Splendid idea! We'll bring the wine. I have a lovely French wine, a Bordeaux, that's…" He drew his fingers together and kissed the fingertips. "You'll see."

"Sounds grand." I rose and extended my hand. "Please arrive tomorrow at seven. I shall have the cook prepare a feast for us to dine over while we discuss our futures."

Malik clasped my hand between both of his and shook it warmly. "You'll see, Balthazar. This plan shall work!"

"I look forward to it," I said, forcing a bright smile before leaving.

The following night, at promptly seven pm, Layla and Malik arrived at my estate. They looked like a handsome couple. He wore a black wool tailcoat, silk lapels, matching trousers, a blue silk vest with decorative mother-of-pearl buttons, a crisp white shirt, and a blue silk cravat. Layla wore a long blue silk gown with intricate beading at the bodice. Her raven-colored hair had been swept up in an elaborate updo with ringlets framing her heart-shaped face.

Alina eyed her like a hawk sizing up a wee mouse, making me nearly splutter with delight.

I handed their coats to the maid and led them into the living room.

The formal living room of our London estate was a feast for the senses. Rich, dark mahogany furniture perfectly matched the dark hues of the Persian carpets that adorned the floor. A grand piano occupied the corner by the window, its polished top reflecting the sunset light drifting in from outside. Dark-green velvet curtains framed the wide windows, and a large crystal chandelier hung from the ceiling, sparkling and throwing prisms of light around the room.

Everywhere, intricate carvings and ornate decorations caught the eye, displaying the wealth and opulence of the era. A heavy fireplace dominated one wall, with a large oil painting of a hunting party above it. Thick tapestries hung from the walls. It was a room made for entertaining, filled with memories and secrets that whispered in the air. And it was all Alina's doing. While I was gone, she had dedicated all her energy to this task. As we gathered around the table, Alina and I discussed our plan to uncover more information about the unknown daggers and Malik's motives. We made sure to pour libations before starting our quest.

Alina led Layla over to the chairs perched around the roaring fireplace.

"I'd love to get to know you," Alina cooed at her, most charming. "Balthazar has told me so much about you."

Malik and I chose the easy chairs close enough in proximity to partake in conversation with the women but far enough away to have a private conversation if we chose. As we all sipped our Madeira, I overheard Alina say, "I love your gown, Layla. You simply must tell me who your designer is."

Layla's cheeks grew rosy. "Actually, Alina, I made it myself. I'm quite handy with a needle and thread."

"Yes, she is," Malik interjected. "She crafted my attire as well. I'm often gone for days, and my beloved fills the time with her sewing."

He smiled warmly at Layla, the love evident in his gaze.

"That's remarkable!" Alina exclaimed. "I'm afraid I'd

look a mess if I were to take it upon myself to sew my own clothes."

"Anyone can sew, Alina!" Layla said. "I could show you sometime if you like."

"Oh, that would be lovely," Alina said. "We could have some fun together."

I nearly spit out my wine. Alina would split her toenails with a cleaving knife sooner than deign to do anything remotely domestic.

I engaged Malik in a conversation on the latest news about parliamentary debates, the monarchy, foreign affairs, and political ideologies, all while keeping my awareness on Alina's conversation with Layla.

Alina's sly smirk widened as she said, "So, what's this I hear about mysterious daggers? Balthazar told me quite a tale. Pray tell, what is this adventure you are so eager to embark upon?"

Layla's gaze flitted in my direction and darted away. "It's truly exciting. They can transform the darkness our lovers wield and stop the cravings they each experience."

"What do you know about Balthazar's darkness?" Alina asked in a whisper.

"Malik has shared with me Balthazar's depravity," Layla whispered, leaning close to conspire. "Your lover is a monster, or didn't you know?"

"Of course, I know. And I love him for it." Alina laughed, but it had a nightmarish quality to it.

I could feel her jealous anger stir the air between us, but I refused to be cowed. I was my own person, and whatever was in my head stayed there unless I was ready to share it.

I continued my discussion with Malik.

"Both of our lovers are born of darkness," Layla said, "although I've helped Malik learn to control his urges to kill.

He now only kills when he absolutely has to—and he assures me he only kills those who are evil."

I clenched my teeth so hard I thought I might shatter them as Alina audibly sighed in distaste. Listening to Layla's words, the truth was indisputable—she was turning Malik into an obedient slave like Cora had done to Mathias, trying to shape him into her concept of morality. Red-hot fury swept through me, and I wanted nothing more than to rip out her throat with my bare hands. But it wasn't the time or place for such drastic action. I forced my wine glass to my lips and drained it dry. Then, I lifted a tiny silver bell and rang it to get a refill from the maid.

All conversation ceased at the sound of the tinkling bell.

The maid appeared, and I requested more Madeira for all. She dutifully refilled each glass and withdrew from the room.

I spoke of Queen Victoria and her role as the symbolic figurehead of the empire and her influence on its global presence, hoping Alina would again draw Layla into a conversation about the daggers.

She didn't disappoint. "So what would you do if you found these wonderful daggers, Layla?"

Layla seemed to climb on her soapbox as she said, "I would make the world a better place. I would help Malik have an ordinary life and not have to kill to sustain himself. He's grown tired of all the killing and wants something different. He and I want to be married and have children. We can't do that if the child's father is still a monster."

She sipped her wine. "I love him more than life itself. It is my fondest wish that he's freed from the curse of his existence—to kill and consume souls or die."

I burned with the evidence I needed to hear. Layla was just like Cora. And soon Malik would become a simpering fool like Mathias, not the well-heeled killer he'd grown to be.

Either that, or he would attempt to outwit me and come out on top.

Layla's gaze traveled across the room.

"My father in Anatolia is a Timehunter," she said, her voice steady and strong. "His whole life, he's been studying these blades and their effects on time and space. They have extreme power and can be used to summon the greatest magic or destruction."

This bit of information intrigued me, and I lifted my finger to Malik to pause our conversation.

Layla outstretched her arms. "So powerful that they can change the course of life and alter the very fabric of space and time. I want to destroy the darkness, and I believe the only way to do that is to harness this power and use it for good."

"You really believe that, don't you?" Alina said gently.

Layla smiled and nodded, a tear rolling down her cheek.

"I do," she whispered.

"I find that an intriguing story," I said, smiling at Layla.

Fired up with determination, she nodded vigorously. "My family has been trying to unlock the mysteries of the daggers for countless years. But if they ever land in the hands of the Timehunters like my father…"

Her words trailed off as a chill of fear shook her body.

Her voice quavered as she said, "My father wanted to kill Malik! That's why we had to run!"

The fear in her eyes was palpable.

Malik cast a soothing glance in her direction.

Their eyes locked in care and understanding.

"Yes, the daggers are powerful and not to be underestimated," Malik said, his voice heavy with warning. "These blades are dangerous, but not just anyone can find them. It takes a special kind of person to unlock their power. You have to know how to solve the puzzle and open the scrolls to get them to work properly. I'm hazy on all the details."

"Do you know where the daggers are?" I asked, my throat painfully dry.

"No," she said. "But we heard that someone from a different time period knows where they are."

Her voice trailed off, and desperation replaced the terror in her gaze.

"Do you have a name and a location?" I asked.

Layla and Malik exchanged a glance.

"Yes," Layla said.

"Splendid!" I said. "We'll all go find them together."

I locked eyes with Alina, and without a word, I knew we were on the same page.

Grabbing her roughly by the arm, I demanded, "Come with me now." As we stepped away from prying ears, we exchanged a knowing glance and nodded in unison. "They must die," I hissed through gritted teeth, my grip on her arm tightening. She nodded back fiercely, determination burning in her eyes. Together, we made a pact to end their lives before they could end ours.

CHAPTER EIGHTEEN
ALINA

S tanding in the hallway with me, Balthazar spoke in a low, venomous whisper. "Layla must be eliminated. Woman to woman. Kill freely, my love. Then, I'll get rid of Malik."

"It can't be that simple." I whispered. "I plan on having some fun with Layla beforehand. You're right—she's sickly sweet, like those Sugar Plum candies sold at the Enchanted Confectionery Emporium on Regent Street."

He pulled me close and rocked me back and forth. "Finally, my eyes are open, and I see how deeply I have been deceived!"

Excitement blazed through me as dark fantasies of revenge and torture filled my head. I regarded Balthazar with lusty arousal, my body humming with the need to fuck.

He chuckled, sensing my desire.

"Later, my sweet," he murmured, and planted a chaste kiss on my cheek. "We can celebrate once we have them ensnared."

"How should we proceed?" I asked, stroking his erection through his trousers.

He tapped his lips and grew thoughtful. "I've got it. You go back and keep them engaged in conversation. I'll procure a powerful sleeping draught I have tucked away. I'll enter bearing an excellent champagne laced with the drugs. Once they've sipped to their heart's content, they'll simply collapse to the floor, and we can drag them into the dungeon!"

I let out a squeal. "Oh, this shall be so fun!"

Balthazar seized me and pulled me in for a quick, brutal kiss. Then, eyes shining, headed down the corridor while I slipped back into the living room.

"My apologies for our disappearance," I said smoothly. "We discussed a celebratory libation to drink to our new endeavors."

Layla and Malik broke apart from their embrace.

"And my apologies for allowing you to catch us in a physical display of affection," Malik said, his emerald eyes shining. "It seems my beloved and I cannot keep our hands from one another."

He flashed Layla a heated look.

She stepped back from him, her cheeks ablaze.

"Nonsense," I said, waving my hand. "True love should be celebrated. This Victorian era places far too much emphasis on modesty, religious piety, and strict codes of conduct. Please, sit. Balthazar shall return shortly with a bottle of Veuve Clicquot."

I let my eyebrows arch dramatically.

"Sounds divine, doesn't it, my love?" Layla reached for Malik's hand and squeezed it.

"Without a doubt," he said, smiling as he gazed into her eyes.

Good god, I wanted to vomit at their love for one another. I forced my eyes not to roll and plastered on a sickly-sweet smile. "If you two don't sit and stop being so affectionate,

I'm afraid I'll be forced to retire to my chambers with Balthazar."

I tittered out a silly little laugh, which sounded forced, even to my ears.

They didn't seem to notice, still focused on one another, but they drifted in unison to the sofa like two lovebirds.

Balthazar's footsteps echoed down the hall, and he appeared in the doorway, brandishing a silver tray, champagne flutes filled with the pale golden liquid, the Veuve Clicquot bottle, and a gleam in his eyes.

"Our finest Veuve Clicquot," he said in impeccable French. He'd arranged the glasses so that two were on one side of the tray, the bottle was in the middle, and the other two drinks were closest to him.

"*Bien, bien. Nous sommes honorés,*" Malik said, his accent equally impressive as he conveyed how honored they were.

Balthazar extended the tray to them.

They each reached for the glasses closest to them, which must have been the right ones, as Balthazar smiled knowingly.

"My love?" he said, handing the third glass to me.

"*Merci, mon amour,*" I cooed with a smile.

Balthazar took the last glass, set the tray on the side table, and held his champagne aloft. "May our course be true as we seek the sun and the moon daggers."

"May we come to swift fruition," Malik said. He flashed Layla another sweet gaze before lifting the glass to his lips, and taking a long swallow.

A look of alarm flashed across his face, and he gasped.

"What is it, love?" Layla said, concerned.

He tugged at his collar. "Can't…breathe."

"Oh, my," she said, pressing her hand to her bosom. "I seem to have become alarmingly fatigued."

"Fuck," Malik said. "What did you…"

His words faded away. He reached for Layla, his movements clumsy and slow. Before he could touch her shoulder, he slumped into her lap. He writhed and struggled like a fish on a hook, trying to overcome the effects of the poison.

"Can't let it…*win*," he wheezed.

Layla collapsed on top of him.

Balthazar and I looked at one another and laughed.

"What a waste of Veuve Clicquot." I reached for the bottle and took a few hearty swallows.

"Oh, I think we got our money's worth," he said, rising from his chair. "Let's work together to get them into the dungeon. The sleeping draught lasts about an hour."

We struggled to get Malik's limp form down the stairs and into cells at either end of a dark hallway.

The air in each cell was heavy with the smell of dampness, sweat, and mildew that clung to the slimy stone walls and dirt-caked floors. The darkness seemed to press in on me as we heaved Malik onto the floor. An oppressive weight lingered here that could only be alleviated by a single slit of moonlight that managed to sneak through the barred windows.

Balthazar stood in front of the dungeon prison cell, looking at the heavy steel door that imprisoned Malik. It was an old-fashioned door made of thick wrought iron with a prominent lock in the middle of it. The lock was of an ancient design, with intricate scrollwork carved into it and a keyhole that seemed too small for any modern key to fit into.

The door was painted with a deep-red paint. On it, someone had written a single word in bold block letters: "Unforgiven."

A glass viewing portal sat above the words, which could be opened or closed at will.

Balthazar smirked and fit a key into the keyhole. He twisted it, and it gave a satisfying snick as it locked. He turned to look at me and said, "Shall we?"

He proffered his arm.

"We shall," I said, grinning as I tucked my hand into the crook in his elbow.

We sauntered upstairs and retrieved Layla's slumbering form.

"Aw, she looks like an angel," Balthazar said.

"She looks like my next unfortunate victim," I said with glee, grabbing her ankles as Balthazar seized her torso.

She was much lighter than Malik and proved a breeze to carry down the stairs.

The two cells seemed to shimmer with magic and were separated by a long, dank hallway. Cobwebs hung from the ceiling, swaying in a draft that smelled of mildew and stale air. A single lantern, the only light source, flickered at the end of the hallway, providing just enough light to make out the silhouettes of rats and other vermin that scurried and skittered through the shadows.

We dropped Layla unceremoniously in her cell and looked at one another.

"I could fuck you right here. Wouldn't that be delightful to be caught in a depraved sexual act when she woke up?" Balthazar said, gazing at me with heavy-lidded eyes. His fingers skittered across my neck like a spider.

I shivered at his touch.

"The best," I said, but then I glanced around.

A gray rat eyed me from the shadows, his red eyes glittering.

"But I'd rather do it somewhere cleaner than this." I sniffed. "I do have my standards."

Balthazar bowed and gestured toward the door. "Then, after you, my love."

"Thank you, my love." I drew myself up, gave Layla a haughty sneer, and said, "See you later."

My first act of torture was to tie Layla to a sturdy timber pole in her prison cell so she could not move or escape. For days, I tortured Layla, using all manner of instruments, from the whip to burning hot irons. Layla could only whimper and scream in pain and terror, her cries echoing off the grim dungeon walls.

But then this proved unsatisfying. I wanted more—more suffering, more terror, more power over her. So I began toying with her mind. I would tell her lies, like Malik had abandoned her or the guards would never let her go free. We didn't have guards, but she didn't need to know that. I fed her false hopes and promises that if she was good enough, she would be allowed to leave, only to dash them moments later.

I wanted to break her spirit, and I could feel it crumbling beneath me with each passing hour. But no matter how much I tried, I could not get her to beg for mercy or tell me anything useful about the daggers. She remained defiant until the very end, no matter how much I tried to break her.

After days of fruitless torture, I convened one day in the drawing room with Balthazar.

"How's it going with Malik?" I said.

"Useless folly," Balthazar spat, yanking his arm away with a sneer. "I'm at my wit's end. But I haven't given up. I

have people who devise concoctions to weaken the spirit—
make one give up on living and welcome death. I was
thinking of contacting one of my associates for that."

"I have a better idea," I said. "I knew a man once—Raul
Costa. He's an Italian apothecary whose family deeply
understands the science of poisons. He is the best in his
field, and his family has made it their life's work to create
the most powerful poisonous agents imaginable. What if I
time travel to Italy in Raul's time and return with some of
his poison?"

Balthazar's face reddened with anger. "No!" His voice
echoed through the chamber, bouncing off the walls like
thunder. "I know Costa. He's a fucking Timehunter. I absolutely forbid it. You won't be going anywhere."

He took a menacing step closer, towering over me like a
vengeful god.

"Everyone is always talking about these Timehunters." I
stamped my foot. "Who the hell are they, and why is
everyone scared of them?"

"They are dangerous to you, Alina. They will kill you
instantly when they learn that you're a Timeborne."

I just stared at him. "Why are *you* so scared of Timehunters, Balthazar?"

"Just fucking let me deal with my people," he growled. "I
can take care of Malik."

My heart pounded harder. Sweat soaked through my
clothes as I struggled to find words to soothe his ruffled
feathers without further provoking his wrath.

I sashayed up to him, rolling my hips seductively. "Balthazar, my darling."

I roamed my hands over his body, exploring every inch of
him with passion. I lingered on his collarbone, tracing it in
circles before descending to the depths of his groin.

He let out a growl and pushed my hands away, attempting to walk past me.

"Look," I said, seizing his arm. "Clearly, your tortures aren't working. The poison you're working with is weak. Raul's poison is superior to anyone else's!"

Balthazar curled his lip into a snarl. "Don't even think about trying to match my power. I'll do what needs to be done, and you'll continue to torture Layla."

His eyes were full of rage as he shoved me aside and made for the dungeon.

When he strode up the stairs after checking on the prisoners, Balthazar hissed, "Malik hasn't weakened at all. He's too powerful."

"It's all because of your puny poison," I snapped. "It's just not strong enough."

We clashed in a heated argument, screaming our grievances at each other until I yelled, "You go to Raul! You get the poison!"

His face turned red, and he bellowed a deafening roar as if to shake the room's walls.

"No!" He slammed his fist against the wall. "You stay here, and I'll go somewhere else to get poison."

His voice was low and menacing, like a distant rumble of an incoming storm.

We relentlessly subjected Malik and Layla to unspeakable atrocities for days, but they wouldn't yield. With each passing hour, their resilience only seemed to grow. They withstood the anguish as if they had formed a silent pact, though they were kept in different cells with no means of communicating with one another.

Rage surged through me as my frustration and resentment boiled over. I had to get my hands on those cursed blades.

Balthazar strutted in front of me, his hand gripping the

blade at his waist. "I'm setting out to find those elusive sun and moon daggers," he declared.

My fists clenched at my sides as I shouted, "I'm coming with you!" The sound of my own voice echoed back at me from the stone walls.

But Balthazar's face was set in determination. "No, you must stay behind and watch over the prisoners." Anger flared up inside of me as he dared to lock me in my bedroom on the night of the full moon, leaving me alone while he ventured off into time travel.

I was apoplectic with rage.

After what felt like hours, I finally managed to pick the lock on my bedroom door and burst into the hallway, my skin flushed with frustration and anger. I reveled in the thought of torture that would soon begin; each strike would be more painful than the previous one. My cackles echoed against the walls as I cracked open the creaky door to Layla's prison cell, ensuring that Layla's harrowing screams reverberated down the hall and pierced Malik's cell. "He can hear your cries for help, but yet he won't come. Do you think now you know why?"

"He loves me," Layla wailed. "Malik loves me with all his heart!"

The agony of waiting for Balthazar's return weighed heavily on me, and my tortures continued unabated. With every passing moment, Layla's resistance became more evident, and I was certain I needed to act. As soon as the full moon appeared in the sky, I left without thinking twice, returning to Raul's time. I knew he would have no qualms giving me what was necessary to finish the job quickly. When Balthazar returned, I would have the answers we sought and two lifeless corpses. A rush of pleasure surged through me at the thought.

I raced up the steps to Raul's estate and rapped on the door. Raul's face lit up in recognition as he beheld me.

"Alina! You're back!" he exclaimed, lunging forward to enfold me in his arms. The passage of time had sculpted a captivating beauty into his visage, making him look unbelievably seductive. "Where have you been, my love? Your family was murdered, and then you vanished!"

I averted my gaze, feigning shame. "I needed time to lick my wounds and heal from the tragedy. But I had no choice but to return. I need your aid."

"You know I'll do anything for you!" he said. "How might I be of service?"

My heart pounded against my chest. "I'm in such peril, Raul! You must help me. Malik and Balthazar are trying to kill me. I need to destroy them, and I need strong poison to weaken them."

At the mention of Balthazar's name, Raul's face grew pale.

"So, you're in league with him? I heard rumors that you and Lord Balthazar were lovers. And now you need my help." He turned away from me, his voice stony as he spoke over his shoulder. "I'm afraid I cannot offer assistance."

I bolted forward and latched onto Raul's arm, gripping him like cold steel.

"Raul, please!" I shrieked, my eyes flooding with tears. "You have to help me! You're the only one who can."

He stared in horror at my vice-like grip, his expression turning to disgust. "Release me, you witch! If Balthazar is involved, you don't need my help. You need someone else."

"Who?" I pleaded.

His gaze burned into mine. "Perhaps a holy man that can perform an exorcism. Obviously, you're in league with Satan himself."

I had to make him understand—somehow. My cries grew louder as desperation took over.

"You can't possibly comprehend the terror of living with Balthazar, Raul. Every single day I'm scourged with fear. I never loved Balthazar. I pretend to love him. He is a *monster*. I'm in a toxic relationship with him and I want to leave him. Yet now Malik, this other demon, wants to possess me and I can't do it. I need to be free of them. I need something more powerful to finish them both off for good! Please, Raul, you must show mercy," I said, hoping my years of practice at faking emotion would pay off.

I fell to my knees and clutched Raul's booted feet.

His eyes flashed with something darker than hope, which made me uneasy.

"Alina, stop," he growled, gripping my arm so tightly I winced. "It pains me to see you so upset."

He hauled me up with a force that left bruises, and I stumbled onto shaky legs.

Before I could speak, his embrace was suffocating, crushing the air from my lungs.

"There, there, my love. I'm sorry I was so harsh," he crooned in my ear. "I can see you live a horrible existence with Lord Balthazar. We are part of a secret society known as Timehunters. You came to the right person because I have exactly what you need to get rid of them or weaken them. We Timehunters love to destroy darkness and kill Timebornes. I will make some for you and send you on your way."

As I looked up at him through blurry tears, his eyes glittered with a calculating glimmer, making my blood run cold.

"You will?" I whispered, knowing this was too good to be true.

He grinned down at me, all teeth and malice. "Yes. But it will come at a price."

"Anything you want," I said. "Anything at all."

"Be careful what you promise. I intend to take you up on your promises," he said, still grinning.

I looked into his eyes and swallowed hard, remembering Balthazar's words. *If you open your legs to another, I shall slaughter you.*

But then I recalled Balthazar's cruel expression moments before he locked me in my sleeping chamber and took off to find the daggers.

Just try it, my lord. Just try to murder me.

"If it's sex you want, I shall accommodate you," I breathed.

"Don't flatter yourself," Raul said, sneering. "I have a wife and a son of sixteen. What kind of upstanding man would I be if I cheated on my wife?"

I stalked around him like a feral cat.

"You, my sweet, are nothing close to an upstanding man if you're as I remember." I brushed my hand across his groin, delighted to find rigid heat beneath my touch. "Or is this merely hot iron, left there by the blacksmith's hand for safe-keeping?"

Raul clutched my hand, staying my desire to get inside his breeches. A dark, husky laugh left his throat. "What a wicked spell you weave, my venomous snake."

"Allow me to keep weaving it, and you won't regret it," I said.

Raul looked right and left before dragging me into the barn.

Being fucked in the hay brought back all sorts of unpleasant memories for me, but I made it worth Raul's while and then some. I was doing this for the ultimate sacrifice and most authentic purposes.

When we'd finished sometime later, Raul hissed at me as

he righted his clothes, "You stay behind. I'll head out first. I don't need gossipmongers stirring up my business or relative peace at home. Come to the back door in half an hour."

"But…" I said, already regretting my actions with him. He was treating me like a common whore, after all.

He silenced me with a kiss that left me breathless, then ducked outside.

I listened to his retreating footfalls as I angrily picked hay from my hair. Nearly an hour later, I sauntered to the front door and rang the knocker hanging from the iron lion's mouth.

Raul threw the door open.

"I told you thirty minutes," he hissed. "And I said the back door, not the front."

"I have no timepiece to tell the time," I said innocently, batting my lashes at him. "And I was in such a daze I did not memorize your words."

I smiled sweetly at him. He could be an ass all he wanted, but he fucked like I remembered—passionately and intensely.

"Alina, I…" he said, but his words were cut off by a dulcet-sounding voice.

"Raul, can you please come here?" a woman said from the back of the house.

"I'll be there shortly, dearest one. I have business to attend to." Without another word, he ushered me outside and slammed the door. He grabbed me by the arm and led me to an outbuilding away from the estate.

"Stop manhandling me!" I whispered, prying his claws from my arm.

"You're going to get me into trouble," he whispered.

"You should have thought of that before you slipped your cock inside me a few short meters from your lovely home," I said.

He let out an exasperated sound and threw open the shed door.

Inside stood row after row of neat shelves with endless jars, carefully labeled with their contents.

"Don't touch a thing," he said as he stalked down one of the rows. "This stuff will kill you."

I snatched back my hand as it drifted toward one of the clear jars.

He plucked a jar from a shelf and seized a cotton cloth hanging from a hand-forged square nail to buff the label.

"Yes, this is the one," he said, his face a grim mask. He shoved the jar before my face. "Open this, and it will cost you your life. Keep it shielded until you're ready to wield its power."

My brow furrowed. "But how can I open it to use it without dying?"

"Are you placing it with a prisoner?"

I gave a single nod.

"Is there a slot that you can slide it through?"

I nodded once more.

"Then proceed with caution. Wear gloves when handling it, and remove them before taking out your hand. Leave the gloves inside. Seal shut the entrance into the cell completely. The deadly vapors of the poison will quickly fill the room and extinguish the prisoner immediately."

I shivered with satisfaction. Balthazar would surely be pleased with what I'd brought. His anger would quickly dissipate when he saw with his own eyes how effective the poison was.

Raul handed me the jar wrapped in the cloth, and his eyes glistened with hunger. "One more fuck before you go?"

My undergarments grew damp with desire. I placed the

jar back on the shelf, not wanting to disturb the contents. "Surely not in here where there is so much poison."

He shook his head. "I have a study around the back. It's where I keep my drawings."

He led me down the row of shelves and jars and entered a dark room. He took me without preamble there, driving himself inside me against the back wall with his hand pressed over my mouth. Once done, he withdrew, tucked his slippery cock away, and sauntered to a large desk with colorful illustrations in tidy piles.

"You can see yourself out," he said, picking up a drawing. "Be careful not to jostle anything. And don't take anything except the jar I gifted you. You won't like the results."

I sneered at him. "Where might I find lodging until I'm ready to return to Balthazar?"

I didn't want to tell him anything about my abilities as a time traveler or where I might be currently living.

He licked his lips. "Does this mean I might get to sample the sweets again?"

"We'll see," I said, already weakening inside.

He let out a low chuckle. "There's a lodge in town not too far away. An old woman runs it. She turns a blind eye to the goings on there. Tell her Raul sent you, and she'll give you a fair price. And leave the door unlocked. You never know who might decide to pay a visit some night."

I eyed his stirring cock as it grew inside his breeches. Oh, I was a dead woman for even considering. But what was I to do until the next full moon? I didn't dare be seen around town. People's memories and actions could be so ugly.

I stayed cloistered in my small room for the next month. The room's furniture was simple yet elegant: a single bed draped with a thick quilt, a small writing desk, and a few wooden chairs gathered around a low table. On the wall hung a large painting of the mountains. A small fireplace offered further warmth and a place to curl up with a book in the evenings. I lived in a fantasy fairy tale for weeks, forgetting the trials of the outside world.

The old woman delivered a food tray to my door each morning, and I waited eagerly for Raul each night. On the nights he came, we fucked with abandon before he slipped out before dawn. I felt cherished by his visits.

Then, his visits ceased, and I paced the room through the night, waiting for the full moon to appear. When it finally arrived, I departed without payment to the old woman. What could she do except demand payment from Raul? He was wealthy enough. He could pay for the room. And besides, with him not showing up for several days, I wouldn't arrive home stinking of another man's semen. I reasoned that he did me a favor even though it stung that he'd abandoned me.

I appeared in the moonlit yard outside the estate where I'd left Balthazar. I crept out of the shadows, my heart pounding heavily in my throat with every step I took toward the estate. Clutching the jar of poison, I slowly opened the door to the entrance.

Before I even had time to breathe, Balthazar roared from inside, "Where have you been, you bitch?"

CHAPTER NINETEEN
ALINA

F ear rippled through my veins as I stood in the dark foyer while Balthazar yelled at me. The paintings of prominent figures hanging on the wall seemed to leer at me, echoing their disapproval of my actions.

Balthazar's face contorted in rage. "Didn't I tell you to stay put and watch the prisoners?"

Bolstering my courage, I yelled back, "I did! But when I got bored of being your guard dog, I went to find Raul so you and I could take out Malik and Layla. They're useless to us. We're wasting our time trying to torture information out of them. We need to kill them. You should be thanking me!"

With shaking hands, I held up the jar containing the lethal poison, praying it wouldn't explode.

Balthazar's transformation into a vengeful beast shook the room and filled my soul with dread. His eyes blazed red with malicious intent as his grotesque form grew larger, maggots writhing like snakes beneath putrid skin. His skin flapped around his bones as he waved his hands.

"I could have done it alone!" he roared, shaking paintings

from the wall. They landed on the floor with a resounding crash.

"Of course, you could," I said, determined not to show fear. Once more, I held up the jar of poison. "But look. This substance is so powerful it could kill us all."

I ducked around him on tremulous legs, fished in the pocket of my overcoat hanging on the coat rack for a pair of opera gloves, and slid them on.

"At least allow me to show you the effects. You can murder me later," I said, hurrying past him, trying to avoid brushing against his maggot-covered skin.

A terrifying shriek coming from Balthazar's monstrous mouth echoed through the hallway, sending shivers down my spine. I staggered in reckless terror down the stairs and into the dank dungeon.

I peered through the viewing port, my heart thumping wildly as I spotted Malik lying on the ground, completely still, his petrified expression frozen on his face. I hesitated, deciding what to do next.

This won't be any fun if he's comatose. Maybe bringing Layla in here will rouse him from his coma.

I set the jar on the ground and pushed past my putrid lover, who stood behind me, rushing to Layla's cell. Once I unlocked the door, I dragged her unconscious form along the stone floor, hoping they stirred each other to life with their sickening love.

"What the hell are you doing?!" Balthazar roared, his one good eye bulging out of its socket.

"Killing two birds with one stone," I said, disgusted at the sight of Balthazar's dangling eyeball.

"You can't have all the fun. I must be the one to make her suffer," he said.

I dropped Layla's legs, and they hit the floor with a thud.

I glared down at her, my stomach turning as I took in the bruises and cuts that covered her body. Even her face was unrecognizable. My tortures had disfigured her entirely.

I shifted my gaze to Balthazar.

"Fine." I waved my hand at him dismissively. "But fix yourself up first. You don't want to terrify them into submission, do you?"

"I thought you found me arousing in my true form." Balthazar leaned forward as if to kiss me.

I couldn't do it now—I couldn't let a monster kiss my lips. Not with the memory of Raul's touches whispering across my skin. "Later, my love. I can't wait to bed you. But first, we have two prisoners to kill."

I stroked the bloody muscle covering Balthazar's cheek and tried to appear adoring.

Thankfully, he returned to his human self before dropping his lips to mine.

We kissed with passion and fury before I pushed away.

"Let's get this done." My gaze dropped to Layla's prone form on the floor beside my legs.

"We still know nothing about the whereabouts of the daggers," Balthazar said, stroking his jaw, now mercifully covered with skin and stubble.

"At this point, I don't believe they know anything," I said, shrugging. "We can find the knives without any information from them."

He stared at Layla with contempt. Then, he said abruptly, "Unlock Malik's cell door."

I held it open for him as he dragged her across the threshold. I shut the door behind them, sealing them all in.

Malik stirred in the corner, frowning. His eyes fluttered open with effort, and he blinked, gazing down at Layla, his true love.

My heart raced joyfully, and I clasped my hands beneath my chin.

We've done it. We've wakened them from unconsciousness. Now we can have some fun.

I could barely hear them through the sturdy door, but the look of joy on their faces sickened me. Malik and Layla embraced as rivulets of blood seeped from their wounds.

"I knew you'd be merciful, Balthazar," Malik said between kisses. "I knew you'd let us both live. Now, we can search for the daggers together. You've had your fun."

Balthazar screamed a guttural cry as he stumbled forward, teetering on the edge of insanity.

My hands flew to my mouth.

Oh, God. He's transforming again.

"Is that what you think is happening, Malik?" he bellowed, half-human and half-monster. He wrenched the pair apart.

Layla screamed and tried to grab Malik. Malik yelled and tried to reach for Layla. But they were both too fragile, too injured, each too weak to fight the impending doom that faced them. There was nothing they could do.

Balthazar stood over them, his face a mask of cold determination. "I'm done hearing her wails. This is dragging on far too long." He seized Layla by her throat, his fingers digging into her delicate neck. She struggled to breathe as he squeezed harder, her eyes widening in fear. Balthazar snapped her neck with a single swift movement, killing her instantly.

Malik screamed in agony; his body too broken to do anything to stop Balthazar. He was powerless as his lover was brutally murdered right before him.

A terrible laugh left Balthazar's lips as he staggered from the cell. Once he stood in the corridor with me, he said, "Do your worst, my love."

I shuddered at his grotesque form, trying to focus on the human parts. Turning away, I fell to my knees and picked up the jar of poison. Hastily, I opened the slot at the bottom of the door and shoved the jar inside, my hands shaking.

The lid was secured tightly, but as I struggled to remove my gloves, it slipped from my grasp and shattered onto the floor. A piercing scream ripped through me as I pulled my bare hands back. The portal door slammed shut with a soft snick, but it did nothing to stop the terror thrumming through my veins.

Would Balthazar and I soon be dead, too? I backed away hurriedly, running straight into Balthazar.

My flesh crawled as maggots, writhing from his skin, burrowed into me. I screamed in horror as I felt them squirming around my throat and face. With a frenzy, I tore at my own skin to free myself of their filth.

Inside the cell, Malik's cries pierced through the air as the toxic fumes crept ever closer. His body convulsed as he held Layla close, his sobs muffled as he clutched her to his chest. His eyes bulged, and veins twisted in his neck as life drained from him. But, the fighter that he was, he released Layla, screamed, and pounded the floor in rage. Violent coughs shook his body as he fell to his hands and knees.

The end was near for Malik, but I didn't want to watch. Instead, I craved Balthazar's body. His half-monster, half-human form turned me on again.

I whirled to face my grotesque lover. "See? I did the right thing by procuring the poison from Raul. We've now achieved the ultimate crime. We're partners through and through."

I ripped at his tattered vest, torn from his transformation. Bloody muscle contrasted with skin-covered flesh.

"Tell me, my love," Balthazar said, half his lips falling

off. "How did you convince Costa to give you the poison? He is, after all, a merchant demanding recompense for his concoction and no Timehunter gives away his poison for free.

Heat and longing surged through my body, remembering the delicious price I'd paid. But I didn't dare tell Balthazar—not in a million years. I tried to direct my arousal toward Balthazar, but a chunk of his ear fell to the floor, filled with writhing, squirming maggots. I focused on the parts of him that were still intact—like his left shoulder. "I told him there's a bad man after me, and you and I were worried for my life."

Balthazar's eyes narrowed—at least, I thought they narrowed. One of his eyelids hung loosely over his eye. "And did you tell him who the bad man was?"

I shook my head, the lies tumbling from my lips. "No. But he was more than eager to help when he feared for my safety."

My fingers trembled as I peeled his bloody vest away from his blood-soaked shirt.

"Why would he care so much about your safety?" One maggot-infested eyebrow rose high on what was left of his forehead.

I closed my eyes. *Good lord, I was having such a hard time staying focused. Raul didn't dissolve into decaying flesh. He was a man, all man.* I frowned. *Who treated me like a whore…*

A rush of arousal for Balthazar ripped through my abdomen. I'd been a fool to bed Raul. But then I glanced at Malik's body writhing on the stone floor.

It was so worth it. He'll be dead soon.

"Let's go upstairs, my love," I said, reaching for Balthazar's bony hand. I tugged him up the stairs, and we crossed the threshold, falling into one another arms. Images of Raul's intact body kept flooding my brain. I squeezed my eyes shut and tried to focus on Balthazar.

He's my true love. There's only Balthazar.

I couldn't stop the stream of sexy images of Raul between my legs, eating me out, or fucking me against the wall of my little room in the lodge. I finally surrendered to it, using my fantasies to fuck Balthazar.

We fell to the floor with a thud and rolled onto the furs before the fire. I undulated against the soft fibers as Balthazar slid his macabre cock inside me. Soon, I didn't know which male was turning me on more—the man who fucked me stupid in Italy or the monster on top of me.

In the throes of our passion, Balthazar cried out. "Alina! I want to have a child with you!"

I was so disgusted by the idea I nearly stopped grinding my hips against him. Having a child was right up there with the worst of the worst ideas.

"Oh, my love," I said with forced gaiety. "You're just high on the night's killing. We don't need a baby to complete us."

Balthazar clutched my hips, forcing me to stop, and gazed into my eyes. "Don't you want a child with me? Think of it. We'll find the blades together and live a normal life with you as the mother of my children."

I wanted to retch all over him, purging his ridiculous notion from my and his mind.

"You'll be my queen, my empress... We shall rule the world and raise a family. Oh, what a splendid idea!" Balthazar beamed on the side of his face, which was still intact.

"I don't want a child, my..." I started to say "lord," but bit my lip. "I don't want children."

"You'll warm to the idea," he said, his hips bucking inside me again. "I'll make sure of it."

"No, Balthazar, I won't. I would never want to bring a child to this world ever. Please don't ask me."

The veins in Balthazar's neck bulged and his face grew bright red with fury. "You have always been a selfish bitch, Alina. You're right—you'd be the worst fucking mother ever."

His cruel words struck me like an icy gust of winter wind, leaving me speechless and numb. He pushed himself off me and stormed away without even finishing having sex, leaving behind hatred in the air and my body trembling in hurt.

I lay there, motionless and paralyzed by fear. All I could think of was the angst I felt when Balthazar demanded an heir from me.

Without warning, a dangerous idea snaked into my head: I was driven by an ever-growing arrogance and greed to have absolute power, a mad desire to enslave the world in my darkness. Even with Balthazar by my side, I could never achieve this goal—women were considered second-class citizens. So I had to leave him behind to pursue my own ambition. I craved the ultimate power that could only be gained through acquiring the ancient blades, a task I would take on alone without any of Balthazar's protection.

His body restored, Balthazar returned holding a bottle of whiskey. He tipped it to his lips and swallowed. When he'd drained the bottle, he threw it into the fireplace where it shattered into a million bits. Then, he flopped next to me, reeking of booze.

I tried to carefully slip away from his side, but as soon as I moved, Balthazar's iron grip snatched my ankle.

"Where do you think you're going?" he growled with his eyes still closed.

"To the chamber pot, my love. Don't worry, I'll be right back," I said sweetly, desperately trying to release myself from his clutches. After a moment that felt like an eternity, his hand finally relaxed and released me.

I sighed and crept away. As I passed through the formal living room, I thought of how we'd given Malik and Layla drugs those many days ago. I knew where Balthazar kept his potions. I'd seen him put them away in his study. Inspiration struck, and I knew what I needed to do. I would drug Balthazar and sneak away. It was the right thing to do. If I stayed here, we would never find the blades. Instead, we would keep getting caught up in our reckless, sexual folly.

An exhilarating rush shot through me. I would strike out on my own and become the most powerful woman the world had ever known.

I tiptoed down the hall and into Balthazar's study.

Balthazar's study was a grand room adorned with several rich tapestries and finely crafted bookshelves lined with ancient manuscripts. A large, ornately carved desk sat at the far side of the room, its surface covered with parchment and inkwells. The room was lit by several candelabras and a few tall, iron-barred windows letting in light and air. The walls were painted a deep crimson, and the floor was composed of dark hardwood planks.

A crystal goblet and a decanter filled with an unusual red liquid sat atop a small side table. On the opposite wall, a large portrait of a mysterious figure stared down at me, his piercing eyes burning like embers.

The painting was the only thing in the room that seemed to hint at Balthazar's true nature. In the picture, the figure had long, pointed ears, crimson eyes, and a set of curved horns. It was unmistakably an illustration of a demon, and it sent a chill down my spine as I looked upon it.

I focused on my task, crossing the room and opening the doors of the ornately carved cabinet. I found the belladonna inside a ruby-red glass vial on a lower shelf. Fearing Balt-hazar would wake at any second, I snatched the vial and crept toward the room where Balthazar lay fast asleep, naked on top of the furs.

I pried open the top of the vial and carefully poured some of the concoction on Balthazar's lips.

He frowned and licked his lips, rolling to his side.

Was that enough to make him weak for a while?

As I stood there, contemplating, he flopped on his back.

"Get me another fur, Alina," he murmured, eyes still tightly shut.

I complied, tucking it around him like a mother might tuck in a child. A dreamy smile spread on his face, and he sighed.

I poured another few drops onto his mouth. But my shaking hands fumbled, and a liquid stream fell onto his tongue.

His eyes flew open as he coughed and spluttered.

"What did you do?" he snarled, but his eyelids drooped. The word "bitch" left his mouth in a mumble as sleep over-took him.

I tried to recall how long Layla and Malik had slept once they'd ingested the respective drugs, but fear made my mind all foggy and jumbled.

Was it an hour? Thirty minutes?

I raced upstairs and gathered a few belongings. I would hide somewhere until the full moon and then travel time. But where?

On impulse, I scurried back downstairs, intending to check on Malik. On the way, I passed Balthazar's sleeping form—his mouth gaped open and noisy snores made the walls shudder.

"I'm sorry, Balthazar. You will never have the blades," I told him with contempt. "I'm done with our relationship and your so-called love for me. I want the power of darkness to be mine alone and no one else's. No more of your ridiculous words about having a baby together. You've taught me to embrace my wickedness and now I must show you how powerful it can be. Goodbye, my dear. Prepare to rot in hell forever as I take the blades and become the most powerful being of all!"

I hastened down to the dungeon to see if Malik had succumbed to the poison. I opened the little viewing portal to his cell. It was covered in glass, so I didn't worry about escaping poison. Malik had positioned himself against the wall, cradling Layla's body. The two lovers lay entwined, even in death. A stab of sympathy pierced my heart. He really did love Layla. But the sentiment quickly passed.

Good riddance—we don't need more star-crossed lovers in this world.

Malik's eyes flew open, startling me.

"You're still alive," I said. "How is that possible?"

He made an almost imperceptible shrug. "He's using you, you know."

"Who's using me?" I said.

"Balthazar. I know him better than you do. He raised me as his own from when I came into existence until now." His voice came out hoarse and weak.

His words stabbed me like a spear smeared in jealousy, but I kept my composure.

"I assure you, I know him intimately. I know his weaknesses and vulnerabilities."

A faint-sounding "Ha!" left Malik's lips. "Keep telling yourself that. You must get away from him. Find the daggers."

My gut pricked with interest. "Do you know where to find them?"

Malik's eyes closed.

"Malik!" I hissed. *"Malik!"*

Is he dead? Damn it all to hell!

I was ready to slam the portal door shut and head away from here when a croaking whisper left his lips.

"Find John James. In the Americas. In the 1700s. He can help you." His head slumped forward, lolling on his chest. His arms grew slack, and Layla rolled from his arms.

Malik, it seemed, had joined his beloved. And I had the answers I needed.

I lunged up the stairs, pounding them with my feet in an explosive sprint to freedom. Gasping for breath, I skidded to a halt in the doorway and held my breath as I listened for Balthazar's snores. As I inched forward, the chandeliers clinked and rattled in protest.

My heart was racing faster than a runaway horse as I snatched up my satchel from the foot of the stairs and tiptoed out of the estate. The horizon glowed pink and orange with the dawn, mirroring my inner glow of liberation.

With trembling hands, I hastily strapped a saddle onto one of Balthazar's prized stallions. Gripping my dagger, journal, and meager belongings, I mounted the horse and spurred it into a gallop. The ground shook beneath us as the horse's hooves pounded out a frantic rhythm, echoing through my body like a war drum.

My heart raced with determination and desire for the forbidden freedom promised at our destination. It was a dangerous game I played, leaving behind all that I knew for a chance at something more. But I had come too far to turn back now. This was my time to seize control and make my own choices, even if it meant going against everything I had ever known, including the intoxicating allure of Balthazar.

CHAPTER TWENTY

ALINA

I awoke from my time travel to an annoying chorus of birdsong greeting the day.

Ugh. Birds and their morning cheer.

I opened my eyes, hoping I was in the 1700s, somewhere in the land known as the Americas. The sun's rays poked through the foliage of the trees, illuminating the lush green grass and the winding stream nearby and painting the sky in a soft orange light. Everything around me seemed so sickeningly quaint and pastoral, even if unfamiliar to me.

It always took me a few moments to orient myself to my new surroundings. I shook my head, rubbed my eyes, and stood. The dew felt cold on my ankles, the chill of the morning air wrapping me in a shiver. I looked around at the trees, the firs and pines standing tall, their branches reaching out toward the sky. The leaves rustled in the slight breeze.

I walked toward the stream, and paused by the water's edge, listening to the gurgling of the water as it slid over the rocks and stones beneath it.

Thoughts of what I'd left behind stormed through my mind. Rage seared through me, an inferno of ire that blazed brighter with each thought of Balthazar. Every bone in my body was filled with boiling animosity toward his deceitful secrecy and terrifying dominion. All the times he left me with no word and refused to tell me where he'd gone grated at my nerves. And that wretched woman who was the "love of his life…" I could no longer suffer his manipulations in silence and had reached the absolute limit of my patience—not after he'd waxed on and on and *on* about the fucking love of his life.

I had a newfound strength coursing through my veins, and I knew that I could do it on my own. I loved Balthazar, but I was also angry. I was sick of his controlling ways. Sick of his secrets. I felt betrayed that he would share details about his first love, and I didn't want to share my own evil power with someone like that.

But then there was our sexual communion…

A wave of dizziness swept through me, forcing me to steady my body on a nearby tree trunk. How could I live without our passionate encounters.

But that's the problem, isn't it? That seems to be all we do when we're together…fight, and then fuck.

As I stepped into the middle of the stream, something caught my shoe-clad foot and held fast. I pulled, only to find my foot stuck between two boulders. A tangle of branches and creek debris wrapped around my ankle. I tried to wriggle free of my shoe without avail. I dipped my hand in the icy water and tried to untie my laces, but a knot had formed in the leather strands. No matter how hard I tried, I couldn't free myself. My shoe was jammed between these two god-damned rocks and the fucking branches.

As I turned my head, my peripheral vision caught a glimpse of a woman walking toward me. Her hair was long and auburn, flowing down her back, and she was wearing a white dress that seemed to float in the breeze. Holding her skirt aloft, she was several meters downstream, picking her way upstream like a graceful deer.

"Hello!" I called out, waving my hands. When she didn't respond, I raised my voice. *"Hello!* Can you help me?"

I drew frantic circles in the air and pointed at my foot.

She still didn't respond, even though she was now within hearing distance.

"Are you deaf?" I bellowed, my veins pulsing with mounting rage. A numbing chill seeped up from the icy depths of the murky water and into my trapped foot.

The woman lifted her gaze to me, a menacing sneer painted across her face, and said, "No."

Her vehemence startled me. I was the one trapped, not her.

"Then, can you help me?" I gestured to my foot. "My foot is stuck in these boulders."

Unhurriedly, she approached and stood next to me. "Oh, you poor thing. You need my help. But why should I help you?"

I blinked, surprised by her answer. "I don't know. Friend in need?"

I tried to smile through my irritation.

She seized my jaw in her hand and squeezed it. "Aw. Look at you. So stuck and yet so very pretty. I'd guess you think I should help you because you're so attractive. Am I right?"

I tried to pull my head away, but her grip was strong. I attempted to claw her hands from my face, but her fingers were immovable. A chill ripped through me.

Who is this woman?

"What's your problem?" I drew myself up. "Why are you so unkind to me?"

Her lips curled into a sinister smirk, her fingers digging into my cheeks like talons. Her wicked eyes glared with evil intent as she forced me to look away in fear. The anger emanating from her made me tremble, and I thought I was looking at the face of death itself.

I shook her off with a few choice curse words. "What the hell? Are you a madwoman?"

"I am the stuff of nightmares, you vicious serpent. I will make you suffer in ways you can't even imagine, and it all begins with my refusal to help you." She glared at me with venom in her gaze, her hands clenched into tight fists as she planted them on her hips.

I cowered in the shallows of the stream as I tried to free my foot from the tangle of branches and debris that was imprisoning me.

The woman stood motionless, her figure silhouetted by the setting sun. Her eyes, a piercing shade of gray, remained focused on me as I flailed in the water. She had an air of poetic sophistication, from her slim frame to the way she held herself with grace. But as I struggled for purchase, she made no move to help me.

It was clear something else was at play here. Something deeper, and darker.

I finally spoke, my voice cold and emotionless. "What do you mean you are my biggest nightmare? You don't know me."

I tried to slap her, but she stepped away from me. With one swift movement, she twisted my arm sharply, and I cried out in pain. She forced my head into the water. With my foot still stuck, I gasped and spluttered desperately trying to free myself.

My hair was twisted into a knot of pain, and I was yanked from my watery fate. With one hand clutching my now-sopping hair, the woman leaned in close to me, her face full of sinister rage.

"You vicious little viper, I do know you," she said. "I know all about you. Except you don't know me. I think you deserve the same punishment you meted out to all your past lovers. Starting with Francesco, the poor stable boy that you told your father violated you, while you were in throes of pleasure. For that I will bring you the greatest pain *ever*."

Her face contorted into a cruel, vicious sneer as she shoved me away from her.

I stumbled, falling into the shallow creek, my shoe still caught in the rocks. A searing stab of pain shot through my ankle. The woman's words sank into me, cold terror washing over me as I saw the shadows lurking beneath her stoic facade. This woman vanished in front of me, only to materialize a split second later with her hands tightening around my throat like an iron vice.

Rage and fear coalesced in my stomach, freezing me solid.

I glared at her. "You! You're a monster like Balthazar!"

"And *you*," she said with bitter scorn. "You shared a bed with him and claim to love him, yet still think of him as a monster? What kind of wretchedness must one possess to be so two-faced?"

She flickered in and out of existence, each time her fingers tightening around my throat, cutting off my screams. I gasped for breath as she squeezed harder, until panic consumed me. This wasn't an ordinary woman; she was an embodiment of the same darkness that had corrupted Balthazar.

When she released me, I fell back with a gasp. "I…I…I *do* love Balthazar. With all my heart!"

I yanked on my foot with all my might. I had to get away

from this woman, even if it meant tearing my foot from my leg.

The woman's voice choked me like a ghostly fog. She vanished in front of me, only to materialize a split second later. "You say that you love him, but all I hear is a hollow echo of what I once felt for Balthazar. Our connection was powerful, a force that enveloped us in an infinite darkness. You and he had *nothing… nothing* compared to the bond we shared. Don't you understand? Nothing could ever come close."

The air seemed to freeze and crackle with her words as if a thousand demons were present, relaying the same warning message.

I sat in the creek, sopping wet, as this woman stared at me with a wild and menacing gaze.

"You're his first love." The words tumbled from my lips in a whisper.

"I am Zara, Balthazar's *only* love…his first and his last. You're just a whore spreading your legs to every man and to him as well." She let out a cackle that filled the air like a murder of squawking crows.

I stared in disbelief. I thought Zara had been killed by my father.

I became frantic, desperate to wrench my leg free. Finally, one of the rocks gave way, rolling to the side with a splash. I scrambled to stand and tried to flee, but my foot was swollen, and my wet shoes could not find purchase on the slippery rocks.

Zara grabbed me by the hair with a superhuman strength, yanking me backward so hard that my feet lifted off the ground. Stream water flew and splashed around us as I screamed in agony, unable to free myself from her grip.

Her voice came roaring out in a savage shriek, full of

anger and vengeance. "You brought unspeakable suffering to Layla. You destroyed Malik with your evil deeds. You've ruined countless lives, and now I will make your life a living hell!"

She threw me through the air like a rag doll. I flew helplessly and crashed into the stream with a heavy thud, my body broken and bloody.

Heaving sobs poured from my lungs. And unlike all the times I'd faked it, these tears were real.

"Balthazar will protect me," I screeched. "He'll find me and save me, and you'll be *nothing.*"

Zara threw back her head and let out a maniacal laugh. "You just said he's a monster! And now you think he's going to save you, after you betrayed him, lied to him, and most importantly broke his loyalty and trust?"

I huddled in the creek bed, the water flowing around me as I contemplated my next move. What could I do to get away? And *would* Balthazar save me if he were here? Not if the tortured feelings he'd shared with me about Zara were true. I was so fucked. I rolled to my hands and knees and crawled out of the creek to dry land. I was cold, wet, and shivering when I emerged. I thought maybe Zara would let me go, having had her fill of torturing me. I was wrong.

Zara's voice rose like a crescendo of hatred and condemnation, taunting me with every dark deed I'd ever committed. She shouted out the names of Davide and Tomaso as if they were curses and recounted the details of my treachery against Balthazar in vivid, twisted detail. She spoke of my sexual trysts with Raul as if she'd witnessed each one.

I pressed my hands over my ears in vain; her words tore through me like pointed blades, each syllable slicing deeper into my soul than any physical blade ever could.

"No!" I screamed. "Enough! Please, for the love of God, put an end to this suffering!"

Zara erupted into a maniacal laughter. "Oh, my dear, you have barely begun to experience the brutality and pain that victims feel when tortured and abused by you. The torment has only just begun, my vicious, venomous snake!"

I dug my fingernails into the dirt and heaved myself up, ignoring the searing pain that coursed through my veins. With a scream of determination, I lunged away from Zara, but she was hot on my heels. Finally, I spun around to face her, the rage bubbling up inside me like boiling magma.

My words exploded out of my mouth. "Every treacherous act I've done—it was all for Balthazar! We share a dream! We will rule this world together with darkness and make it evil!"

Her expression twisted with rage. "You think Balthazar loves you? That he'll ever love you like he loved me? I gave him a family and children, a life together in darkness. He's so blinded by what happened in the past that he can't see straight. He's blinded by your lies. He can barely see what's real. You're nothing more than a toy. I gave him love, family, children… I gave it all to him."

I staggered backward, horrified. "You gave him children? You and Balthazar were a family?"

"Yes. Everything was taken away from us. *Everything.*" Her shoulders sagged, weighed down by the burden of grief. "We were two powerful forces of darkness whose bond was unbreakable. We were inseparable from one another. But to him, you are nothing more than the daughter of Mathias, his sworn enemy and yet he still takes you into his bed and claims to feel love for you. If that was truly the case, wouldn't he have opened up about his past in full detail, revealing who I am, our family, and how I fit into his story. Instead, all he has shared is a shallow version of events."

A surge of emotion rose inside me as I screamed, "Balthazar loves me!"

I hoped desperately to make it true, my voice ringing out with a passionate intensity that bordered on desperation.

"You are ignorant of Balthazar's innermost feelings...completely oblivious," Zara said. "Whenever he spoke of his past, you refused to listen. What gave you the right to deny him the family he so desires? All you can think of is yourself and your own petty wants. You are nothing more than a self-centered shrew!"

"He said you were gone!" My cries echoed through the forest.

"And yet here I stand," Zara said, her arms flung wide open. "He makes many errors when his temper gets the best of him. It appears he doesn't even realize I am still alive. And we are going to keep it that way—for now, anyway."

She seized my upper arm, her nails digging into my flesh like claws.

"Who sent you? What do you want from me?" I screamed.

"Aw, you poor thing," she said. "Every mistake you make I will know, and I will chase you and haunt you for it. My beloved Balthazar has so much pain still and can't let go of the past. He can't see straight. And now it's time for you to pay for your mistakes."

The she-demon hauled back and struck me hard until darkness enveloped me from all sides.

I came to, wildly disoriented, lying on a strange bed in a small, dimly lit room. I sat up, startled.

The walls were made of wooden planks, and the pine floors were covered with straw mats. One small window covered with a torn, stained curtain regulated the amount of light and air entering the room, which wasn't much. A simple wooden dresser sat against the wall, holding a wash basin and a porcelain pitcher of water for basic hygiene.

My body ached, and I let out a groan, falling back on the uncomfortable straw-filled pillow.

Fear nibbled at my insides. Had Zara brought me here to further torture me? Did I need to escape before being subjected to more violations? I honestly didn't think I could endure any more pain.

As I was contemplating my escape, a man entered the room. I let out a screech and attempted to pull myself into a ball. But my wounds were extensive, and I yelped in pain.

The man held up his palms and spoke to me in English. I was familiar with the language but didn't want him to know that.

He was a tall man, roughly thirty years old, with broad shoulders and strong arms that spoke to years of hard labor. His skin was weathered from days spent in the sun, and even in the dim light, I could make out the shades of blue and green in his eyes that seemed to have captured the depths of the sky and the forests. His hair was chestnut in color, short, and swept back on his head, framing his strong features. He wore a simple linen shirt rolled up at the sleeves, trousers, and boots that had seen better days.

"You've been badly hurt. Who hurt you? Where did you come from?" While his voice was gruff, there was a kind of warmth and sincerity in his words that made me feel at ease.

"*Non ti capisco,*" I said repeatedly, speaking in my native Italian. *I don't understand you.*

The man propped his hands on his hips.

"Hmmm," he said, frowning. He held up a finger and stepped from the room.

I lay there with my palms pressed into the mattress, panting like a bitch in heat.

When the man returned, he carried a cloth. He filled the basin with water from the pitcher, rested it on the floor at my side, and wrung out the cloth. Then, he proceeded to dab at my face and neck.

"No!" I shouted, pushing his hand away.

He sighed and let out another, "Hmmm."

Then, he spun, strode from the room, and returned bearing a broken piece of looking glass. He held the glass before my face, and I gasped.

My cheeks were cut and scratched, and my lips and nose were swollen and red. Angry purple-and-red blotchy bruises made me look disfigured. My hands trembled as I pushed my hair back from my face to examine the jagged edge of a long, thin cut that snaked down the side of my neck. I touched the warm, sticky trickle of blood that had dripped onto my collarbone from the wound. I didn't want to know what lay under my dress, but I could feel the throbbing aches and pains.

Layla's bloated face—the face left grotesquely misshapen by my heinous tortures—floated before me.

Oh, God! I look just like her! This must be what she felt like at the end of her life!

Rage bubbled and boiled, making me want to throw things or hit something. But I was as weak as a kitten.

The man reached for the cloth in the basin again, wrung it out, and held it up, seeming to ask permission to dab at my face.

"No!" I shoved his hand away again. I didn't deserve kindness.

He dropped the cloth into the water and stood there, watching me. As he studied me, he frowned.

Even that was painful. I was a beautiful woman, used to being fawned over by men, not pitied. I didn't want to be watched, scrutinized, studied, or examined. I rolled away from him and threw my hands over my head.

The slow sound of his footsteps indicated he'd left the room. I waited for some time until I was able to stretch out on the bed.

I was alerted to the presence of a horse and buggy outside. I heaved myself out of bed and hobbled toward the window to see who had arrived.

A dapper-looking mustached man wearing a black coat and trousers climbed from the buckboard. He retrieved a black leather satchel from the back of the wagon.

Behind him, the sun had begun to set, casting a dull orange glow over the parched earth. The fields were dry, with only sparse tufts of grass dotting the landscape. A broken-down barn, its paint faded, stood as a lonely sentinel in the distance. The mustached man disappeared, striding out of view toward the house.

Heavy footsteps tromped in my direction, and the man who had tried to care for me appeared in the doorway with the new visitor.

"Hello, miss," the newcomer said in halting Italian.

I sat up, and a torrent of words tumbled from my mouth. "You can speak in Italian? Where am I? Who brought me here? Who is the man who tried to take care of me?"

"Wait, wait," the mustached man said, pumping his arms up and down. "You must speak slowly. I am not fluent in Italian. But first, introductions. This is Philip Weston, and I am Dr. Clive Carson. What is your name?"

I shook my head, pretending not to understand him. "*Non ti capisco.*"

"Philip tells me you've been unconscious for days," Dr. Carson said. "He said he found you laying on the plains when he returned from war. He brought you home, bloodied and beaten. Who beat you?"

"I don't recall," I lied in Italian. "I was attacked in the forest."

"Pity. You're severely injured," Dr. Carson said in Italian. "That is the phrase I was searching for. May I examine you?"

I eyed him and then Philip. I shook my head.

"Please, dear. I fear you won't get better without proper care. Please allow me to assess your wounds. Philip will step out of the room, won't you?" Dr. Carson flashed Philip a stern look and then turned his kind eyes toward me.

Philip nodded and retreated.

I sighed and shrugged.

Doctor Carson opened his black satchel, revealing forceps, herbs in glass vials, some kind of sawing device, and other medical equipment. He peeled apart my dress, maintaining my modesty as best he could, and poked, prodded, and examined. When he was done, wordlessly, he left the room.

When he returned, he said, "I don't know where Philip has gone. He must have stepped out. I have news which I hope is welcome."

He smiled grimly. "You're...I'm afraid my Italian is quite rusty. I don't know the word. You're..."

He rocked his arms like he was holding a baby.

A chill rippled across my scalp, and I shook my head, eyes wide.

"No, no, no," I shouted. "This can't be!" It had to be Balt-hazar's.

Oblivious to my wounds, I lunged from the bed and seized the doctor's throat.

"Get out! Get away from me!" I said. "I must leave at once!"

Dr. Carson shouted as he ripped my hands away from his neck.

"Philip!" he called, and Philip burst into the room like a raging bull, joining Dr. Carson in subduing me onto the bed, trapping my arms beneath their combined weight.

"She's gone mad!" Dr. Carson said in Italian, with a string of vicious curses in English. "We won't hurt you. We want to help. I'm going to give you something to calm your nerves. Will you please calm down, dear?"

I writhed and wrestled beneath their grip.

Dr. Carson muttered something to Philip, and Philip seized both my arms. He held me down like he was made of iron while the doctor rooted in his bag. He held a glass vial over my mouth.

I thrashed my head back and forth, but Dr. Carson seized my jaw with a grip so strong I couldn't move. Then, he poured some of the bitter-tasting concoction into my mouth. I spluttered and tried to cough it out, but Dr. Carson pinched my lips shut.

"This is going to help you feel better," he said.

My limbs became heavy under the influence of whatever substance he'd given me.

Cautiously, both men released me, their hands hovering over me, ready to pin me again. Then, slowly, they backed from the room. A door opened and closed, and their voices sounded like they were coming from outside.

Hot tears rolled down my face as I lay there, unable to move.

A baby will get in the way of my plans. I must get rid of it. I must do what's best for me. I need those blades for myself.

With effort, I rolled to my side and spied the looking glass on the floor. As if moving through water, I reached for the mirror. Its edges were sharp, perfect for what I had in mind. I began to slash at my abdomen, but my movements were clumsy and lethargic.

The air grew heavy and thick with an invisible presence. I felt as though every cell in my body was suffocating with fear.

Zara materialized like a ghostly apparition, slowly fading into view. Her black eyes pierced right through my soul.

In one swift movement, Zara grabbed me and slammed me into the wall. I heard the thud of my body hitting the hard surface and felt the pain jolt through me, but I didn't scream. It would do me no good—I was completely at the mercy of the demon. Her icy fingers lingered on my neck as her malicious laughter echoed through the room. She grabbed a fistful of my hair and smashed my head repeatedly against the wood until my ears rang and stars swam before my eyes.

Eyes flashing, teeth bared, she snarled, "You're going to keep this baby, or you'll see a worse side of me. For starters, I'm going to rip your fingernails off one by one." She seized my hand, pinched one finger in her vicious grip, and snarled, "What do you say we start now?"

I let out a muffled cry and wrestled my hand from her clutches.

Zara laughed maniacally and faded from sight as footsteps strode through the house.

My entire body hurt from being slammed repeatedly into the

wall. I sobbed uncontrollably. My heart broke into pieces. Balt-hazar's face flashed before my eyes and I knew that he could not, would not save me this time, even if he knew where to find me. My treacherous heart had betrayed him, and I was left wallowing in a sea of despair and anguish. Tears of remorse cascaded down my face as the crushing weight of self-pity descended upon me.

Philip appeared in the doorway, balancing a tray of steaming food. "I come bearing sustenance," he announced with a smile. "You look like you could use some comfort." His soothing words wrapped around me like a warm embrace.

My tears evaporated, replaced with an icy determination as a plan began to form. Devising a quick scheme, I knew I had to make him fall in love with me, fuck me, and make him believe this baby was his own. I would start looking for the blades myself.

I wouldn't allow anyone to stop me. No matter the cost.

CHAPTER TWENTY-ONE

BALTHAZAR

My mouth felt stuffed with cotton as I woke up shivering on the cold floor. A fur lay nearby in a heap like I'd wrestled with it during my slumber. I blinked, trying to orient myself, but my eyelids scraped across my eyes like sand across boulders.

As I stumbled to my feet, every muscle in my body screamed with pain. My vision blurred, and my head spun as I shuffled across the worn carpet of the living room, grasping for support on the luxurious couch and coffee table. My mind raced, trying to figure out what foul concoction had been slipped into my drink.

"Alina! *Alina!*" My voice bounced around the house, echoing in my ears. "Where are you, bitch?"

I stormed through the house, looking everywhere on the main floor and upstairs. Rage surged through me with every movement, sending heat through my body. I felt no remorse as I moved furniture and ripped open drawers, searching for any trace of her.

My outrage grew. I tossed furniture, which splintered as it crashed against the wall. I threw her clothing and jewelry on the floor. I rifled through papers and documents, desperate to find something—anything—that would help me discover what had happened to her.

My heart raced as I fought to control my emotions. I refused to believe that she was gone, yet I was plagued by my own doubts and fears.

I sank to the floor in the master bedroom, the rage and grief dissipating. The full moon had been last night. Alina had left me—again. Only this time, she'd given me poison and left no clues. She didn't want to be discovered. Until I found her, I would never be able to rest.

The floor was hard and unyielding beneath my ass, and I felt a jolt of pain that brought me from the dissociative fugue. It was unimaginable—I had thought Alina worshiped me, and yet here she was, turning her back on me and leaving without so much as a word.

I felt a strange void inside as if I no longer had a purpose. I had been so sure of Alina's love that I had never considered a life without her in it. Now, I was forced to confront the reality of a world in which I was utterly alone.

She had struck the death knell for our relationship. I lay on the floor for a long while, motionless. I had no idea if I could ever stand up again. All I knew was that the world had shifted, and I was now completely adrift.

Time drifted and surged, slowed, and sped as I slumped on the floor, unable to get my body to move. Finally, with a groan, I stood. Everything in this room was in a chaotic disarray, just like my heart.

Moving like an ancient man, I shuffled into the hall and down the stairs, each footstep landing like an iron anchor. I dragged my feet across the main floor and headed for the dungeon.

When I stood before the portal door to Malik's cell, I was

stunned to see him still alive. Tears streaked his face as he cradled Layla who lay stiff in his arms.

An unwelcome stab of compassion pitchforked my heart as I regarded him. I knew how he felt. But then my rage bubbled up from some distant place where it had been hiding for the last few hours.

I pounded on the door. "Where's Alina? Where's that fucking bitch?"

Malik turned to look at me, the effort of movement obvious in his lethargic movement and pained expression.

"I imagine she left you," he croaked, his voice as dry as dead leaves.

"Why would you think that?" I battered at the unyielding door.

"I told her to leave you. I said you were using her." One eyebrow lifted on his forehead. "Isn't that what you do? You befriend people. You even get them to fall in love with you, then you discard them and throw them away when they have outlived their usefulness."

I was so angry I couldn't speak. I longed to storm into the prison cell and tear Malik apart, limb by limb. But the poison still lingered in the air around him and, if I were to enter, I would be dead or dying, too. With my heart pounding, I frantically looked for anything I could destroy, but my gaze met with solid stone and metal. There was nothing left to do but to let out a primal cry of rage before turning back toward safety.

My soul burned with fury as I stormed back upstairs. I had no doubt where I'd find her—with *Costa.* She would regret the day I found her; I was sure about that. But my hands were tied until the next full moon.

The moment the full moon crested over the horizon, I readied myself to time travel toward Costa's estate in Italy. Adrenaline raced through my veins as I faced the unknown of where I would find Costa and what I planned on doing to him.

I took a deep breath and felt myself being pulled into a swirling vortex of colors and sensations.

As I traveled through time, I experienced a disorienting mix of emotions and physical sensations. I could feel the rush of wind against my skin, the weightlessness of being suspended in space, and the tingle of electricity in my veins. My mind was bombarded with images and memories, mine and those of the people I was about to meet.

And then, just as suddenly as it had started, the whirlwind stopped, and I found myself standing in a completely different place and time.

With the bloated, orange-yellow sun hanging heavy in the sky, it was midday. I stormed toward Costa's front door like a tempestuous wind, eager to exact my revenge. I battered the door with my fist, the wood creaking and groaning under my assault. The door splintered, and I powered into the house.

A man's shout came from the back of the house. I sprinted in that direction, approaching Costa as he rushed from a back room. I crowded him, preventing egress, and glanced through the doorway into the room where he'd emerged.

A young teen cowered in the corner; his eyes filled with terror as I locked eyes with him. My cruel sneer widened, and my teeth glinted as he shivered in fear.

Costa reached for the doorknob in a desperate attempt to shut the door. I slammed my palm onto it with a loud bang, pushing it back open and filling the room with a sinister dread.

Costa pulled himself up to his full height, towering before

me and preventing me from keeping my hand on the door. He leaned forward, intimidating me with the intensity of his glare.

"Lord Balthazar!" His voice was a menacing growl. "So, we finally meet in person. You should have told me you were coming—I could have arranged an opulent feast."

I seethed with rage, my eyes blazing. "Shut up! All of you Timehunters are fucking despicable!"

Costa just shrugged, infuriating me even more. With one swift movement, I attempted to barrel through him and enter the room he had blocked off, but he stood motionless like a stone wall in my way.

My fists clenched as I stepped back with a growl, consumed by anger and resentment. "Where the fuck is Alina?"

I tried to peer around him into the bedroom where the teen cowered. I figured the boy and Costa were taking turns with Alina and she was now hiding in the armoire.

"Alina?" Costa feigned innocence.

I grabbed his shoulders and hurled him to the side. "Stop being coy. You know very well who Alina is. Where is she?"

I blasted across the room, my footfalls thundering.

The teen pressed himself into a corner and shook with terror.

Costa raced toward the boy and shielded him with his body as I dashed around, flinging open the armoire doors and looking under the bed.

"Where is she? Where have you hidden Alina!"

"I don't have her!" Costa spread his arms to protect the teen. "Why would you think she was here?"

I lunged toward him and grabbed his shirt, lifting him into the air.

Costa's legs pinwheeled and his eyes bulged. "Put me down! Alfonso, *run!*"

The teen pushed away from his dangling father and tried to bolt from the room. I dropped Costa, faded from view, and reappeared at the door, slamming it shut before the boy took his next step.

Alfonso screamed like a girl.

I seized him and flung him across the floor. He skittered like a rag doll and crashed into the wall.

"You! Stay there. And you!" I faded and reappeared in front of Costa. "I want you to be honest with me. If you don't, I shall kill your son!"

"No!" Costa scrambled to his feet. "Spare my only child."

"Then, speak the truth! Why did Alina come here before?" I felt myself starting to transform into my true self, rotting skin and writhing maggots. I willed my body to stay human.

Costa trembled as he spoke. "She said you were both monsters, you and someone named Malik. She was terrified. I could see it in her eyes."

His skin was clammy with sweat as he stared at me, his fear so strong the air seemed to hang around him.

I waited for him to continue.

"She begged me to give her something. So, I relented." A subtle shrug made his shoulder rise and fall almost imperceptibly.

I clenched my teeth. "You Timehunters never give something for nothing. What did you get in return?"

Costa's gaze shifted to the right. "I was willing to do it for free."

My hand flew to his throat, my fingers tightening around his windpipe. "What did you take in exchange?"

Pulling himself out of his fear, Costa bared his teeth in a cruel grin as he spoke.

"She pleaded with me," he said, the words dripping with arrogance. "Begged me for mercy. But then, she realized what power I had over her and offered herself to me."

His eyes gleamed with malevolent triumph, relishing the depravity of the moment.

"And let me tell you," he said, his voice dropping to a dangerous whisper, "it was an offer that I couldn't refuse."

The pulse in my throat began to pound, loud and insistent.

"We had a great time. I fucked her in every way possible until she had to leave. She's one horny bitch." Costa grabbed his crotch.

Letting out an animalistic roar, I hurled him across the room.

Costa slammed into the wall, making the room shake.

Alfonso whimpered and shrank inside himself like the pathetic worm he was. I stalked over to him, picked him up, and shook him so hard his teeth clacked.

Holding the boy in the air like a prize, I said, "It's because of you, Costa, and your despicable Timehunters that I became this angry, dark demon. You fucking destroyed me. And now, you will pay!"

I felt my cheek crack apart, followed by the writhing sensation of maggots. A couple of them fell to the ground and squirmed about.

Alfonso let out a mewling whimper like a wild animal whose leg had been caught in a trap.

Costa crawled toward me, leaving a trail of blood behind him. His hands and knees were torn and bleeding as he lunged forward, wrapping his desperate fingers around my ankle. He blubbered uncontrollably, tears streaming down his face in an endless stream of grief.

"Please…" he begged, his voice cracking with desperation. "Please put my son down… Spare him… He's only sixteen... He has so much to live for… Please don't do this… I beg of you."

I looked into his eyes, filled with nothing but cold, unyielding malice. I let my arm drop and the lad fell to the ground. He let out a high-pitched scream as I dragged him out of the room.

Costa seized my ankle again. I shook him off like the dog he was. His elbows thumped on the hardwood floor as he fought to grab onto his son's legs.

With a vicious growl, I retrieved my dagger faster than the eye could comprehend. "I'm going to destroy you and your life just the way you destroyed mine long ago."

I grabbed Alfonso's hair, bared his neck, and sliced through it.

Costa let out a deafening, guttural scream. "No! Alfonso, no! My boy! You fucking monster!"

He lunged to his feet and seized my neck. But I was already transforming, and his hands wrapped around bone and cartilage. Horrified, he snatched back his hands and stared at the maggots that squirmed on his fingers.

"You know, Costa, Alina played you," I snarled. "Did you really think she was just a normal girl? She is a Timeborne, and your own secret society knows that you should never spare a Timeborne or Timebound. But instead of fulfilling your duty as a Timehunter and eliminating her, you let her manipulate and toy with you like a puppet. Just imagine what your father or the leader of the society would say if they found out that you failed to follow their orders!"

Costa spluttered and backed away. "I did not know Alina was a Timeborne."

"Oh yeah?" I sneered. "Because all you cared about was

having an easy lay with her and ignoring the consequences. Now your son has paid the price for your recklessness."

"I'm going to kill you, Balthazar!" Costa growled through gritted teeth. "I will make sure you suffer for this."

"How can you kill me if your poisons are far from you, hmm? I got my vengeance on my children's murders long ago, but I vow to destroy your society one day. You try one more move like that, and I'll cut off your balls. And if you ever try to fuck Alina again, I'll fry those same balls in hot oil and force-feed them to you. Do you understand me?"

He collapsed to the floor next to his dying son and sobbed.

On the night of the full moon, I headed back home. When I manifested in the gardens, my home was engulfed in flames. Shards of memory I had buried deep in my mind, of the day I'd lost my children, came roaring to the surface.

I sprinted for the door, unaware of the flames and heat, and raced through my house. The stairs to the upstairs were gone, charred beyond recognition, and ceiling timbers lay burning on the floor.

I headed for the dungeon, taking the steps two at a time. Flames licked at every place that wasn't stone, metal, or glass. Inside the prison cell, Malik lay dead. I thundered up the stairs. Someone coughed in the nearby charred rubble.

"Who's that?" I said, whirling about.

"Master, it's me, your groomsman, Peter. I came inside to save you," he croaked, then coughed violently. "When I couldn't find you, I assumed I was too late."

"Who set fire to my home? Did you see anyone?" I glanced at his skin, pearly white from the severity of the burns. He would never make it.

"It was a…a…" Another coughing fit ensued. "It was a woman, master."

"Good god, it was Alina!" I roared, pacing the hallway like a caged beast. "What kind of fool am I? For all this time, she's been using me! She's betrayed me in the most horrible fashion imaginable. She slept with Costa. Not once, but countless times."

I beat the stone hearth until my fists were bloodied as my mind filled with seething hatred. Pain pierced my heart, leaving me gasping for breath. "She lied to me the whole time we were together. All she wanted was ultimate power...and power over me!"

Insane with rage and heartbreak, I staggered from my burning estate, determined to leave it all behind. This life was gone. There was nothing left for me to do but kill.

For days the town was terrorized by me, an unstoppable killing machine. I took pleasure in the deaths of my victims, brazenly murdering them whenever the opportunity arose. Each killing was unique. Sometimes I would take my time to carefully orchestrate their agony, dragging out their final breaths before releasing them from their misery. Other times I attacked with relentless ferocity, slaughtering without remorse. Not a single soul was spared, and death followed me wherever I went.

Soon, I grew bored and empty. The slaughter wasn't slaking my heartache or calming my rage. There was nothing left for me here. I went into the fade and reappeared in a hunting lodge of mine in Scotland.

My sprawling estate was nothing short of majestic. Nestled in the forested part of Scotland, it was a looming black structure made of obsidian stone, its ancient timeworn walls of granite, and its heavy Gothic spires reaching the heavens. The grounds were so vast that the estate could be seen for miles, with the sun glinting off the turreted towers.

I strode through the wrought iron gates at the entrance,

oblivious to the well-manicured lawns dotted with ancient oaks, oleander bushes, and vibrant wildflowers. I scowled at the clear, bubbling brook that trickled through the lush vegetation.

There was nothing that would make me happy except for the murder of Alina Tocino.

Desperately, I longed for joy and the warmth of love I'd had with Zara and my children to fill my life. I'd hoped Alina could be the one to bring me bliss again, but instead, she'd ripped my heart to shreds with her lies and betrayals. She'd broken my soul apart, leaving me crushed in a sea of unending sorrow.

The air was heavy inside the house, with a musty scent left behind in my absence. I dragged my feet through the drawing room, with its stately mahogany walls, tall velvet drapes, thick, ornate carpets, and flopped on the sofa. A cloud of dust puffed around me. I coughed, threw my arm over my eyes, and tried to blot out everything.

A gentle touch startled me, and my arm flew away from my face. The ghost of Zara stood over me.

My eyes shot open, wild with terror, as I gasped at her spectral form.

My voice came out a strangled whisper, "No more! Get away from me, spirit! Stop your hauntings!"

The ghost remained, unmoved by my desperate plea. "Balthazar, my love, stop your mad ravings. You're in pain, and your suffering rips me apart."

She reached out, soft fingers caressing my jaw.

I screamed at the top of my lungs, "Stop this! Get out of here! You don't exist any longer. You were slain before my eyes!"

A tortured cry broke out from my lips as I begged for peace. "Why won't you stop hurting me? You have ripped apart my life like a wild animal. My love for you was never-ending, and we had a family, five innocent daughters, slaughtered on that fateful night because you weren't there to protect them. Now everything is gone. First, the girls, then my heart when you left me for Mathias, and now Alina has abandoned me, too. Is there no end to my misery?"

Hot tears streamed down my face as the phantom before me shattered into a million pieces. My heart pounded with a savage fury as I realized the twisted truth of my own deeds.

"This is what happens when I take too much life," I said to myself, my voice shaking with repressed anger. My vision blurred until all I saw was a murky red haze.

A howl of hatred and regret escaped past my lips as I reminded myself that it had been me who chose to fuck Alina, seeking love in all the wrong places, only to be inevitably betrayed and lose everything.

I lurched to my feet, staggering across the tiled floor. I screamed out in mindless rage, my voice echoing through the stillness of the house and reverberating off the walls.

"No one is loyal to me! My first love betrayed me! Mathias and Amir stabbed me in the back when I thought they were my friends! Malik turned against me. Timehunters slaughtered my family! I thought I could find a new life when I found Alina, but I was wrong."

I was a complete fool to have been swayed by Alina's words. My mind had been clouded with her lies and I didn't question it until it was too late. Anger roiled inside me like a raging inferno, blinding me to the truth that had been right in front of me all along.

The ghost of Zara reappeared, looking more beautiful than ever. Knives stabbed at my heart, and I stumbled backward, falling to the floor. I grabbed my head, pulling at my hair, wanting these delusions to stop.

"Balthazar!" she said. "What has happened to you? You were never like this before! You have gotten angrier through the centuries. You carry enormous pain, and to what end?"

I slapped my ears with my palms. "Stop talking to me. You're nothing but a figment of my imagination. I never want to relive that life again."

Zara's ghost pried my hands from my head, feeling very much like flesh and blood. She wrapped her arms around me and tried to kiss me, but I pushed her away. How could I kiss a ghost? Yet, the likeness my imagination took was unreal.

"Balthazar, look at me, my love."

"No!" My raging scream echoed in my ears as I pressed my eyelids shut.

"I heard you murdered Raul's son."

My eyes shot open, a predator's stare piercing the darkness. "What did you say? How could you know about that? Of course, you know. You know *everything*. You are nothing but the manifestation of my inner insanity."

An unhinged cackle spilled from my throat.

"Why did you kill him?" the ghost of Zara asked.

"Why? *Why?*" I stalked in a furious circle, my hands fluttering around like lost birds. "I killed his son because *his* people killed *my* children. *You* betrayed me. You left me. You left me to be with Mathias."

The ghost got in my face. She felt so real. Her breath warmed my face. "You were so angry, you forgot I was grieving, too. I lost them, too! I reached out to you desperately for comfort, but you kept pushing me away, blaming me for everything. Your words were cruel daggers cutting through my heart and every time I sought solace in your arms, you turned away. You had become a monster out to consume my soul, and when someone tried to help us both—the one man who offered me compassion—you lashed out at him too. And so it was then I walked away from you, bleeding and broken, as I left behind all hope of reconciliation."

A guttural, feral scream ripped from my throat and echoed around the room. "*Enough*! Cease your conniving lies and leave me be! I won't have it. There can be no doubt that he commanded those Timehunters to slaughter our children!"

As the sound of innocent children's giggles echoed through the room, my heart pounded. I spun around, searching for their faces, but they were everywhere and nowhere at once. My daughters' angelic voices echoed through the room, their laughter and giggles filling my heart with love. But as I reached out to hug them, they disappeared like wisps of smoke, leaving me grasping at empty air. The cruel illusion taunted and teased me, reminding me of what I had lost.

"Freya! Astrid! Tove! Revna! Meya!" I screamed, my voice choked with agony.

They only laughed cruelly as they slipped from my grasp like smoke.

"Freya," I said in a sing-song voice. "Revna. Where are my precious little girls?"

I tiptoed toward the paintings on the opposite wall, immersed in a game of hide and seek.

"Astrid. Meya. Where *are* you?" I cupped my ear with my hand and tiptoed around the room. "You're such good hiders!"

Five sets of little girl voices emerged from the understairs closet. I skulked across the room, held my finger up to my lips, and whispered, "Shh."

I threw open the door only to be met with cobwebs.

My eyes brimmed with tears of frustration and despair as I realized that my daughters were gone forever. The only thing left was their haunting laughter, echoing endlessly in my mind until it becomes an ominous crescendo, consuming everything else in its wake.

I tore at my hair, shrieking from the pain in my scalp and the agony in my heart. My five little girls were long dead, just like Zara. I fell to my knees and pounded the floor, beating at my own pain.

"Stop making me relive the past! I don't want to re-experience the horrible loss of my family!"

I crawled across the tiles, heading for my liquor cabinet. I clawed my way to standing, seized a dusty bottle of amber liquid, uncorked it, and glugged it. The alcohol blazed a fiery path down my throat. I continued to drink in greedy, grasping swallows. Soon, my body was infused with the 80-proof whiskey, and I began to sway.

That's better.

I smiled and pivoted, coming face to face with Mathias Alastair.

I laughed bitterly.

"Look at you, old man! Look at you! You're pathetic!" I repeatedly stabbed the air in front of Mathias. "You're not real! Leave. I will not rest until I have finished what I started and eradicated every last trace of your legacy. Just like I know you killed my family and sent those fucking Timehunters to kill my children. My family didn't deserve to die. You had no mercy, and the Timehunters you sent to slaughter my children only proves it.

"Every breath I take is filled with burning rage knowing you were responsible for this injustice. I will slaughter your daughter and every single offspring she bears, snuffing out the chance of them ever seeing the light of day. I will track down the sun and moon daggers, unleash nightmares upon this land, and in the end, my victory will be absolute!" I cackled in glee, rubbing my palms together.

Mathias' expression darkened and he shook his head in disbelief. "Oh, Balthazar. You have no idea the power that I hold. Trust me when I say that I will have the last laugh. Despite all I've done for you, all the lessons I taught you, you still view me as the problem?"

His voice cracked like thunder as his anger and sorrow collided in the air. His form dissolved into a fog of pure agony, evaporating in the wind until nothing was left but echoes of misery.

I collapsed against the cabinet in a fit of rage, sending crystal and glass clinking and clattering as they crashed to the ground. I held my head in my hands as thoughts of revenge raced through my mind. I wouldn't stop until I had the sun and moon blades in my hands and Alina kneeling before me. She wouldn't have all that power anymore. I was determined to take what was rightfully mine and start again. With a cry of vengeance, I rose to my feet, determined to start my search.

Those blades would be *mine*.

CHAPTER TWENTY-TWO

ALINA

1785

It had been exactly seven months since I left Balthazar, determined to leave my old life behind and embark on a journey of self-discovery. During these seven months, every step forward was shrouded in uncertainty as I ventured into unfamiliar territory. The passage of time was marked by the constant struggle to maintain a façade with Philip, who seemed to revel in pushing my patience to its limits. These seemingly endless seven months felt like an interminable quest, filled with challenges and revelations at every turn.

I rolled back and forth on the bed I shared with Philip. This place, these furnishings, that *man*—everything was shabby, worn, a neglected shadow of my former life of luxury. If I stayed put in this cabin, I would go mad. I had to *do* something, to set out on my search for the man Malik had insisted held the key to finding the sun and moon daggers—John James.

The object of my pursuit had proved remarkably elusive. The appellation "John James" seemed to shadow my every step, a spectral presence that defied confirmation or refutation. As I searched, I encountered various John James—a butcher, a dashing rogue who brazenly courted me despite my obvious pregnancy, a farmer, and a banker. Yet, the specific individual I sought, the one urged upon me by Malik, remained elusive. Doubts began to stir, making me suspect Malik might have orchestrated this predicament. He knew I was evil—I had spent weeks torturing him…and wanted me to *fail*.

Nonetheless, the most challenging aspect of my expedition was not the pursuit of John James.

It was my growing resentment toward Philip. Even the sound of his voice set me off. It was getting increasingly difficult to play, "Let's pretend you and I are happily in love." An unsettling sensation of deceit gnawed at me, a feeling that he possessed knowledge I lacked. Philip had been unusually quiet and reserved when I asked for his help in finding John James. His eyes held a furrowed brow, deep in thought, as he mulled over my request. I could sense the weight of his silence, like a heavy cloak draped over our conversation. My words were carefully chosen, revealing only the bare minimum of information about the importance of this task. Despite his reassurances of, "We'll locate him, no need to fret," believing him proved difficult in light of the unfavorable course events had taken.

I had been with him for seven months, and nothing had changed except my growing belly, which I'd tricked Philip into thinking was his. I'd known who the father was the second the child was conceived—it was Balthazar's. At every turn, an overpowering sense of isolation enveloped me. Were it not for Philip, I would have faced complete solitude. I had vowed never to place my faith in anyone.

However, something else plagued me—I couldn't help

but feel I was being manipulated by everyone. It was as though I was becoming a pawn in an intricate scheme of deceit on a grander scale. My caution around individuals had been a constant since my departure from Balthazar. Yet, this seemed to resonate as a component of a larger design, a plan orchestrated by some higher force.

It felt like Karma for my sins. The same Karma that had taken my family away from me and that had made me a target of abuse and manipulation. The same Karma that had taken my hope away from me and replaced it with a sense of dread and loneliness. The same Karma that had drawn Zara into my life.

My thoughts kept returning to Malik. Had the bastard set me up?

However intense my suspicions, I remained resolute in pursuing the elusive man and the puzzle fragment that would ultimately grant me absolute power. I was prepared to unearth the sun and the moon daggers and cast darkness across the world, no matter the cost.

This notion propelled me forward, and with unwavering determination, I was committed to emerging from this nightmare, channeling every ounce of energy until I succeeded.

Golden rays of sunlight poured through the bedroom window, illuminating the dust particles dancing in the air. I had been lying here for what felt like hours, lost in thought and reminiscing on my life's journey. The warmth from the sun's embrace was comforting, but also served as a reminder of the time passing me by.

In an abrupt surge of emotion, I whispered, "Balthazar, I love you. Maybe it was a mistake leaving you."

The confession escaped me spontaneously, its authenticity overpowering my hatred. Salty hot tears rolled down my face like lava, burning me with the realization of how far I had sunk. The immense power I sought had driven me to a point of no return, darkness consuming my soul with its inexorable greed.

My stomach seized with such a great and shocking pain that I doubled over. I cried and hugged my belly, which was squeezing down on the baby with such force that I thought I might pass out. When the pain passed, I lay on the bed, panting. Another contraction seized me. Then, another.

This loathsome baby was coming.

Philip entered the room, his eyes wide with concern. Embracing me, he held me close, offering solace as I wept into his chest. He brushed away my tears and murmured, "Everything will be alright. I'll arrange for a midwife to assist us."

"No! No midwife," I said.

"But, sweetheart, you're in pain." A pathetic smile spread across his face. "And while I might prove helpful with the cows or the sheep when they give birth, I'm afraid I'm rather helpless when it comes to a woman."

I glared at him with hate-filled eyes.

Philip didn't seem to notice. He kept insisting that a midwife would be helpful.

The contractions became more and more violent.

"Alright," I said, panting. "Get her."

Philip trudged from the room, a thick blanket of gloom cloaking his every step. The front door creaked open.

"Greetings, Philip." The sound of Philip's name, spoken in a low, menacing tone, made the hairs on my neck stand up.

"How do you know my name?" he stammered.

"I'm a midwife," Zara said. "We're trained to know all that matters about our patients. I came to check on Alina. How is she?"

"She's in labor! Come right in!" His voice was tight with urgency.

Zara entered the room like a gust of deathly air, sending shivers down my spine. She gazed upon Philip with cold indifference before he hastily departed. She then swiveled toward me, her eyes filled with venom and loathing.

"What's wrong with you? Childbirth should be a joyous event." Her voice was sharp and cold. "I never even flinched when I gave birth, whereas you're an absolute wreck."

She towered over me, empowered by my fear.

Terror surged through me as I looked up at her, and I wanted to run away as far as I could. My heart raced with hate for her and the child, wishing they would be cursed for an eternity of suffering in hell.

"Why are you suddenly so quiet? Does your terror of me stifle your throat?"

"What do you want from me?" I cried out in agony as another contraction overtook my body.

"I'm here to save the child," she said. "To ensure that no harm comes to it and that you will never be able to hurt it."

I gritted my teeth, holding back a scream. Sweat poured down my face, and my entire body felt on fire. I clenched and unclenched my fists, my breathing becoming more labored as the pain intensified.

I pushed and pushed, trying to force the baby out as my cries echoed through the room. The darkness seemed to close in around me, and the world was silent.

A scream pierced the air. I opened my eyes. Zara hovered over me. Her expression was one of pure satisfaction as she watched the baby slowly emerge from my body.

I gasped, tears streaming down my face as a sudden wave of relief washed over me. Hours of agony had finally ended, and my baby was here.

Zara held the infant in her arms, her eyes moist with tears. "You're a beautiful little girl. Balthazar always has beautiful girl children. I'll watch over you and keep you safe from your monster of a mother."

She bit the umbilical cord and assisted me in expelling the placenta. Then, she placed the baby in my arms.

"Care for her," she said, with a malicious glint in her eye. "Don't do anything stupid—don't even think of harming her. I'm going to go dispose of this."

She picked up the placenta with her bare hand and held it aloft.

"And then I'll be on my way." She started to turn, then hesitated. Her pointed gaze met mine, reaching inside and seizing my soul. "I'll be watching you."

She was gone, leaving a wake of bloated silence.

I stared detachedly at my child, this infant with whom I felt no connection. She was a beautiful little baby, as far as babies went. Dark blond, wet curls clung to her scalp as she regarded me with her soulful blue eyes. I pictured Balthazar's joy over this baby. He would be ecstatic if he knew. A well-spring of fondness filled my aching heart as I thought of Balthazar. This baby was what he'd begged for. And I'd refused him.

My wickedness was my own secret power, something that I loved and reveled in. Every bad thing I did brought excitement through my veins, and I embraced the pleasure and darkness of it all.

Philip walked into the room, marveling at the tiny newborn cradled in my arms. "She's so beautiful! She's wonderful!"

He reached for her, taking her tenderly in his arms.

As he rocked her, his face shifted to a look of surprise. "What's this?"

He lifted a necklace with a charm that looked like a tiny dagger around her neck. I had never seen it before.

Oh, my god, I gave birth to Balthazar's child, and a necklace appeared; I had no idea where it came from or what it meant. All I could think of was that Balthazar had somehow known I had given birth and had sent me this sign—as a warning.

Philip looked at me, his eyes wide with fear and confusion. "Where did it come from?"

"It was my mother's," I lied, my eyes not meeting his. "I placed it around the baby's neck. My mother would have loved her. God rest her soul."

Philip looked at me, then back at the baby. "But it wasn't there a minute ago when I picked her up. I swear."

"You were probably focused on her beautiful face." I forced myself to gaze at him and smiled.

Philip's frown deepened, but he said nothing.

Fear overwhelmed my senses as I realized I had to leave right away. Balthazar knew where I was, and he would hunt me down. I was sure of it. With the next full moon weeks away, now was the only option. But where could I go?

"What shall we name her?" Philip asked brightly, utterly unaware of my inner turmoil.

"You name her," I said, barely able to keep my facade of composure together.

Philip mulled it before settling on something. "Emily. We'll call her Emily."

He stroked her tiny cheek with his thumb as the two studied one another.

"Perfect," I spat, knowing that this name would haunt me forever.

Several days had passed since Emily's birth, yet I grappled to bring her contentment. Despite my efforts, her unrelenting cries persisted. I carried the weight of understanding that the fault lay with me—I had not desired her arrival, and she seemed to sense it.

The only thing that could keep me from bursting into tears was the thought of finding John James. I had to find him before Balthazar hunted me down. I had to leave Philip and Emily to do it, but every time I tried, something held me back. I packed everything in the barn in a satchel: clothes, belt, knife, and some food—jerky and pemmican. All I required was the bravery to depart.

I held the certainty that if Emily were to one day uncover my identity, her feelings toward me would transform to disgust. She would despise me. With a heavy heart, I acknowledged that it was best for her to never know me. As I made my way toward my bedroom, preparing to dress for the day, this notion weighed heavily upon me.

Philip called out from the kitchen and asked if he should make breakfast for Emily. His voice sounded so hopeful; he wanted nothing more than to make his new daughter smile at least once before the day ended. Each day, he tried everything he knew.

I had to leave—now.

I walked back over to him without a word and hugged him tightly, then kissed Emily on the forehead before whispering, "It's best if you never know," into her ear. Then with tears in my eyes, I left the room.

Philip's and Emily's cheery voices faded as I tiptoed from

the house. I hastened to the barn, grabbed my rucksack, and fled.

I traveled for days, moving from inn to inn, using the small amount of money I'd taken from Philip. I had to get far, far away from Philip and Emily. Philip would be looking for me. When my money ran out, I sold my body for a night of warmth in a soldier's arms, then killed him and stole his paper money, Spanish dollars, and British pounds.

My feet ached as I trudged deeper into the unknown wilderness. I glanced over my shoulder every few steps, jumping at every shadow and rustle of leaves. My heart raced as I imagined Balthazar's menacing figure emerging from behind a tree or galloping toward me on his black stallion. The fear was paralyzing, making me see him in every dark corner and passing shadow.

As I ventured deeper into the unknown, my mind began to play cruel tricks on me. Whispers and cackles filled my ears, taunting me with doubt and fear. The images before me began to twist and distort, morphing into grotesque versions of reality. Despite my efforts to push them away, the voices inside my head grew louder, reminding me of my past mistakes and predicting my inevitable failure.

Native Americans or soldiers would attack anyone who strayed into their territory, or so I had been told. I disregarded their advice, thinking I was a beautiful woman—who would want to hurt me? I could seduce my way out of any situation. Yet, as my fears grew, I wanted to retrace my steps and seek forgiveness back home.

Despite my fear, I took a deep breath and continued my journey. Suddenly, I found myself surrounded by a group of fierce warriors, each decked out in vibrant tribal clothing and sporting intense scowls. I couldn't understand their language and had no weapons to protect myself against their aggressive advances.

"I'll give you what you want," I told the tallest man. I sidled up to him and brushed his smooth jaw with my palm.

He grinned, licking his lips and eying me hungrily, even though we did not share a language. Then, he said something to the others, and they all laughed.

I was dragged through the forest, kicking, and screaming, my heart pounding in my chest, until we reached a small cabin at the top of a hill. I was greeted by another man, a Caucasian, who spoke the same foreign language. His eyes were filled with kindness, and he seemed to understand my plight. The man gestured for me to stay. He said something to the warriors and gave them a bushel of corn, and some animal hides.

They nodded, satisfied, and departed. Relief flooded me. I'd been spared. But then I eyed the man before me—what fate would befall me with him?

"Do you speak English?" he said gently.

"A little," I said, eying the doorway.

"Good. I won't hurt you." He extended his hand.

I viewed his hand through narrowed eyelids. I was filthy, having traveled for days without bathing. My beautiful hair was a snarled mess. Why should I trust this man?

He waved his hand up and down and repeated, "I won't hurt you. I promise. My name is John James."

The floor rushed up to meet me as I lost consciousness, everything going black before I even hit the ground.

CHAPTER TWENTY-THREE

ALINA

I awoke with a start, searching for the source of the sound that had roused me from my slumber. I lay there, trying to orient myself before the noise came again, growing louder and closer until I could recognize it as a voice muttering in English.

A man crouched in the corner, his back turned to me as he fiddled with unusual documents and objects. "Must not have these lying about. Not with the company around. No!" He shoved them into a rucksack, his movements frantic and fumbling.

I sat up and peered over his shoulder at one of the parchments in his hand, reading the words "time travel" in a neat, flowing script.

He's the right John James!

I cleared my throat to get his attention, and he spun around, his eyes wide with surprise.

"I've been looking for you," I said. "If you're trying to hide your documents relating to time travel, don't bother."

John James blinked twice, then sighed, his body relaxing. "What are you doing here?"

"I'm hiding from a man named Balthazar. He's a monster," I said, wincing slightly at the thought of referring to him as something loathsome.

An unmistakable dread shimmered in John James' eyes. Then, the fear vanished, and I questioned if I had imagined it all.

"I need to find the sun and moon daggers. I'm a time traveler," I said.

John James studied me, taking in my words with a newfound understanding. He stood up slowly and stepped toward me, his gaze never leaving my face.

"You're a time traveler?" he said with wonder and skepticism.

"I am," I said, pulling back from his approach.

"Your accent…" He paused, rocking back on his heels, and pointed at me. "You sound like you come from foreign lands. So you've learned some English."

"Yes," I replied, my voice barely more than a whisper. My English is not perfect, but I understand it and can speak some."

I was lying, of course. I'd known rudimentary English when I arrived and learned even more living with Philip. But I still pretended not to understand when it suited me.

"What is your name?"

I hesitated. Philip never knew my name—to him, I was always "Francesca." But it seemed best to tell John James the truth.

"It's Alina."

"A beautiful name! I'm so pleased you're a time traveler! This is wonderful!" John James patted my shoulder. "Don't worry, my child, I will help you. We've been waiting for someone like you. Once you've rested, I will introduce you to Dancing Fire. He's a good man. His tribe are good people."

I whimpered. "No, no! I won't hear of it!"

I was terrified of meeting this stranger, Dancing Fire, and his tribe—especially after being captured.

John James knelt to take my hands in his own. His gaze was steady and comforting. "I won't let anything bad befall you. You're safe here with me. You'll see."

I wanted to believe him. I wanted to trust that I was safe in this strange land, despite all the tales of its violence and danger. I nodded slowly, and John James smiled, squeezing my hands in reassurance.

His gaze hardened with resolution. "But you'll need help finding the blades. Dancing Fire is another time traveler. It's best to work as a pair rather than alone."

Another time traveler? Is he a darkness, too?

I recoiled at the offer. If I'd wanted a partner, I would have chosen Balthazar, the man I loved, not some stranger. No matter who it was, I refused to give an ounce of my power away.

"I would rather go on my own."

"No," John James said, his icy stare sending shivers of dread through me. "You wouldn't. And I wouldn't dream of letting you go alone."

A cold sweat broke out over my body. A million questions raced through my mind about what he knew of the blades that I did not. My body trembled with an illogical fear, once more questioning if Malik had trapped me in a web of deceit.

John James' posture softened, and his face appeared friendly.

"Come now," he said, rising to his feet. "Let's get you something to eat. You'll want to be restored when we meet Dancing Fire and his people."

As he stepped out of the wooden cabin, the hinges let out a low, eerie squeal. I sat on the edge of his bed, anxiously tapping my foot against the creaky floorboards. My heart raced with anticipation as I waited for him to return from the dark outbuilding beyond the trees.

The cabin was sparsely furnished but held several inter-esting artifacts, most of which were unfamiliar to me. The bed I sat on was made up of what appeared to be animal hide stretched tightly between two thick logs, pushed up against one wall. A large, make-shift wooden desk filled a corner, and the top was littered with strange contraptions and odd, myste-rious-looking tools. A thick book leaned against a stack of parchment paper, and a half-empty bottle of dark liquid stood next to a bowl containing what appeared to be medicinal herbs. An old oil lamp with a faintly flickering flame hung from the ceiling, providing a dim light that illuminated the cabin.

I started to get up and snoop around, but John James returned, carrying an armful of food. He deposited these in the middle of a small table shoved against the back wall as if seldom used.

My stomach growled at the sight of salted pork, dried fruits, and some kind of pickled vegetable.

He heaped some of everything onto a tin plate and handed it to me. The scents wafted up from the plate in bursts of flavor, making my mouth water. My stomach growled as I reached for the food, and I wolfed it down with the gusto of a starving dog. I couldn't remember the last time I had a good meal.

John James sat on a hewn log as I ate and asked, "How did you find me? Who told you to look for me?"

He plucked a pickle from the jar and popped it in his mouth.

"There's a man named Malik who told me to find you," I said, with my mouth full.

John James rocked back. "Ah, Malik. How is he? I haven't seen him for quite some time. He came here with Layla, and I told them where to find the daggers you seek."

I paused, unsure of what to say. I couldn't tell him the truth—that Balthazar and I had tortured and poisoned them. I blubbered that Malik and Layla were dead and Balthazar had killed them. I had enough practice at lying to be convincing.

John James' jaw dropped, his lips trembling as he tried to speak. But only a choked sound escaped from his throat. His eyes were wide with disbelief and heartbreak as he turned away, unable to hold back tears.

"Oh, lord! So tragic!" He rubbed his eyes with his thumb and forefinger. "Give me a moment to process this terrible news!"

"Of course." I hung my head and forced a sniffle as John James tromped outside.

When he returned, his eyes were swollen and red.

I folded my hands in my lap and pretended to look sorrowful.

John James shook his fists and stalked back and forth. "You were right to come to me. I loathe this man, Balthazar. We must hasten to the tribe and find Dancing Fire! Then you can be on your way and find the daggers." He looked at me. "Did you...how did you know Balthazar?"

Aching for Balthazar was like a rusted nail stuck in my chest. My body surged with passion and longing like a potent poison flowed through my veins.

"We were together for a while. As lovers. I was a fool!" I shot to my feet. "He tried to kill me many times. I don't know why I stayed with him! You've got to help me find the sun and moon daggers. I must destroy Balthazar once and for all."

"I will help you," John James said, touching my shoulder. "You have my word."

Two hours later, after tromping down the hill and trekking through a dusty, grass-covered plain, we entered a world far from the luxury I had left in my past with Balthazar. Animal hide tents dotted the horizon. People were half-clothed and dirty everywhere I looked—some of them were even barefoot. They looked like they'd sprouted from the earth like Philip's stupid cornstalks.

John James, however, walked with ease among them, greeting them in their own tongue. He led me into a circle of people, the presumed elders of the tribe. In the center of them was a handsome man, tall and proud, with a face that seemed composed of leather and stone.

"Alina," John James said, "this is Dancing Fire. Dancing Fire, this is Alina. She came to me seeking my help."

I stepped before the imposing bronze-skinned male, flustered and ill at ease. As I looked into his shrewd brown eyes, I could feel an unspoken understanding between us, as if he already knew everything about me—including that I was a liar and a fraud.

I took an immediate dislike to him.

"Speak!" he said in a voice that could shatter glass. His English was razor sharp. "Explain why you requested this audience with me."

I shrank back, my heart racing inside my chest. His piercing golden-brown eyes peered at me like a falcon seeking out its prey before diving, talons outstretched.

Trembling, I pointed to John James, who stood near a white-haired woman, engaging in idle conversation. I hated how this Dancing Fire dismantled all my defenses, leaving me weak and afraid.

Dancing Fire continued to stand tall and menacing, glaring at me with contempt.

I swallowed hard. "I…I came to John James to seek help.

I was a dangerous man's lover and am now trying to hide from him. I need two daggers that John James knows about to help protect me from this man."

Keeping his gaze pinned on me, Dancing Fire said, "Don't trifle with me, woman. I've recently lost my two sons, Swift Hawk, and Hunting Wolf. I am in mourning. I only agreed to meet with you because John James is a close friend and ally."

My eyes traced the weathered features of the elders, each one etched with deep lines of sorrow. Even the usually boisterous Dancing Fire had a somber and distant look in his eyes, as if his grief weighed heavily on everyone around him. I shifted uncomfortably, feeling out of place among these grieving faces, like an outsider intruding on their sacred mourning.

In a whisper, I said, "I am a time traveler. John James indicated it wasn't safe to look for the daggers alone. He told me you're a time traveler, too."

Dancing Fire's face hardened into granite, and he slowly shook his head.

Dancing Fire had me in his sights, intent on extinguishing the fragile flame of my life. But I found strength and courage from within.

"I'm sorry your sons are no more. But now's your chance to do something good and help another human being in need."

"No."

My heart sank to my stomach.

His eyes shifted from bright and alert to dull and menacing, paralyzing me with fear. Standing before a powerful enemy who knew all my secrets, I felt more alone than ever.

Shaking the fear from my body, I sashayed toward Dancing Fire, my hips rolling seductively.

"I can help comfort you in your time of need," I said, letting my finger trail across his smooth, warm chest.

He snatched my hand, strong enough to crush the bones in my wrist. I screamed in pain as I tried to jerk away, but he held me tight and refused to let go. His grip was relentless and sent a chill of terror through me.

"I don't trust you," he hissed, his eyes as black as midnight. "You wear the face of an angel, but there is something vicious about your character. Pretty looks but sinister intentions."

He flung my hand away in disgust.

Rage bubbled up within me. I held back, my teeth gritted with temper and fear.

"Me? You think I have sinister intentions?" The words dripped from my mouth like poison. "I'm a good person. I've saved people!"

The inferno of his eyes burned into mine.

"You'll never fool me," he said with an icy voice. "I can sense a liar."

A chill sank down my spine as I realized his power over me. If he ever found out my dark ways, he could easily kill me in the blink of an eye. I had to find those blasted daggers, which meant I had to be on his good side.

"Balthazar is real, and he's hunting me. He could easily destroy us both," I said, hoping to instill fear in him.

Instead, he chuckled.

"You really think to make me afraid? You're more of a fool than I thought. I know who Balthazar is and the evil he's capable of." His features transformed into something unreadable, impassive. "I will help you. But not for the reasons you imagine. I have no interest in protecting you from Balthazar."

His words prickled, awakening a chasm of fear. I wished

I'd never come here to face Zara and Dancing Fire. I was in uncharted territory now.

John James lumbered toward us, interrupting my fearful thoughts.

"I see you two are getting along nicely." He beamed.

Dancing Fire and I eyed each other warily, the tension thickening with every passing second. Even as John James carried on his conversation, Dancing Fire's gaze bore into me as if to determine my motives for being there.

I barely tracked John James' commentary; I was too focused on Dancing Fire.

But when James said, "According to my connections, you are to look in England in the 1400s to find the daggers," I took notice.

"The 1400s?" I said, dragging my gaze away from Dancing Fire. Relief flooded my body as the connection between us was severed.

"Yes, yes," John James said, nodding.

Dancing Fire's eyes met mine again, and a sharp, discordant wave of electricity surged between us, sealing an unspoken promise. We both knew we would be on our way to England when the next full moon rose in the night sky. Our fate had been sealed.

As we trudged through the streets of 15th-century England, Dancing Fire's frustration radiated off him in waves. We had been searching for the elusive daggers for three long years and still had nothing to show. We exhausted every possible source of information—libraries, scholars, even commoners on the street—yet our quest remained fruitless. It didn't help that Dancing Fire was seen as an outsider, shunned by the locals and unable to gain their trust. I couldn't help but feel that his presence was hindering our progress.

Dancing Fire's piercing stare held me captive, never allowing me a moment of respite. He would often furrow his brow and narrow his eyes, as if scrutinizing my every move. His constant questioning made me feel like I was under suspicion, even though I had done nothing wrong. He seemed determined to make sure that I was not conspiring with anyone else. Every passing day, my animosity toward him festered, fueled by the burning question of why he believed he had the right to dictate my every action. My head throbbed with anger, consumed by thoughts of his suffocating hold on me and the seething disgust I felt toward him.

All I could focus on was the urge to rip his head from his neck, fueled by an uncontrollable fury that boiled up within me.

I started suffering from crippling hallucinations. Every time I would turn a corner or walk down an alley, I could see Balthazar's silhouette lurking in the shadows, only to discover someone else leering at me maliciously. Balthazar's visage tortured me, waking me up from nightmares in a cold sweat and sending me to bed each night with dread.

For years, I tried desperately to gain sympathy from Dancing Fire, spinning tales of woe that I had concocted.

"My adopted family was slaughtered by Balthazar before my eyes—it was terrible!"

But no matter what I said, he never believed me.

"Don't you see my scars? I was tortured and beaten when I found out I was pregnant, and someone cut open my stomach!"

"Why are you telling me these ridiculous stories?" he said. "I honestly don't care about you or your wretched life."

Finally, after three horrid, fruitless years, I'd had enough. I sat in a tavern across from Dancing Fire and stared into my ale.

"I think we need to go back and get more information from John James," I said coldly.

"And why do you think that?" He stared at me from across a great chasm, his eyes as dead as our search for the daggers.

"Because," I said slowly, digging my fingernails into the worn wood. "We haven't found anything. Or haven't you noticed?"

I tried to match his cold gaze.

He scoffed and looked away. "And you think I'm to blame, no doubt."

"Of course, you're to blame! No one wants to talk to you!" I flung my hands about. "You put off this unapproachable energy like you're ready to slit someone's throat."

He leveled me with a sinister gaze. "Yours perhaps."

I wanted to run away but held my ground. My blood boiled in frustration as thoughts of John James came flooding back.

"John James promised us that we would find the blades here! How could I have been so gullible? He lied to me! Everyone always lies!" I let out an exasperated growl. "And we must defeat Balthazar! All we've met here are dead ends."

I drained my mug, letting the warm ale soothe my temper.

"Are you done with this little display?" Dancing Fire sneered, gesturing wildly between us.

"Stop patronizing me! I'm sick of it!" I slammed my stein on the table.

"I'm through playing your games," Dancing Fire said, his voice echoing off the walls.

The few patrons sitting in the tavern turned to stare at us, eyes wide.

"Keep your voice down," I hissed.

"Or what?" he snarled.

"Or…Or…I don't know." Exhaustion seized my limbs, and I wanted to rest my head on the table and sleep. But we had to forge on. "We need to return to John James. I don't like being lied to."

With a sigh, Dancing Fire rose, tossed a few coins on the table, and walked away.

"Wait!" I scrambled to my feet and rushed after him. "Where are you going?"

Dancing Fire glanced over his shoulder at me. "Back to see John James, like you said. The full moon is happening right now."

We time-traveled back to John James' era during a heat wave. Sweat poured down my body as I slogged up the hill to his dwelling. When his cabin came into view, John James sat outside on a stump beneath a tree, fanning himself with a parchment. He blinked in surprise to see us.

I was too tired to storm toward him, shouting accusations. Instead, I said, tiredly, "We didn't find the daggers. You lied."

He pulled himself up and said, "I certainly did not lie. I gave you an answer based on what my sources told me."

"Well, they lied, then. Lies, lies, lies… That's all I get are lies." I flopped down in the dust next to him.

John James and Dancing Fire exchanged a look.

"I never guaranteed you'd find the daggers. I only said that was a good place to look based on what my sources said…" John James looked at me pointedly. "What if I told you where to go next for answers?"

"You'd probably tell me to go to hell," I said. "Believe me, I already live there."

John James scoffed. "I'm serious."

I glanced at him, eyes narrowed, my head tilted. "I'm listening."

He leaned forward, his forearms resting on his thighs. An undeniable spark of excitement danced in his eyes. "I've come across some fresh information since you've been away. You're going to want to hear this. It's about my twin brother, Jack. He's the key to all of this."

I regarded him skeptically, the seed of suspicion still lingering. "Why should I go looking for Jack James?"

A triumphant smile played on his lips. "Because he holds the answers you've been seeking. He's immersed himself in the future, specifically in 1988. He's become an expert in time travel."

I squinted, trying to process the information. "Is there anything else you're not telling me?"

John James raised his hands in a half-shrug. "Well, there's one more thing. Something that might tip the scales for you. We're both Timebounds if that means anything to you."

Heat surged through me, making me feel like I could combust. "Wait, hold on. You and your brother are both Timebounds? What is that? And why was this never mentioned earlier?"

CHAPTER TWENTY-FOUR

ALINA

My mind struggled to make sense of John James' words as he spoke beneath the shelter of an oak tree. Timebounds? Connect with his brother in the future? I had many questions, yet he seemed to be expecting something else from me—a sign of understanding I couldn't give.

His gaze shifted between my face and the ground. He seemed evasive.

"What is a Timebound? What do you mean?" I asked. "And why are you here and your brother there?"

I waved my hand toward the horizon, indicating the future.

John James nodded, his face a mask of determination. "My brother and I were born in this century, separated as little children. When you are a Time*bound*, you can only time travel with the help of a Time*borne*. Babies can time travel. Even infants can be transported to other times and places with the help of a Timeborne. It's a rather magical relationship."

He cast a gaze in my direction, anticipation evident in his eyes. The inquiries were apparent, a silent plea to discern my belief in his words, to ascertain if the enigma of the narrative held me as it had him. Before I could formulate a reply, he pressed on.

"During the initial weeks of our lives, my brother and I were transported to disparate eras. The details of his vanishing—where, why, and by what means—remained shrouded in mystery."

The heat, or maybe his words, grew too intense for me to bear. Parched, I wiped my sweaty face with the sleeve of my dress.

"I need some water." I swayed where I stood.

John James bolted to his feet and gestured for me to sit on the stump. "Of course. I'll be right back."

I slumped to the hard log, practically melting on contact. I glared at Dancing Fire.

He should have told me this. I'm certain that he knows.

That same damn stony, impassive expression of his met my glare. Inwardly, I growled. Doing a face-off with Dancing Fire would get me nowhere. Besides, it was too hot.

I turned my thoughts to Emily. Had the little necklace charm been a key of sorts? Did it appear around her neck as an exclamation of her arrival on earth as a Timebound?

My thoughts were interrupted by John James's slow clomp as he labored in our direction, bearing two jars of water. He handed one to Dancing Fire and one to me.

"Thank you," I said out of forced politeness.

I poured some water down my parched throat. It was too warm and had a wood taste, probably scooped from a barrel. It did nothing to quench my thirst.

"Let me show you how Timebound travel works," John James said, proffering his hand. "Let me see your dagger."

I eyed him suspiciously before retrieving my dagger from my waistband.

"Here," I said curtly. I glanced at Dancing Fire, still staring at me like he was a statue. "You knew about this, didn't you?"

He shrugged a shoulder.

I shot to my feet. "Why didn't you tell me about it?"

"We don't exactly talk, now, do we?" Dancing Fire took a couple of steps and leaned against the trunk of a gnarled oak tree. He tipped his head up and drained the jar, making a satisfied "Ahh" when finished.

I growled and gritted my teeth.

John James' gaze bounced between us before settling on my knife.

"Watch, Alina." He grasped the hilt of my dagger and gave a gentle tug. Opening it revealed a hollow space with a sort of keyhole. "The necklace charm fits in here. For the necklace to activate, the Timebound must draw blood from their hand and place it on the pendant. After that, they must insert the charm. Once done, the time traveler will cut their hand and speak the ancient words aloud to travel. Both parties will travel together."

I gazed at him, struggling to comprehend his words. Perhaps I was just not ready to accept them.

"We were brought here—my brother and I—when we were three. I stayed here." John James' gaze flitted to the dirt at his feet, to the tree where Dancing Fire stood, to the distant horizon. He never met my gaze. "All I know is that we have the same face and are passionate about time travel. There are many resources in the future."

"How do you know this?" I squinted at him. "Have you been to the future?"

"I have connections."

"Is there anything else I need to know?" I swiped at my

face again. Sweat was pouring from my skin in steady rivulets, and I didn't like it.

John James glanced over his shoulder as if a ghost hovered nearby.

"Just that if a Timeborne dies," he said in a near-whisper, "the Timebound is stuck there."

"What?" I said, my brow furrowing.

John James raised his voice and waved his hand in an agitated gesture.

"You must have more important things to do than keep questioning me," he said. "You need to move on and head to 1988."

He started to turn, but I grabbed his arm.

"Wait! Why 1988?"

"That's where my brother is. Based on my calculations, it has to be true."

"Based on your calculations?" I spat; gaze locked with his. "You want me to head to the future based on some theory? What if you're wrong like you were about 1400?"

"You'll just have to trust me, won't you? What alternative do you have?"

My mind reeled with shock and confusion. John James had sent us on a wild goose chase to the 1400s, yet he expected me to trust him now?

"Do you even know if your brother knows you exist?"

John James shook his head. "I highly doubt it. We were three years old when we separated, after all."

"Then why do you remember things that he doesn't?"

John James glared at me with intense anger.

"Alina, enough with the questions. Listen to me and head straight to Canada. That's where he is, last I heard." His face softened, and he added, "Look, Alina, I'm your friend, and I'm only trying to help you."

"If you were truly my friend, you would tell me *everything*!" I snarled.

"If I told you *everything*, I wouldn't live much longer...I'd be dead." He paused before saying, "I'm your last thread of hope, Alina. Your last thread."

He lumbered away, leaving me in a wake of chilling mystery.

But he was right. I had to follow the threads wherever they led.

On the next full moon, Dancing Fire and I catapulted through time and found ourselves in the land of the bizarre. Vancouver, BC, 1988 was overwhelmingly strange and chaotic at first. Metal machines zipped across smooth roads or flew overhead. Everywhere we looked, it seemed impossible to make sense of it all. People in all manners of dress and undress scurried about. A cacophony of nonsensical noises invaded our hearing, and the smell of unknown fragrances and odors assaulted my senses.

Amid all this chaos, one thing was certain: this was not the world we had left. It was a world without darkness, where the lights never went out, and something called "technology" ruled the land.

Armed with the knowledge of time travel and adaptation, we took to the streets, blending in with the crowd and trying to decipher what was happening. Even though we could comprehend the words, we didn't understand the meaning when people spoke.

As I grew accustomed to the culture of Vancouver, BC, and its nuances, however, I became more outgoing. Life here, for women, at least, seemed freer than the restrictive, male-dominated cultures I'd experienced so far. Women could have multiple partners. No partners. Issues like Continued Advocacy for Gender Equality, Reproductive Rights, and awareness about domestic violence, sexual assault, and harassment were topics of conversation. I wholeheartedly embraced these issues, becoming an advocate.

Dancing Fire, or Moon Lee as he requested to be called in this era, seemed to pull into himself.

"Come on, Lee," I told him one afternoon as we wandered along the Burrard Inlet in Emerald Cove Beach. It was a warm day, and I'd dressed in hot-pink leggings, a neon-green mini skirt, and a slouchy black tank top. The beauty of the park enveloped me like a warm hug.

I was captivated by tall fir trees that stretched toward the sky, their tops swaying in the breeze. The air smelled of cedar and pine, and the occasional salty sea air from the nearby ocean delighted me. The paths were lined with wildflowers, leading us through a verdant forest toward the beach. I paused to admire purple lupines, vibrant yellow dandelions, and delicate white daisies.

"Come on, what?" he said in a sulky voice.

"Admit it—you like the freedoms women take in this era." I spread my arms and twirled in a circle.

He afforded me a grunt but said nothing.

"Surely you're not ashamed. Life is like that song, Express Yourself—the one that singer Madonna wrote. 'Don't go for second best, baby,'" I sang. "'Put your love to the test.'"

Lee gave another grunt.

"It's live and let live, baby," I said, resuming our walk. "Women are equals here. We're not relegated to the kitchen."

"When were you ever 'relegated to the kitchen?'" he asked. "You've lived a privileged life of your own design."

"Under the thumb of a control freak." I frowned, thinking of Balthazar. I plucked the petals from a flower and set them free to flutter away in the wind.

"Yeah," Lee said, giving me a sidelong glance.

I stiffened as anger coursed through me like boiling water from a kettle. I turned to face Lee, my lips tight, my good mood fluttering away like those flower petals. "Yeah, what?"

All I could hear was our breaths mixing together in the silence.

He sneered. "That's the thing. I can't tell if you want to end Balthazar or ride him hard and put him away wet. I hear you yelling 'I love you, Balthazar,' at night when you writhe in your bed like he's on top of you."

"Stop spying on me," I snapped.

"It's kinda hard given that cracker box of an apartment we're staying at."

"What? You're the one who vetoed me selling my body for cash." I huffed.

"You're right. You could get *arrested*. Thrown in jail. Women's rights haven't gone *that* far." He stalked along the path, heading toward the sand.

I hurried to catch up to him. "Get a better job, then!"

"I'm at least working. What do you do all day?"

I scoffed. "You load trucks full of produce all day."

"And get paid *cash* under the table. We're not exactly legitimate citizens with driver's licenses and social security cards, are we?" He glared at me. "You just flit around town."

"I'm not just flitting," I shot back. "I'm looking for Jack James like we're supposed to be doing. That's our one goal."

The tension between us popped and crackled.

I sighed. "Can't we at least be friends after all this time? Allies? Or get along?"

"I doubt it. I don't trust you or your motives. Not when you whimper for Balthazar in the night. He's a demon, or have you forgotten?" Lee's jaw set into a granite block.

I sighed again. "You don't get it. When you're a darkness, you have a different kind of love. There are all these intense cravings. They're difficult to control. I vow here and now that I will hunt down Balthazar and tear him to pieces for his wickedness. My every breath will be dedicated to finding the blades to rid the world of this malevolent force, once and for all."

"Whatever," Lee said, veering to trek across the sand toward the road. "Let's get something to eat. I have enough cash in my pocket for a couple of sandwiches."

As we stepped on the sidewalk, a flyer on a telephone pole caught my eye.

Enroll today at McMont College. Exciting programs for all.

Lee turned to see what I was staring at. "You should enroll. You might learn something useful."

I couldn't tell if he was baiting me with sarcasm, so I let it go.

"I'm serious, Alina. Your English is much better. Your Italian accent is fading."

I side-eyed Lee. "I've been practicing how to blend in. People look at me strangely when I lapse into Italian. They judge me. I'm trying to talk like a normal citizen of North America."

"And you're doing great. I barely notice the accent anymore."

Is he being nice to me?

I tore the flyer from the phone pole. "Do you really think I could do it? I don't know what to take."

I stared at the paper with a Xeroxed photo of a college campus and several smiling students.

Lee snatched the flyer out of my hands and scanned it. "There's a campus not far from here. We can get something to eat along the way, and you can talk to someone there."

Could I really do it? The thought sent an adrenaline thrill through my body, igniting a fire in my chest that refused to be extinguished. *Yes, I can and will do it. I must.* With grim determination, I declared, "Let's go, we have to see what this place offers."

We arrived at McMont College, the intimidating facade looming over us with its grandeur and prestige. Who said a demon couldn't strive for greatness? But there I stood, brimming with fierce determination and ready to shatter every stereotype. Little did I anticipate the daunting obstacles that would threaten to crush me into submission.

CHAPTER TWENTY-FIVE
ALINA

When Lee and I sauntered through the doors of the Office of Enrollment at McMont College, we were struck by a putrid combination of smells: the stench of over-brewed coffee, the musty odors of paper and ink, and a biting tang of printer toner. I leaned my forearms against the smooth white counter.

The woman behind the desk glowered at me, her glasses perched atop her nose like a hawk. She rapped her knuckles against the "personal computer" she had before her. "What do you need?"

Her nameplate read Sonia Collinsworth. The woman's frail frame was draped in loosely hanging clothes, revealing the delicate lines of her bones. Her eyes held a quiet sadness. Despite her stoic demeanor, it was clear that she had spent her life fading into the background and now approached her inevitable obscurity with a sense of resignation.

I smiled at her and feigned courteousness. "I'm new to the area and hoping to enroll. Is that possible?"

A spark of annoyance flashed in her eyes. She rose from her desk and crossed to the counter.

"What are you interested in taking?" She reached beneath the counter and retrieved a college catalog. She flipped through the pages. "We have courses in Arts and Humanities, like literature, history, philosophy, languages, and visual arts. The Sciences include biology, chemistry, physics, mathematics, and computer science. Social Sciences include psychology, sociology, economics, political science, anthropology…"

"Archeology," I said. "I like to dabble in the past."

Lee snorted.

Mrs. Collinsworth frowned at him, and then her gaze returned to me. She thumbed through the catalog and tapped one of the pages. "An archeology degree, like the one we offer, is taken in different levels, starting with a bachelor's degree. If you're serious about it, you'll want to advance to a master's degree or even a Ph.D. You'll want to start by enrolling in an anthropology bachelor's degree program."

As I peered at the course content, Mrs. Collinsworth said, "Your coursework will cover archaeological methods, cultural anthropology, archaeological theory, ancient civilizations, and more. It's an exciting program."

"Uh-huh," I said, still skimming the page. "I'm uniquely familiar with past civilizations. Is there a way to shorten the course? You know—hurry it along?"

"You'd have to discuss that with your professor, dear. I have no idea." She scanned my face like she was trying to figure me out. "You might consider gaining fieldwork experience through internships, volunteer opportunities, or summer excavations."

"Oh, yes! I'd like that very much!"

"Someone is lecturing on something related to the past in Jacobson Hall. Room 14. That's out this door, across the green space, and enter the building on the right. Why don't you go have a listen, and, if you like it, come back?" A tight smile formed on her face and disappeared. "We can get started on paperwork."

Lee and I exchanged a glance.

I shrugged. We had nothing else to do, so I thanked Mrs. Collinsworth and left the Enrollment Office.

Inside Jacobson Hall, we trekked down the white-speckled tile toward Room 14. When we rounded the corner, voices emerged through the open doorway.

I paused, clutching Lee's sleeve. "Do you hear that?"

"What? I hear many things," he said, shaking free of my grip.

I pointed toward the open door, where taunts, jeers, and defensive explanations emerged. "That voice sounds like John James. What if it's him? What if that's his brother?"

Lee cocked his head and listened. Then, he rushed toward the door.

I scurried after him.

We both huddled just outside the door, listening.

"Mr. James," a male voice said, "what have you been smoking?"

Laughter rang out.

"My research is sound," said the man who sounded like John James. "At the solar eclipse, there's a moment of utter darkness. If a child were to be born at that moment, the baby would be born with a dagger. That dagger would enable the child to time travel."

"Oh really, dude?" another male shouted. "Darkness? Daggers? Dude! No fucking way."

The audience roared with laughter.

"It's him, Lee. I know it is," I hissed. "That's Jack James."

He wiggled free of my grip. "Okay, so make your move.

Rush in and tell him you're here to discuss time travel and find out where the sun and moon daggers are."

"Right." I rolled my eyes. "That won't arouse suspicion, will it?"

"I was being sarcastic," Lee said. "Of course, I don't expect you to do that."

Jack said something about how physics proves his theory, but I barely listened. I was trying to formulate a plan.

A series of boos and hisses rang out.

I turned to Lee. "I almost feel sorry for him."

Lee scoffed. "You? Feeling sorry for someone? I sincerely doubt that."

"Come on. He's a…What do they call it?" I snapped my fingers. "He's a *nerd*. Nerds are super smart. He's being targeted for his intelligence. I know what that's like."

An expression of derision flashed across Lee's face. "You've never been targeted for your intelligence. More like your predilection for evil."

I chuckled.

A man sped out of the room.

I jumped back. "That's him! Let's catch him."

My feet pounded against the tile as I tried to catch up with the mysterious man. I lunged toward him and grasped his arm. Fear flashed across his face.

"No need to be scared," I said softly, attempting to put him at ease. "What's your name?"

His lips curled in revulsion. "Everyone here knows my name. It's Jack James. The weirdo who talks about time travel."

Trying to appear fearless yet seductive, I lowered my eyelids and formed a secretive smile. I could tell this guy was a challenge...but maybe that was part of the fun. "I don't think you're weird. I'm fascinated by time travel."

He squinted at me. "You're just messing with me."

"I'm not. Truly, I'm not." I touched his arm. "I'm new here. I'm interested in archeology. Are you a student here, too? Maybe you could tell me what courses to take since we share the same fascinations."

He cocked his head to the side and studied me. "How do you know what *fascinations* I have?"

"I just heard you speak. I could hear the passion in your voice." I swept my hand across my collarbone like an invitation.

His gaze dropped to the tops of my breasts, which peeked out the tank top. Then, his gaze zipped to my eyes like he'd lapsed in sin. "Yes, I'm a student here. A grad student."

"What courses do you take?"

He rattled off names like Anthropology Advances and The History of Ancient Civilizations. He looked up, startled by the commotion in the hall, as his classmates spilled from the door of Room 14. Without another word, he spun on his heel and sprinted away.

I turned to Lee, who leaned against the hall wall. "Let's go get me enrolled."

Two of his courses were held in huge auditoriums. I slipped into those classes as if I belonged there and sought him out to sit near or beside him. I conversed with him over the coming weeks whenever possible. He was a tough nut to crack, always suspicious of those around him. He would be friendly and chatty when he wasn't scanning the room for eavesdroppers. But when someone happened to glance his way, his whole body tensed, and he would take off like a shot.

After a couple of weeks of this, I grew discouraged. I didn't come all this way to be repeatedly rebuffed.

My classes were over for the day, and I clomped up the stairs to Lee's and my apartment. The building had seen better days, with its peeling paint, dusty hallways, and creaky staircases. Inside, the walls of our apartment were painted white and grimy with age, and the ceilings were low. The gray sofa was frayed but comfortable, and the coffee table was an old trunk we'd purchased at a thrift store. But at least there weren't gaps in the walls that let in the wind and dampness, like at Philip's cabin.

I dropped my textbooks on the sofa and flopped next to them, leaning on the back of the couch. I was not making much progress in getting to know Jack James, which was frustrating. He was too cagey…too evasive…too scared. His eyes were sunken deep into their sockets, dark circles sparking fear in anyone who met his gaze. His gaunt frame looked like it had been put through a wringer of torture and strain, his mind unraveling from the long days and nights of torment. He resembled a mad scientist, with all the students giving him a wide berth due to his unhinged look. They taunted him relentlessly, daring him to snap and unleash whatever demons he had locked within.

How could I get close to him?

When Lee arrived home, I was still sitting in the same place I'd sat for the last hour, trying to devise a scheme to get to know Jack better.

"What do you look so sour about?" Lee said, his arms full of groceries. He strode toward our tiny kitchen, which had a single window overlooking the city below and counters lined with mismatched dishes and utensils.

I watched him unpack horrible items like "Mac and Cheese" and "Spaghetti-Os." But we were living on Lee's paltry income, lucky to eat at all.

"I can't seem to get close to Jack. He's like this weird little rat who skitters away at the slightest provocation."

Jack scoffed. "And your master skills at seduction aren't working?"

"No," I said, glowering at him. "What if we were to get a dorm room? Or could I get a dorm room? You know, I could be more available to him on campus."

"Absolutely not. Not if I'm paying." Lee slammed a can of coffee on the countertop.

"You know what I can do for money, right?" I fluttered my eyelashes at him.

"Fuck, Alina." He tossed a bag of noodles in a cupboard. "Do what you want, but do you really want to end up in jail? I won't bail you out. Let's get that clear. You land in jail for prostitution, and you're staying there, got it?"

"Okay, okay, okay. I got it. Selling my body for sex is a no-go." I sighed and pouted. "So, what can I do?"

"Don't ask me. You're a clever woman. You figure it out." He folded up the paper bags and shoved them in a cupboard. Then, he reached into the fridge for a cold beer. He twisted off the top and took a long swig. "Anything else?"

I shook my head at him.

"Good. I'll be in my room."

After he left, I headed out the door, intending to go to the library and do some research. When I arrived, I wound my way through the stacks of the McMont College library. A muffled sound caught my attention as I scanned the shelves for books on ancient civilizations. It was a quiet sob that seemed to be coming from behind one of the bookcases. Was someone crying in the library? I had to investigate. Carefully, I made my way to the darker corners of the library, where the sunlight rarely penetrated.

A figure sat huddled in a chair draped in shadows, his head bowed low, and his face hidden from view. He was muttering to himself, the desperation making his voice tremble.

"I can't take this anymore. Where are you? You promised me you'd come back, but it's been forever. I'm all alone here, and I need you."

Who is he talking to?

I searched around him for any sign of another soul.

"This is getting harder every day," he said. "Everyone ridicules me when discussing time travel, but I'll keep trying until you notice me. You're the only one that matters to me in this world. Please, come back to me."

I tensed, uncertain whether to speak or retreat. Finally, I found my voice.

"Jack?" I whispered. "Is that you?"

His body jolted with shock as his eyes snapped up to me. He scoured the area for an avenue of escape, but impenetrable walls of darkness seemed to close in on him from every direction.

"What are you doing here?" I asked.

"Hiding," he said quietly. "I just needed a place to be alone."

My heart wrenched at the sight of him, so small and help-less. My mind raced with a hundred ideas of how to take advantage of this vulnerable moment. Could I exploit his naivety and use him for my own gain? I had to know. I had to get close to him.

"Who were you talking to?" I took a step closer.

He stiffened.

"I know what it's like to leave everyone and everything behind," I said, inching forward.

He narrowed his eyes.

"Everything and everyone I ever loved betrayed me.

That's why I'm here. I'm searching for answers." I took one more small step in his direction.

He bolted from his chair, pushed past me, and sprinted away.

I sighed, settling into the warm seat he'd just abandoned, and I propped my head in my hands. My curiosity about Jack was insatiable, and the mission to find the sun and moon daggers took a momentary backseat to my desire for knowledge.

My pulse quickened with anticipation as I imagined uncovering his secrets, which he might have kept hidden for centuries.

I must know more.

CHAPTER TWENTY-SIX
ALINA

A s the days went on, I followed Jack James around, hanging back until he noticed me or wondered how I had managed to find him in the throng.

"This man is the weakest man I've ever met," I muttered as I watched him from across the cafeteria. He ate alone, as usual, head ducked, trying to appear as small as possible. "I'll bet he's still a virgin. He lives in his head. And look at his hair! It's flying everywhere, disheveled and wild, making him look crazy."

Yet, I knew if I wanted to gain the knowledge and locate the treasured sun and moon daggers, this strange man was my only hope, no matter how crazy he seemed. His extensive understanding of time travel was like a key to unlocking unlimited possibilities.

I "ran into" Jack outside the bookstore one day. He looked worse than usual, his clothes in shambles and his hair more disheveled than ever.

"Jack," I said, "you don't look so good. What's going on?"

"I'd rather not talk about it," he said, getting ready to bolt.

I reached for his arm, and he jumped from my touch.

"Tell me what's wrong." I looked into his hauntingly desperate eyes.

His hands trembled as he tugged at his hair like a tornado had taken over his body. Without so much a word in response, he made his way across the campus with a frenzied urgency. Eventually, he stopped at a park and sank on a metal bench. His movements were charged with electricity as he jittered and quaked.

"What is it, Jack?" I said, genuinely concerned. "What has you in such a twist?"

He let out a groan. "Today's the day I present my research culminating from all the years of sweat and blood I've given to the topic of time travel."

"That's wonderful!" I said.

"Is it?" he said, his expression bleak. "I hope it will be well-received. I hope this will be the launch into the prestige and recognition I've longed for. I long to be one of the most respected in science—not my geeky thirty-two-year-old self who lives on Top Ramen and Chinese take-out because he's too distracted to prepare a meal."

I listened, not wanting to interrupt his train of thought.

"For years, I've had headlines appear before my eyes, stating things like 'Jack James proposes Brilliant New Concept on Time Travel.'" He swept his hand before his face. "But… I was supposed to give my dissertation in room 15B, the cozy room I've been practicing in. Only it's unavailable. Instead, I'll be speaking in the auditorium."

He let out an anguished groan.

I held back a chuckle, unable to believe he was fretting over a venue change. "What's wrong with that?"

"The auditorium is just…well, too big." He rocked on his seat. "Listen. I know time travel is possible—my entire life has been devoted to the topic. Yet, I'm worried that my mind will become a void. All thoughts, words, and carefully-constructed phrases will be sucked into the web of deep space."

This man on whom my fate rested was just so… *weak*. He was a pathetic example of a human being. But it behooved me to be *nice* to him.

I pulled any inkling of sympathy into my mind and touched his shoulder. "I'm sure your dissertation will be a success.'"

He looked at me, really looked, as if seeing me for the first time. "You're just saying that. I shouldn't have said anything."

And then, like always, he was gone.

I went to my Anthro 101 class, lost in thought about Jack James. Professor Jones stood before us at the end of class and said loudly, "Everyone! I have an announcement to make. At 4:30 P.M. in the Jacobson Hall auditorium, a grad student, Jack James, will present his dissertation on time travel." His body shook with mirth, his face red with the effort to contain it. "Go check it out if you want a good laugh. Class dismissed!"

This was my chance to interact with others and find out more about Jack.

"That Jack James," Rick Marshall said in the hallway. "What a loser."

"I can't believe he thinks his theories are true," his girl-friend, Monique, said. "Want to have a listen? I could use a good laugh."

She hooked her hand around his elbow and led him out of the building.

I wandered along behind them, heading for Jacobson Hall.

When I got there, I took a seat in the back.

Jack was already onstage, pacing back and forth. He paused occasionally, staring out at the audience as if looking into a black hole that he wanted to crawl into and disappear through time and space.

Several fellow students shuffled into the room and sat in the back, snickering. I took a seat in the corner. The rest of the audience consisted of professors, scientists, and diplomats, staring blankly at him.

Dr. Tim Wong, the department chair, sat with a grim demeanor and beard like an angry Billy goat. His eyes darted to his watch before sliding to the exit in the back of the room, catching my gaze. I stared him down fiercely, challenging him to utter one word of ridicule against Jack James.

I shifted my attention to Jack. Onstage, he was whispering something, almost as if he was pleading with himself or desperate to remember the right words so nothing would be left unsaid.

Finally, he stood solemnly before the podium.

"In 1905," he began, "Albert Einstein proposed the theory of special relativity. This theory suggests that photons can travel through space at a constant pace of three hundred thousand kilometers per second. Not only is this speed difficult to achieve, but it's also impossible to surpass. Yet, across space, particles are accelerating."

"We all know the theory of special relativity, Mr. James," Professor Rubenfield, a woman who looked more like a football player than an instructor, said.

"Right, right," Jack said, sweat pouring down his face in rivulets. "Understood. But I'm leading up to my theory."

"Well, get on with it then," Professor Rubenfield said with a dismissive wave of her hand.

Dr. Wong glanced at his watch again.

Jack cleared his throat. "In 1915, Einstein proposed the theory of general relativity, where gravity curves space and time, and time slows or speeds relative to how fast you move. This process is known as special relativistic time dilation." He rushed through the long sentence, then smiled at Professor Rubenfield, adding, "I know you know this, too. Bear with me."

Professor Rubenfield's lips flattened.

Dr. Wong snorted.

Several of my classmates snickered.

This was so painful to watch that even I wanted to flee.

"So, given these two theories, I've also been studying solar eclipses," Jack said. A stain of wetness spread beneath his armpits.

The voice of the woman who sat beside Professor Rubenfield cut through the auditorium like a razor.

"Wait, I'm confused," she spat out, each word dripping with contempt. Her thick glasses amplified the intensity of her gaze as she peered at Jack with suspicion, her eyes boring into him like nails. "So, now you've jumped from Einstein to solar eclipses?"

Jack swallowed hard, tugging at his collar. His mouth opened, but before he could respond, the woman leaned forward and jabbed a finger in his direction. "You better get your facts straight before wasting our time with this nonsense."

"Give me a chance to explain!" Jack said, his face red with anticipation. "The legend of Eclipsarum Obscura: The Celestial Convergence has been handed down through time. Surely you've heard of it."

"That's nothing but a bullshit myth," someone called.

"But it's not!" Jack cried, dabbing at his sweaty face with a handkerchief. He dropped it on the podium and then continued. "Eclipsarum Obscura is a cosmic phenomenon that occurs when two mighty black holes collide in the distant reaches of the universe. As these celestial titans converge, a mesmerizing celestial dance ensues, releasing powerful waves of energy that warp the fabric of space and time.

"During this extraordinary event, a unique celestial alignment opens a temporal rift that grants individuals born under its influence the extraordinary ability to traverse through time. Babies born during Eclipsarum Obscura are believed to be chosen by the cosmic forces, marked with a celestial birthright that links them to the temporal currents unleashed by the collision of the black holes."

Several people laughed. "This is preposterous!"

Jack swallowed and continued, "These gifted individuals, known as Timeborne, grow up with a profound connection to the ebb and flow of time. As they mature, they discover their latent ability to manipulate temporal threads, allowing them to navigate through different eras and witness the unfolding of history."

His words carried a weighty promise, and his gaze was feverish with excitement.

"That's fucking bullshit, dude," Rick said, bolting to his feet. He grabbed his girlfriend's arm and stormed from the room.

A few others exited, too.

Jack's voice quivered. "Eclipsarum Obscura only happens occasionally, and people worldwide wait for and wish to see how the sun and moon join. But imagine if a child, a small infant, was born during the solar eclipse when these two black holes collide. That child would have the ability to time travel. But…!" He lifted his finger. "There's a catch. The collision of the black holes also creates an unintentional catalyst for the release of malevolent forces. As the black holes merge and the celestial energies surge, a dark and ancient entity known as the Umbrum Void is inadvertently awakened from its eons-long slumber."

By now, the room was nearly empty.

"The Umbrum Void, a force of pure darkness and malevolence, feeds on the chaos and disruption caused by the collision of the black holes. It seizes the opportunity to exploit the destabilized fabric of the universe, slipping through the rifts in space and infiltrating various realms. The cosmic shockwaves created by the Celestial Convergence act as a gateway, allowing the Umbrum Void to permeate the universe, corrupting the very essence of existence. At the birth of a Timeborne, beings of pure darkness are unleashed into the world. It's up to the Timeborne to destroy and cleanse the world from the evil that was born with it."

The room grew quiet.

Dr. Wong studied his watch.

Professor Rubenfield whispered to the woman next to her.

Jack plucked his handkerchief from the podium and dabbed at his damp brow before continuing. "Many different nations and cultures believe in this idea and wait for a Timeborne to appear and show everyone that time travel truly exists and is possible. The Native Americans believe that their ancestors witnessed Timebornes and the ensuing evil many years ago. The Mayans and Incas witnessed the birth of a child during that critical moment when the Eclipsarum Obscura occurred. The child born during this event can time travel during each full moon." He wiped sweat from his neck and brow with a trembling hand. His voice dropped to a whisper. "One last thing. There are two daggers—the sun and the moon daggers."

Mesmerized, I shot forward in my seat. My heart pounded in my chest like an echo in an empty chamber.

His voice was steady as he said, "The city of Ugarit was thrown into chaos during the first solar eclipse when two razor-sharp blades emerged from the darkness. These blades can pierce through time and grasp onto events, twisting them around in a powerful vortex that could rewrite history. If evil forces were to seize control of these daggers, the world would be engulfed in chaos, and anyone with the power to wield the sun and moon daggers would be able to manipulate time. The world would be thrust into pure evil if the daggers got into the wrong hands."

The few remaining audience members sat in stillness, considering his words.

Then, someone said, "What a crock of drivel, man. You've got some nerve putting forth all your so-called 'theories.'"

A few people next to him agreed.

Jack's expression fell. With a shaky breath, he rested his palms on the podium. "Thank you all for your time and listening to my time-traveling theory on the solar eclipse."

No one cheered or applauded. Instead, Jack was met with blank or disbelieving stares.

I glanced toward the exit, wondering if I should leave. But how would that look to Jack James? I couldn't afford to cast a wedge between us.

Dr. Wong shifted in his seat. "Mr. James, I have to say you sure have a wild imagination. Light and dark, good versus evil. What happens after the Timebornes time travel? Do they fly and have superpowers?"

"No, professor, they don't have magic powers. They are regular humans like you and me," Jack stuttered.

"So, where is your proof?" Professor Rubenstein asked.

"I don't have proof, professor, but I have vital research

that time travel could exist. Someone could time travel if they were born during the solar eclipse."

"You need proof, Mr. James," Professor Rubenstein stated. "How can the department board award you with a Ph.D. if you have no actual physical proof of a Timeborne? When someone develops a theory, they must have two things: strong evidence behind their theory and physical proof that their theory is real and legitimate."

"So, you're asking me to bring you proof or evidence of a Timeborne?" The words slid out of his mouth like gravel, squeaking with the desperation of an adolescent schoolboy.

The crowd erupted in loud guffaws that echoed off the walls, piercing the air and masking all other sounds.

"That's exactly what we're asking, Mr. James," Dr. Wong said. "Explaining is one thing, but validation is essential for securing your Ph.D. But today, you just made a laughingstock of yourself."

"Time travel is possible," Jack said. "I know it for sure, and if you just listen to me, you'll understand, too!"

He flung his arm across the podium, scattering his notes and charts on the floor. Then he spun on his heel and sprinted off the stage.

"Wait! Where are you going?" I yelped, leaping to my feet. I charged down the aisle, ramming through people trying to leave.

When I reached the backstage area, Jack was nowhere to be seen.

CHAPTER TWENTY-SEVEN

ALINA

My heart raced as I hurtled down the barren hallway, desperate to escape the auditorium's murkiness. Unstoppable momentum drove me out into the blinding daylight.

Jack powered toward the clock tower ahead. With one final effort, I pumped my legs faster and lunged forward, following in his wake.

What's he doing? He doesn't want to kill himself, does he?

My stomach twisted at the thought of what he was about to do. Was he really going to do it? He was so weak, so helpless, yet I had to save him.

He vanished into the clock tower as I charged across the vibrant green lawn. My heart pounded with a sense of urgent anticipation. Even though rescuing people was far beyond my capabilities, I had to try to save him. I needed those sun and moon daggers.

I skittered beneath the stone archway. *There. The stairs!*

My feet pounded against the ancient stones of the clock tower as I bounded up the spiraling steps, desperate to find Jack. Sweat poured down my face and dripped onto the stairs.

I took the steps two at a time until I reached the top, where I collapsed against one of the pillars, gasping for air. My chest heaving, I braced my hands on my knees and searched for any sign of Jack.

He stood, one foot braced against the windowsill as if to climb out.

Unaware of my presence, he muttered, "I've never been accepted. That Carlton Smith, the chubby moron who made me his target all through sixth grade, reveling in the humiliation of watching me struggle with sports he found so easy. Then, Amanda Ray from high school, her voice dripping with disdain when her friend asked if she was taking me to prom. 'Jack James?' She spat out before breaking into a cruel laughter. 'No way. He's like a brain in a jar or something. I'm going with Dylan, the quarterback. Muscles are much more attractive.'"

He stared out the window at the ground below, his entire body quivering.

His voice shook with indignation as he continued. "Jeremiah Schmidt, my high school philosophy instructor, used to humiliate me. 'Mr. James,' he said one day, a mocking smirk on his face and an open invitation to join in the laughter of his students. 'If you can't keep your head out of the clouds with all these ridiculous fantasies on time travel, why don't you transfer to a course that teaches science fiction? This class is for more serious topics suitable for the brilliant minds here.' I've been made fun of and humiliated my entire life. No one has ever had faith in me or given me support. I'm the biggest failure alive."

With a fire burning in my belly, I wanted to scream out at Jack, *Man up! Stop cowering under the perception of others and take responsibility for your life!*

Anger and contempt coursed through my veins as I

listened to Jack complaining about stupid things. All I could think about was Balthazar—his strength, courage, and spirit —a real man who never needed to grovel like this. But my mission remained clear, and it steeled my resolve even if I wanted nothing more than to hurl *myself* out the window.

"Jack," I said softly.

His head whipped around. "You again! What do you want? Why are you here?"

I took a tentative step forward.

Jack dropped his foot over the windowsill. One leg out. Another leg to go. Then, he could simply push off and die.

"I felt the truth of your dissertation," I said, my voice tight. "You dared to present a taboo subject like time travel, and I admire you for it."

The muscles in his face hardened, and he threw his other leg through the window. His lower limbs hung out of the window defiantly, defying me to move an inch closer.

"Think about it, Jack. The skeptics are idiots, like those who believed the world was flat. You and I—we're not like that. We're forward thinkers." I took another step closer.

His gaze darted out the window.

My words hung on my tongue like lead weights as I tried to coax him into loving me, wanting me. Once I had what I desired so desperately—information about the daggers—then I could kill him.

"Your time travel theory is amazing. It's just the kind of thing I needed to hear. I've lived my whole life wishing I knew someone who shared my beliefs."

Jack's face twisted into bewilderment. "You really believe me? That time travel is possible?"

"Of course I do!" I said as I held out my arms. "C'mon, let's go. Grab your stuff, and we'll head to my apartment."

My words seemed to spark something in his gaze.

"I have a roommate who loves time traveling just as much as me," I said. "His name is Moon Lee...or just Lee for short. Let's go meet him and discuss this further, alright?"

I stepped forward, my voice filling with anticipation. "What do you say?"

"Someone actually believes in me," Jack said, staring out the window as if surprised to be sitting on a windowsill, about to fall to his doom. He scrambled backward right as I lunged forward, catching him before he fell to the hard, stone floor.

I helped him right himself and brushed off his clothes. "There. You did it. You made the right choice. It's really okay that you have detractors. A lot of people don't like me, too."

Jack blushed. "I find that hard to believe."

A bitter laugh left my throat.

"Oh, you'd be surprised," I held out my hand. "So, are you ready to come to my place?"

Shyly, he took my hand. "Yes. I'd like that very much."

When we climbed the steps to my apartment, it was a warm, sunny day, but it felt strangely cool inside. Jack stood in the doorway, looking a bit disoriented.

"Come in, come in, don't be shy," I said, practically pushing him through the door.

He stumbled inside as if unused to having legs.

Lee exited the bedroom at the sound of all the ruckus and began chatting with Jack, sizing him up.

Lee must have decided that Jack was alright because his demeanor shifted. He began to talk more openly about his heritage—the stories of his Native-American ancestors, the long history of his people, and the values he still held close to his heart.

Jack seemed to be genuinely interested and asked him questions.

I stood in place awkwardly, unused to being ignored. As I was about to interrupt them, Lee said, "You and your brother look so much alike."

Jack looked taken aback. "I didn't have a brother. I'm an only child."

"Oh, wait—I was talking about someone else," Lee said, quickly correcting his mistake.

I glared at Lee, who, of course, ignored me.

"I'm going to go out and get some food," I said. "Do you want to come, Jack?"

"No, thank you. I'm enjoying my conversation with Lee," he said. His smile, which I'd never seen, made him almost handsome.

"Suit yourself," I said dismissively before departing.

When I stepped onto the sidewalk, a man hobbled toward me. He was a slight man, around fifty or so, wearing round spectacles. He looked like a scholar who belonged in a classroom or poring over ancient old tomes. His face was nondescript and utterly unremarkable.

I was about to move around him when he blocked my path.

"Excuse me," I said, taken aback. "You're in my way."

The man looked up at me with a strange intensity, and the hairs on the back of my neck stood on end. His eyes were black and emotionless, and the rest of his face was shadowed beneath a hood.

"I know about you," he said in a low, raspy voice. "I've never met you face-to-face before, but I know who you are."

I stood on the sidewalk, frozen with fear and confusion.

"Did Zara send you?" I asked, my voice shaking.

The hooded figure didn't answer right away. Finally, he spoke in a deep, gravelly voice that sent a chill down my spine. "I don't know anyone named Zara; I just wanted to thank you personally for saving Jack today. Jack is very important to me, and I want to make sure that you won't hurt him, betray him, or kill him. Because if you ever hurt him or betray him, I will personally destroy you. Do I make myself clear?"

I nodded, unable to speak.

The man stepped forward, his eyes burning and intense. He pointed a finger at me.

"Remember," he said. "This is your one chance. Don't fail."

"You don't know me," I stuttered, my voice tight with terror. "I would never kill Jack."

The man gave me a long, appraising look, his dark eyes boring into mine. My heart raced, and I took an involuntary step backward.

"I know exactly who you are," he said finally. His voice was deep and quiet, like distant thunder. "I've watched you for a long time. You're a vicious little serpent. But I can still kill you."

"Kill me?" I sputtered, a laugh rising in my throat. "You're hobbling. You look old and frail."

"Appearances can be deceiving. Your thirst for the power of the blades is unquenchable and you have lied to all who have crossed your path. But I know your darkest secrets. And if you make one false move, I will snuff out your life in an instant. You only saved Jack for your own motives. But Jack James is very precious to me." The man's lips twisted in a cruel smile. "Don't underestimate me or my power. I made you a Timeborne and I have the power to easily take it away from you."

He stepped forward. A searing pain ripped through my chest. I gasped and fell to my knees, clutching my heart.

"Now," he said softly, "do not make the same mistake twice. If you harm Jack, I will make sure you suffer."

I stumbled back. Warmth radiated from my chest, as if he had branded his warning into my soul. My blood surged through my veins in a crescendo of strength and resolve.

"You have no idea who Balthazar is, do you? He's my lover. He is not one to be toyed with, and if I commanded it, he could reduce you to ashes instantly!" My words hung heavy as I stared him down, daring him to contradict me.

A mirthless laugh left his lips.

"Oh, Alina," he spat with contempt. "You used Balthazar's naivete to your advantage. You kept him in the dark while you poisoned his mind against Malik. Then you turned on him and sought the power of the blades for yourself. Your lies are pitiful. I can see right through them."

Each word was a hammer pounding nails into my broken heart.

He sneered. "Cross me, and I will unleash Balthazar upon you in a cataclysm of searing tortures that will rip the breath from your lungs. You are playing a fatal game with forces beyond your darkest imaginings, and I will not spare a single mercy if you attempt to defy me."

Icy fingers clawed up my spine. I was skirting a dangerous line between choices. One false move, and everything would unravel before me.

The man vanished before my eyes. I stumbled back inside the apartment, shaken to the core.

Jack and Lee sat on the sofa, drinking beer, and laughing. But then Lee noticed me shivering like a frightened mouse.

His eyes bore into mine, the intensity of his gaze jolting me to attention.

He furrowed his brow. "Where's the damn food?"

I struggled to steady myself, my voice barely above a whisper as I stammered, "It's too hot to go shopping."

Jack's eyes sparkled with excitement. "Come on, girl, grab a beer and join us. We're having a wonderful conversation."

"Thanks, I think I will," I murmured as I stumbled toward the kitchen.

Against the counter, I gasped for air, my heart pounding. The power emanating from that man was like nothing I had ever encountered. It was suffocating and terrifying. My hands shook as I wondered who he really was and what he could do.

The fear that gripped me went beyond rational thought. I wanted to run away and never look back. But I had to get it together and pretend to be normal.

I took a deep breath, squared my shoulders, and opened the fridge. I grabbed a beer, twisted off the top, and took a long swallow. As the buzz of alcohol hit me, I felt more in control.

I headed back toward the front room and perched on the arm of the sofa. "Tell me about yourself, Jack. Who's your family?"

Jack's voice dropped to a whisper. "I'm an orphan. No family, no friends. But I've always been passionate about time travel and sun and moon daggers."

"What do you know about the daggers?" I said, intrigued at the thought of unlocking their secrets.

His eyes lit up with a strange fervor, and his expression shifted to something almost fanatical. His eyes blazed with excitement.

"The power the first ever eclipse contained was so strong

that one giant sword blade split into two," he said, his hands moving in a flurry of motion to illustrate his point. "It is a reminder that anything is possible—whether good or pure evil—and can never be predicted."

He frowned and disappeared behind a veil of thoughts. When he refocused on us, he said, "The blades are said to have been created in the ancient city of Ugarit."

"Ugarit?" I repeated.

"The city was destroyed when the blades were created, but that could only be a myth. I've read a lot of books about time travel, talked to scholars, and done my research." His eyes met mine, and he gazed at me dreamily.

I smiled and said nothing.

Lee glanced at me, then at Jack, and said, "Jack, will you excuse us for a moment? I need to discuss something with my roommate."

Jack looked puzzled, then shrugged. "Sure thing. This beer is getting to me anyway. Where's your bathroom?"

As Jack wobbled to the bathroom, Lee hissed, "Jack's a really nice guy. He's growing sweet on you. If you value your life, keep everything on the lowdown. Don't you dare mess with him. I won't stand for you harming him."

I bristled, remembering the menacing warning of the terrifying man outside. "What does that mean? I understand what I must do."

"Do you, now?" Lee said. "I still can't help but question that."

"Please, stop doubting me," I hissed.

"Listen, Alina," he said, his voice hoarse with urgency. "We don't know if there are Timehunters here—you've got to act normal. Pretend as if your life depends on it. Don't tell Jack anything. Don't let anyone learn about us!"

I clenched my fists, anger boiling. "I know that! Play the part, act like a good little student. I've got it!"

My blood ran cold. Could that man outside have been a Timehunter? No. He was far more powerful than that. But, then, who was he?

What was he?

Draining my beer in one gulp, I stormed into the kitchen, and tossed the bottle in the trash. I stopped cold when I glanced out the window. A chill of dread rippled down my spine as I gazed upon him. The sinister hooded man stood outside the complex, staring up at the window from the ground below.

Just waiting.

CHAPTER TWENTY-EIGHT

BALTHAZAR

I had been looking for Alina for years, and my hope was fading. I encountered dead ends everywhere I went. It was as if she had vanished into thin air. Nothing made sense anymore, and my life felt like a void.

My only consolation was the thought of the happy times I'd had with my children before they had been taken from me by the Timehunters. It was a long time ago, but the memories had been as vivid as yesterday. But even that was becoming increasingly distant, and I felt like I was losing myself in pursuing my revenge.

I had been searching frenetically, barely sleeping, only stopping to drink. I killed constantly, leaving a wake of destruction. I had almost forgotten what it felt to be truly happy before all this had happened, and I ached to rebuild it all—but I feared it was too late.

I stumbled home under the heavy blanket of night, inebriated and consumed with thoughts of a past that I could never reclaim. My estate was vast, yet it felt like a tomb. There was no one to share it with.

My footsteps stopped when I caught a familiar glimpse of

a ghost-like figure in the corner of my eye. I was too drunk to react quickly, and the figure slowly materialized into the form of a woman—Zara.

My throat constricted, and I couldn't bring myself to look at her face. I could only glance in her direction. This must be a fever dream. But she looked so *real*.

"Balthazar…sweetheart, you look miserable," she said.

"I am," I said through a sob. I reached for the half-empty decanter of bourbon sitting on a walnut cabinet and took a long swig. "My life is empty. Nothing but a void."

I weaved side to side, unsteady on my feet. I planted my hand on the wall to keep from falling.

"Listen to me. I'm speaking to a ghost. A ghost! Ha! What a fool I am." Drool spilled from my lips, and I wiped it off with the back of my hand.

"You miss what we had together. I do, too. I know you think about the children," Zara said gently.

I waved my hands through the air. "Their silken tresses sparkling like gold in the sun… Their smiles… Their laughter… The way they ran to me when I returned from a raid."

A foolish smile spread across my face.

"Yet you've never gone back." Zara's voice felt like a caress upon my weary brow.

"True," I choked out, my voice barely a whisper. I swayed where I stood, trying to process what was happening. In a desperate attempt to make sense of the situation, I said out loud, "Maybe I can save them. Maybe if I go back, they were never killed. I'll reclaim my family, and all will be okay."

But I knew, even as the words left my lips, that it was a futile dream. As I turned to Zara, the words died on my tongue. Her sad smile and gentle touch on my back reminded me of the life I had lost and could never regain, her otherworldly presence adding to the weight of this realization.

"If only it were that easy, my love," she said.

Then, like the ghost that she was, she disappeared.

A cry of anguish ripped from my throat, and the bottle slipped from my hand. It shattered on the floor, spraying shards of glass everywhere and drenching my rug with bourbon. I fell to my knees, despair clawing at me like a demon, overwhelming my senses.

"Zara! Oh, Zara!" I dropped my head in my hands and wept, crying my way into a dark pit of oblivion.

When I awoke, it was the witching hour, the time when the world was still, and darkness began to give way to light. Outside, the full moon shone through the window, high in the sky, beckoning me. I pushed to my feet and staggered outside, bleary-eyed and still swimming with the drink.

There was nothing left for me here. Nothing. The only thing that could save me was starting over, returning to the past to reset my life to its former glory.

I'd done this so many times that I'd grown accustomed to the sensation of my body slowly fading away. It started as a subtle shimmering at the edge of my vision, like ripples on a pond. The edges of my body began to blur until I was completely transparent, like a ghostly apparition made of shimmering light. Even through my drunken haze, I could still feel the grass beneath my feet and the wind on my skin. But it was as if I had become a part of the air itself, a memory in the sky. The air around me crackled with energy, and then, I was gone. I had traveled back in time.

I arrived in my former Viking settlement in the tenth century, coming to awareness in a mud puddle.

Christ, I thought as I dragged myself from the sodden mess. Offal, pitched from someone's window, and animal waste clung to my fine wool coat. I removed the coat and flung it away from me. My hair was a tangled mess, and my clothes were sodden from the mud. My heart raced with excitement and nerves.

I blinked at the landscape before me, the bright-blue sky, the salty breeze, and the vastness of the sea, all of it painfully familiar. I stood at the edge of the settlement I knew so well, where wooden huts were scattered, some with thatched roofs and others with simple wooden shutters.

I slunk past the huts, keeping to the shadows. Someone's clean clothing hung in a small courtyard near their door. I snagged a pair of trousers and a linen tunic and donned them, pitching my wet, stinking clothes in the street. Then I began my trek through town.

The morning spread its light over the fjord, giving me a sense of hope, even in my unkempt state. It was impossible to deny that this was a familiar place, even though it had been many centuries since I had been here. The air smelled of salt and smoke, and the bright seagulls called out in the distance, piercing the peaceful silence. The sun glinted merrily off the crests of the waves, and people moved about with a rhythm that seemed quintessentially Viking.

Everywhere I looked, people hurried around, and children ran and played. The town smells were just as I remembered. The settlement was bustling with activity, people tending to their crops, hammering swords into shape, fishing in the nearby bay, rowing out to explore the open sea. A sense of community prevailed everywhere, a small world with its traditions, beliefs, and secrets.

I felt a strange sense of belonging here, a connection with my past. Distant memories ripped through my heart, pushing through the walls I had erected over time. I had been happy here, truly happy.

My heart skipped a beat when I spotted Zara, the woman I had loved so long ago. She walked toward me with a determined stride, looking as beautiful as ever. I tried to run toward her, to take her in my arms again, but as I tried to move my feet forward, it felt like they were glued to the ground. I was aware of the air passing through my body and the sensation of my hands reaching out. Still, somehow, I was unable to interact with the living world around me.

As Zara drew closer, I was filled with nostalgia and regret for all the years we had spent apart. I wanted to apologize for my mistakes, to tell her how much I had missed her and how sorry I was for leaving her. But when I opened my mouth, no words came out, and all I could do was stand there like a ghost, silently observing her from the sidelines.

A hale young man jogged down the street, a child on his shoulders, three more laughing by his side. When he caught up to Zara, he slid his arm around her waist and kissed her cheek. The child—Freya—reached out her arms for Zara, and Zara took her from the man's—from *my* shoulders.

That's me! And those are my children!

My heart felt like it would burst with pain. It surged around me in an invisible wave, carrying the echoes of the past that haunted my every step. I saw them as though they were right before me, yet when I reached out to touch them, they remained just out of reach.

I tried to say something to Zara, but she didn't hear me. She was engaged in a conversation with the other Balthazar, and I felt like I was intruding on some private moment, even though I had been part of it once in a different timeline. A pang of regret seared through me that I hadn't gone back before it was too late. A life once lived could never be altered. Now I was being denied the opportunity to share in the joy that was surrounding me.

Too much time had passed, and I was no longer the person I had been. I wanted to take the children in my arms and hug them, but I knew the moment would never come. I was stuck in some hell realm now, and the past was only a memory that held me back from achieving whatever it was that I wanted.

My heart yearned to touch Zara. I wanted to say something meaningful that would make her understand how much I still cared for her, but the words wouldn't come. Instead, all I could do was turn away, knowing that I had left my heart forever with her in this place I'd once lived.

I shook my fists at the heavens with an ear-splitting roar of pain. My cry echoed as I cursed any god who would hear me. "Let me at least feel my babies' embrace. Let me wrap my arms around them to soothe their cries! Let me kiss my wife's lips and feel her warmth just one last time!"

But no one heard me. No one responded. There were moments of joy and connection everywhere I looked, and I felt a deep ache in the pit of my stomach. I wanted to run over, scoop my children up in my arms, and tell them all I wanted was to be a part of that life again, but that would never happen. Instead, my family and the other Balthazar, the me that was no more, walked right through me, trampling my dreams to the ground.

Rage built inside me, a fury that reminded me of the past I wanted to forget. I had to turn away, had to focus on something else, or I risked exploding in anger. I stumbled into the closest bar, desperate for some form of distraction. The barkeep—someone I didn't recognize—raised his eyebrows in surprise, probably thinking it was too early to drink. He could see me—a *stranger* could see me.

Of course. The people I long to see me cannot, yet this simple man can interact with me.

I ordered a drink, then another, and then another. Maybe if I drank enough, the pain and the memories would just disappear. But no matter how much I drank, I could not escape the truth: I was not the same man I used to be. I was a wretch. And I could not make the pain stop.

Finally, the barkeep said, "Sorry, man, but you've had enough. It's barely noon. I think you need to go somewhere and sleep it off."

Rough hands seized my tunic and hauled me off the stool. I was guided to the door and shoved outside, where I stumbled and fell.

Ragnar and Thorstein, my old friends, sashayed past me, oblivious to my presence. Their faces looked as haggard as mine, and they staggered a little.

"Hello, old friends!" I called out, lifting my hand in greeting.

Ragnar paused, his brow furrowed. "Did you hear something?"

Thorstein propped his hands on his hips. "Like what?"

"I don't know. I thought I heard a voice I recognized," Ragnar said.

Thorstein cuffed him on the ear. "You're probably hearing your wife's shrill nag. She'll tan your hide for being out all night."

Ragnar thrust his hips a few times, with his hands poised like they were clutching a woman's ass. "I know how to make her forget."

They both laughed and sauntered away.

I dragged myself to my feet and stumbled toward my home, where I'd experienced so much joy. It was exactly as I remembered—a cozy longhouse built by my own hands. Smoke coiled from the chimney. Stacked wood lay neatly beneath the shed roof. Goats and sheep grazed contentedly on the hillside. I pictured them all inside—that other Balthazar and my family. I slumped on top of a smooth stone. I wept, dropping my head in my hands.

The day my life had changed roared into my mind. All the details spilled around me in vivid detail. Holding my children's dead bodies. The sea of blood. The flames that consumed my life. And I'd blamed Zara for everything.

Gentle waves lapped against the shore near where I sat. The faint bleating of goats could be heard in the distance, a reminder of my former life that I had once taken for granted. The sound carried on the wind, a melancholic melody that tugged at my heartstrings and brought back memories of simpler times. Memories of chasing after mischievous kids and milking the herd with my family flooded my mind, making me long for those carefree days once again. But now, as I stood alone in this unfamiliar place, all I could do was listen to the echoes of my past.

A gentle hand rested on my arm, and I opened my eyes. To my surprise, Zara's ghost stood next to me, her smile shining like a beacon of hope. And miraculously, she could see me, just like I could see her.

The sun shone brightly behind her, lending an angelic halo to her demonic form.

"I know you miss them," she said, her voice soft yet strong.

My heart filled with remorse. "I just wish I didn't screw up. I should never have pushed you away. I assumed everything without appreciating its value. In the blink of an eye, everything was taken from me."

Zara nodded, her warm eyes understanding.

"It's alright," she said, and I knew she was speaking to me and her heart. "We all make mistakes. Just remember that you are never truly alone."

Tears flooded my face. "You're the only one for me. Darkness with Darkness. We were destined to be together."

"You should never have gone running after Alina," she said. "We did things right. Our cruelty was justified, but we followed the rules. I'm shocked that you continued to pursue Alina, after you constantly telling me that Mathias, her father, killed our children. Why be with the enemy's daughter?"

An icy chill permeated through my body as she spoke. My hands shook. If I dared touch her, my fingers would slide right through her form.

A lump formed in my throat as I whispered, "I miss you. Your wisdom, your love, and everything about you. But you're a ghost…"

"I'm as real as you," she replied with conviction. "I'm only a few steps away."

Her gaze was piercing, and her words cut through the air like a hot knife.

My heart thumped painfully in my chest.

"Balthazar, my love, we can have it all back if you get the blades from Alina. Don't you want to save our family and be together again?" Her eyes begged me for a response.

"Yes, Zara," I replied with a pained whisper. "More than anything I want our girls back and us together again."

She nodded. "You must go to 1990 and find her at McMont College. You will find the blades there and you will find Alina. Balthazar, put aside the drinking and focus your mind on this mission—get the blades and bring our daughters back."

I tried not to listen, my thoughts hazy with the fog of alcohol, but her words penetrated me like daggers.

"You're a ghost, Zara. You aren't real! How can I believe you? It will all be a goose chase yielding nothing."

She stared at me, fire burning in her eyes. "I'm tired of

you not believing me. Your daughters would be disappointed. I'm disappointed in you."

My heart stopped as she turned away and disappeared, leaving nothing but a wake of frozen silence. A frigid sensation ran down my spine. I was terrified that this ghost wouldn't leave me alone.

I stayed in the same place all day, unable to tear myself away. I watched the other Balthazar play with his children and hug Zara. I stared as Zara tended to the children while gardening. When the other Balthazar danced with Freya, Revna, Tove, Meya, and Astrid, I held out my hands. I waltzed in a circle, pretending it was me dancing with my children. I imagined them laughing with me, not *him*, as I made funny faces and told them tales of distant lands.

This was torture. What would I do next? Would I go to 1990 as the ghost of Zara had advised? Or would I stay and torture myself, endlessly watching the ghosts of my past as they frolicked and loved one another?

The answer was obvious. Staying here would only bring me continued pain. If I cast myself into the future, I might have a chance at revenge.

That night, snowflakes fell with a soft whisper, blanketing the small longhouse in a calm silence. My family huddled inside their home, and it was a night of rest. But for me, this night was far from peaceful.

I stood at the fjord's banks, looking up at the sky with a wistful gaze. My mind drifted back to the day my beloved family had been taken away from me. I thought of my children, their precious faces fading from my memories. I thought of my wife, her loving embrace fading from my heart.

And yet, I still found myself standing in the same spot on

this night of the gibbous moon. I thought of what could have been, what might have been, if only I had acted differently.

A strange commotion sounded in the distance, and a vision unfolded before me. I squinted, focusing on the small group of cloaked figures moving purposefully through the snow.

The Timehunters. I witnessed that fateful night. They descended upon my home with brightly burning torches. They held their torches to the longhouse, which burst into flames. Children's voices wailed in terror.

My children. The Timehunters were burning my loves to charred ash, and I stood there helpless to save them.

Zara and that other Balthazar arrived home, terror in their eyes. The other Balthazar drove his dagger into one of the marauders.

A shiver traveled along my back as one of the Time-hunters burst from the house carrying a limp body. He moved quickly as if trying to escape. His eyes glinted with an unfathomable cruelty, and my stomach churned. Seeing the other Balthazar, he extended the limp body like a prize. It was Tove.

Tears flooded down my face like a torrential rain of despair, feeling helpless and impotent against the evil in front of me.

Another man appeared out of nowhere. He seemed slight, a nondescript sort of man wearing glasses, too frail to be a Timehunter. He looked like he belonged behind a podium in front of a group of academics. He didn't participate in the mayhem. Instead, he crept away from the burning wreckage.

I followed the figure, determined to find out where he was going. He disappeared into a snowbank, and a faint cry for help issued from beneath the blanket of white. The bespectacled man plowed through the snowbank and uncovered the face of little Freya.

Freya whimpered and clung to the bespectacled man as he hurried away with her.

"My Freya!" I wailed. "She lived through the attack!"

All this time, I'd thought her dead. My only evidence was her little shoe wedged in a snowbank. I looked up at the night sky and thanked the stars for delivering Freya from her attackers. Freya, who had been taken that fateful night during the full moon, was my only surviving child.

The man holding her paused as if sensing me. He turned, and our eyes locked. His steely gaze penetrated me like a shard of ice, sending shockwaves of dread up my spine. He was no ordinary man. An air of cunning and mystery surrounded him. I couldn't move, rooted to the spot as he disappeared from my sight.

The entire scene vanished, leaving me standing in the stillness of night, with snowflakes drifting all around.

A tiny glimmer of hope burned in my chest—my Freya was alive! Who had saved her? Where was she now? My daughters were gone, and my family ripped apart. I had to bring them back together, no matter the cost. Zara had told me that the daggers could do just that. With a burning desire to reclaim what was taken from me, I would stop at nothing to get those blades, even if it meant hunting down Alina and ending her life to earn them. How foolish had I been for indulging in passion with my enemy's daughter? But now there was no more room for weakness, only rage-fueled vengeance.

I was coming for Alina and no force on this earth could stand in my way of reclaiming my family and destroying Mathias' legacy forever.

CHAPTER TWENTY-NINE

BALTHAZAR

When I arrived in 1990, I hated this place. I hated the people, the time period, the zipping, whirling machines catapulting across roads, and how it all felt so removed from who I was.

I was wandering around, getting accustomed to my surroundings, when I came upon the university Alina supposedly attended. McMont College. And there she was—my wretched Alina. I stopped in my tracks. Two young males fawned over her, carrying her textbooks and books, while she walked with a regal presence.

As I approached her, a sharp pain shot through my chest. I gasped for air and my knees buckled. I was dying. I could feel my life force leaving my body.

I looked around in desperation. People passed by without noticing my predicament, and a swell of panic rose in my chest. I could feel my strength slipping away and couldn't understand why. I'd killed enough people recently to be invincible. Why was I collapsing now?

Alina walked away toward the edge of the campus, and I attempted to call out to her. Instead of words, only a weak moan escaped my lips, and she didn't seem to notice. My vision blurred, and a burning sensation grew in my chest, like a physical manifestation of despair.

A looming male stood before me, casting a long and eerie silhouette in the dim light. He was exceptionally tall and had a rather gaunt, almost skeletal appearance, with limbs that seemed disproportionately long and thin. His face bore a feral expression, etched with an unsettling intensity that sent shivers down my spine. His gray eyes, like storm clouds on a cold morning, pierced through me, locking onto my very soul.

As he advanced closer, every step deliberate and measured, an overwhelming sense of dread enveloped me. My legs quivered, and my breathing became rapid, the sound echoing in my ears like a drumbeat of fear. Despite the instinct to flee, something inexplicable compelled me to remain rooted in place, as if I were caught in the grip of an invisible force, paralyzed by the power emanating from this enigmatic and foreboding figure.

I closed my eyes, feeling completely helpless. When I opened them, the man continued to watch me. A smirk crept across his face, and with a satisfied swagger, he strode away, leaving behind a trail of proud arrogance.

The pain continued, and I clutched my stomach, writhing in pain.

A young woman rushed to my aid. "Can I call an ambulance? Do you need CPR? Maybe you're choking."

I pushed away her attempts with a menacing snarl. "Get out of my way! I don't need your help!"

She stood tall, unflinching in the face of my wrath.

"You aren't going to hurt me," she said, determined.

Rage boiled within me, threatening to explode. Without

warning, I let her glimpse my true self, the beast that lurked beneath the surface, ready to consume all it encountered.

Her eyes widened with terror as she backed away slowly. "I mean you no harm, sir."

"Don't call me *sir*!"

Her head whipped around, her gaze landing on a park across the street. "Let me help you to that bench over there."

How odd that she showed me kindness. I'd just showed her my true self. But I was in too much agony to protest. Clutching her extended hand, I rose and hobbled toward the grassy green park, where I crumpled on the wooden bench.

"Water! I need water," I wheezed.

She reached into the roomy bag by her side and produced a too-bright pink-and-purple container with a slender, hollow tube protruding from its top.

"Here." She thrust the container at me.

I recoiled. "What's this?"

She laughed. "It's a water bottle, silly. It's got water inside."

I took it, holding it gingerly. Unlike the glass, metal, and ceramic containers of the past, it possessed a remarkable lightness and flexibility. Forgetting my pain, I gently squeezed the bottle. It gave an impression of fragility, though it was surprisingly resilient. It felt smooth to the touch, with a slight coolness akin to polished horn or bone. Yet, it lacked the heft and solidity of traditional vessels.

The young woman tapped the hollow tube. "You look like you've never seen a water bottle. How is this possible?"

I turned it side to side, hearing the water slosh inside.

"You suck on the straw. Like this." She took it from my hand, pursed her lips around the tube, and sucked. Then, she handed it back to me.

I mimicked her. Liquid poured into my mouth. The taste

of the water contained within this novel vessel was an enigma to my palate. Unlike the familiar flavors of natural spring water drawn from a crystal-clear stream or the earthy notes of well water, this liquid bore no distinct taste of its own. It seemed strangely neutral, almost as if the vessel had imparted a sterile character to the water it held.

Shaking my head, I handed it back to her.

She frowned. "Don't you like it?"

"It's not to my liking, no." I began to tremble in pain without the water bottle to grab my attention. I wanted to be taken away from here. A mixture of emotions flooded through me as I thought of the stranger standing in front of Alina. I felt my blood boiling with rage, but also a sense of fear and confusion. Who was this person and why were they preventing me from reaching Alina? My mind raced, trying to make sense of the situation, but all I could feel was a bubbling fury and helplessness.

A faint whisper came from nearby. With my heart pounding, I listened, my entire being focused on the words of the woman before me.

"Sir. Sir. Do you need help? What do you need?" she said.

"My name isn't sir!" I roared. "It's Balthazar!"

The woman kept her composure and replied with a cheery voice, "What a wonderful name! It's so powerful. My name is Scarlett."

I wanted to spit insults at her but was dumbfounded by her serenity.

"Do you need a place to stay?" she asked with an air of suspicious pity.

I collapsed onto the ground. I tried but failed to get up as a crushing weight clung to my chest like iron claws. I could scarcely breathe.

"I can get a place," I croaked, desperation seeping into my voice.

Her gaze softened as she hovered over me. "You don't have to do this alone. Let me help you. Come with me to my place. You can rest there."

I hesitated, then, with a nod, accepted her help. "Fine. Take me."

Trying to keep myself together, I followed her as she wove through the streets. Finally, she led me up a set of decrepit concrete stairs.

Her apartment was small and cramped, on the fourth floor of an aging building in a less-than-desirable part of town. From the outside, it looked like any other apartment building, but inside, it was a world of its own, which I found far too unpleasant for my liking. Its shabby interior looked like the result of years of neglect. The walls were peeling, the floors were stained, and the curtains were a faded, tattered mess.

"Let me show you around." She took my hand and led me from room to room.

The living room was cluttered with piles of books, clothes, and knickknacks. The furniture was sparse and mismatched, the sofa lumpy and uncomfortable, and the floors covered in threadbare rugs. A tiny kitchenette was tucked away in the corner. The only thing that seemed to be in decent condition was Scarlett's bed, though even that was nothing to write home about.

I surveyed each room with disdain, unable to comprehend how someone could choose to live in such a place. I was used to luxury—vast estates sprawling across acres and acres, gardens that stretched as far as the eye could see, and kingly furnishings that could inspire awe in even the most well-traveled individuals. This place was downright ugly.

Oblivious to my disgust, Scarlett said, "Please, settle yourself on my sofa. You must be hungry? Want mac and cheese?"

"Mac? Who's Mac?" My forehead pinched together as I perched on her lumpy sofa.

Scarlett laughed. "It's not a who. It's a what. It's macaroni. You know…pasta."

"Ah. Pasta." That was a word I recognized.

She took out a covered container from a white storage device, possibly an icebox. After removing the film, she placed the bowl into a small cupboard with a black and silver design. Then, she pressed a button, and the inside of the cupboard illuminated and whirred.

I jerked in alarm.

"I made the mac and cheese last night," Scarlett said, noting my reaction. "I promise it won't kill you once it's microwaved."

I mutely nodded, having no idea what a "microwave" was.

The strange cupboard dinged. Scarlett opened it and removed the bowl, adding a fork from the drawer. She tore off a piece of paper from a paper roll and brought everything over to me.

"Here you go." She thrust a bowl of orange noodle goo at me. "Here's your napkin. Sorry, I don't have anything fancier."

I picked up the fork and hesitantly poked at the orange cheesy mess before cautiously taking a bite. The taste and texture of the dish were alien to me; I recoiled in shock, my face contorting in disgust. I pushed the bowl away, and my appetite was completely lost. I had never seen or tasted anything like this before. It did not resemble any food from the past.

"I'm sorry. I've lost my appetite." I set the bowl on the small table next to the sofa.

"That makes sense. You were in so much pain. Are you feeling better?" Scarlett said, sitting next to me.

I glanced at her, *really* looking at her for the first time.

Scarlett was a petite and pretty young woman. Her eyes were brown and clear, like a riverbed flowing through a lush green forest. They were tranquil and inviting and showed no signs of malice. Her wavy brown hair hung down to the middle of her back in shimmering chestnut-colored waves. She smelled of honey and lemon, of sweet and tangy, a bouquet of some exotic flower. Her hair held the scent of a spicy sea salt, a beach on a tropical island. Her gentle voice belied her strong determination, and her smile had the power to brighten any space. She blushed under my scrutiny, casting her gaze at her lap.

"Have you heard of a woman named Alina?" I said.

Her head snapped back as if she had been hit by an electric jolt. "Alina?"

"Yes, yes, Alina Tocino. She's a student at McMont College," I said.

"There are so many people at McMont College, sir," Scarlett replied, her timid voice almost drowned out by my rage.

I grabbed her shoulder and squeezed, my fingers like iron bands around her skin. "Don't call me *sir*!"

"Okay! Alright! Balthazar! Your name is Balthazar!" She whimpered and tried to shrink away from me. "Is she your daughter?"

"What? No!" I bolted from the sofa.

I tried to control my anger. This pathetically sweet woman had only wanted to help me, and I couldn't take out my anguish on her. I took several long, deep breaths, willing myself to calm, and then turned to face Scarlett.

"I apologize for my anger. I've had a rather stressful day." I forced a smile. "Alina and I are old friends. I've known her a long time but have lost touch with her. I must find her and speak to her."

Scarlett smiled radiantly, her fear forgotten. "It's okay. I know what it's like to stress out and lose your shit."

My brow furrowed. *Lose your shit?*

She sprang to her feet.

"You stay put," she commanded, her voice far too sunny. "I have to go to class. Don't you dare stroke out on me!"

She gathered her belongings and bounced out of the apartment.

Stroke out?

My frown darkened. It seemed like an insane thing to say. I wanted desperately to leave, but a fresh wave of pain struck me down before I could move. I collapsed in agony, clutching my chest with white-knuckle ferocity. I lay there helplessly against the unforgiving floor, feeling darkness creeping closer and closer.

I rolled back and forth, clutching my stomach on the floor as the sounds of crazy metal machines on the road outside filled the air. 1990 was far too strange for my tastes. What was happening to me that was preventing me from finding and killing Alina? From seeking the sun and moon blades. From finding my beloved daughter, Freya. I was utterly impotent, wracked as I was in pain.

I rose and staggered around this wretched apartment, still feeling the lingering effects of my encounter with Alina and that strange man.

I peered out the window. A menacing figure stared back from outside. Despair slammed into me.

It's him. It's that man who watched me with mocking satisfaction as I lay helpless, unable to move.

The shadowed figure shook his head before vanishing.

With a wild cry, I slammed my fist against the wall, crumbling it into dust. I slumped to the floor and sat there, despondent.

I had to form a plan.

When Scarlett returned, I had managed to crawl to the sofa and collapse into an uneasy rest.

She limped into the apartment, her steps uneven and halting. Her face was swollen, her right eye blackened, and a deep cut spread across her forehead. She tried to smile at me, but fear filled her eyes.

I clenched my hands into fists. "Who hurt you?"

She looked away before finally responding.

"It's fine," she said softly. "My ex got mad when he thought I was seeing another man. I'm fine."

Anger built inside me. I wanted to protect her, but I couldn't do anything if the perpetrator was still out there. Before I could say anything else, someone pounded on the front door.

"Scarlett, open up! I know he's in there!" a man yelled.

"Go hide," Scarlett said to me, her voice shaking with fear.

I would do nothing of the sort. I had to prove that I was still made of darkness and steel.

I hauled myself from the sofa and threw open the door with a deafening slam.

A smarmy-looking brute of a man stood at the door, his eyes overflowing with rage. "See? Bitch! I was right. You've got a man in there."

I grabbed him in one swift move. My grip around the man's throat tightened as I lifted him off his feet.

His feet dangled helplessly, and his face filled with terror.

"You fucking piece of filth," I said through gritted teeth. "You wretched coward. How dare you assault a woman! Your stench fills my nose. You reek of despair and cowardice."

"Balthazar, stop it!" Scarlett pleaded in a shrill voice. "He's intoxicated. He won't do anything. Put him down!"

"There is no excuse for what he did to you." Rage coursed through me like an unstoppable river. "I'm going to make sure he faces justice."

I slammed the door behind me as I stormed outside, dragging Scarlett's tormentor in my clutches. Once I was in the alley, where metal bins overflowed with garbage, I choked the life out of him. As I inhaled his spirit, a surge of power filled my veins. I tossed his lifeless body into a dumpster. I was still the darkness, and its tricks were still effective.

When I returned, Scarlett was washing the blood from her face in her tiny toilet room. She avoided my gaze. "What did you do to him?"

"That man will never be a problem," I said. "I chatted with him, and he'll never bother you again. I told him I would kill him."

"You what?" Scarlett stilled, holding the wet cloth aloft.

"It's an expression," I said lightly. "Nothing but a threat, I assure you."

I had to leave. I couldn't rely on a mere stranger to help me find Alina.

I hesitated before saying, "I'll be on my way."

Scarlett whirled to face me. "No, please stay. I'll help you find Alina. I promise!"

Her voice cracked as she spoke. I could feel her desperation, her need to keep her word. But I could not stay.

My heart sank as Scarlett's face fell.

With a heavy heart, I made my way out, leaving Scarlett in the safety of her home. The solemn expression on her face as she watched me go stayed with me long after I'd departed. But I had to make good on my mission.

I had to find Alina.

CHAPTER THIRTY

BALTHAZAR

Every morning, I woke up with one goal in mind: to find a way to get close to Alina. But as the days passed without any progress, my mood sank lower and lower. I felt like I was drowning in a pit of despair with no way out.

Whenever I saw her I was struck by a wave of pain that I couldn't suppress. Why couldn't I get close to her? My frustration boiled over, and it pissed me off.

At my wit's end, I headed back to Scarlett's apartment. Maybe she could help, after all. As I lifted my hand to knock, the door flew open.

"Oh!" Scarlett's eyes widened in surprise, and her cheeks flushed pink. She shuffled her feet and twisted a lock of hair around her finger, unable to meet my gaze. "I was just on my way to class."

"Hello, Scarlett! How are you?"

"I'm doing okay," she replied. "Did you find Alina?"

I sighed, shaking my head. "I'm still trying to find a way to connect."

Scarlett hung her head. "I hoped you'd return, and I

wanted to help you. I looked her up in the phone book. Every time I approach her, though, she walks away. I tell her she's pretty and smart. I ask her about her classes. I try to get to know her, and she just walks away. Don't worry. I think I'm wearing her down. I'll invite her over, and we can have pizza and beer. That way, you can talk to her without feeling so awkward."

I smiled, grateful for her thoughtfulness. "Thanks, Scarlett. That would be great."

"Would you like to come in?" she said shyly.

"I thought you said you have a class to attend," I said.

"It's Economics 101. I can blow it off," she said.

I pictured her holding a dandelion by its stem and blowing, the seeds scattering to the wind. These phrases of the 90s were baffling. But I nodded as if I understood.

"Yes, please, I'd like that."

Scarlett stepped aside, and I shuffled in, dragging the weight of my frustrated search behind me.

Something looked different.

"Did you get a new sofa?" I stared at the clean lines and simple geometric forms of the wooden frame of her new couch, which held one giant off-white cushion.

"Yes!" Scarlett's eyes sparkled. "It's new to me, anyway. A friend was getting rid of her futon. It turns into a bed, see?"

She grabbed the backrest and yanked it down until it hit the floor with a deafening thud, revealing an ominous expanse of ratty mattress.

"I hoped you might come back." Her words flew out of her lips with the force of a person desperate to cling to something they could not afford to lose. "And I thought, if you did, you'd probably feel more comfortable having your own bed."

"I see," I said, staring at the mattress with an overwhelming sense of disgust and fear. I tentatively patted it, repulsed by the thought of having to sleep on it. The thin mattress was worn and stained, and it looked barely large enough for a sleeping child, let alone an adult. I wrinkled my nose and could have sworn I even detected a faint smell of mildew from where I stood.

"It stinks, doesn't it? Don't worry, I bought a fabric freshener." Scarlett zipped toward her tiny kitchen and returned with a small metal canister that read, "Wonder Spray." She ripped the white flexible lid off and jabbed her finger onto the tiny white knob. A deafening hiss echoed through the room as a powerful, fragrant mist exploded, engulfing us in a dizzying wave of sickly-sweet stench. The overpowering smell was like walking through a field of wilting flowers, heavy with rot.

"Good lord, what have you done?" I exclaimed, moving away from the odorous scent.

"It's a deodorizer. I think it smells better, don't you?' Scarlett waved her hand before her nose. "Sit. I'll get us something to drink."

As she hurried back to the kitchen, Wonder Spray in hand, I sat on the futon's wooden arm. There was no way I would sit on that disgusting cushion.

My frustration boiled to a seething rage as I contemplated how close and yet so far I was from confronting Alina. Every time I moved closer to her, my body screamed in agony, like thousands of tiny needles piercing my veins. It had to be the work of the too tall, gray-eyed man. What could possibly explain his motives?

Scarlett returned carrying two icy bottles. She thrust one into my hand so forcefully that the cold beverage splashed onto my skin. Without hesitation, I gulped down half the ale.

"It's absolutely imperative that I find Alina," I said. "The truth is, I know her parents. They died recently, and they left her a vast sum of money. If she doesn't claim it soon, the government will swoop in and seize it all."

"That's so sad. And fuck the government. Don't worry. I'll help you find her." She took a long swig of her ale and side-eyed me. "You look so tense, Balthazar. You need to let off some steam. What do you say we smoke a joint?"

"A joint?"

"You know… Reefer. Dope. Weed. Mary Jane." She sprang to her feet and hurried out of the room. When she returned, she waved a small translucent bag full of dead leaves. "This is pretty good shit. I scored it from the same friend who gave me the futon."

I stared at her in puzzlement as she sat on the futon, grabbed a shiny publication from the side table, and poured out some of the leaves. A mound of bright-green buds spilled out.

She grabbed something from the side table and pulled out a small piece of paper. With skillful fingers, she sprinkled some of the leaves on top of the paper. She began massaging and tucking the contents until they were evenly distributed like a tight, uniform cigarette. She placed the cigarette between her lips and lit it with a match. Inhaling deeply, she held her breath and then exhaled a skunky and earthy-smelling plume.

She extended the burning cigarette to me and said, "Here you go. Have a hit."

"No, thank you." I waved my hand in front of my nose. The cigarette's scent mixed with the noxious floral fragrance Scarlett had sprayed, creating a repulsive smell. "I'm fine with this."

I hefted my ale and emptied the bottle.

"Suit yourself," she said, before sucking in another draw.

She fell back on the futon as if tired. "I could give you a massage, you know."

She rolled to her side and rested the burning "joint" in a nearby ashtray.

"I'm pretty good with my hands," she said, wiggling her fingers.

"No, thank you," I said again.

"Oh, come on, dude. You're obviously tense over your whole search for this Alina chick. Let me help you regroup. Take a load off. Find your inner bliss." Her eyelids grew heavy.

"What would it entail?" I asked.

"You with your shirt off. Me with my hands all over you, helping you relax. Doesn't that sound amazing?" Her voice sounded dreamy and far away.

It had been a while since I'd had sex. And Scarlett was pretty. What could it hurt?

"Fine, but not in here."

Scarlett grabbed the joint, inhaled again, and lurched to her feet. Through a lungful of smoke, she said, "No problem. I just changed the sheets."

She extended her hand and guided me to the bedroom.

Scarlett's bedroom was sparsely decorated, with a double bed and a dresser against one wall and a small bookshelf against another. A few novels, an old dictionary, and several knick-knacks were on the bookshelf. The bed was covered in a patterned quilt.

"Take off your shirt and lay down," she said as she tugged her long-sleeved shirt over her head. A colorful tattoo of a snake coiled up her arm.

As my gaze locked onto Scarlett, I couldn't help but be mesmerized by her many tattoos. Each design seemed to tell a different story of her past. But the sight of her voluptuous breasts made my mouth water, full and heavy with temptation as they hung from her chest like ripe fruit. My cock twitched in anticipation as I removed my fine, linen shirt.

Scarlett perched on the edge of her bed and patted the mattress. "Right here, big boy. On your stomach."

I stood before Scarlett, my body tense and powerful like the coiled springs of a machine. My muscles rippled with power, and eons of experience radiated from me. I waited for her, giving her time to take in every detail of my form. She allowed her gaze to wander across me slowly, hungrily. Her tongue darted across her lips.

I took my time, crawling across her bed and sprawling face down. I propped myself on my forearms and looked over my shoulder at her.

Scarlett straddled my hips and grabbed a small bottle from the side table. She poured some fragrant oil into her hands and swished her palms together. With a heavy-lidded gaze, she said, "Relax, baby. I don't bite."

She let out a throaty laugh as I melted onto the mattress.

Her hands caressed my back with a slow swish.

"Mm," she said, kneading and stroking my muscles. "You're so strong, Balthazar. I had no idea you had such a powerful body. I'll bet it feels good when you're inside a woman, doesn't it? You seem like you're all man."

Oh, yes. My cock liked the direction this was headed. Most definitely.

I allowed Scarlett to continue her massage. Her touch was firm and slow, deep and practiced. When I felt sufficiently relaxed and more than aroused, I murmured, "How would you like to find out how it feels to have me inside you?"

WICKED LOVERS OF TIME

I awoke sometime later, naked, stunned to find myself next to Scarlett, who was also naked. I hadn't felt the need to kill her after sex. She looked so peaceful, so beautiful, as she slept next to me.

Her eyes fluttered open, and she stretched and yawned. "Wow, B. You're like the best lover I've ever had."

Of course, I am.

Scarlett hadn't been bad either. While she may not have had Alina's crazy raw energy, she had potential. I could show her a thing or two to ignite her passion and make our love-making more explosive.

Should I stay for a while? Maybe. This could be a waystation while I searched for Alina. Yes, it would do nicely. But we couldn't stay here. The thought of remaining in the squalor of her apartment filled me with dread.

I insisted we let her apartment and all its furnishings go. Scarlett moved in with me to a luxurious waterfront home in the Jericho Park neighborhood of Vancouver, BC. The owners had "suddenly died," leaving the house vacant with no survivors to claim it. I'd made sure of that before I dispatched the residents and inhaled their souls.

Nestled in the lush foliage of the Pacific Northwest, its view of the nearby beach was breathtaking, its walls drenched in sunlight and greenery.

The home itself was a marvel of modern design. Its interior was a harmony of soft curves and natural light, with touches of warmth and comfort throughout. The living spaces were airy and inviting, and the kitchen featured all the finest appliances. Upstairs, the bedrooms were spacious and comfortable, with grand windows that opened up to stunning views of the sea. Outside, the yard was an idyllic mix of manicured greenery and mature trees, and the patio and deck were perfect for outdoor entertaining.

Not that I entertained.

It was a home fit for a king and suited me far better than Scarlett's tawdry apartment.

We lived in relative harmony while Scarlett pursued her studies. I followed my futile quest to get close to Alina. I was getting no closer to Alina, which frustrated me—each and every time I was assaulted with pain.

Scarlett waltzed into the room as I stood in my office gazing at the garden.

"Balthazar!" Her voice held traces of alarm.

I turned to her. "What is it, my dear?"

"I'm so sorry to tell you this. I've just come from the women's clinic. You know, I've been using a diaphragm for birth control. But it failed! I'm pregnant!" She wrung her hands.

I stood there in shock, unable to comprehend what she had just said. I had put up with the mess of her birth control and reveled in the pleasure of our passionate sex, assuming the latex device filled with goo did what it was supposed to do. Now, she was pregnant?

"With whose child?" I asked, my words laced with fury.

Scarlett's face blanched as she realized the implications of my question.

"Yours, asshole! Surely, you're not accusing me of sleeping around, are you?" Her voice trembled.

I glared at her, no longer recognizable in my rage.

"I'm faithful to you. I don't sleep around. I'm *not* that kind of person." She hesitated, her limbs trembling. "But it's okay if you don't want it. I'll get rid of it. I'll make an appointment at the clinic."

"What did you say?"

"You know. An abortion. I'll get rid of the baby. I don't

expect you to raise a child. You don't exactly seem like father material."

"No!" My eyes blazed with fury. "What kind of people are you in the 20th century? You would kill an innocent child to avoid responsibility? Have you no decency?"

Desperation clawed at my throat.

"I'll take care of the child," I said, tears streaming down my face. "My prayers have been answered. I've been waiting to have a child."

"You have?" Scarlett's face brightened.

"Yes, dear Scarlett. I've been desperate to build a family again. I'm more than ready." I rushed toward her and took her in my arms. "Oh, Scarlett. You've made me happy. So very happy. This is wonderful news."

"I can hardly believe it, but I guess we're having a child." She stepped away from me, her features heavy. "I also have news for you—about Alina."

I narrowed my eyes as I searched her expression. "What is it? You have news?"

A mysterious smirk curled up the edge of her mouth. "I was going to keep this to myself in case you were mad at me for the pregnancy. But since you're happy, here goes. Alina's seeing someone. His name's Jack James. Rumor has it they're engaged."

This news slammed into me like a ton of bricks, pushing the air from my lungs as her words registered in my brain. Alina—*my* Alina—was about to get married? Oh, I was so going to kill her this time.

I had to find a way to destroy her once and for all.

CHAPTER THIRTY-ONE
ALINA

1993

I t had been three years since I married Jack, a decision I had never planned for, yet one I made all the same. We were consumed with our research on the ancient sun and moon daggers.

The weeks flew by in a blur of work and research. Jack poured over his books and notes each night, constantly learning and growing. His dedication and focus were inspiring.

Our sex life, however, as well as any form of intimacy, was a barren wasteland of mediocrity. Jack stayed confined to the monotonous missionary position, never daring to explore something new or thrilling. Even when I did attempt something different, I would nearly drift off into an endless slumber without ever feeling any pleasure.

I lavished him with unending compliments and praise in the bedroom, living room, and everywhere else. Every time I offered him words of affirmation, his face would light up with a glow that would make me forget the feelings of being imprisoned in a loveless marriage.

The hobbled, old man, whom I decided to call the Scholar, said I must never do anything to hurt him, so I resorted to feigning enthusiasm and admiration just to avoid my own boredom. I had to keep on pumping him up to protect myself from harm. Yet, everything about this marriage was exhausting.

Further, Jack's demeanor was sullen and withdrawn when he wasn't immersed in research. I couldn't even pry details from his childhood. No matter how much I prodded, he never unburdened himself.

Jack was a fortress, hovering silently in the shadows of his past. He told me he was an orphan, but I knew there was more to the story he never revealed. Even as I tried to pry out of him, he gave me nothing, leaving me in the dark about the secrets and reasons for his guardedness. I discovered later that Jack was abandoned on the street with no one to turn to. But that was it. Other than that, I knew nothing.

Rather than go mad with frustration, I poured myself into finding the daggers, studying historical texts, scouring libraries and obscure bookshops, and talking to anyone even remotely interested in the sun and moon daggers.

Every lead had been a dead end, and every hope had been dashed. I was exhausted and disheartened, wondering if my quest was a fool's errand.

As I trudged through the streets of Vancouver, lost in my own thoughts, I noticed someone standing in my path. It was Lee, looking as suspicious and distrusting as ever. He swayed slightly as if his afternoon had been lost in a bar.

"Hello, Alina. How is your quest going for the daggers?"

I told him of my despair over all the dead ends and growing doubts that I would ever find the daggers.

Lee listened. "There's a shop called Quill & Codex Antiquarium. It's a bookshop that caters to those interested in obscure and historical texts. It's run by a friend of mine, and he deals in rare and ancient artifacts. I'm sure he'll be able to help you."

His gaze shifted to something behind me, causing his eyes to grow wide with fear. I whirled around, half-expecting to see a dangerous threat lurking behind me, but all that greeted me was an empty street, with the only sound coming from a distant dog barking.

An icy chill snaked up my spine, and my heart pounded like thunder. "What was it? What did you think you saw?"

He paused for what seemed like an eternity before answering. "Nothing."

He quickly gave me directions to the shop, then rushed away without another word.

I went to the Antiquarium. Lee's friend bore no new information.

Outside the Quill & Codex Antiquarium, a man approached me. He bore the disheveled appearance of an archaeologist with his dusty clothes, smudged face, and mud-covered boots. He was an older man with white hair, and he stood out among the bright colors and sounds of the city. He was holding a package, and when he saw me, he smiled.

"Are you Alina Tocino?" he asked, his accent betraying his Eastern European homeland.

Startled, I nodded. "Do I know you?"

He shook his head and held out the package, which, upon closer inspection, revealed itself to be a bundle of carefully wrapped papers.

"I have something for you," he said, slightly trembling. "I believe this will lead you to one of the daggers you seek."

I gasped, my heart racing. Was this mysterious stranger

what Lee had seen? Could it really be true that he brought me information about the daggers? And if so, who was he, and why was he helping me? I opened the package, and inside were maps, letters, and long-forgotten documents that seemed to point to the dagger's whereabouts in a place called Eyjaf-jallajökull.

When I looked up to thank the man, he had already folded into a crowd of tourists bumbling along the sidewalk with cameras hanging from their necks. I stood transfixed, a voyeur to the strange scene unfolding before me. The tourists stumbled and lurched like marionettes whose strings had been cut, their bodies writhing in spasms as the enigmatic stranger folded into their presence. With each step, he disappeared around the corner until only the echo of what transpired remained.

The documents in my hands trembled with supernatural energy, and my hair stood on end as I clasped them. I raced home to Jack, the desperate urgency of our mission palpable.

We were off to Iceland in pursuit of the first dagger that would unlock my destiny.

"Jack, my love," I shouted as I threw open the front door. I rushed through our apartment with its chaotic mix of old and new.

I threw my backpack on the antique couch that had seen better days, its faded velvet upholstery fraying at the edges. Around it sat mismatched chairs, some modern and plastic, others with carved wooden frames that had once adored Victorian parlors. A colossal bookshelf, made of old crates cobbled together and filled to bursting with books, dominated one corner. The walls were a patchwork of posters and photographs, some of them vintage black-and-white prints, others hand-painted in vivid colors.

"Jack!" I called. "I have exciting news!"

"In here, Alina!" he yelled.

I hurried into the bedroom, which, much like the living room, held a mismatched array of antiques and salvage. Our sizeable four-poster bed, draped in white mosquito netting and piled with blankets and quilts, stood in the middle of the room. The room was small and cluttered, with two desks on opposite sides. One held a manual typewriter, its keys worn from years of use. The other was piled high with papers and an old portable computer, its screen flickering with each keystroke. Above the desk hung a tall, gilt-framed mirror, reflecting the chaotic scene below.

The air was thick with the smell of incense and old books. Jack sat at one of the desks, his glasses perched on his nose, his hair a wild, unkempt mess.

He removed his glasses and rubbed his eyes.

"What have you got there?" he said, peering at the documents in my hands.

"The daggers! Or at least one of them. I know where to find it!"

Jack looked at me with a puzzled expression. His gaze slid to the bundle in my hand and then to my face. "Can I see?"

"Yes, yes!" I spread the documents all over his desk, pointing to pertinent facts. "It's all here! We're going to Eyjafjallajökull!"

Jack snatched up a map and several letters, his eyes blazing with determination. He studied them, his lips pursed in concentration as he flipped between them.

I wanted to scream at his slow, laborious perusal of what I knew was true. The dagger was within our grasp.

Finally, his excited gaze met mine. "I think you're right, Alina."

"So, when can we go?"

"To Iceland?" he frowned. "There are steps to follow to perform a dig, you know that."

I barely kept my temper in check. "Of course I know that. So? Are you in?"

Jack sprang from his seat with an energy and fervor that could not be contained. Without warning, he grasped me in an embrace filled with such wild joy and passion that I felt my heart swell with emotion. "This is great news, Alina! All our hard work will be rewarded!"

It took several months to obtain the necessary permits, but finally, we had them in hand. Full of exuberance, we set off to Iceland.

The modest archaeological excavation site nestled within Eyjafjallajökull, Iceland, exuded an eerie tranquility. An oppressive chill clung to the air, enveloping the desolate landscape in a shroud of mist and dampness. The flat terrain seemed to stretch endlessly toward the distant horizon, devoid of any signs of vibrant life, save for the occasional birds passing overhead, bound for warmer destinations.

Hidden amid the tall grasses, the excavation site revealed itself only through a handful of inconspicuous flags demarcating its boundaries. At its heart lay a substantial crater, its once-formidable sides, and bottom eroded by the relentless march of time and the capriciousness of weather. Earth and dust had settled within this crater, bearing witness to the ages. Fragments of shattered pottery and ancient stone tools lay strewn about the crater's rim, like whispers from the past.

In this hushed landscape, the sole audible notes were the gentle murmurings of the wind and the sporadic echoes of trowels meeting stone as Jack and I toiled diligently to unearth one of the daggers. The site exuded an aura of profound mystery, its secrets concealed beneath layers of dirt and debris, tantalizingly out of reach. For the present moment, however, all remained undisturbed and serene.

Jack and I worked hard under the pale sun, struggling against the exhaustive archaeology dig all day. Our trowels relentlessly scraped against the ancient soil, clinking against rocks and pebbles as we delved deeper into our work. Despite the tedium of our labor, our shared determination was unwavering. We were on a quest to uncover the legendary sun dagger, an ancient artifact whispered about by only a fortunate few.

As the sun began its slow descent, my heart sank. We had found nothing—again. My movements, however, began to mimic the gradual fading of the daylight as if I were entering a trance-like state. At irregular intervals, I would pause, crouching low to scrutinize the earth and stones before me, only to return to my rhythmic digging.

My trowel struck something unyielding and sleek, sending a jolt of exhilaration coursing through me. Methodically, I unearthed the treasure from its earthen cocoon: a venerable ceremonial dagger, its golden sheen radiating in the twilight. It appeared to be made of pure gold, though its surface was now dulled and weathered by centuries of use. The handle was adorned with intricate carvings, depicting scenes of battles, gods, and sacred rituals.

But it was the blade that held the most fascination. Made of dark, unknown metal, it gleamed in the light of the sun, casting an otherworldly glow. Its edges were razor sharp, and it seemed to hum with a strange, almost magical energy.

The sun dagger, at last, lay before me.

My trembling hands cradled the artifact, and my gaze

flicked to Jack. A tempting impulse beckoned me to conceal this discovery, to harbor it selfishly as my own. The allure of greed whispered to me, urging me to keep the treasure hidden from my husband.

I stared at its dusty hilt, tracing my thumb along the age-worn surface. The age-old symbols inscribed on the handle glowed faintly in the evening light.

Behind me, Jack shuffled his feet and cleared his throat, eager for the recognition of his presence. I closed my eyes and took a deep breath. I had to turn around and show him the dagger, but my mind screamed to keep it to myself. I was terrified of the power it held, the energy it could unleash, and the secrets it had been protecting for so long.

Finally, I turned around slowly, the dagger gripped in my hands and met Jack's gaze. His cerulean eyes were wide with anticipation, and I gave a gentle nod.

"I found it. We've got the first dagger," I said reverentially, holding it aloft.

Jack stepped forward in awe. He grazed his fingers over the surface of the knife before he looked up at me, his eyes sparkling with wonder.

The blade pulsated with a heat that seemed to come from within, and its symbols glowed brighter in the fading light. A wave of energy passed between us, and at that moment, neither Jack nor I could doubt the power of the artifact I held.

I was consumed with aching nostalgia for my beloved Balthazar, an unbearable yearning in my core. Jack's eyes were full of desperate longing, stirring a potent desire within me that I could not deny. I pulled him close and kissed him passionately—how I used to kiss Balthazar, unrestrained and feverishly, like it was our last moment together.

Jack and I fell to the ground, our bodies entwined together and the treasure between us. We explored each other with a fierce tenderness, a desperate desire that was as beautiful as it was wild. Our movements were primal and instinctive, our souls intertwining and merging in a way that transcended time and space. Yet, I was lost in thoughts of Balthazar. I felt as if he were here, thrusting inside me, using Jack's body to convey his love for me.

When we finally reached our climax, the world shook around us. The intensity of our pleasure was so powerful it seemed to reverberate through the very fabric of existence. Afterward, we lay there panting and exhausted. The dagger between us still gleamed in the waning light.

Jack murmured sweet phrases in my ear as he stroked my sweaty, dust-covered skin. "That was beautiful. I've never seen this side of you."

"Yes," I said, my voice thick with emotion. "It's been locked away all this time."

My vision blurred as I squeezed my eyes shut, tears streaming down my cheeks. My heart felt like it was being stretched and pulled in two, aching for the love of Balthazar and yet knowing that our paths had long since diverged. Even though I'd chosen to forsake him and set out alone to find the blades, claiming the power for myself, I still longed for his embrace. Not Jack's—never Jack's.

"Well, let's set this beast free," Jack said, drawing his tongue up my neck. "I want more of this."

His cock, usually so eager to be tucked inside his trousers once finished, stirred against my thigh.

As satisfying as this had been, I couldn't bear to partake in another round. Not when every fiber of my being longed to be with Balthazar.

"We will, Jack, I promise. But, for now, let's take the dagger back to camp and examine it."

A flash of disappointment flickered across his face, but he

rolled to his side and pushed to stand, straightening his clothes. He offered his hand to me, but I hesitated. Jack was already sinking into a bad mood, and I had to try to lift it quickly. His disagreeable moods pulled everyone down, especially me.

"Don't you see, darling?" I said, trying to put on a supportive face. Lord knew I had plenty of practice. "Our names will be spoken of among scientists! You can finally prove your theories!"

My optimism was slowly consumed by a gnawing dread coiling around my heart like an unrelenting python. I knew something had changed during this discovery, though I could not give it shape or name. But I could sense the coming of an inevitable transformation that promised darkness and despair.

Jack brightened at my words. "Do you think so?"

"Yes! You will, at long last, be lauded, not scorned. You will contribute something immense to society!" I reached for his hand.

"You've made me so happy. I love you, Alina," he said, brushing his lips across my knuckles.

My lips refused to move as if sewn together with barbed wire. Jack's searing gaze pierced through me as seconds stretched into an eternity, but I couldn't make the words escape my throat.

I finally said, "I care for you too!"

Truthfully, what I really cared about was power. It was mine and mine alone, not something to be shared with anyone —not Jack, and definitely not Balthazar.

CHAPTER THIRTY-TWO
ALINA

When Jack and I returned from our journey to Iceland, I was eager to tell Lee about what we had found. My heart pounded as I walked up to his condo, and a storm cloud of conflicting emotions came rushing at me. I was eager to share the news with him but scared of how he would react. We were never best friends.

"Alina!" he said as he opened the door. He seemed surprisingly cordial. "This is a surprise. Come in, come in."

He led me through his front room and headed for the kitchen. Every wall was adorned with artifacts: ancient leather drums, intricately carved masks, and tapestries bearing symbols of the indigenous people that were once abundant in the area. Shelves lined the walls, and each was filled with arrowheads, feathers, ancient pottery, and various jewelry pieces.

My pulse raced as I stood in the kitchen. "Lee, I did it. I found the dagger."

A look of astonishment crossed his face. "I'm impressed, Alina. You really found it?"

I nodded.

He paused, stroking his smooth jaw. "You've changed so much since Jack. You're not the same woman you once were. You've become a better person."

I forced a smile to mask the true fear that threatened to consume me. The man with the glasses could be watching me.

"I'm sorry I ever doubted you," Lee said, his expression filled with unease. "I don't trust easily for a very good reason."

His face turned to stone, obscuring what turmoil might be beneath that he dared not let anyone else know.

I shook my head. Lee was always filled with secrets. But I held secrets of my own.

"I saw Balthazar," Lee said in a hoarse whisper. "He was standing there, watching us as we walked down the street. One moment, he was there. The next, he was gone. I think he's been looking for us."

An electric current of fear surged through my body, making every hair on my neck stand at attention. As Lee's words sank in, my mind raced with desperation as I concocted a plan to deceive Balthazar. I had one of the blades, but he didn't need to know that. My heart pounded relentlessly against my chest as I tried to drown out his menacing voice with visions of ultimate power. I would stop at nothing to claim it for myself.

"Don't worry," Lee added. "Maybe I drank too much that day. It was that day I sent you to the Antiquarium."

"I see," I said, and changed the topic back to the sun dagger. Still, I could not shake the chill of dread lodged in my heart like a shard of ice, paralyzing me with fear.

CHAPTER THIRTY-THREE

BALTHAZAR

At the prestigious McMont College, Scarlett's eyes widened in concern as she watched me stumble toward Jack James as if entranced. I had been determined to find a way to get close to Alina, but my attempts thus far had been futile. Desperate for a break-through, I took Scarlett's suggestion to approach Jack and began making my way over to him through the sea of students bustling around us. The intensity of my focus on Jack was almost palpable, as if he held the key to unlocking everything. Sweat beads formed on my forehead as I nervously approached him, hoping that this would finally be the solution to my quest for Alina's attention.

The college campus overflowed with students, and they weaved around me as if I were a stone in a stream. I was used to evoking fear and helplessness, but with each step toward Jack, the same agony I experience when approaching Alina washed over me. It had to be that wretched, gray-eyed man torturing me. I let out a growl, and a nearby young female yelped and scurried around me.

There. That's better.

As I became closer to my target, an intense, almost debilitating pain stabbed in my ears, followed by an urge to vomit. I doubled over and clutched my stomach, struggling to keep the contents inside as I groaned.

Scarlett flew to my side. Her grip on my arm was vicelike as she hauled me backward away from Jack. Unrelenting, despite her late stage of pregnancy, she managed to yank me off the ground with a superhuman effort.

"We need to take you home," she said.

I stumbled beside her, barely making it back to my house before I collapsed onto the floor.

Scarlett ran to get me water and medicine, but the pain persisted. I couldn't focus on anything else but the searing agony that kept me from doing anything. I screamed at my powerlessness to bridge the distance between Alina and her charlatan husband. Jack James seemed no more interesting than soggy toast.

Scarlett handed me the pills with a heavy sigh, her swollen belly stretching further than my imagination could grasp. After nine months of waiting and hoping, the baby still showed no signs of coming soon. My frustration boiled within me uncontrollably, threatening to tip over into something far more sinister.

I staggered to our spacious bedroom and flopped on the mattress, pulling a pillow over my head. I groaned as Scarlett bustled around the room, closing the curtains as if I were an invalid on death's door. But I was too weak to protest.

Scarlett chirped in her typical fashion, saying this and that, but I paid her no mind. Instead, I slipped into the bliss of the void and dreamt of endlessly reaching for Alina, choking the life out of her, only to have her slip from my grasp.

The high-pitched screech of a wounded creature jolted me

from my dreams. I shot up in bed with a start, fear coursing through my veins.

"Good God!" I said, alarmed by the otherworldly noise that echoed through our bedroom walls.

"Balthazar!" Scarlett shrieked, her voice shaking with terror. She gripped the dresser for support.

"What is it? What's happening?" I yelled, trying to get my bearings.

Scarlett sobbed. "The baby! It's coming."

"Well, then, lay down. March in place. At least give me time to wake up," I growled, flinging back the covers Scarlett had tucked around me. Then, it dawned on me—the baby— *my* baby was coming.

In a panic, I jumped out of bed and yanked Scarlett's hands. "Take my spot! Lie down now!"

I pounded the silk sheets with my fist.

Scarlett doubled over as another contraction ripped through her womb, clenching her belly muscles like a metal clamp. She staggered onto the bed, her face contorted in pain.

I raced around the room, gathering supplies and preparing for Scarlett's impending labor. I felt helpless in the face of such an immense task, but I tried to project confidence and efficiency for Scarlett's sake. I hadn't participated when Zara had my children. She'd had a midwife. Only now did I regret not paying more attention. Yet, I wanted to make this birth something special for Scarlett, something memorable and magical. She was having *my* child, after all.

Scarlett's contraction ended, and another started minutes later.

"I need to go to the hospital," she said, her voice strained with fear.

"What? No! You're staying here," I bellowed, my voice echoing in the room. "You'll have the baby here."

Scarlett shook her head. "No! No one has a baby at home."

"People have been having their children at home for centuries!" I grabbed her hand and pulled her against me, determined to make her understand. "You're having it here. This is *my* child, and I insist it will be born here in my house!"

Scarlett looked up at me, her fear palpable.

"Okay, okay," she whispered. "We'll have the baby at home. But what happens once our child is born? Are you going to cast me aside? You're talking like I have nothing to do with *our* ba—"

Her words cut off as another contraction seized her. She grabbed my wrist and squeezed with the force of ten men.

I endured the searing pain, my jaw clenched tight. "Of course you have something to do with the child! You're the vessel carrying our child, right?"

No matter how hard I tried, the smile on my face was nothing but forced.

Scarlett's widened eyes brimmed with disbelief and suspicion.

"Please," she said as another contraction wracked her body. "We need a nurse."

"I'll deliver the baby!"

"Do you know how?" Her voice trembled with doubt.

"Yes, I know exactly what to do."

As the hours dragged on, I watched Scarlett's brow furrow with every contraction. She gripped my hand tightly and I could feel the dampness of her palm against mine. The room felt hot and stuffy, filled with the sounds of heavy breathing and muffled moans.

When the baby finally emerged, a sliver of light from the window caught the glint of sweat on Scarlett's forehead as she pushed with all her might. And then, suddenly, a tiny head emerged, followed by arms and legs flailing in the air. My heart raced with both fear and awe as I reached out to help guide the baby into the world.

A Timebound necklace sparkled around the infant's neck. I ignored it and turned my focus back to the crisis: Scarlett was bleeding profusely.

What do I do?

"Balthazar!" Scarlett gasped. "I need medical care. Take me to the hospital now!"

Without hesitation, I summoned a dark, thunderous cloud that enveloped us and hurtled us toward the hospital.

Scarlett screamed as we zipped through time and place. "What's happening?"

"Shh," I soothed. "It's nothing that you'll remember." The storm's chill swirled around me as I cradled both Scarlett and our newborn child in my arms. Fear and desperation filled my heart.

As we entered the hospital, Scarlett shook her head, coming out of a daze, and clutched my sleeve. "Promise me you'll name our baby Tristan—after my grandfather."

Her words shocked me. "You're talking as if you won't make it out alive."

"I might not." Her face drained of color.

"No!" I growled. "You're going to live!"

I insisted on accompanying Scarlett into the emergency room. I loomed over her, clutching the baby, willing my beautiful Scarlett to live. "You're going to make it. The doctors will take good care of you."

A nurse bustled in. "Mr., uh…"

She glanced at the folder in her hand.

"Call me Balthazar. That will suffice."

"Balthazar." She forced a smile. "I'm going to have to ask you to leave for a moment. We have to perform some tests and give her blood. Would you mind stepping into the waiting room?"

Would I mind? Of course I minded. I wanted to stay by her side.

"It's just procedure, sir. We'll come collect you shortly so you can be back by her side."

I growled as I left, holding the baby. As I headed for the waiting room, I couldn't help but marvel at the tiny miracle of life I held in my arms. My child, here in my arms, filled my heart with a love I never thought possible. The joy and contentment were like a warm embrace after years of solitude and pain.

But as I stumbled past the bathroom, I sensed something was off. The door was slightly open and a single eye peered through before quickly shutting. A chill shot down my spine, warning me that danger lurked behind that door. And then I heard it—my child's wail piercing through the peaceful air. Panic gripped me as I felt an ominous weight pressing down on me, foreboding of something terrible about to happen.

I shushed my child, but I couldn't shake the sense that something was wrong. Dread hung heavy in the air, curling around my shoulders like ribbons of smoke. I rushed away, but I knew with every step I took, something sinister lurked close behind.

CHAPTER THIRTY-FOUR

ALINA

The sense of doom had been my constant companion since our return from Iceland, especially after speaking with Lee. I constantly awoke feeling nauseous and tired, as if I hadn't slept a wink. My skin grew pale and translucent as rage simmered underneath my surface. Boiling anger bubbled out of me in sudden, unpredictable outbursts. Jack carefully kept his distance.

After weeks of feeling increasingly ill, vomiting daily, I finally mustered the courage to visit the doctor. She listened to my symptoms and took notes, then handed me a little cup and told me to go pee in it. I frowned. I was at death's door, and she wanted a urine sample?

"Just do it, Alina. I think I know what the matter might be," she said with a smile.

I did as she asked and left the sample in the collection window in the bathroom.

When I entered the exam room, the doctor silently wrote on a notepad without looking up. I knew it was terrible news without her having to say anything. She finally looked up at me, her expression both grave and kind.

"You're pregnant."

"What?" It was like a gut punch. I had no idea what to say or do. Tears filled my eyes, and I couldn't find the words to express the complexity of my feelings.

I trembled with fear. How could I be pregnant? Then, I remembered the day Jack and I had found the dagger, and the passion we had shared.

The doctor handed me a tissue, and I wiped away my tears. I thought of all the possibilities ahead for myself and my future. I didn't want this baby. The thought of motherhood, of being pregnant again, disgusted me. I had already been a mother in the 1700s. Why should I be one again in this century? When I arrived here, my sole purpose was to find the sun and moon daggers, take over the world with darkness, and make Balthazar kneel at my feet. I felt his presence lurking in the shadows, a predator on the prowl. And then there was Zara, Balthazar's former lover, her mocking laughter echoing in my mind like a twisted symphony of torment. I was trapped, surrounded by enemies who delighted in my suffering.

On top of that, I was stuck in an unhappy marriage with Jack, forced to bear his hateful child. I could not stand anything or anyone.

I stormed down the hallway, my jaw clenched and ready to explode. I yanked open door after door, trying to find the exit. My mind was so foggy I lost my way.

I nearly fell to my knees when I rounded the corner and entered what had to be an emergency room.

The scene before me couldn't be real. My heart sank as rage filled my veins like molten lava. Balthazar stood in a room with a baby in his arms, weeping over a beautiful woman in the hospital bed. She looked pale and wan.

His betrayal cut like an icy blade. This woman had stolen

my man! I would kill her! I would force Balthazar to raise a child alone while I sought the moon dagger.

"Can I help you?" A nurse stepped into my line of sight, blocking me.

"I…I…Exit," I mumbled, trying to peer around her.

She placed her hands on my shoulders and pivoted me around. "That way. Straight ahead and turn right at the end of the hall."

I was consumed with fear and rage. Had Balthazar seen me? Would he track me down and murder me?

I moved forward until the nurse disappeared down the hall. Then, I crept back down the hall in the direction from which I came. I had to take Balthazar's lover out before anyone noticed me.

I slipped into the bathroom when Balthazar stepped away from her room. I kept the lights off and opened the door a slit to watch. As Balthazar passed by, he gazed in my direction. *Shit.* I quickly closed the door and waited several long beats. When I opened it, Balthazar was gone. I exited, grabbed a cart of medical supplies, and shuffled down the hall.

The bitch's hospital room was filled with the scent of disinfectant and the low murmur of voices. A doctor in a white coat led a group of nurses toward the bedside, where the bitch lay pale and still. They spoke in hushed tones as they examined her, taking notes on their clipboards.

In the hallway, I crouched behind a corner, heart racing. Sweat dripped down my forehead as I watched them leave the room and head toward the elevator. I waited until they were out of sight before darting into the room.

The victim's face paled when she saw me, and a surge of anger and jealousy shot through my veins. Without hesitation, I grabbed a pillow from the bed and pressed it over her mouth. She struggled weakly, but eventually fell still under the weight of my hand.

I quickly scanned the room for any evidence that could link me to the crime. Satisfied that there was none, I fled into the night, adrenaline coursing through my veins. No one would ever know of my involvement in her death—or so I thought.

CHAPTER THIRTY-FIVE

BALTHAZAR

Hours later, the doctor came to the waiting room. His face was grave, and my heart plummeted.

"She didn't make it," the doctor said, his voice heavy with regret.

I took a step backward. "She what?"

"She died, sir. Your wife. We don't know what happened. She was stable. Her vitals were good, and color was returning to her skin. The nurse and I stepped out into the hall to confer, and when we returned, she was gone."

"What did you do to her?" I flew at the doctor, ready to kill.

He pried my fingers from his coat as he blubbered, "We tried to save her! She was going to make it, I swear!"

I threw back my head and screamed.

"Sir! Sir! Not so loud!"

The words sailed over my head. I glanced at his nametag. *Frank Clark, MD.*

"I want to see her, *Frank*," I demanded. The baby whimpered in my arms.

"It's Dr. Clark," the doctor said.

"Fine, *chum,*" I snarled. "Take me to see my lover."

"But, sir…" Dr. Clark began.

"Take me to her *now!*"

Dr. Clark trembled as he beckoned me to follow.

The sterile hospital room was a flurry of activity as nurses bustling about tried to clean up the blood that had been spilled. Scarlett lay motionless in the bed, surrounded by the eruption of movement, her gaze fixed on the blankness of the ceiling. She was gone, and the tragedy of it hung heavy in the air.

Clutching my child, I stood in the doorway, horror and sadness dripping from my pores. The reality of the situation had left me battered. I wanted to move, to do something, but I was frozen in place, paralyzed by grief.

I inched into the room, my eyes fixed on Scarlett's still form. I rested the baby next to her lifeless body. I couldn't take it in. She was so beautiful, even in death. I wanted to reach out and touch her, to feel the warmth of her skin one more time.

I took her cold hand in mine and let the tears fall freely. I would never see her again, and the pain of it was too much to bear.

Dr. Clark interrupted my shock. "You shouldn't have had a home birth. You should have, at the very least, called a midwife."

My rage was unleashed like a storm. "It was *our* choice. *Our* decision."

"I'm sorry, but she had a chance at life if you had brought her to the hospital. You shouldn't have had a home birth."

I let out an animalistic roar, gripping the doctor by his shirt collar and shaking him violently. My fists clenched, my jaw tightened, and I could feel the heat radiating off me. Tears streamed down my face, mixing with the anger that boiled in my chest. It was suffocating, as if the room had shrunk to contain only my intense emotions. "*You* should have done more. You're the fucking doctor. You should have saved her!"

The baby wailed, his arms and legs flailing.

Dr. Clark's voice boomed through the room. "Call security! I need help in here now!"

The nurses nearly tripped over themselves as they rushed out of the room, their eyes bulging with fear.

I released Dr. Clark, and the room fell into an eerie silence. The doctor slowly backed away, his fear palpable. In my grief, I had unlocked my demonic rage. A maggot squirmed on my cheek and dropped to the floor.

Dr. Clark's eyes widened in horror as he stepped back, crossing himself with shaking hands.

"Dear God," he said, voice trembling. "What are you?"

Fury coursed through my veins as I smiled, and chunks of flesh sloughed off my face.

"Your worst nightmare made real," I snarled. "You'd be wise to call off your security, before it's too late."

"Of course," he stammered. "At once."

"Now, would you mind giving me and my dead lover a moment of peace?" I grinned at him. More maggots fell to the ground.

Dr. Clark let out a shuddering groan and backed out of the room, closing the door behind him.

I turned to Scarlett, feeling a deep chill as if my soul was being ripped from me. I couldn't believe it. I had lost dear, sweet Scarlett and failed her in the worst way. I resumed my human form, picked up the baby, and rocked him in my arms.

"There, there, little one. We'll manage on our own." I gave him my pinkie finger to suckle. "So, what do you think of the name Tristan? Do you like it?"

He sucked my finger, staring at me.

"I agree. It will do. For now." I turned back to Scarlett.

My face was like stone, my breathing shallow and measured as I faced the truth. Scarlett, the mother of my child, was dead. I had held her hand hours earlier as she strained to give birth. Now, her skin was cold, her eyes empty. There I was, standing in the hospital, the most powerful man in the world, a demon capable of unfathomable death and destruction but unable to save her.

A deafening roar in my ears made me feel like I was being dragged down into a bottomless abyss.

I thought of all the times she had taken care of me and the moments we had shared. I thought of our child's future and what might have been.

And now she was gone, just like Zara and my beautiful daughters.

Hot tears overflowed from my eyes, scalding my cheeks as I collapsed to the ground in a fit of uncontrollable sobs. The pain in my heart was unbearable, fueling a deep-seated anger that consumed me. In that moment, I made a dark and twisted decision—to raise this child in my image, with all the evil and cunning that coursed through my veins. Together, we would conquer and dominate the world with fear and chaos as our weapons of choice. I had no idea how wrong I'd be in my quest for dominance.

CHAPTER THIRTY-SIX

ALINA

My feet pounded against the pavement as I hurried home, constantly glancing over my shoulder, consumed by fear. The test results weighed heavy in my pocket as I burst through the door of our cozy kitchen. Jack's back was turned to me as he bustled around, chopping vegetables and sizzling meat on the stove. I took a deep breath and mustered up the courage to break the news.

"Jack," I called out, my voice wavering with nerves. "I have some important news from the doctor."

He stopped what he was doing and turned toward me, his eyes full of concern. "What is it?"

I hesitated for a moment before blurting out the truth. "I'm pregnant."

For a second, there was silence as we both processed the information. Then, his face lit up with excitement and joy. "That's incredible!" he exclaimed, pulling me into a tight embrace.

"I don't want it," I said.

"What? Are you sure? We can take a break from our

search for the second dagger and pursue other endeavors until the baby is born."

"I'll be the worst mother ever," I blurted. "We don't need a child to complete us."

I slumped on the sofa.

Jack sat next to me.

"I want this child," he said. "It will make me so happy. I've felt so alone lately, and now you're giving me something priceless."

"But I don't want a baby." I sighed. "Please don't make me do this."

Perhaps the baby would make Jack happy, but what about my happiness? A baby would change my life, and not for the better. I was consumed with terror of Balthazar's former lover, Zara, and the Scholar. My mind raced with visions of the horrifying punishments they would enact on me if they were to learn I had done something to Jack, or this cursed child inside me. I feared Balthazar taking my life if he ever found out what I'd done to his lover. My heart hammered wildly in my chest. But despite my fears, I made the ultimate decision—I would keep the child, if only to save my own life from my wretched tormentors.

I had been pregnant for what felt like an eternity. Every day was a struggle, and the months crept by in a blur of nausea, misery, and a deep longing for the days before I conceived this child. I had never wanted a child, and now my body was betraying me by holding on to this one.

Each day, my hatred for the pregnancy grew as my body changed. My morning sickness was relentless, and the fatigue was unbearable. I felt like my life was out of my control. The helplessness filled me with dread and resentment.

I counted down the days until its arrival, wishing and praying that it would all be over soon. I just wanted my life back. I tried to forget I was ever pregnant. I wanted to return to the woman I was before this nightmare began.

It felt like I was constantly being watched, my every move quietly scrutinized by the Scholar, Zara, and Balthazar.

As the months ticked by, a single thought consumed me: *Balthazar must never discover the baby growing inside me. He'll kill me for getting pregnant with another man.* I was consumed with paranoia of him finding me.

Dark circles had begun to form under my eyes, my racing thoughts causing me almost unbearable anxiety and sleepless nights. Each morning, I awoke feeling slightly more exhausted than the day before. I had developed a habit of glancing over my shoulder every few minutes, scanning my surroundings for any suspicious sign.

After trying in vain to get some sleep in the afternoon, I awoke to Jack's excited cries.

"Alina!" He burst into the room, clutching a stack of papers. "I've found it! The other dagger!"

"What?" I forced myself out of bed and staggered to his side. "Where is it?"

He spread a map on the bed and stabbed it with his finger. "It's here! It's in Peru! It's at an excavation that's already in progress! I can go find it and return before the baby is born."

"Where did you get this information?" I asked.

Jack's chest puffed up. "I followed a lead."

I seized his shirt. "What do you mean '*I* can go find it?' *We'll* go to the dig together."

"But, Alina," Jack stuttered, "you've been so ill with the pregnancy."

"I don't care how ill I've been," I screamed. "If I don't get to go to this dig, you'll be sorry!"

I glanced around the room, waiting for the Scholar to materialize and choke the life out of me.

I recanted my words: "I'm so sorry, Jack, sweetheart. You're right. This pregnancy has tortured me. I don't mean to take it out on you, but I think a trip away will do me wonders."

He stared at me with skepticism. "Alina, if anything happens to the baby…"

"Nothing will happen to the baby, sweetheart. We'll be together. That's all that matters." I kissed his cheek.

He seemed to consider his options before agreeing.

I let out a sigh and placed a hand on my swollen belly. We would head to Peru before this wretched "life event" commenced. And maybe, if I was lucky, the child wouldn't survive the journey. Zara wouldn't harm me if the death was an accident, would she?

CHAPTER THIRTY-SEVEN

ALINA

I was so mesmerized by the ancient excavation site in Peru, I nearly forgot I was pregnant. The arid breeze carried the scent of desert dust while the midday sun cast its golden glow upon the surrounding ruins.

"Let's call it a day," Jack said as he walked beside me.

Ignoring him, I scraped a garden trowel across the dirt, keeping my eyes trained on the site beneath me.

"Nothing," I muttered. We've been here for weeks, and I still haven't found anything significant. Please hand me a broom."

I extended my hand without looking up at him.

Jack removed his backpack, retrieved the whisk broom, and placed it in my outstretched hand with a sigh. Then, he shrugged the pack back on his back.

I swept the patch of land I had just troweled, still gazing at the dusty, dry soil. "Nothing, nothing, nothing! It's endless days of paltry finds. If I don't have anything to show for myself when we return, I'll…I'll…I don't know what I'll do."

I ran my hand through my messy, short-cropped hair and turned, giving Jack my full attention.

He started to open his mouth to say something. I gasped and placed my hands over my swollen stomach as searing pain shot through me.

"What is it?" Jack asked.

"Shit," I muttered through clenched teeth while slumping against the nearby wall.

"Are you going into labor?!" His eyes widened in horror.

"I don't think so," I groaned, trying to keep calm. "I've been having false labor all day."

"Why didn't you tell me! We need to get out of here." He began gathering our supplies. "You could be going into early labor!"

"Don't be ridiculous, Jack," I said, smiling wanly. "Braxton-Hicks occur during the second or third trimester. They're preparing my body for the real thing, but the baby isn't due for a month."

Jack's face paled to an ashen hue. "What if you go into labor out here? We're stranded in the abyss of wilderness without any hope of cell service. Our only lifeline is a distant ham radio that connects us to the remote village miles away —but what if it's too late by then?"

A guy named Omar, an excavation team member, raced toward us from the white tents set up as living quarters and a makeshift office. "Mrs. James, come quick!"

My voice burst with urgent desperation. "What is it?"

"Moon Lee is trying to reach you via the ham radio..."

"Moon Lee? Why? What does he want?" I said.

"Follow me." Omar took off as I lumbered behind him, with Jack at my side.

Omar threw back the tent flap and stepped inside, tugging

me in after him. He rushed to the small wooden desk, grabbed the black radio receiver, and said, "Mr. Moon Lee, I have Alina here. One moment."

A sinister static tore through the air.

He paused and said, "Mr. Lee, can you repeat that? Our connection isn't clear."

Grabbing the radio from Omar's hand, I shouted, "I'm here!"

The agonizing feedback making its way through the speaker shattered my ear drums. I could make out Lee's low, gruff voice murmuring words like "my ancestors," "ancient artifact," and "la Cueva del Fuego," but nothing else.

"Lee, I can't hear you," I squinted with impatience as I spoke into the device.

Jack grabbed a chair for me to sit in as more jumbled sentences erupted into the room.

"Look for the dagger in La Cueva del Fuego," were the most decipherable words, and my body trembled.

I asked, "So, I'm supposed to look for a knife in the Cave of Fire?"

The connection hummed louder as Lee replied, "Yes, yes! Look in La Cueva del Fuego. That is where you are to search."

I pushed from my seat. "Okay, okay! Thank you, Lee! Thank you!"

Before I could say anything else, a disheartening crackle erupted over the speaker, and our connection was lost.

But one thing was clear—we had to find La Cueva del Fuego and the second dagger.

Outside the tent, my skin crawled as I overheard snippets of conversations between the team, including words like "solar eclipse" and "total darkness in several hours." The chill that overcame me was so powerful it made my teeth chatter.

I spun around to Jack. "Will there be a solar eclipse today?"

He shifted nervously and muttered a barely audible, "Yes."

My voice rose with rage. "Why didn't you tell me?"

Jack threw his hands up in exasperation. "You've been moody and emotional throughout this whole pregnancy, and if I dared to mention that the Eclipsarum Obscura solar eclipse meant our baby might be born during this time, you'd lose your mind!"

"What?" I shrieked. "It's that mystical solar eclipse you spoke of during your dissertation? How do you know?"

Jack's cheeks reddened. "I have my sources."

"I won't have this baby today!" I stomped toward the Jeep. "Let's go!"

There was no way I would go into labor during the so-called Eclipsarum Obscura solar eclipse and prove whether Jack's theory was correct. I wasn't ready for the consequences of Jack's being right, and I did *not* want to birth a Timeborne.

I clutched the map Omar had given me, telling myself to calm down and "not take things out on Jack." If the Scholar were to show up here in Peru and murder me, he would have plenty of places to hide my body, and no one would ever find me.

Jack silently approached the vehicle, no doubt fearing a shouting match.

"I'm sorry, I'm sorry, I'm sorry, Jack. Sometimes I just can't control my temper. I'm hot and miserable with this baby inside." I reached out and squeezed his hand.

He gave a tentative smile.

My apology was interrupted by another Braxton-Hicks.

Jack's face colored with alarm.

I held out my palm like a stop sign. "Not a word from you. This is *normal.*"

I ground my teeth together and endured the pain.

Jack stayed silent for the grueling drive as we followed a dirt road and then simply unmarked land.

I shifted my attention between the map and the terrain. Finally, I pointed. "Over there."

We continued up the terrain with the Jeep pitching and jostling side to side. Jack parked the Jeep between two ginormous boulders, taller than us combined. He retrieved his backpack and slung it over his shoulders, and we trekked for the cave entrance.

An icy silence stretched between us.

Jack kept sneaking glances at his watch.

"What?" I snapped. "Are you timing something?"

He shook his head.

"You're counting the minutes until the eclipse, then."

His grim silence told me the answer.

My heart raced. "When does the solar event happen?"

Jack's monotonous response did nothing to calm my nerves. "The moon would pass between the sun and the earth in just over an hour, plunging us into darkness."

As if that wasn't enough, my body decided now was the best time for a Braxton-Hicks contraction.

I tried to steady my breathing and command my body to hold onto the baby for just one more month. Jack and I needed to focus on our next move inside the cave. But every step deeper into its depths made me more anxious. Water dripped from stalactites and echoed in the darkness while my mind raced with thoughts of what could go wrong.

As we paused to plan our next move, I couldn't help but

grimace in pain. I ignored Jack's concern and pointed him toward the pool deeper into the cave.

"I'll follow," Jack said, reaching for his backpack to retrieve his lantern.

As we ventured further into the abyss, I realized that the unknown terrors lurking in every shadow were not nearly as daunting as the conflict growing within me. This baby might be born during the solar eclipse.

"Let's go," I said with forced resolve.

Jack flicked on the lantern. It let out a dim glow like the batteries were dying.

A shudder ran through my body as I stepped into the depths of the cave, a place so dark and damp that it felt alien. Then, the sunlight cascaded in from a hidden crevice and illuminated the pool before me, glowing with such intensity that it seemed to be a reservoir of ethereal magic.

My foot caught on a rock, and I crashed to the ground, slamming my head into the wall with an almighty thud. A cry of pain escaped my lips as the world around me shimmered.

Jack rushed to my side, throwing himself to the ground beside me.

"Are you okay?" His voice was full of panic.

I blinked a few times, struggling to clear my head.

"I'm not sure," I muttered, lifting my trembling hand up to feel the back of my head. My fingertips met with something wet and sticky, and when I drew them away from my skull, they were covered in a layer of hot, crimson blood.

"Don't worry, I have medical supplies," Jack said, heaving the pack off his back. He yanked open the zipper of the khaki-colored canvas and retrieved the small medical kit. After donning latex gloves with trembling hands, he grabbed two-by-two gauze squares, a roll of gauze, and a bottle of saline from the kit. Then, working quickly yet precisely to clean and dress the wound, he stated, "It doesn't look bad, Alina, but we should head back and get it checked."

"No! We can't stop now."

I shouted in agony as Jack tied the bandage around my head.

He yanked my arm, trying to help me to my feet. "Omar's a trained paramedic. He'll be able to get us back here before you know it."

A beam of sunlight illuminated his face in a sallow hue. The shadows shifted wildly, giving him an almost terrifying appearance.

My khakis flooded with liquid, and Jack's face contorted with disbelief.

He gasped. "No! What the…?"

Unable to contain my fear, I screamed, "My water broke! I'm going to have the baby right now! It can't be happening! It just can't!"

I lay against the cave wall, my breaths coming in shallow pants. Every ounce of my being was consumed with pain and fear.

"This is all your fault!" I screamed at Jack. "You insisted I have this baby!"

Rage and desperation surged through my veins as I grabbed at my belly. With wild eyes, I reached to grab a sharp rock, intent on killing the baby in my womb.

Jack grabbed my wrist. "No, Alina, don't do this! You have to stay strong! You can make it through this!"

I fought against his hold, knocking the lantern away. It crashed against the wall, and its light extinguished.

I let out a guttural sound, pressing my hand on my stomach as the pain radiated throughout my body. I tried to breathe deeply like the birthing coach had instructed, but it was easier said than done.

Jack's presence only made me more anxious. His attempts at comfort felt like empty gestures and did nothing to quell my rising panic. Was I really ready to give birth? Doubts swirled in my mind as I struggled to regain control of my breathing.

"I can't do this," I muttered, half to myself and half to Jack.

But deep down, I knew that giving up wasn't an option. The baby was coming—whether I was ready or not. As another wave of pain hit me, I steeled myself for what would come.

Terror seized me as the sunlight was sucked from the cave. The solar eclipse had temporarily blocked the sun from the sky. The sudden darkness was replaced with chaotic energy as I fought against bringing this wretched child into the world.

"No!" My screams and cries echoed off the cave's walls as I struggled to resist my body's powerful contractions, fighting against the forces of nature and my own body. I cursed at God, and everyone else, as the shadows of the eclipse continued to smother us.

At the apex of the eclipse, a crescendo of cries pierced the air as the baby burst forth from my body. The cave was engulfed in darkness, and every drop of water dripping into the pool seemed to punctuate the moment with haunting echoes. A chill swept through the cave as if death itself had come to witness the newborn's arrival.

The child continued to wail as Jack fumbled with it. "She's here, Alina. She's here. Keep pushing. You have to get the placenta out."

The lantern flared to life in a burst of light. At my side lay a black dagger, gleaming with arcane symbols inscribed along its blade and handle. Something dark surged from the edge, coalescing into an unnerving darkness before it was sucked away as if by some unseen force. My heart raced in terror as I understood what I had unknowingly unleashed—a force of evil, just like me.

CHAPTER THIRTY-EIGHT

ALINA

The plane banked sharply as it approached landing. I gripped the armrests of my seat, trying to hold onto my composure, but I felt like everything was slipping away from me.

I glanced over at Jack who cradled our baby in his arms, tears of joy welling in his eyes. All the way home from Peru, I had been struggling to come to terms with the fact that my child was a Timeborne, a rare and powerful being who could manipulate the very fabric of time and space. It was a knowledge that filled me with dread.

I knew that this power would make her a target, and I was already filled with the fear that Balthazar, the love of my life, might one day come to take her away. He might come to love *her* instead of me. I would not allow that to happen. I had to shield her from the knowledge of her own abilities, even if it meant destroying the very thing that made her unique.

I glanced over at Jack. His eyes widened with manic glee, his breaths coming in short bursts. "It's a miracle! She's a Timeborne! She can travel through time!"

I wanted to grip his throat and choke the words out of him.

"Your theory is wrong, Jack," I said through clenched teeth. "And if you don't stop talking right now, you'll regret it."

The threat hung heavy in the air as Jack's glee faded.

Shit. I'd done it again. My heart sank as I realized that I was trapped with Jack, my pathetic excuse of a husband. I had managed to escape without Emily, leaving her behind with Philip. But I couldn't do that with this child or my husband. I understood that if I didn't keep Jack content and our baby alive, the Scholar would come for me, and Zara would hunt me down like an animal. Then there was Balthazar, a shadow lurking nearby, biding his time and waiting for the perfect moment to strike. I was sure he must have been alerted by some unknown force once the baby was birthed.

I was being watched by *everyone*.

I glanced at Jack.

"I'm sorry, sweetheart." I had never apologized as much as I did with Jack. I felt like a puppet being jerked around by unseen forces. "But we can never speak of your ridiculous theories about time travel again. Nor can we search for the Moon dagger. I'm done."

Jack cocked his head and studied me. "What is it that has you so afraid?"

I squeezed my eyes shut. Oh, how I wished I could tell him, could tell someone. But I couldn't. I wouldn't.

"I'm just tired," I said, meeting his gaze.

"Post-partum depression," he said, nodding. "We can get help for you with that."

I shook my head. There was nothing that could help me.

Jack stared at my swollen breasts.

"Are you going to nurse her?" he asked in a desperate whisper.

I gave him a stern look. "No. You said you'd help and do everything. You can feed her formula."

The baby's features contorted, her hands squeezing into rigid fists as she kicked and flailed with all her might.

"But she's hungry *now*," Jack said weakly, not wanting to oppose me but still desperate for his daughter to be fed. "You have to keep feeding her until we get home."

I gritted my teeth and reached for the nameless baby. I hadn't even had the heart to give her a name. She latched onto my aching breast, helping to relieve the swollen tension. But I felt no warmth as I fed her. I had no nurturing impulses to give to her or anyone.

Once we were back home, I sat in the kitchen and listlessly picked at a salad we'd bought at the grocery store on the way home. My appetite was gone. I informed Jack I needed to see Lee.

"You want to see Lee? Why?" Jack held the baby over his shoulder, rocking her back and forth.

"We need to tell him about the baby. He'll want to know."

Jack's disappointed expression burned into me like hot coals. His words cut through me with a sharp edge as he spat out, "Whatever. *Someone* must watch over our child, so it's up to me now."

He bounced her fiercely on his shoulder, and she seemed strangely content with the rough treatment. At least I'd given my children fathers who would care for them.

Jack looked at the baby with a visible sense of awe. "This little beauty must have a name worthy of her. What should it be?"

The child gurgled and waved her arms with delight, seeming to understand the question fully.

"Olivia! Olivia is in Shakespeare's 'Twelfth Night,' one of my favorite plays, where she's a strong, independent, and complex character. That's it!" Jack said, looking up from his bundle of joy. "What do you think, Alina? Shall we call her Olivia?"

My heart stuttered, and I hesitated before responding with a defeated voice, "It's fine. I don't care what you call her."

"Your mommy doesn't care," he said in a sing-song voice. Olivia squealed.

"She doesn't care one bit," he said, tickling her tummy. "But I think she really does care."

He swirled her around as he waltzed out of the room. "Let's see if our neighbor will watch you while Mommy and I go visit Uncle Lee, okay?"

I lurched into Lee's condo, desperation washing over me. Jack followed me like a mongrel.

"Alina," Lee said in greeting, standing aside for me to enter. "Jack!"

I side-eyed Jack and said in a low voice to Lee, "I need to speak to you in private."

"Will you excuse us for a moment, Jack?" Lee asked.

Jack's gaze slid between me and Lee before he nodded.

Lee led me into the kitchen and sat at his small table. A half-eaten sandwich and a nearly empty bottle of beer rested before him. "You look awful. I heard you had the baby in Peru."

He took a bite of his sandwich and gestured for me to sit.

"Who told you?"

"I have my sources. How are you doing being a new

parent? How's the child?" he asked with uncharacteristic gentleness.

"We have to go away," I said, settling onto the hard wooden stool. "We have to time travel together, away from here."

His eyebrows rose, but he said nothing as he chewed his food.

"A dagger appeared by her side. Olivia is a Timeborne and must be hidden from the darkness, or else Balthazar will find her. He'll find us." I reached into my purse, withdrew the dagger, and handed it to him.

He sucked in a breath at its beauty.

"You must hide this," I said, desperate. "Olivia must never know of her abilities. She can't know she's a time traveler."

Lee continued to stay silent, lifting the beer to his lips and draining it. His sharp eyes bore into mine while he ran his tongue around his teeth in a mocking gesture.

"I will hide her dagger and ensure no one ever finds out about her. As for you..." He jabbed a finger at me. "You better take care of that baby."

He fixed me with a steely glare, the weight of his words settling like a rock on my chest. The old wooden chair groaned as Lee leaned back so the front legs lifted off the floor.

"Alina, you have to stay out of trouble. I'm going to hide the dagger and get away from here for a while. Take care of her and Jack. We'll need to be apart until this settles down. No time traveling or looking for the other dagger. Just remain in one place." He brought the chair's front legs to the floor with a loud thunk, making an exclamation point on his words.

Jack appeared in the doorway, glowering. "What are you two talking about?"

"We were just discussing your beautiful child, Olivia," Lee said, smiling broadly. "At the time of the full moon, if the dagger cuts Olivia's skin, it is said she can time travel."

"I knew it! I knew my theories were true!" Jack said.

"The cutting of flesh with the uttering of sacred words on the knife will supposedly take the Timeborne to another time and century," he said. "But it will also release the darkness."

"The Umbrum Void?" Jack said, looking confused.

"Never mind. Lee's telling tall tales again." I shot him a sharp glance. "In any case, he's going to hide the dagger. He'll oversee it, and we won't speak of this time travel nonsense again."

"But—" Jack said.

"Not a word. I'm sick of the topic."

Lee took the dagger from my hands, then we said our farewells.

"You just don't understand," Jack said on the ride home. "Time travel is my life...my passion! I can't *not* speak about it just because it makes you feel uncomfortable. You don't get it. You gave birth to a remarkable child with remarkable abilities. She's going to want to know about it!"

I frantically searched for a way to get us out of this situation. Taking a deep breath, I lied through my teeth. "Lee and I are on the same page about time travel—it's all completely bogus."

Jack frowned. "Lee said that? But what about when he told us about uttering the sacred words?"

"That's the *legend,* not the reality. He told me that before you entered the room."

Jack's face fell.

"He laughed, saying something about La Cueva del Fuego being littered with artifacts like the dagger we gave to him."

"He did?"

"Yes, sweetheart. I'm sorry. I know it hurts you to hear that, but we've got to face facts. Olivia's just an ordinary child meant for an ordinary life." I put my hand on his thigh.

Jack seemed surprised by my kindness. I absentmindedly rubbed his upper arm. As I reached out to comfort Jack, a war waged inside me. On one hand, I had promised Lee that I would stay out of danger and stop searching for the moon dagger. But on the other hand, the thought of possessing such immense power and being able to negotiate with Balthazar was tempting. Was it really breaking my promise if I had already agreed to go after the dagger? A mischievous smile crept onto my face as I contemplated my options.

Yes, this felt right. It was what I was destined to do: possess the sun and the moon daggers.

CHAPTER THIRTY-NINE

BALTHAZAR

I had been consumed by the need for revenge against Alina ever since she had left me so long ago, and I had spent decades planning and scheming to make her pay. But when my son was born, everything else faded away. I wanted to be the best father I could be, and the old anger and desire for revenge were replaced by a newfound joy and vigor.

Rather than relying on nannies and other caretakers, I decided to raise Tristan myself. I was determined to be there for him at every step, and the time I spent with him was some of the most fulfilling moments of my life.

As Tristan matured, I tried to instill evil in him. Violence, death, and destruction were ways of life, and I wanted to pass that lesson on to my son.

"Make sure if someone pushes you, you hurt them. Punch them. Kick them. Do whatever it takes to make sure they never mess with you again by instilling pain and fear. "

But no matter how many times other children provoked him, Tristan's response was always the same—tears streaming down his face as he refused to fight back. Months went by, and still, my son never showed even a hint of aggression. I began to worry that he was too kind for his own good. I tried to instill in him the importance of not showing weakness, but though Tristan listened intently, it seemed like the lesson just wouldn't stick. I had to come to terms with the fact that my son might never possess the cruelty and malice that I so desperately wanted him to have. As much as it pained me, I had to accept that he was just too pure-hearted for his own good—or, for *mine*.

Instead, he was *nice*.

I noticed with dismay that my son had an innate ability to calm people down and make them feel at ease with his gentle words. He was also soft and caring. This disturbed me. He was too much like his mother. Too much like Cora, Mathias' sugary-sweet wife. My burning ambition was to have a son like Malik, but instead, I got Tristan, the meek and gentle boy who could never live up to my expectations.

Every day that passed was a reminder of my failure. My resentment grew like wildfire until nothing was left but a determination to find retribution, a need to unleash vengeance on the one responsible for my misfortune. I planned on resuming my hunt for Alina.

CHAPTER FORTY

ALINA

Eight years of torment had passed since my child was born. Eight unbearable years.

Hatred burned through my veins like acid, corroding the patches of joy that used to be scattered throughout my life with Balthazar. I loathed myself and everything I had become, an enslaved worker to my own offspring. Every day, an unending routine of nourishing and tending to this creature, as though it held the key to redemption. Nevertheless, no matter how diligently I endeavored, the hollowness within me remained untouched.

The days were long and lonely, and I felt increasingly isolated from the world around me. I spent my days gathering antiques for the store *Life after Life*, which Jack and I purchased when Olivia was two. It had kept me occupied for a time, but now nothing kept me from my tormented thoughts.

I tried to hide my inner turmoil but soon found that I couldn't keep up the facade anymore. I started to hear strange voices in my head, taunting me, telling me I was a loser and that I was pathetic and weak.

I thought I might be going crazy, but I was determined to prove that wasn't true. One night, when I thought I heard voices outside the antique shop downstairs, I rushed down the stairs leading to the back of the store.

I gasped. Balthazar stood at the window, his black clothing glowing silver in the moonlight. He stood tall and proud, his dark hair tousled by the wind. My heart raced as I sprinted out the door, my mind consumed with him. Ignoring any sense of caution, all I wanted was to taste his lips, run my fingers through his hair, and feel his strong embrace. The air around us seemed electrified with anticipation as I closed the distance between us, my longing for him overpowering any fear of danger.

As the front door clattered shut behind me, Balthazar whirled to face me, his eyes glittering with menace. He took a step toward me, and I froze.

"Balthazar, I abandoned you!" I yelled. "I admit it. It was the only way to get the daggers. Every second I've been apart from you has felt like an eternity. I did despicable things just to find those blades. I married an imbecile for his knowledge of their whereabouts. I cannot express my regret that I had to leave you behind. Despite it all, you are still my beloved King, and I am your devoted Queen."

His gaze shifted and he paused, assessing…calculating.

I approached him and fell at his feet, pressing my forehead on his boots. "Please forgive me. I can't live another day without you."

He grabbed a handful of my hair and wrenched me up to face him.

The pain in my skull, sharp and intense, was exquisite.

"You fucking whore," Balthazar roared, his voice shaking with rage. His face twisted and flushed an angry shade of crimson. "You deceived me. You wanted those blades for yourself, thirsting after ultimate power."

"I know, I know, my…" I almost slipped and uttered the words "my lord." Instead, I interjected, "My King."

His expression faltered. Then his hand shot out and seized my throat.

Maggots popped through his forehead and squirmed on the surface. His skin fell away from his eyes and nose, leaving behind bloody bone and cartilage.

It aroused me, making me wet.

He crashed his lips to mine. He tore apart his trousers revealing his thick, engorged cock. "Do you want this? Do you?"

"Oh, yes, Balthazar. Please!"

"You don't deserve it!" he roared, spraying my face with spittle.

"Please, Balthazar." My mind and body were in a frenzy of longing. "Please fuck me. Give me what I've longed for."

With a sudden force, Balthazar spun me around, ripping my skirt away and savagely tearing my panties down. He pounded like an uncontrollable animal, pressing my face against the glass with one hand while I silently endured every second of it.

Though it was far from romantic, it still exceeded any of the terrible sex I'd shared with Jack, who couldn't begin to match up to the sheer passion and drive of Balthazar.

"Oh, my love," I said through gritted teeth. "I'm so glad I murdered Scarlett for you."

Balthazar stopped abruptly. "What did you say?"

My confusion made it hard to think straight. "I... I didn't say anything."

He spun me to face him. His grip on my throat tightened

until I could barely breathe. Fear ran through me. This might be it—the end of everything.

I fought with all my might against Balthazar's hold, but it was like fighting a force of nature. He transformed into his demon self, and nothing would halt his frenzied wrath. He flung his arms in the air, releasing me, and let out an ear-splitting scream that shook the very foundations of the earth.

I scrambled away from him, terror gripping my heart as I watched in horror at the monster before me.

"What's happening?" I screamed, my voice cracking with fear.

Balthazar wrapped his clawed hands around his head, letting loose another blood-curdling scream. "Stop! Make it stop!"

As I backed away slowly, his eyes blazed with madness, his body wracked with uncontrollable spasms.

I crumpled to the pavement, heart racing. Ahead, on the darkened sidewalk, a dark figure stood there, a sinister grin on its face. Balthazar disappeared in a puff of smoke, and as much as I wanted to believe it was all just a nightmare, my throbbing body told me otherwise.

I scrambled inside the antique shop, slamming the door behind me and locking it tight. Balthazar would come back for me soon enough, and this time, I had to be ready.

Endless arguments with Jack filled my days.

"You always side with Olivia!" I yelled, throwing my hands up in exasperation. "She's just a child and already you're spoiling her."

Jack, hunched over his keyboard in the bedroom office,

tried to reason with me, his voice calm and measured. "She's our daughter, Alina. We should be on the same side."

But I was relentless. "You never listen to me. Our marriage is falling apart and all you care about is our daughter."

On one occasion, I'd had enough. I stood in the center of the living room, my arms crossed and my face stern. Each tick of the antique clock on the sideboard hammered at my brain.

"I told you initially that I would only bear Olivia for you. I can't be expected to toil constantly to care for her." We'd been locked in a battle of wills for the past hour, but it seemed he wasn't getting the point.

Jack bolted from the sofa and threw up his hands. "You've got to make an effort, Alina!" Frustration rolled from his shoulders like tumultuous waves. "I'm happy to be her primary caregiver, but at least a little affection from you wouldn't harm her."

"When I'm in her presence, I'm civil and polite," I snapped.

"'Civil and polite' does not a mother make. Kindness and commitment go a long way." Jack's face was blotchy and red from the exertion of quarreling with me.

"I'm so sick of your 'better than thou' attitude. You're nothing but a worthless loser." I sneered. "I should've never saved you. Our sex is ridiculous to non-existent, and everything to do with you is repulsive."

He looked like he'd been punched in the gut. My words were harsh, but I had finally found the courage to voice all the things that had been eating away at me for years.

Jack was speechless, the anger in his eyes transforming to disbelief and hurt. He had once thought I was his savior. His one true friend. Now, with those few words, I had destroyed the fragile bridge between us, splintering it like decaying wood.

I expected him to fight back, to lash out and tell me I was wrong. But he didn't. Instead, he simply looked at me with hollow eyes, his skin ashen, his body shaking with a mixture of emotions. Pain was etched on his face, and a pang of guilt shot through me for the first time in a long time.

The voices of Zara and the Scholar shouted in my head with taunting threats. Their intimidating warnings were like an unshakable vice around my heart. I hadn't seen or heard from them in months, but their words echoed in my mind, a constant whisper of fear I could not escape. The pressure of their unfulfilled promises weighed heavily on me. I shook with fury at the thought of being manipulated by unseen forces and vowed to break free from their ghostly power. I was done acting like their well-heeled dog.

Jack and I stood there for what seemed like an eternity, both of us unsure of what would happen next. Finally, he spoke, his voice low and broken.

"Is that it?" he said.

"Not really." I stepped forward and grabbed him by the arms. I locked eyes with him, my gaze cold and determined. "This isn't working. I don't want to be married to you anymore. I want a divorce."

Jack crumpled as if I'd thrown a bowling ball at his abdomen. "I knew our marriage has been strained for months, but I had never imagined it would come to this."

Olivia bounced into the kitchen like a puppy dog, over-flowing with joy.

My hands flew from Jack's arms, and our argument ceased. Jack and I smiled like we always did when Olivia was around. Only Jack's smile was genuine—mine was forced.

"Hello, Olivia, darling," I said.

"What's up, buttercup?" Jack said, reaching for her.

Olivia threw her arms around his waist, hopping from foot to foot. "Come and watch me jump on the mini trampoline! I can do it really high."

She demonstrated by leaping into the air, reaching up until her fingertips nearly touched the low ceiling.

Jack's eyes went wide with astonishment. "You can go that high?"

Olivia smiled proudly. "Sure can!"

He ruffled her hair. "I'll be right there, little monkey. And your mom, too?"

He glanced in my direction.

I returned a strained smile. "Of course, kiddo. We'll both come and watch you."

After Olivia scampered away, I hesitated. I took a deep breath and said, "I'm sorry, but I can't do this anymore. I feel so...resentful...toward our daughter. I never wanted her in the first place. I just can't bring myself to play with or be around her."

Jack's chin quivered, but he offered a solemn nod. His voice cracked as he said, "I think you're right. It's time for us to stop pretending that things between us are normal or that you're a parent who cares."

The sentiment crashed over me like a wave, surprising me with its finality. This was the first thing we had agreed on in what felt like forever.

"Tell Olivia her mom had something urgent to attend to," I said in a voice as cold as the snow outside. I closed my fingers around my purse handle, brushing the worn fabric of the sofa.

"Where are you going?" Jack asked, his voice heavy with disinterest. His face was expressionless, but his eyes flicked down to the brown leather bag.

"To Lee's." I opened my purse and ran my thumb along the spine of my journal, its pages filled with secrets. Satisfied that it was still there, I shut my handbag and faced Jack.

"I thought Lee was gone," Jack said.

"He is. He's *always* gone," I spat back. Taking a deep breath, I turned away from him and added, "I just need some space from *you*." My gaze fell upon Jack's face, a torrent of guilt and turmoil surging through me. The weight of our troubled marriage crushed down upon me, begging the question —was it even worth the agony to continue?

CHAPTER FORTY-ONE
ALINA

My horrible life was serving no one. I was sick and tired of Balthazar chasing me, of Zara's and the Scholar's leering threats. Thoughts of them tormented me, intent on breaking me. I needed help as well as space from Jack, so I headed to Lee's.

I knocked frantically on the door, my heart pounding against my ribcage as I waited. I assumed he was gone but when I started to fish out my key, the door swung open wide.

I reared backward, surprised to see someone other than Lee.

"Good. I've been waiting for you." The male towered above me like a giant, an unearthly figure with limbs that stretched on for miles. His feral expression was a chillingly unnerving sight, and had my heart frozen in terror. His gray eyes were like a midnight storm, razor-sharp, as if they had the power to unravel all my secrets with just one glance.

"Who are you?" I asked, my voice trembling ever so slightly.

"Salvatore," he replied. "I am your ally."

"My ally? I don't think so."

Salvatore's dark eyes pierced through me, and a sense of calm washed over me despite my fear.

He stepped aside to let me in. I brushed past him, entering Lee's cluttered front room, feeling safe and protected for the first time in weeks.

I perched on the worn sofa, eying him with suspicion. Two empty beer bottles sat on the side stand, evidence of Lee's continued drinking. "Where's Lee?"

"He's not here."

A chill rippled through me. "You didn't…he's not dead, is he?"

"Of course, he's not dead. I have no desire to harm him." Salvatore laughed. "Worry not. I'm here to help you." His eyes took on a satisfied glint. "We're going to work together to deceive Balthazar."

A tumultuous blend of emotions surged through my body, leaving me feeling dizzy and uncertain. I searched for some sense of familiarity or trust in Salvatore's storm-colored, brooding eyes, but he was still a stranger to me. Despite this, there was an undeniable aura of immense power surrounding him, making me feel both intimidated and desperate. With no other options left, I knew I had to put my faith in him.

"Deceive him? How can we possibly achieve such a feat? He's a cunning monster."

He exhaled sharply, his grin widening. "We are going to draw him out. Play with his mind. My powers are far greater than Balthazar's. You will meticulously re-write your journal as though it were a love letter to Balthazar. But deep down, its contents should be crafted with the intention of depicting you as one who loathes him and is frightened of him."

My heart raced as I contemplated his words. Desperation clawed at me. I could do this.

"What about my daughter?" My voice cracked with

emotion. "Should she ever be given the power of time travel, I wish to ensure her blade carries a deadly poison. I won't let her suffer the same fate as me."

Salvatore tsked. "Let's not pretend you don't fear her power. You want her dead."

I cringed at his honest assessment of my motives but said nothing to confirm. "To what end are we doing this? Drawing Balthazar out?"

"You'll see," Salvatore said. "It's part of a greater plan than your own selfish motives. Go to Raul Costa. Beg his forgiveness if need be. Trust me, he will help you create something perfect and deadly."

Raul and I hadn't exactly departed on good terms, so this might prove challenging. "Okay, so I obtain poison from Raul. I rewrite the journal. Then what?"

"Go to John James. Ask for his help."

I looked at Salvatore incredulously. "Go to John James? What kind of game are you playing?"

"It's a game of deceit, my dear," he replied, the corners of his lips twitching into an evil smirk. "We are dropping subtle hints along the way, creating a breadcrumb trail for Balthazar to follow. Ask John James for assistance. Pretend to be a hapless female, frightened of Balthazar. He will point you in the direction we want. He will tell you where to take your rewritten journal and the sun dagger. Follow his instructions to the letter."

He took a step forward, his eyes boring into me with an intensity that made my skin crawl. "This is our plan. Do not fail."

"I won't fail," I said solemnly.

After he left, I prepared to follow his plan. It was time to destroy my past. My fingers trembled as I reached into my purse and pulled out my weathered notebook. I gasped as I thumbed through the pages containing stories and entries about my life before I decided to leave Balthazar and start over. Even though I had few recollections of the details, the pages before me spoke of a darker version of myself, one who partied hard, tortured others, and lived recklessly. It had been a good life, one that I treasured.

Now, I had to move on. I had to create a new narrative with the intention of deceiving Balthazar. Taking a deep breath, I grabbed my pen and focused on writing a fake journal full of false hopes, dreams, and tales of a person that would never exist.

My pen moved quickly, recording a new story and life for myself, dropping hints to Balthazar.

I spent the next two days absorbed in my writing. I crafted characters that sprung to life with every pen stroke on the page. I conjured up settings, scenes of grandeur and sorrow, and painted them with my words. I even concocted complete fabrications of truth and fiction blurred beyond distinction, creating a story as captivating as it was challenging.

I wrote late into the night, often forgetting to eat or sleep. Every moment felt like a lifetime, and my fingers ached from the long hours of scribing. I was lost in a world I had created, slowly discovering new details and nuances that surprised me. There was an undeniable thrill in watching a story emerge from nothing but the power of my words. With every keystroke, I felt like I was birthing something beautiful and unique, and I was immensely proud of my creation.

Finally, after two days of intense labor, I stopped writing. I blinked, my vision slightly blurred after so many hours of staring at the parchment. I smiled, satisfied with what I had achieved. A wave of fatigue crashed over me, yet still, I was overcome with a surge of energy. I had written my masterpiece with such power that I transformed my image from an evil force into a vulnerable quarry before my own eyes. Balthazar would indeed be deceived.

Clenching my fists and gritting my teeth, I fought against the growing exhaustion that threatened to overwhelm me. Refusing to surrender to sleep, I stumbled through Lee's condo. Despite knowing him for years, I felt like a stranger in his home; so many mysteries were left unsolved and endless secrets were hidden within his walls.

Could I glean some truth about him? Everywhere I looked, there were Native American artifacts that Lee had collected over the years. Some were in glass cases, while others were scattered around the room.

As I entered Lee's bedroom, a wave of nauseating affection smacked me. Every inch of the walls was plastered with photos of Lee, Jack, and Olivia, their smiling faces beaming down at me from every angle.

On a corner table sat a dagger—*her* dagger—the one that would enable Olivia to travel in time. It gleamed dangerously under the muted light, calling out to me like a siren's song. My heart pounded as I approached it, stretching out my hand until my fingertips brushed against its cold metal hilt.

All this time, Lee had hidden it away in plain sight, just like he had done with everything else.

My mind raced as I tapped my lips, searching for a plan to save myself. I had no choice but to destroy the original journal and plant the incriminating diary with someone—the perfect someone. I didn't know who that was, but I would figure it out. Then, I had to find Raul and obtain the poison. My heart clenched at the thought of him, but I had to try to win him back if my plan would succeed. Before that, I would have to face Jack and tell him I was taking a long trip searching for the moon dagger. I hope he wouldn't see through my story and discover the truth behind my motives.

The original journal had been my only confidant and companion through the darkness of my past. Its sturdy pages recorded my vile deeds, detestable thoughts, and heinous actions. Now, it was time for that part of my life to end.

I stared at the diary in my hands. Half of my life was inscribed within its pages, yet I could not keep it any longer.

Carefully, I ripped each page from its binding, feeling deeply sad as I did so. When I was finished, I consigned the pages to the flames of Lee's fireplace, watching them burn. I sighed, feeling both relief and sorrow. The journal was gone, but so was the last remnant of my wicked past.

A strange sense of completion shrouded me in Lee's cluttered front room. I felt cleansed, ready to start my new life. I took a deep breath and headed home to Jack.

I walked into the house with a heavy heart, expecting to find Jack waiting eagerly to talk. Maybe he hoped for reconciliation. But as I stepped into the entryway, I was met with a strange and eerie stillness.

I wandered from room to room, searching for him, and found him sitting in a chair by the window, his back to me. I could tell from the stillness of his posture that he was deep in thought.

I cleared my throat, but there was no reaction. I took a few more steps toward him, thinking he hadn't heard me, but he still didn't turn.

Then, I noticed the unmistakable chill that hung in the air. Jack was intentionally ignoring me.

Why did this hurt so badly? I was the one who wanted out. I was sure, given the chance, Jack would want to work things out.

I steeled myself against the wave of rejection that threatened to overwhelm me and spoke softly. "Jack...are you okay?"

There was no response.

Jack's indifference toward me said more than words ever could. I couldn't bear to look him in the eyes for fear of what I saw there.

"Jack, I'm sorry, my love, but I'm leaving for a bit," I said. "I'm going to go find moon dagger. We need to separate."

Jack nodded slowly, his eyes betraying a sad resignation as if he had expected this and yet still felt the sting of loss.

"I think what broke our marriage apart was stopping pursuing something we believed in—finding the daggers," he said quietly.

The edges of my lips turned up in a reluctant smile as I recalled the days when we both believed so strongly in our shared mythos. We used to talk endlessly about how the ancient sun and moon daggers were said to possess unimaginable power.

Jack's angry expression softened slightly as I told him about a fake mission to search for the dagger, and for a moment, it felt like the old us was back. The bruised bags under his eyes were evidence that his nights had been as sleepless as mine. I looked deep into his eyes, feeling guilty for the secret I was withholding from him—that I wasn't leaving to pursue the moon blade.

"I'm going to do this, Jack," I lied, gripping his hands. "I'm going to bring the daggers home, and when I do, I'll return to you. I promise."

With a heavy heart, I pressed my lips against his soft cheek before turning away—my mind already full of ideas on how to successfully create a new me without Jack ever knowing.

A cold shiver skated down my neck on the night of the full moon. It was time to put my devious plan in motion. I pulled on my cloak and slipped out the door. I time-traveled to John James' time, where it was midday. Sultry heat gripped the land like a sweaty hand as I climbed the hill to his cabin.

I moved through thick air that felt too heavy to breathe and held fast against every step forward. My satchel hung from my shoulder like an iron weight. Heat radiated from the ground in waves. When I reached John James' familiar little cabin, he was out by the creek filling an urn with water. I approached him slowly so as not to scare him.

He rose and squinted, trying to see me through the misty heat. "Hello! Who goes there?"

"It's me, John James. It's Alina."

"Alina Tocino?" he said, creases forming in the corners of his eyes.

"One and the same," I said. "It's so good to see you!"

John James wrapped me in his arms in a bear hug. Even this friendly hug felt more substantial than the lukewarm embraces I endured from Jack.

"What brings you to these parts?" he said, beaming.

"I wanted to tell you I found one of the daggers."

He clapped his hands together.

"Did you? That's wonderful news—simply wonderful. Please come and sit with me and share the details." He gestured to his spot beneath the trees. "It's far too hot to be indoors."

I followed him and perched on a tree stump.

"Can I get you some water? It's fresh and cold." He hefted the urn with one arm, his muscles straining.

"Yes, please. That would be lovely," I said, aware of how parched my mouth felt. After living on the Pacific West Coast for many years, I had forgotten what Midwestern heat felt like. I was not used to the humidity and heat that prevailed here in the summertime.

When he returned, I regaled John James with the heroic story of my adventures to Peru, where I had unearthed an ancient dagger, embellishing the story to suit my purposes. I proclaimed the courage and determination I had shown by embarking on this excursion while pregnant and how Jack and I had stood together in our mission. It was all an elaborate lie, but John James seemed to eat it up. His eyes locked onto me, transfixed by my exploits as if I was sharing a legendary myth.

"Honestly, Alina, your fortitude is admirable," he said once I'd finished.

I glowed, thinking how easy it had been to craft a tale for my nefarious purposes. This kind of storytelling was in my blood, honed since I was a youth.

A sly smirk curled on my lips, and I leaned in close, the words barely audible when I spoke. "I've brought the sun dagger with me. Would you like to see it?"

John James' breathing came out in short, ragged gasps, and his eyes shone with avarice. "Show me."

The intensity emanating from every syllable was almost tangible.

I lifted my satchel from my shoulder and unzipped it. From within, I pulled out a long, slender dagger, its bone handle intricately carved with symbols. I pressed it into John James' hands, feeling its weight and power in my palms even after it had left me. His eyes widened as he examined its beauty and might. With a deep breath, I explained that this and my beloved journal were two items Balthazar would use to track me down, so I had to entrust them to him for safekeeping. Tentatively, I met his gaze, pleading for help without speaking.

John James' pupils dilated. "I can't risk it. I'm not willing to keep them for you. If they are ever in my possession, Balthazar will relentlessly hunt me down."

His voice trembled, and he shivered as if caught in an icy wave.

He popped up from his seat and stumbled backward, barely catching himself before he fell. Wringing his hands, he said, "Here is my advice. Separate the items. Don't take any chances." He slammed his fist on his palm, emphasizing his point. "You must entrust these items to a compelling individual—someone who can defend themselves if Balthazar decides to attack."

His vehemence made me flinch.

"Do you have anyone in mind?" I asked, a hint of desperation in my voice.

"Yes!" His voice cracked like a whip through the trees. His face drained of color, and his eyes blazed with urgent intensity. With shaking hands, he clutched my wrist. "Take the sun dagger and give it to Giovanni Zampa. He will keep it safe for you."

"Signor Zampa? Yes, I know him." The words came out in a rush.

John James scanned our surroundings as if someone was shadowing him, then looked back at me, gripping my arm.

"You must travel back in time and bring your diary to Eyan Malik," he said urgently. "He lives in 1582."

I gasped in shock. "Malik is dead!"

My throat constricted as John James said, "Eyan Malik is very much alive."

The last time I saw Malik, he was a captive in Balthazar's dungeon. I had tried to poison him and failed. Now he was living? How could this be?

"Go!" John James said. "Find him! And get these cursed

items away from here before Balthazar appears and leaves our corpses in his wake."

The fear of death pressed against me like a smothering blanket, but I had no choice. I would time-travel back to 1582. I hoped fate would grant me enough time to seek out Eyan Malik before Balthazar caught up with me. In truth, either darkness might try to kill me. I had to assume I was making the right choice.

I grew suspicious as the daunting task settled into my mind. "How do you know Malik is alive?"

"My sources have told me that Malik's in a different time-line," he said. "1500s Italy."

I rolled my eyes. John James was always so secretive with this information.

"Fine, I'll go to 1500s," I said through gritted teeth, becoming more frustrated by the second. "Why don't you tell me who your sources are?"

John James visibly paled and shook his head.

"I can't. I'll die," he murmured.

"Curse you and your brother!" I spat. "You're both fools!"

John James winced, his eyes filled with fear and desperation. Then he appeared to gather strength from within and spat, "Balthazar is hunting us. You must do as I say if we are to survive. Take the blade to Zampa. Find Malik and give him the journal before it's too late. He is our only hope against the evil Balthazar. For the love of God, do this quickly, or else all will be lost."

CHAPTER FORTY-TWO

ALINA

In a blinding flash, I materialized in the sun-drenched cobblestone streets of 1582 Italy. I was stunned by the vivid beauty around me. The bustling crowds moved with intent like scurrying ants, the sweet smell of fresh bread wafting from the ovens of local bakeries like a siren's song. I felt the warmth of the summer breeze against my skin, but my heart ached with grief. It was here that I first met Balthazar.

A violent shudder ran through my body at the thought of Balthazar, followed by an inferno of yearning that nearly brought me to my knees. I hadn't felt such a scorching passion since leaving him. But I also hadn't encountered such overwhelming terror. I'd committed the ultimate betrayal against Balthazar—cavorted with another man, Raul, and then abandoned Balthazar without warning. He'd threatened, in no uncertain terms, that if I ever spread my legs for another man, his retribution would be swift and deadly. As much as I craved to be near him again, I had to push away those cravings. Instead, I had to find Giovanni Zampa.

Then the image of Balthazar's bitch girlfriend, Scarlett,

SARA SAMUELS

flashed through my mind, eclipsing any other thought. Uncontrollable rage seethed within my gut at the injustice of Balthazar demanding loyalty and fidelity but then fathering a child with another woman.

I knew where Signor Zampa used to live. Would he still live there? Perhaps he was in town. As I searched the small village's bustling streets and alleyways, I felt a sense of hope that I was getting closer to finding my quarry. And then, as if by some divine intervention, I spotted someone in the distance that fit the description I remembered of Signor Zampa.

He was a tall, thin man with a long beard and a sharp gaze. He was wearing an old, tattered cloak and looking around cautiously, perhaps expecting someone to arrive. Was he searching for me? Did he have foresight as to my arrival?

As I walked toward him, his eyes widened, and his jaw dropped as he recognized me. He fumbled for words, trying to compose himself, but the shock was too evident on his face.

"Alina? Is that you?" His voice quavered like that of an old man.

"Yes, yes, Signor Zampa."

A sharp intake of breath escaped Signor Zampa's lips as he peered at me.

"Is that *really* you?" he asked incredulously, squinting to make out my features.

"Yes," I said. "It's me, Alina. I need your help."

"What can an old man like myself do to help you?" he asked. His back was stooped, yet his gaze was unwavering.

My hands shook as I said, "Balthazar, he's trying to kill me. I found the sun dagger."

"Come, child. We cannot discuss such a perilous topic in public," he said, looking left and right as he took my elbow and guided me off the busy street. He tugged me into a shadowed tavern.

The air inside the cafe was thick and humid, with a hint of sweet smoke lingering in the background. The smoke hung in the air, illuminated by the light that filtered through the half-closed blinds. It was a heavy, oppressive atmosphere, yet strangely intoxicating. It reminded me so much of when Balthazar and I were in love.

Signor Zampa gripped my arm and dragged me through the inn. A gentle hum of conversation drifted from groups of people scattered around the room, punctuated by laughter and calm clinks of glasses. We wove through the crowded tables until Signor Zampa finally stopped, motioning for me to sit opposite him at an unoccupied table.

I sat, expectant, unsure of what to say or do. I started to speak, but he put his finger to his lips.

I waited, silent until a rotund tavernkeeper wearing a loose-fitting, knee-length woolen tunic, hose, and leather shoes trundled toward us. "What'll it be, Signor Zampa?"

"Two tankards of mead, if you please."

The tavernkeeper nodded and shuffled away, limping slightly.

"Wait until he returns," Signor Zampa said, "before you share your story."

The innkeeper returned shortly bearing two metal tankards. He plunked them before us and waited while Signor Zampa fished a few coins and tossed them to him. Then, with a grunt, the man walked away.

We both took a long sip from our drinks. The spiced, fermented honey water tasted delicious to my parched throat.

"You say Balthazar is trying to kill you?" Signor Zampa said in a low voice. The feeble figure that had shuffled along the cobblestone road moments before was gone. In its place sat a robust and well-built man with sharp eyes and a commanding presence.

"Yes," I replied in a quivering voice. I told my story, carefully chosen words painting a portrait of me as the distraught victim of an evil man.

Oh, I was good at this play-acting. My performances were getting stronger with each passing day.

When I finished, he asked, "And how can I help?"

"I've been advised to leave the blade in your safekeeping. I can't keep it as it will serve as a tracking beacon for Balthazar." I reached into my satchel, pulled the dagger from its sheath, and slid it across the table.

Signor Zampa glanced right and left before taking the sun dagger. The gold-inlaid stone hilt glimmered in the lamplight, reflecting a soft, orange hue. He ran his fingers along the edge of the blade.

"This is no ordinary weapon." He paused, lifting his gaze to mine. "This is a weapon of power, the magnitude of which I cannot comprehend. This might be a responsibility I am not prepared to shoulder."

I briefly considered throwing myself at his mercy, offering him sexual favors or servitude. But the thought of sex with such an old man turned my stomach. So, I waited as he considered, my chest tightening with each passing second.

Signor Zampa continued to study me before nodding. A flicker of fear flashed in his eyes before settling into a defeated resignation. "I will take this," he said, his voice wavering, "and keep it safe."

I exhaled a deep breath of relief, reaching across the table to clasp his hands in gratitude. His grip was warm and firm, reassuring me that all would be alright.

"Thank you, Signor Zampa. I'm indebted to you."

The tavern was raucous, with laughter, song, and clinking

tankards competing for attention in the smoky, low-ceilinged room. We finished our mead in silence before Signor Zampa pushed to his feet.

"Wait! I need to find someone else here in Florence," I said. "Do you know a man named Eyan Malik?"

He glanced around warily. "No, dear. I'm afraid I don't. But I'd best be on my way."

Without further hesitation, he folded himself into the crowd and disappeared.

I had no idea where I could find Malik, so I decided to take a chance and visit Raul. As my stomach filled with nerves, I took a final sip of the mead before me, but the sweet liquid felt like churning waves instead of providing any comfort. Anxiety coursed through my veins at the thought of the impending reunion.

Outside, the beginnings of sunset drenched the air in vibrant colors. Raul lived a ways from town, and I had to find a way to get there besides walking. It could be midnight before I arrived on foot, and I would be exhausted. I had to steal a horse.

I stood in the shadows of the tavern, my heart pounding with anticipation. A group of horses stood tied to a tethering post, their heads low. I glanced, searching for any sign of danger, before I crept forward. I stayed within the shadows, my steps swift and light as I moved to one of the horses. I paused to stroke its muzzle and whisper soothing words in its ear, and when it didn't shy away, I knew I had made the right decision.

In one swift motion, I untied the horse, grabbed the reins, and vaulted onto its back. I dug my heels into its sides and galloped away, the wind stinging my face as I left the safety of the shadows and raced into the waning light.

When I arrived at Raul's estate, the sky had turned the

color of milky ink. An air of melancholy hung around me as I dismounted and approached his front door. The soft glow of candlelight shone in one of the windows, but the rest of the house was dark.

I hesitated before lifting the heavy iron door knocker. Once I sounded it, there would be no turning back. I sharply snatched the iron knocker off the door and slammed it against the wood. The sound of its resounding thud echoed through the air, reverberating with a feeling of finality. I waited for an answer. Despite my pounding, the ancient oak door gave no answer except for the haunting silence that echoed back. With a frustrated exhale, I pounded on the knocker again and again until my hand throbbed with pain.

At last, a plain-looking woman opened the door, wearing a simple, loose-fitting long linen skirt and a close-fitting bodice over a long-sleeved blouse. Her hair had been tucked in a linen cap. Her eyes widened in fear, and she stepped toward me, wringing her hands together.

"Um, ma'am? Are you here to see the master of the house?" she asked, her voice trembling slightly.

"Indeed," I said. "I'm here for Master Costa."

Raul barreled toward the door. His face contorted into a twisted combination of fury and terror.

"Noemi," he growled, "get out of here now!"

The maid fluttered away from the door and disappeared.

"You!" Raul snarled at me. "How dare you darken my door?"

In his mid-40s, his handsomeness was dimmed by lingering grief. His face was contorted in bitterness, a lifetime of sorrow hardening his features like aged parchment.

"It's so good to see you, Raul," I said, trying to mask my fear.

He grabbed me by the throat. "You bitch! You set me up!

Because of you, Balthazar murdered my son and stole my life away. I lost my wife soon after. I lost everything! You played me for a fool!"

His voice grew louder with every word, reverberating through my senses as if it were battering against a wall of stone. The hatred in his eyes was burning hot, searing into me with an intensity that left me trembling in fear.

"Raul, let me explain!" I gasped, clawing at his hand.

He shook me before shoving me away. I stumbled backward, catching myself before tumbling down his stone steps.

"Please let me explain," I repeated. "I always cared for you but couldn't be with you. Balthazar is a treacherous demon. I lived in fear for my life when I was with him. He's hunting me now. That's why I'm here. To beg mercy and repair the rift between us."

I palpated my aching neck.

"You want my mercy?" Raul roared. "You want my forgiveness? I should simply kill you the way Timehunters are supposed to kill people like you."

He seized my arm and dragged me away from the house.

I stumbled through the overgrown grass surrounding his estate to the back. He threw open a door and hauled me down a staircase into a circular room.

A curtain of oil lamps hung from the wall, lending the space an eerie, golden glow. Daggers had been arranged in a sunbeam pattern along the shiny surface of a round table; chairs surrounded it. Thin cracks spread across the hilt surfaces from being handled over time, and the blades glinted like eyes under chiseled stone brows.

Raul snatched up a knife as we passed the table. I screamed in terror as he dragged me through a door into a separate chamber, where bones of all sizes were scattered across the floor like a sickening mosaic. Torches lined the room, creating a flickering pattern of shadows and light.

My chin was forcefully lifted, forcing me to face the walls adorned with a collection of skulls, their empty sockets staring out in chilling terror.

"Behold! These are all those who've dared cross us—Timebornes, Timebounds, and soon enough, you too will join them."

My legs gave way beneath me, and I collapsed in fear. "Raul, don't do this! Please, I'm begging you!"

He hauled me to my feet. His eyes filled with an insane frenzy as he shouted, "I was demoted by my own people. Balthazar was *in my home*. He should have been my victim, not the other way around. I was reduced to a lower rank in the society of Timehunters. Killing you will be my ticket back into my rightful place at the top."

He tightened his fingers around the hilt of his knife.

In a fit of desperation, I tore my shirt open, revealing my breasts. Heat radiated off Raul as I stood before him, his marble-like body sending shivers down my spine.

"I love you!" I screamed. "I ache for you. I want to be with you! You were always amazing. You helped me poison my parents. I'll be your queen."

Raul started to soften, though I could tell he was still holding back. I stepped closer and ran my hands along his chest, feeling the hard ridges of his muscles beneath my fingertips. I moved my hands lower, tracing the contours of his stomach and hips, and he shuddered beneath my touch.

No longer able to resist, Raul allowed himself to be seduced, his body shaking as I continued to caress him. His face softened into a satisfied smile, and I knew I had reached his passion. Sparks ignited between us when our lips touched, and an inferno of need consumed me. I clung to

Raul's body as if my life depended on it, feeling his hands roam up my sides and back with uninhibited adoration. His kiss was so potent that I gasped for breath when we finally parted.

"Raul," I whispered, my voice carrying the desperation of being unsatisfied for too long, "I can't bear it anymore. I need to be with you. I'll do anything to make this happen."

Fire glittered in his dark eyes.

"Anything?" he asked, a sinful promise in his tone.

My breath caught in my throat. Raul's eyes burned into mine as he licked his lips hungrily. I expected a confession of dark secrets or an illicit pleasure.

"Promise me you will bear me a child."

His words hit me like an unexpected wave. Every muscle in my body tensed with shock and fear of the unimaginable request.

"Why, Raul, do you want a baby with me?" My heart pounded in my chest.

"Because of you, I lost my child," he snapped. "If you give me a baby, I'll make you queen of my house, but only if you promise never to travel again, or else I swear on my life that I will turn you over to the Timehunters!"

His eyes blazed with conviction.

I bit my lip. "Okay. I'll do it."

What would it hurt? I could give him the baby he wanted and then leave before dealing with any real consequences.

"If I promise you this, I require something in return," I said.

"You're in no place to bargain, my darling," he said, his lip peeling back in a cruel sneer.

"Yes, but this request is simple. I only need some of your poison."

He rose one of his elegant eyebrows. "What for?"

"There is someone I need to poison," I said. "She lives in an era in the future."

He licked his lips, savoring his newfound power over me. "Let's see how things go between us. Then, I might grant you this one favor."

I sighed. I would have to agree to this exchange. I had no other options.

CHAPTER FORTY-THREE

ALINA

In 16th-century Italy, courtship was a long and complicated ritual governed by strict rules of etiquette. As the weeks unfolded, true to his word, Raul followed every practice to the letter. Every day, Raul would bring me the most exquisite gifts, like a crystal necklace or a bouquet of freshly picked roses. He constantly wrote me love letters, pouring out his heart and soul in the eloquent handwriting of a prince.

When we were together, Raul would often bow down on one knee and kiss my hand, treating me with all the respect and admiration I deserved. Whenever I had a need that arose, he was always there to provide it, never hesitating to go out of his way to make me feel like I was the most cherished woman in the world. He gave me the royal treatment I deserved every step of the way.

We made love constantly, and we fucked with abandon. I became pregnant within weeks of my arrival to Italy. I no longer had to insert gooey diaphragms coated with oozing spermicide into my vagina. I embraced the idea of bearing Raul's child. Plus, Raul's family had told me if I gave birth to a firstborn son, then he would take on the characteristics of his mother. I couldn't wait to see signs of evil in my child.

The feeling of Raul's arms around me was a security I had been missing for decades. Zara and the Scholar became mere memories, their threats fading with each embrace. I felt safe and content in Raul's presence, my worries dissolving like snow in the sun.

Since I arrived, I had been begging Raul to teach me about poisons, but he forbade it while I was pregnant.

Now that Angelo was born, Raul turned to me and said, "Today's the day, my queen."

"And what day is that, my love?" I said, rocking Angelo in his spacious room. Angelo's eyes were transfixed upon the cherubic angels dancing among flowers and lambs on his ceiling. I'd protested such an angelic scene for my son, but Raul had won, for now. When the baby was older and showing signs of his evil nature, I planned on having demons painted on the ceiling who ripped off the heads of the angels.

"When you arrived, you asked me for poison to eliminate someone. I said we would see. But you have proved your loyalty and love to me. Today, I shall take you to the Phytomancer's Den and teach you how to create your own poison." He beamed at me, dropping to one knee, and taking my hand to bestow a kiss.

"Oh, Raul!" A shiver rippled up my spine. The poisons were stored in a shed near the estate, but Raul concocted his formulas in the Phytomancer's Den. And now he would share his secrets with me? I was overjoyed.

"We can go as soon as you're finished with our child. In fact..." Raul rose and lifted Angelo from my arms. "I shall take him to the wet nurse so we can proceed."

He made silly noises to Angelo as he danced through the room, waltzing past the heavy velvet curtains drawn to let in the light of this warm summer's day. Our child shrieked and laughed. A sunbeam illuminated the shelf holding Angelo's many intricately carved wooden animals and soft, stuffed creatures. Raul snagged a woolly bear and danced out of the room, his feet moving effortlessly across the polished marble and colorful rugs.

Outside, we pushed through the ancient, overgrown forest near Raul's estate to the Phytomancer's Den.

"Who knows about this place?" I asked as Raul helped me over a fallen log.

"Few. It's nestled deep within the trees, hidden from prying eyes. Its location is known only to those initiated into the sinister art of poison-making—the Timehunters."

The den appeared ahead as a dilapidated stone tower covered in creeping vines and surrounded by gnarled trees and poisonous flora. The air outside the structure was thick with an eerie, greenish mist that shrouded the tower in an unsettling aura. Several loud hisses announced our arrival, followed by the rustling of vegetation. Raul put out his hand to stay my movement.

"What is it?" I asked. "What's making that sound?"

"The guardian serpents," he said. "Move not a muscle. They will strike without warning."

He spoke in a strange tongue, the air filling with eerie hissing as if an invisible orchestra of snakes were tuning up their instruments. The atmosphere was so thick with tension that it felt like I breathed through a straw. I *loathed* snakes. Hated them. Could think of nothing worse than touching a serpent.

Raul continued chanting and making strange gestures with his hands. The rustling noises stopped. I could sense the creatures watching, listening, waiting to determine our fate.

Finally, Raul stopped his incantation. "Okay. It's safe now."

"Are you sure?" I clutched his sleeve.

"Of course. I've been the overseer of the guardian serpents for a long time."

Raul's words only slightly mollified me. I trembled as we approached the door, knowing one wrong move could mean death by fang.

Raul uttered more strange incantations with accompanying hand gestures as we stood before the intricately carved wooden-and-metal door. Several rows of symbols had been carved into the wood. When the glyphs started to glow, he pushed the door open and stepped aside for me to enter. I cautiously stepped across the threshold.

"Besides the guardian serpents outside, there are many sentient, carnivorous plants within these stone walls," Raul said. "They can sense when someone seeks to endanger the poisons. Their deadly skills can be awakened with a snap of my fingers."

Was he warning me or simply informing me? I shook with fear and arousal as I entered this hallowed chamber.

Inside the tower, the laboratory was a labyrinth of shelves lined with rare and deadly plants, grotesque animal specimens, and a collection of eerie glass containers filled with what I assumed to be vibrant poisons. A series of glowing, bioluminescent plants illuminated the dimly-lit space, casting an eerie, otherworldly glow. My steps echoed through the musty shop as I crept past the shelves of strange relics, their half-glimpsed forms visible through the murky glass.

Raul's voice seemed to bounce from wall to wall, filled

with sinister pride as he lurked in my wake. "Here you'll find an array of exotic and rare ingredients, including venomous serpent fangs, hallucinogenic mushrooms, and the petals of a flower known as the Widow's Bloom, which is rumored to be the most potent poison in existence."

"I see," I said, captivated by the room's deadly contents. "I want to create a poison using the Widow's Bloom."

Raul whirled me around to face him, then leaned in for a kiss. When he withdrew, he murmured against my lips, his warm breath skating across my skin, "Nothing would give me greater satisfaction, my love. But the Widow's Bloom is only to be handled by a *master*. And you are a willing but unskilled student. I shall teach you to use the Belladonna. It will serve your purposes nicely."

A twinge of egoic recalcitrance tightened my belly.

"As you wish." I stepped away from him coldly and continued my slow perusal of the laboratory. "Tell me. How did you come to be a Timehunter?"

I rounded the end of the aisle, glancing at Raul.

His chest puffed with pride. "It passes from father to father. Generation to generation."

"Is there a leader?" I eyed this cavernous laboratory filled with elaborate distillation apparatuses, cauldrons, and alchemical tools. Intricate diagrams and handwritten scrolls detailing poison recipes covered the walls, revealing the secrets of Raul's craft.

Raul's eyes shuttered. "Of course. I don't know who he is except through legend. People have told me he lives forever. But that could merely be a theory. He supposedly resides in the Ottoman Empire and is said to wield enormous power. The Timehunters in that region are the most powerful in the world. Our society here isn't as strong as in the Turkish Empire."

"How can I meet this mysterious stranger?" I asked, drawn to such power.

"You cannot." He picked up a jar of some strange substance and shook it. The contents burst into glowing stars. "If I were to open this lid right now, we would die within seconds."

He smirked as if enjoying the power he had with his mastery of poisonous substances.

"Then, pray, do not open it," I said, shivering.

Raul stalked toward me, slow and deliberate in his movements. He pressed me against the back wall and rucked up my skirt. His skilled fingers stroked up my inner thighs. "My darling, before I share my secrets of poison alchemy, I must ask for a favor."

"What is it?" I breathed as his fingers slid between my legs. I widened my stance to grant access.

He traced lazy circles around my clit.

I moaned, and my head fell back against the wall.

"You are to join the Timehunters." He pressed a kiss to my neck.

I stiffened. "What do you mean?"

He slid his fingers inside me, coaxing my surrender. "Exactly as I said. If I am to teach you my craft, you must become a Timehunter. And you must promise me you will continue to conceal your status as a Timeborne, or I shall be the one to give orders to execute you."

He urged his entire hand inside me, and I embraced the sensation as my body opened wide. He curled his fingers into a tight fist that moved with determined force within me while his rigid erection pressed against my hip. His heavy breathing caressed my cheek like a tantalizing whisper.

"Promise me you'll do this," he said with an intensity that sent shivers down my spine.

The pressure of his thrusts demanded that I focus wholly on the sensation of pleasure surging through me. I had to remain relaxed to avoid succumbing to the fear of him taking control and allowing his fist to seem like an unwanted intrusion. Each thrust seemed to bring us closer together, creating an indescribable feeling of pleasure and connection.

"Promise me," he breathed again.

What would be the harm in joining this loathsome society? Wouldn't it be better to stand with them than remain hunted prey? After all, the Timehunters were the sworn enemies of every Timeborne and had a notorious reputation for their ruthless tactics and dedication.

As I looked into Raul's eyes and saw the deep admiration in his gaze, something inside me stirred. I had never felt anything like it, a primal surrender that seemed to come from deep within my soul.

Raul kept his gaze steady and unwavering as he slid his fist in and out. Slowly, I began to realize the gravity of his request and the importance of the decision. If I refused, I would be denying not only Raul's wish but also my own life. With a deep, shuddering breath, I nodded in agreement.

A tingle of electricity coursed through my veins, and my heart raced in anticipation. I had made my choice and was ready to join the Timehunters. I would learn to craft a poison to kill my daughter should she venture into the world of time traveling. Everything in my life was going according to plan. But as I surrendered to the pleasure coursing through my body, I could not help but notice the shadows filling the Phytomancer's Den. Something about this new plan seemed fractured.

Deep down, I knew nothing would go according to plan.

CHAPTER FORTY-FOUR

ALINA

The shrieks of Scholar's evil voice invaded my mind three months after my son was born, tormenting me relentlessly. Paranoia consumed me, and the hallucinations grew more vivid by the day. I was never free from their insidious murmurs, no matter where I went. They spoke in my ear constantly, a relentless cacophony of wickedness.

"You think you can run away and hide in Italy? I see everything," he said. "Do you honestly believe you're safe? I watch you constantly."

I couldn't escape. He wouldn't leave me alone. A quiet whisper in the back of my mind said, "But why hasn't he killed me?"

Sometimes, I would tear at my hair, screaming, "What do you want from me? Why do you continue to torture me?"

But, at these times, he always chose to remain mute. Endlessly silent. Quietude engulfed me, forcing me to fill the silence with my own paranoid thoughts. There was no relief from my suffering.

My beautiful son had already started to show signs of his true vicious nature. He would scream and howl as if he were possessed. I wanted to stay and nurture his dark abilities, but when I heard voices in my head, I knew I couldn't. Staying would only bring heartbreak to us all.

The thought of leaving Raul and my beloved son filled me with unbearable pain. All the moments we had shared—the conversations, the laughter, and the passion—were precious to me. I wished I could freeze time and stay there forever.

Raul had left for the Phytomancer's Den early that morning. He thought he would return from his day's work, thinking all would be well. I, however, knew I had to leave at once. I couldn't take the torment any longer. I had to find Malik and obtain answers.

Even thoughts of leaving the Phytomancer's Den left me with a heavy heart. I had spent the past weeks studying the art of poison, learning to create powerful mixtures, including the belladonna elixir I had prepared for Olivia. But there was so much to learn. I had crafted the concoction, but it still felt wrong. Raul had never allowed me to touch the deadly Widow's Bloom or any of the more dangerous plants they had in the Den. I had to put my hope in the poison I had crafted from Belladonna.

As I made my way out into the yard, I was reminded of all I had learned and was leaving behind.

This place—this estate, the Phytomancer's Den—none of it was my place anymore. I had made a choice, a necessity I forced myself to accept. I had to leave.

I stood in the yard of the estate as shadows stretched in the waning light. I was hidden from view by a weeping willow tree, tears rolling down my cheeks, hot and heavy, every sob ripping at my soul. I bowed my head and said a silent prayer, asking for strength and courage as I prepared to leave my loved ones behind.

Once emptied of sorrow, I packed some essentials, grabbed my revised journal, and fled from my home. I ran through the night, away from the haunting voices and the strange feelings that had taken hold of me. Fear and desperation radiated off me like a heat wave.

My feet pounded the ground like a drumbeat until I was drained of every ounce of energy. The sky started to bleed with morning hues, and I pushed myself to the limit until my limbs felt like leaden weights. I collapsed in exhaustion just as the sun became a golden globe, highlighting my failures. I hadn't thought this through. I was running scared, trying to escape the inescapable.

All this time living with Raul, I had been living a fantasy. A life of make-believe. I'd stupidly thought I'd found safety here in Florence, but I'd only been granted a reprieve. A measure of peace with which to gather my strength. Nothing more. I was, once again, the hunted.

The town was barely stirring. Smoke wafted from chimneys, and a few lost souls stumbled down the streets from their night of carousing. My heart pounded as I rounded the corner.

A looming figure materialized from the shadows. He was tall and gangly with a feral expression, his gray eyes drilling into my soul like daggers in the early morning light. As he advanced closer, my legs shook, and my breathing quickened, yet something compelled me to stay rooted in place.

Salvatore.

"So, you're looking for Eyan Malik like I suggested," Salvatore said. His voice was low and gruff, and his gaze seemed to peel my skin apart.

I tensed at the mention of Malik's name.

"What makes you think I'm looking for him?" I asked, trying to keep my voice even.

His lips curled into a smirk. "I hear things. I already told you how powerful I am. Remember, I'm your ally. I'm here to protect you. I'm proud of you."

He held out his hand to me in invitation.

The air surrounding his arm shimmered with a strange energy, like a million tiny diamonds encased in glass.

I stretched my arm forward, driven by some unknown compulsion.

As our fingers made contact, an electric sensation coursed through my skin, and an inexplicable connection seemed to materialize between us. His touch was tender and warm, while his eyes held a mesmerizing blend of light and shadow. I found myself utterly captivated, unable to break our gaze. He drew nearer and traced my face with his fingertips, evoking waves of pleasure previously unknown to me.

My body ached for his touch, a craving so deep and powerful that I feared being lost in it. But I fought against the compulsion, an inner voice warning me of the peril lurking beneath the smoldering sensuality.

"My darling, Alina," Salvatore said. "You have been blessed by Balthazar and know you love him. But you will learn to love me too. I will protect you, and nothing will ever hurt you again. Nothing will ever take you away from me."

He smiled at me as if it were normal to meet this way. "You will find Malik in 1323 A.D. in a small cottage near the city's north edge."

"What city?" I pleaded. "Is he here in Italy?"

"Britannica." The word drifted through the air like a feather. Salvatore faded away, seemingly as if he had never been there. I was left with a feeling of want and a deep-seated, primal arousal. I wanted to know more about him, who he was, and why he was better than Balthazar. He was an enigma, an ever-present mystery waiting to be unraveled. And I wanted to unravel it.

For several days, I lurked at the city's edge, skirting the edges of taverns and cafes in my search for food scraps. Everywhere I went, I heard of Raul's search for me.

"She left him with no warning. Didn't even take the wee child," an ancille murmured as the maids gathered in the courtyard to exchange gossip. They took delight in spreading the news with one another. "We are to inform Lord Costa at once if we hear word of her whereabouts."

They would titter and exchange insults about me.

"She's a strange one, she is. She had Lord Costa wrapped around her little finger. He treated her like a queen, he did, always buying her fancy gifts. But, in my mind, she weren't nothing but a common whore, that one."

Their words stuck in my skin like shards of glass, but I felt too weak to deal with them. Besides, I had other, far more important things to deal with—like finding Malik.

On the night of the full moon, after days of little nourishment or sleep, I time-traveled to Britannica in 1323.

I asked everyone I met if they knew where Malik lived. Most shuddered and backed away from me. One gentleman, perhaps hoping for a night of sexual favors, told me his address. I thanked him, declined his advances, and hurried away.

As I approached Malik's imposing manor, the wind howled, enveloping me in its fury. Perched atop a hill, the ancient stone house seemed like a foreboding sentinel, and each step I took up the driveway reverberated in the silence. The leaves on the trees overhead rustled as if they were spectators awaiting the imminent events.

I grasped the weighty metal knocker and let it crash against the door with a resounding thud.

The door creaked open, revealing Malik, his visage twisted in anger. The atmosphere crackled with tension.

"What are you doing here, Alina?" he snarled. "How did you find me?"

"I…I…" I stammered, taken aback by his fury. "I discovered the sun dagger."

"It doesn't matter," he said. "I am no longer interested in the dagger."

As he tried to shut the door, I wedged my foot to prevent it from closing.

"Wait, Malik. Don't cast me aside so easily. I left Balthazar long ago," I said.

"Don't you utter that monster's name in my presence!" Malik stormed out of the house and slammed the door behind him.

"What changed you, Malik?" I said, dumbfounded. "Why do you hold such animosity toward me? The last time we talked, we were still friends."

"Last time you saw me," he whispered, his voice chillingly flat, "I was chained to a prison wall, enduring relentless torment from my former master, while you stood by and watched. Then I had to witness the death of my true love while you two cackled with glee."

"It wasn't like that. I swear!" My feeble words landed at his feet like dead flies.

My fingers shook as I dug my journal out of my pocket. I held it tight against my chest, then plucked up all my courage and thrust it toward him.

"Take this," I said, my voice strong, even if my body trembled. "It's everything that's happened to me. Everything I've been through."

Malik threw up his hands. "Why are you giving this to

me? What do you expect me to do with it? I don't give a damn about it."

"Read it," I said fiercely. "This journal contains all my secrets and truths. I want you to protect it, please."

I flipped through the diary and pulled out the photo of Olivia with her birthday cake. I thrust it in front of Malik. "Look! This is my daughter. I gave birth to her, a Timeborne, and cannot bear to lose her. You must protect her at all costs."

His lip quivered, and he became transfixed.

"Isabelle. Oh, my Isabelle," he whispered.

"Isabelle? No, this is Olivia," I said, my forehead creased.

He slammed me against the wall. "Why are you tormenting me? I want nothing to do with you!"

"We are on the same team and allies! You told me to find John James and I did! You urged me to find him to discover the daggers, and I did! We are all on the same side. I'm a good person, Malik, and I care for you." I desperately wanted to believe this was true.

A deafening baby wail came from inside the house. We both whipped around to the open window in alarm.

"Malik, is that a baby?"

He didn't answer me. Instead, he snarled, "I want you out of my life, Alina. I'm a man on the brink of survival, and if you don't disappear now, I will make sure you are dead instead."

The baby howled louder and louder.

"Malik, I'm sorry for everything. But please just take my journal and protect my daughter from Balthazar. He will kill her without a second thought."

Malik roared. "After I barely made it away from Balthazar, I swore that I would live an ordinary life. I wanted to vanish from the world. My only reason for living is not linked in any way to Balthazar. I've lost two essential people, and I refuse to be involved with you or your chaos any longer."

The infant's wailing reached a fever pitch, and I sprinted through the front door. My heart raced as I burst into the nursery, and my stomach dropped at the sight of a tiny baby girl lying in her crib, tears streaming down her cheeks. A glint of silver caught my eye—a Timebound necklace adorned her neck.

Malik pushed past me and cradled her in his arms until she finally dozed off. He stared at me with steely determination. "Leave now! Don't ever come back here again."

I stood my ground, even with the threat of violence looming in the air. "Do you really think you can protect your child forever? One day, she will grow old enough to see the monster hidden inside you and turn away from you in disgust."

His eyes burned with a feral fury, illuminating the shadows around us.

My heart beat faster as I took a step back in fear.

"You were aware of all the darkness Balthazar carried, yet still you chose to be with him despite everything he had done. I'll use every ounce of strength I possess to safeguard my daughter from anyone who has harm in mind for her. And I will gladly give up my own life if it means protecting hers— something that can't be said about you." He thrust his arm forward, slicing through the air between us.

I panted hard, taking in the child's room. The walls were lined with lush tapestries depicting scenes of tranquil countrysides and bedding adorned with delicate lace and embroidery. The furniture was carved from dark, polished wood, and the floor was covered with a luxurious Persian rug. An ornate cradle was placed in the center, draped with a soft blanket of feathers and gold. A few stuffed animals were arranged around it, and a set of painted wooden blocks sat neatly on the windowsill. It was an inviting and peaceful atmosphere, yet I felt anything but tranquil.

"All I ask is that you protect my daughter," I whispered.

"I will not protect your daughter! I have my own to protect!" His face contorted in rage.

The air filled with palpable tension, challenging me to oppose him.

He sneered. "Admit it, you still burn for Balthazar. You can't bear the thought of your daughter meeting him and being taken under his spell. You'd rather die than see them together and know he loves her more than you. Your fear is so powerful that you would even kill her to ensure she never meets him. That's what makes you weak—your desire for power and control."

I staggered back, stunned. How did he know I wanted to kill my own daughter? "You're wrong, Malik! I love my daughter. That's why I want you to keep this journal. Only you have the power to protect her and keep her safe."

Malik set the sleeping child in her cradle and advanced toward me, pushing me back with every step. His voice was a low rumble like thunder in the distance. "You always run away. You have the power to teach your daughter how to end Balthazar's reign of terror, yet you choose to manipulate and gain from those around you."

My rage exploded. "You are a weak man! You're too cowardly to face Balthazar yourself, so instead, you want us all to suffer while you seek a normal life. Your precious child, our very lives will all be taken by Balthazar's hand!"

Malik sighed and let his shoulders slump. "Go get help from someone else, Alina, not me."

I spun on my heel, a fiery determination rising in my

chest. As I reached the door, I said, "We'll see each other again, dead or alive."

Hot tears stung my cheeks as I departed. I hid in the nearby woods, watching his house as it gave way to night. When all the lights were out, I crept back to leave behind my journal, tucking it neatly into the baby's window as a parting gift.

Having completed my mission, as disheartening as it was, I had no choice but to return to Jack and Olivia.

CHAPTER FORTY-FIVE

ALINA

When I returned to the States, Olivia was ten, a little girl on the brink of womanhood. When I walked in the door, she fixed me with a gaze that burned with intensity and recognition. Her eyes dissected me, deconstructing every part of me until I was in pieces. Then, the moment passed. She blinked and ran to me, arms outstretched.

"Mom!"

I wondered if Zara and the Scholar were right about Olivia. Would she be my undoing? I shook my head, forced those thoughts away, and spread my arms wide.

She wrapped her arms around my legs and hugged me tight. "I missed you, Mom!"

Olivia paused as the door creaked open, and Jack trundled into the room. He took one look at me, and his face was drained of color.

"Mom's home," Olivia said with exuberance before skipping away.

"Jack!" I cried out, my heart thumping wildly against my chest as vivid memories of the past year and a half overwhelmed me. I had been in an intense and passionate union with Raul, producing an unexpected child and learning to brew poisons to take the life of my own daughter. I'd met with John James and Malik. My wicked soul had concealed itself behind a pretend mask of goodness.

I shuffled up to him like a lost lamb, my voice barely above a whisper.

"I'm sorry I was gone so long," I said, trying to appear sincere.

Jack's aura of stillness made the air heavy and cold. His arms were crossed, and he stood like a sentry, making it clear that I was not welcome in his home. Taking a deep breath, I reminded myself that I would live my life no matter what happened here today.

I said sorry again, my voice small and meek in the silence. Jack's face was frozen in a grimace. He remained mute, and the air between us thickened with unspoken tensions.

"I searched far and wide for the moon dagger," I said.

He cocked his head and squinted at me through one eye.

I shifted my weight under his intense gaze.

"It was all folly. I come home empty-handed." As I tried to sound sincere, my voice wavered. "But I'm different, Jack. You've got to believe me. I love you and don't want to divorce."

His expression softened slightly as if my words had found their way into his heart, and he moved closer to me. His eyes glittered with emotion as he reached out his hand.

"Okay," he said in a voice as thick as molasses. "We can try."

We hugged tightly, and as I melted into his embrace, my mind raced with comparisons between Raul and Jack. Raul's passionate lovemaking left me weak in the knees compared to

Jack's bland embrace. Raul's fiery temper could so easily transform into stormy lust. Sex with Jack was like endless days of boredom. The contrast between them made it hard for me to let go of my reservations and surrender to Jack.

When we withdrew from one another, Jack said, "You should go see Lee. He's been worried sick since you've been gone."

I nodded. "It's so good to be back. I'm so happy you're willing to make amends."

I didn't wait for his response, before rushing toward the front door. I had to do more than simply visit Lee. I had to smear Olivia's dagger with the poison I'd created under Raul's tutelage. Before leaving, I grabbed a few necessary items and scurried away without saying goodbye.

I timidly knocked when I arrived at Lee's condo.

No answer. Good. He's out.

I unlocked the door using the key he'd given me and tiptoed inside. The smell of stale beer hung thickly in the air. My eyes darted to the dozens of bottles scattered around, and a wave of rage washed over me.

So, he's a drunk now. Nice.

I hurried to where I'd found Olivia's dagger and squeezed some poison on the tip. The clatter of footsteps outside startled me, and I hastened to put Olivia's blade back where I found it. I attempted to calm my rapid heartbeat and sauntered toward the front room.

Lee opened the door and halted, glowering at me. "Where were you? You were supposed to stay and protect Olivia, not time travel!"

His words tore through me like a serrated blade.

Lee scowled. "How long have you been in my house?"

"I just got here," I said.

He barreled into the hall with a thunderous roar, his face drawn and pale. He was gone for an eternity until he emerged again, clutching Olivia's dagger in a white-knuckled grip. The silver blade shimmered in the dim light.

"Why was this stored in one place, yet I found it in another?" His eyes were wild with rage, and a shiver of fear snaked down my spine. I couldn't help but think that if he touched even just a millimeter of the deadly razor-sharp edge, death by poison would ensue instantly.

A lump formed in my throat. "I...I put it there. I wanted to make sure Balthazar wouldn't find it."

"Sit down, you lying bitch! I have a few questions for you." Every muscle tightened with anger as he spat venomous words at me. "You think I'm a fool that you can lie to my face? Let me tell you something. You'll regret ever crossing me!"

I stumbled toward the sofa and collapsed.

"I know exactly who you are. Do you think your lies will save you? I know you're a monster." Lee lunged to the side table and snatched up a manila folder, thrusting it into my face. With shaking hands, he opened it, revealing brownish and crumbling pages, taped together: my diary that I had tried to burn in his fireplace. The icy chill of fear settled over me like a fog as I looked upon the scorched evidence of my villainy.

"You're nothing but a liar! I found your journal all burned up in my firepit. Did you think you could hide this from me? I re-pieced the remnants together, though," he said, shaking the folder. The papers fluttered to the floor like leaves. "I know what your agenda is—to get the blades and set this world on a path of darkness and violence. That's pure evil."

I frantically searched for a way to break his verbal attack. Dozens of empty beer bottles littered the coffee table. Not thinking twice, I threw one of the bottles across the room. It smashed against the wall, splintering into tiny pieces. His face became red with anger.

"You've been busying yourself drinking while I was away!" I shouted, my entire body shaking with rage. "This is how you chose to express your worry about my disappearance? Nice."

"You're wrong, bitch!" He shot me an icy stare of resentment. "You're wrong about *everything*. I'm so sick of your bullshit. I'm going to do everything in my power to protect Olivia. And I guarantee it—you're going down. Get the fuck out of my house."

The intensity of his demeanor frightened me. I scurried out of his house and headed straight to my car.

I was just about to unlock my vehicle. A man stood across the street. The Scholar. His face was lined with age and experience, and he smiled at me warmly, like we had been friends from long ago. His cane thumped against the asphalt as he hobbled closer. A chill of uncertainty crept up my back. Had I dreamed a narrative about him being dangerous?

"You're impeding my progress," I snapped. "Get out of the way. I'm finished with your deceit."

"Alina, I'm only trying to help," he said.

I lunged forward. "Only trying to help, Scholar? By keeping me in a prison of fear? What a joke!" My lips curled in scorn. "You and your so-called scholarly, benign appearance."

With a single swift movement, I snatched his glasses and

snapped them in half as he recoiled. Then, I grabbed his cane and threw it away from him.

The Scholar swayed where he stood, and I feared he might topple over.

"It's obvious Balthazar sent you and Zara here! But don't think for one second that I'm scared of you!" I spat, my face twisted in anger.

He shot me an icy glare. "I have a name. It's Lazarus."

I feigned a laugh. "Oh, that does sound quite scary. Ha-ha. The name of a charlatan. You're nothing but hocus pocus! Are you here to try and scare me away? Let me tell you something—someone far more powerful is watching over me. His name is Salvatore, and he is my ally. You have no idea how powerful he is. So it would be wise to step aside or suffer the consequences."

With that, I stormed away, leaving him in my wake of indignation.

"Is that right?" Lazarus' voice struck me in the back like a blade of ice, slicing through my courage and rooting me to the spot. "*Salvatore* has promised you safety and deliverance? Astonishing. I'm in awe."

With dread, I turned to see Lazarus' hand shoot flames into the building next to him, the heat waves crashing like a tidal wave against my skin.

"If you think that will do you any good, be my guest," he said with a menacing grin. You're a stupid woman, Alina. Do you think that by joining forces with Salvatore, you can outwit me? I'm not so easily fooled!"

His eyes burned like two fiery pits. "Do you understand the gravity of this mission? You have been playing your games, spinning your lies with Balthazar, trying to poison your daughter's blade, and putting on a facade of benevolence while secretly loathing Jack! But no matter how you feel about him or what tricks you have up your sleeve, I will not let Olivia fall again—I will defend her with my life!"

"Again?" I shrieked.

I felt the cold scales of a dozen snakes slithering up my legs, and a chilling fear crept through me as they began to wrap around my limbs like a writhing prison. I screamed behind sealed lips as they poked their heads against my face, trying to force open my mouth. Every ounce of strength evaporated as I closed my eyes and clenched my jaw, desperate to escape the nightmare of squirming serpents undulating across every inch of me. I fought and I screamed but their writhing power was too much for me.

Lazarus glared at me with venomous hatred. "I created you as a Timeborne. Your plotting and scheming to construct a forgery of that journal will get you nowhere. You thought you could obliterate the truth, but I remember every detail, darling. You are the vilest, most underhanded serpent I have ever encountered. I recognize all your fabrications for what they are—stories spun with devious intentions."

For one brief second, I wondered what he meant. How could he create me at all? I thought that was all the work of the Eclipsarum Obscura?

I feared fainting from the horrible writhing snakes smothering me. I couldn't move, couldn't breathe. My heart raced, threatening to climb from my throat. I could only stare at Lazarus, who stood there cool and collected in his mocking tone.

One second, he stood several yards away. The next, he appeared before me out of thin air, his crushing hands clamping around my throat. The snakes bore down, too, as if under the spell of their master. I tried to shout but couldn't get a sound out.

"Your ultimate punishment is coming." His eyes glittered

with malice and strength that I had underestimated. My heart hammered in fear as I realized the danger I was in.

"Let Salvatore's twisted games begin," he bellowed, his eyes blazing with an unholy fire. "For I, Lazarus, am here and watching him from afar, waiting for the perfect moment to strike. I will see him at the end of the dark tunnel and have the last laugh."

His gaze pierced my soul like a fiery burning spear, scorching me with an intensity that promised revenge. "I'm going to enjoy watching you both suffer."

And then, like an evil wind, he was gone.

CHAPTER FORTY-SIX

ALINA

I stumbled into Jack's and my antique store, avoiding our apartment upstairs, barely able to keep my footing. As I forced my way through the door, a current of desperation and dread coursed through me with every step. With each progression forward, shadows gathered around me in thick clusters, pressing in until the walls seemed to close in on me like an impenetrable barrier. It felt like every direction I turned ended in failure.

I stared blankly at the array of pocket watches behind the glass case, a dense fog of desolation submerging me. Hopelessness and weariness weighed down my soul as I stood motionless, my gaze rooted to the timepieces that meant nothing.

Olivia came bounding around the corner, sparkling with life and energy. "Hi, Mom! Mr. Keys gave us an assignment today. We have to write about something *interesting* for class! I think I'll write about this store and all the weird stuff we have here!"

My senses stirred from their stupor, my heart heavy with wretchedness.

"Huh? What?" I barely managed to mumble.

She faced me on the other side of the counter, hopping back and forth. "What I just said. I'm going to write about something *interesting*!"

More compelling than snakes consuming you and terrifying demons choking the life out of you?

"That's nice, dear."

The tiny bell jangled on the door as a mysterious figure stepped inside the shop. I glanced at the customer, then resumed my vacant staring at the watches.

The sound of a throat clearing startled me. I peered up to find an ancient woman looming over me, her eyes glinting with secrets untold, and a paper bag clutched in her gnarled hands.

"Can I help you?" I asked, barely able to conceal my apprehension.

"Oh, I sure hope so." She chuckled as she yanked out a porcelain dolly from the depths of her sack. Its lifeless eyes gazed upon me, full of mystery and warning.

"My, this one is, um, unique," I said, reaching for the doll. I turned it side to side.

The doll was wrapped in a tattered, blood-red cloak with a hood that framed an abomination of a face with melting features and wild, oily black hair. Its skin seemed to be both dirty brown and sickly white. But the eyes struck fear into me; the twisted orbs followed my every movement with a wicked malignancy. Whatever this thing was, it was hideous beyond comprehension.

Shuffling feet announced Olivia's presence.

I held up the doll to her.

"What do you think? Should we get it?" I asked, repulsed.

She pointed a finger to her chest. "Me?"

"Yes, you. I asked for your opinion," I snapped.

Olivia shook her head back and forth like a weathervane caught in a tornado.

"I hate it!" Her words echoed off the walls. "Get it out of here!"

"I have no interest in your offer," I told the woman.

She glared at me with contempt. "But I'm giving you a great deal."

"It doesn't matter!" I replied through gritted teeth and leaned across the counter toward her, using my intense gaze to show her that my patience was wearing thin.

She quickly stuffed her grotesque doll in the paper sack and stormed out of the store, muttering.

As the strange woman finally left, Olivia's shoulders dropped, and she heaved a heavy sigh. I rubbed my lower back, trying to ease the strain from dealing with her. The room felt lighter without her presence.

"That was certainly an odd doll, wasn't it?" I asked. I couldn't shake the feeling that the doll was some sort of warning.

"It was creepy, Mom," Olivia said.

"What do you say to ice cream?" I asked, looking over the rim of my glasses at her. "I think we can take a break, don't you?"

I brushed away the feeling of snakes crawling all over my body.

"Goody!" She clapped her hands together. "Ice cream! Who will watch the store?"

"Why, your father, that's who," I said, then called for Jack through the door leading to the back room.

"What?" came his muffled reply from behind the doorway's wood frame and iridescent glass paneling.

"Olivia and I will go get some ice cream at Cool Scoops. Do you want a cone?" I asked.

With one arm propped against the doorframe, Jack leaned casually into the room, a wide grin spreading across his face that seemed almost too big for his features. His hair was messy, and as usual, he wore an old T-shirt with holes around the collar and sleeves that used to be white but were now yellowed with age. "A double scoop of fudge brownie for me, please."

"I want a scoop of fudge brownie and vanilla chocolate chip in a sugar cone!" Olivia said, hopping up and down.

"Then let's do it!" I reached behind the counter for my purse. "We'll be back in a few," I said to Jack.

I took Olivia's hand and led her out of the store.

The sky was dark and ominous, heralding an impending thunderstorm. "Olivia, you go back inside before the storm hits. I'll run out to my car and grab my umbrella."

She nodded and skipped back inside.

Frantically, I scurried across the bustling street, dodging umbrellas, and puddles. The rain was relentless, pelting against my skin and drenching my clothes. Finally reaching the parking lot, I fumbled with the keys to unlock the car door. Retrieving the dark blue umbrella from the back seat, I shook off the excess water before quickly opening it. And there he stood, just a few feet away, his dark hair plastered against his forehead and his clothes sticking to his body. Despite the chaos around us, our gaze locked, and time seemed to stand still in that moment.

Balthazar! He was dressed entirely in black, and his eyes blazed like lasers as he stood there, staring at me.

I felt as if the air itself had frozen. His midnight-black hair clung damply to his face, framing a visage that still boasted the same piercing blue eyes, strong jawline, and soft, inviting lips.

The years had changed me in ways I hadn't expected, and

a wave of emotions crashed over me. I'd meticulously set him up, writing a fake journal and leading him on a wild goose chase. Yet, I'd thought of him daily, conjuring up memories of us running away together and fucking everywhere. I'd missed him more than life, yet there he was, standing before me as if no time had passed.

I felt a love more potent than anything I'd ever known. I wanted to reach out and touch him, to make sure he was real, but I couldn't move.

He stepped forward, breaking the spell, and in an instant, I knew that nothing would ever be the same again.

My heart raced as I considered what to do. Should I stay and talk or leave *for the shop?*

Every second felt like it stretched forever, and I couldn't decide.

A chill traveled down my spine as Balthazar's cold, glacier-blue eyes bored into mine. His lips twisted in a hateful sneer.

"Wait! I can explain," I said, my hands outstretched. "I swear, I still love you. Our time apart only made me realize how much."

His dark brows furrowed, and he stepped forward, prowling closer like a lion about to attack its prey.

"It had to be this way," I stammered. "If we'd gone on the quest together, we never would have been able to keep our hands off each other."

"Couldn't keep our hands off one another," Balthazar spat out the word, his voice dripping with disdain. "Past tense. I hate you and despise you."

The words cut through me like a jagged knife, tearing apart my heart and leaving a deep wound. I tried to deny the hurt, but the pain kept reverberating until I felt like drowning in it. Despite it all, I still yearned for his embrace.

"We can find our way back to the love we once shared."

Olivia's face appeared in the shop window, her eyes widening in shock as she watched us unravel from afar.

"I'll do anything to make amends."

Balthazar's eyes flashed with rage, and he balled his hands into fists. "You *bitch*. You took everything from me. You left me broken. Now you're going to pay."

I fumbled for my purse, but it was too late. He grabbed my throat. "I told you I would kill you. You're a deceitful, lying demon, just like your father. You betrayed me, just like he betrayed me. You are all disgusting serpents."

He squeezed harder, and I gasped for air, desperately searching my handbag for anything to save me. Finally, my fingers grasped the cold handle of my dagger. I drew it out, thrusting it toward him to protect myself. In a single motion, he wrenched it from my hand and plunged it deep into my chest. The pain was unbearable as I collapsed onto the sidewalk.

My world went dark.

Everything around me began to float. I was in a dream and could feel my consciousness drifting away.

Balthazar's voice whispered in my ear. "I loved you with all my heart."

His lips touched mine in a tender kiss, his body warm against mine as the cool afternoon air blew past us.

Why was everything fuzzy all of a sudden? The pain lanced through my chest, and I heard someone scream.

Olivia? Don't be scared.

Jack yelled and shook my shoulder. Onlookers crowded around me as my grip on reality slipped from my grasp. It would be so easy to drift off into nothingness, to finally give up the fight against time and death. I had spent so long running from my destiny, but destiny always catches up to us in the end...

"BP is 90 over 50," someone said. "Pulse is high. Sats are below 80. We're losing her."

I didn't care. My grip on life was fading fast.

"Attach the AED. Now!" someone shouted. "Start compressions."

Hands pumped my ribcage, crushing bones in the process.

"Stop CPR. Do not touch patient. Analyzing," a mechanical voice said. "Shock advised."

"Clear!" a male called.

Electricity surged through my body, jolting me like a bolt of lightning. Every muscle seemed to contract at once, as if my entire being was on the cusp of shattering. The world became a blur of white-hot pain, and my vision danced with bright spots.

"Resume CPR," the mechanical voice droned.

As the hands pumped my shattered ribcage and paramedics bustled around me, a figure loomed in my inner vision.

"Don't be frightened," it said.

"Salvatore?" I squinted, trying to focus. "Is that you?"

"Yes, dear. It's really me. I've been waiting for this opportunity." His voice sounded like the bone-melting lull after satisfying sex.

He stroked my cheek. A wicked smirk crept across his face as his eyes glittered in the moonlight.

"Oh, my darling," he purred. "You actually did it and followed my orders. Now we must get to work. The ultimate beginning has started now, and it's time to claim what always belonged to me."

I blinked as tears stung my eyes.

My savior. Salvatore has come to rescue me.

"That's it," he said. "I'm here to save you from death. We have much to do."

A cruel grin ripped across my features as a fire lit inside my soul. Zara had been mistaken. Lazarus had been wrong. Salvatore was the only one who had seen the truth, and I welcomed his sinister schemes with open arms.

We would bring about a new age of terror and despair, where I would be crowned the supreme ruler of all. Inevitably, my dreams of complete power and domination would finally be realized as I stepped into a future shrouded in darkness. My sacrifices would not have been in vain.

The world, at last, would be mine.

The Journey Continues....
Blade of Shadows Book 4: Timehunters
Coming Spring 2025

THANK YOU FOR READING!

Enjoy *Wicked Lovers of Time*? Please take a second to leave a
review!

OTHER BOOKS IN THE BLADE OF SHADOWS SERIES

TIMEBORNE (BOOK 1)

DARKNESS OF TIME (BOOK 2)

TIMEBOUND (BOOK 3)

WICKED LOVERS OF TIME (BOOK 3.5)
Balthazar and Alina's Story

TIMEHUNTERS (BOOK 4)
COMING SOON 2025

LOST LEGACY OF TIME
(FINAL SAGA BOOK 5)
COMING SOON

JOIN THE BLADE OF SHADOWS!
https://www.authorsarasamuels.com/

Join the Club!
Blade of Shadows Book Club
(Facebook Group)

THANK YOU

TikTok
Instagram
Facebook
BookBub

APPRECIATION

Writing *Wicked Lovers of Time* has been an absolute thrill for me. Exploring the villains' stories and seeing the world through their eyes has been an exhilarating experience. Balthazar, in particular, holds a special place in my heart. Crafting his journey and uncovering the reasons behind his actions was a labor of love. I hope that as you read his story, you'll feel the same connection I do—whether it makes you love him or hate him even more. Now with Alina alive and showing her true wickedness, who knows what chaos she'll bring? I hope you're ready for the next book—it's going to be an unforgettable ride!

Chaela, where would I be without your endless support, friendship, and love? You've been my rock, and I can't thank you enough for every bit of encouragement and every shared moment that means the world to me. You light up my life, and I'm so grateful for it.

Rainy, your magic touch on my manuscript turned it into something I could only dream of. Your eye for detail and your insights have been game-changing. I'm beyond lucky to have had you on this journey, and I'm so thankful for your dedication.

Charity, your feedback lit the way when I needed it most. Your belief in my vision and your insightful suggestions have deeply enriched my work. Thank you for everything; I couldn't have done this without your invaluable input.

Briana, I can't thank you enough for all you do for me!

Seriously, you're not just my assistant, you're my rock and my best friend. I'm so grateful for every moment we share and all the laughs along the way. Thanks for being you and for being on this crazy ride with me. You're the best!

A big shout-out to Krafigs Design for making my book cover a true work of art. Your creativity turned my ideas into a beautiful reality that speaks to anyone who sees it. I am forever grateful for your brilliant contribution.

Sarah and Liam, you both have brought my characters to life in ways I never imagined possible. Your talent in narrating their stories has touched my readers' hearts. I'm so grateful for your enthusiasm and the soul you've brought into this adventure.

Finally, a huge thank you to my amazing beta readers, ARC, and street team. Your enthusiasm and dedication to spreading the word have been incredible. Every post, reel, comment, and video has helped build an incredible buzz, and I am so appreciative of your efforts. You are the best supporters an author could ask for. Your support means the world to me.

ABOUT THE AUTHOR

SARA SAMUELS is the author of the Blade of Shadow series. When Sara isn't daydreaming about her stories and time travel, she spends her day reading romance, cooking and baking, spending time with family, and enjoying life. Sara loves to connect with readers on Instagram, TikTok or by email, so feel free to email her, or message her on social media because she will reply back! Follow her on Instagram or TikTok @storytellersarasamuels to get related updates and posts. Email her at sara@authorsarasamuels.com

Visit her website at https://www.authorsarasamuels.com/ and sign up for the mailing list to stay informed about new releases, contests and more!

www.ingramcontent.com/pod-product-compliance
Ingram Content Group UK Ltd.
Pitfield, Milton Keynes, MK11 3LW, UK
UKHW031429300325
5226UKWH00022B/82